Cara Colter shares her life in beautiful British Columbia, Canada, with her husband, nine horses and one small Pomeranian with a large attitude. She loves to hear from readers, and you can learn more about her and contact her through Facebook.

Christine Rimmer came to her profession the long way around. She tried everything from acting to teaching to telephone sales. Now she's finally found work that suits her perfectly. She insists she never had a problem keeping a job—she was merely gaining "life experience" for her future as a novelist. Christine lives with her family in Oregon. Visit her at christinerimmer.com.

SNOWBOUND WITH THE SINGLE DAD

CARA COLTER

SAME TIME, NEXT CHRISTMAS

CHRISTINE RIMMER

MILLS & BOON

First Published in Great Britain 2018
by Mills & Boon, an imprint of HarperCollinsPublishers,
1 London Bridge Street, London, SE1 9GF

Snowbound With The Single Dad © 2018 Cara Colter
Same Time, Next Christmas © 2018 Christine Rimmer

ISBN: 978-0-263-26549-1

1218

MIX
Paper from
responsible sources
FSC C007454
FSC
www.fsc.org

This book is produced from independently certified FSC™ paper to ensure responsible forest management.

For more information visit: www.harpercollins.co.uk/green

Printed and bound in Spain
by CPI, Barcelona

SNOWBOUND WITH THE SINGLE DAD

CARA COLTER

To Carol Geurts,
who shows dignity, courage and integrity
through all of life's storms.
You are an inspiration.

CHAPTER ONE

"THERE'S MY LITTLE Christmas star!"

Noelle felt a swell of joy as she watched her grandfather, Rufus, shut down the tractor and climb down off it. He paused to lift the old black Lab, Smiley, out of the cab. Then he turned and came through the snow toward her, Smiley shuffling behind him with his happy grin in place, despite the dog's pained gait.

She was relieved to see that, unlike Smiley, her grandpa was agile, surprisingly strong-looking for a man of seventy-eight years. He was dressed for cold, in a thick woolen toque, mittens and a lined plaid lumber jacket.

His embrace, too, was powerful as he came and hugged her tight, lifting her right off her feet.

He put her down and regarded her. "You haven't been losing weight, have you?"

"No," she said quickly, although she wasn't at all certain. She had always been a slight girl, but she hadn't been near a weigh scale since the abrupt end of her engagement. Noelle was fairly certain you could not lose weight eating chocolate ice cream for supper. And also, sometimes, for breakfast.

Their worry was mutual. It was to be their first Christmas without Grandma McGregor. In those months after Grandma had died, there had been something in her grandpa's voice on the phone, which Noelle had not heard before—a weariness, a disconnect, as if he was not quite there. Sometimes he had made mistakes about what day it was, and seemed confused about other small details of daily life. Other times he had reminisced so obsessively about the past that Noelle had been convinced he was declining, too, dying of a broken heart.

Then, a few weeks ago, she had noticed an improvement. To her great surprise and relief, he'd actually seemed excited about Christmas. It had always been such a magical time of year in her family, partly because it was her birthday, too. Would it be too much to expect a Christmas miracle that would begin to heal their losses this year?

But when Noelle had driven into the yard and seen her grandpa had not put up a single decoration, she had felt her heart fall. Then, when she had noticed the tractor tracks, heading off into nowhere, she'd been frightened. He didn't have cattle anymore. Where was he going? She'd followed along the tracks with great trepidation.

"Grandpa." She sighed, feeling that sense of coming home. She got down on her knees and gave Smiley a long hug and an ear scratching before she got up and surveyed her grandfather's project.

He seemed to be clearing snow in a large square in the middle of what used to be a cow pasture. "What on earth are you doing?"

His arm looped over her shoulder, he turned and looked with pleasure at his handiwork.

"I'm building me a helicopter landing pad," he said, and her sense of well-being plummeted.

"A what?" she stammered.

"You heard me. Don't go giving me that have-you-lost-your-mind look. Come on, we'll go to the house and have coffee. You brought everything you need for a nice Christmas at the ranch?"

She thought he might want to take the tractor back to the house, but instead he turned with her and walked the pounded-down snow of the tractor track, Smiley dogging their heels.

"Yes." Noelle hesitated, and then asked, "I wondered why you didn't have any decorations up yet?"

"I thought it would be good to do it together."

Even though she had never helped with things like putting the outside lights up, she loved the idea of them working together to re-create Christmases like the ones they had always enjoyed.

"That sounds fun. I'm so looking forward to the break. I'll be here now until just after New Year's."

"Ah, good. Good. Everybody else will leave Boxing Day, so we'll have a bit of time for just you and me."

"What do you mean everybody?" she asked, surprised.

"Oh, my goodness, Ellie," he said, calling her by his pet name for her, "wait until I show you what I've gone and done. Have you ever heard of Me-Sell?"

She cocked her head at him quizzically.

"You know, the place on the interstate where you put the ads up?"

"The internet? Oh, you mean I-Sell? That huge online classified ad site?"

"That's it!"

The thought of her grandpa on I-Sell gave her pause. He still heated his house with wood. He received two channels on his old television set—if he fiddled with the rabbit ears on top of it long enough. He did not own a cell phone, not that there was signal anywhere near here. He and Grandma had never had a computer, never mind the internet.

"I go down to the library in the village and use the interstate," he said.

"Internet," she corrected him weakly.

"Whatever. I decided to sell some of my old machines out in the barn. Just taking up space. Ed down the road got a pretty penny for his. He did it all on I-Sell."

"Do you need money?" she asked, appalled that somehow this had passed her by in their weekly telephone conversations. She got out here to visit him at least once a month. Why hadn't she noticed he was pinching his pennies? Had her own double heartbreak made her that self-involved?

"Good grief, no! Got more money than I know what to do with since I sold off most of the land except for this little parcel around the home place."

Another of the recent heartbreaking losses had been that decision to sell off most of the land that had been in the McGregor family for generations. There was no one left to work it. In her fantasies, Noelle had hoped one day she and Mitchell would buy it back.

They came over a little rise, and both of them paused. There it sat, the home place, prettier than a Christmas card. Surrounded by mounds of white snow was a large two-story house, pale yellow with deep indigo shutters, a porch wrapping around the whole lower floor, smoke chugging out the rock chimney.

If her grandmother had been alive, the house would have been decorated by now, December 21. There would have been lights along the roofline and a huge wreath on the front door, the word *HOPE* peeking out from under a big red bow. The huge blue spruce in the front yard would have been dripping with lights. But this year there was not a single decoration, and it made Noelle's eyes smart, even if her grandfather had waited for her to do it.

Behind the house was a barn, once red, now mostly gray. In the near distance the foothills, snow dusted, rolled away from them, and in the far distance the peaks of the Rockies were jagged and white against a bright blue sky.

They passed the barn on the way to the house, and two large gray horses with feathered feet and dappled rumps came running out of a paddock behind it.

"Hello, Fred, hello, Ned," she said affectionately.

Noelle went over to the fence and held out her hand. Fred blew a warm cloud of moist air onto her hand. She reached up to touch his nose, but just as she did, a tiny little horse, as black as Smiley, exploded through the snow from behind the barn, and the other two took off, snorting and blowing.

The tiny horse, having successfully chased away the competition, strained its neck to reach over the fence, and nipped at where her fingers dangled.

She snatched them away, and the pony gave an indignant shake of its scruffy black mane and charged off in the direction it had come.

"Who—or what—is that?" she asked.

"That's Gidget," her grandfather said. "She seems like a nasty little piece of work, but you'd be surprised how hard it is to find a pony close to Christmas."

"A pony for Christmas?"

Noelle shot her grandfather a look. Again, she had the terrifying thought her grandfather might be slipping, that maybe he thought she was a little girl again.

"She's a Christmas surprise."

"Oh! You're keeping someone's surprise pony until Christmas?"

"Something like that. Look at you shivering. City gal."

He took his toque off, revealing a head of very thick silver hair. He placed it on her own head and pulled it tenderly over her ears, as if she was, indeed, twelve again and not twenty-three. This time, instead of terrifying her, the casual gesture made her feel deeply loved.

He moved to her car, an economy model that had struggled a bit on the very long, snowy road that led to his place from the secondary highway. Her grandfather wrestled her suitcase out of the trunk. It was a big suitcase, filled with gifts and warm clothes, and her skates. The pond behind the house would be frozen over. The suitcase had wheels, but her grandpa chose to carry it and Noelle knew better than to insult him by offering to help.

When they walked in the back door into the back porch, the smell of coffee was strong in the house, though she immediately missed the just-out-of-the-oven aroma of her grandmother's Christmas baking.

They shrugged out of jackets and boots, and left the suitcase there. Noelle pulled off her grandfather's toque and smoothed her hair in the mirror. Her faintly freckled cheeks and nose were already pretty pink from being outside, but she knew herself to be an unremarkable woman. Mouse-brown hair, shoulder-length, straight as spaghetti, eyes that were neither brown nor blue but some muddy moss color in between, pixie-like features that could be made cute—not beautiful—with makeup, not that she bothered anymore.

The dog had already settled in his bed by the wood heater when she got into the kitchen. While her grandfather added wood to the heater, Noelle looked around with fondness.

The kitchen was nothing like the farmhouse kitchens that were all the rage in the home-decorating magazines right now. It had old, cracked linoleum on the floor, the paint was chipping off cabinets and the counters were cluttered with everything from engine pieces to old gloves.

The windows were abundant but old, glazed over with frost inside the panes.

Aside from the fact that her grandmother would not have tolerated those engine pieces on the counter, and would have had some Christmas decorations up, Noelle felt that sigh of homecoming intensify within her.

Her grandfather and grandmother had raised her when her parents had died in an automobile accident when she was twelve. In all the world, this kitchen was the place she loved the most and felt the safest.

"Tell me about the helicopter pad," she said, taking a seat at the old table. The coffee had been brewing on the woodstove, and her grandfather plopped a mug down in front of her. She took a sip, and her eyes nearly crossed it was so strong. She reached hastily for the sugar pot.

"Well, it really started when I was watching the news one night." He took the seat across the table from her and regarded her with such unabashed affection that it melted her heart and the intensity of that feeling *home* grew.

"There was this story about this girl—not here, mind, England or Vancouver—"

Both equally foreign places to her grandfather.

"—who was going to be all alone for Christmas, so she just put an ad on something like I-Sell and all these people answered her, and she chose a family to have Christmas with."

Her grandfather was beaming at her as if this fully explained the helicopter pad he was building in his cow pasture.

"Go on."

"So I was on there anyway, trying to figure out how to put up a posting for my old junk in the barn, and I just had this thought that I missed Christmas the way it used to be."

"You and me and Grandma?" she said wistfully, thinking of music and baking and decorating, and neighbors dropping by.

"Even before that. You know, TV was late coming to these parts. It was better without it. And a whole lot better without the interstate."

No point telling him again. Noelle waited.

"Don't even get me going on what cell phones are doing to the world."

"I won't," Noelle said, though in truth she knew it wouldn't be long before she missed all her social media platforms. Or more to the point, relentlessly and guiltily spying on someone else's newly exciting life through their prolific postings.

"We used to have big gatherings at Christmas," her grandfather said longingly. "When I was a boy, on Christmas Day the whole community would show up at the old hall, and there would be a Christmas concert, and dinner, and games. Those tables would be groaning under the weight of turkeys and hams and bowls of mashed spuds and pies. Oh, the pies! The women would try to outdo themselves on pies.

"People sang, and talked together. They exchanged gifts with their neighbors. Not much, you see, a homemade whistle, a flour sack, bleached white and embroidered with something nice, like *Bless This House.* If you knew a family that was having a rough go, you made sure all the kids had a present, and that they got a big fat ham to take home."

Noelle's sense of worry was gnawing at her again. As lovely a picture as he was painting, her grandfather had never been like this. Grandma had pretty much looked after Christmas, he'd done the outside decorating and hitched up the old horses for the mandatory Christmas sleigh ride, usually after much nagging! Until Grandma had died, he had never been given to reminiscing. He was pragmatic, not sentimental!

"So," he said, "I got me an email address and I just put a little ad on there, inviting people to an old-fashioned Christmas, if they wanted one."

"Here?" Noelle asked, stunned.

"Well, sure. Can you think of a better place?"

"Grandpa, you can't invite strangers off the internet to your home!"

He folded his arms across his plaid shirt. His craggy face got a stubborn look on it. "Well, too late for your good advice, little miss Dear Abby, I already done it."

"People replied?"

"All kinds of them," he said with satisfaction.

"But how do you know if they're good people?" Noelle asked. Was that faint hysteria in her voice?

Her grandfather patted her hand. "Oh, Noelle, most folks are good. You've just lost a little faith because of that fella, Michael—"

"Mitchell," she corrected him weakly. She did not want to think of that "fella" with his newly exciting life right now!

"Does this have something to do with the helicopter pad?" she whispered, full of trepidation.

"Yup, indeed. Some kind of Mr. Typhoon is coming here."

"Tycoon?" she asked, despite herself.

"Whatever."

"Oh, Grandpa!"

"With his little girl, who lost her mommy."

"Grandpa! Tell me you didn't send anyone any money."

"Well, I did send somebody money. Not the typhoon, someone else. They wanted to come to my Old-Fashioned Country Christmas, but my goodness, them people have had a run of bad luck. Couldn't even put together the money for a tank of gasoline."

Noelle felt sick. How far had this gone? How many people had duped him out of his money? Her hopes for a healing Christmas were evaporating.

Her grandpa was an absolute innocent in the high-tech world. All kinds of people out there were just waiting to prey on a lonely old man; all kinds of villains were trolling the internet to find the likes of her grandfather. She hoped he hadn't spouted off to anyone else about having more money than he could use.

"Grandpa," she said gently. "It's a hoax. If the *tycoon* hasn't asked you for money yet, he will. You're probably being scammed..."

Her grandfather was scowling at her. "It ain't like that."

"How do you know?"

"Because they sent me this." He produced a piece of paper from a heap of papers leaning off one of the counters. Noelle took it and stared at it. It appeared to be specs for building a rudimentary helicopter pad.

"Oh, no, Grandpa," she said. This was how easy it was to fool an old man. The drawing could have been done by a child.

Her grandfather cocked his head.

"Hear that?" he asked triumphantly.

She stared at him. She heard absolutely nothing. She felt the most heartbreaking sadness. What a year of losses. The land. Her grandmother. Then, weeks after her grandmother had passed, her fiancé announcing he just wasn't "ready." To commit. To live in one place. Apparently to hold down a job in the oil industry that had employed them both. Mitchell had gone off to Thailand to "find himself."

If his favorite social media page was any indication, he seemed to be being helped in this pursuit by a bevy of exotic-looking, bikini-clad beauties who had made No-elle newly aware of her lack of boldness—she had never worn a bikini—plus her own plainness and her paleness.

So, she had lost her family ranch, her grandmother and her fiancé. It was true she had held on to hope for a ridiculously long period of time that Mitchell would come to his senses and come back, even after his final betrayal.

But now, this felt as if it would be the final blow, if she was losing her grandfather, only in quite a different way. His mind going, poor old guy. She'd heard of this before. Moments of lucidity interspersed with, well, this.

He had pushed back from the table and was hurrying to the door.

"I can't not be there when they land," he said eagerly. "And I better throw some hay at that pony, so she's on the back side of the barn. Don't want that secret out yet."

Even the dog looked doubtful, and not very happy to be going back outside.

"Grandpa," she said soothingly, getting up, "come sit down. You can help me take my suitcase up. Maybe we'll go find a tree this afternoon, put up some decorations—"

Her grandfather was ignoring her. He laced up his boots and went out the door, the reluctant dog on his heels. Moments later his side-by-side all-terrain vehicle roared to life and pulled away, leaving an almost eerie silence in its wake.

And then she heard it.

The very distinctive wop-wop-wop of a helicopter in the distance.

She dashed to the back porch, put on her grandfather's toque, grabbed her jacket, shoved boots on her feet and raced out the door.

CHAPTER TWO

"KEEP BACK FROM IT!" her grandfather shouted over his shoulder.

Noelle arrived at the landing pad, breathless from running. The blades of the helicopter were throwing up so much snow that for a moment Noelle lost sight of her grandfather, the dog and the helicopter.

And then the engines died, and the snow settled, and it was very quiet. She peered at the helicopter. It was a burnished gold color, wrapped in a word, *Wrangler*.

Behind the bubble of a window, she could see a man doing something at the controls. He had a shock of dark hair falling over his brow, a strong profile and aviator-style sunglasses. From this distance she couldn't make out his features, and yet, somehow she knew—perhaps from his chosen entry—that everything about this man would be extraordinary.

As she watched, he took off the earphones he was wearing and the sunglasses, which he folded into his front breast pocket. He got out his door with an easy leap. He acknowledged Noelle and her grandfather with a slight raise of his hand and then moved to the passenger door.

He was wearing a brown distressed-leather pilot's jacket lined with sheepskin. His shoulders appeared impossibly broad, and dark slacks accentuated the long lines of powerful legs. He moved with the innate grace of a man extremely confident in himself.

Noelle could see now his hair was more than dark, black and shiny as a raven's wing. His features were strong and even, with the faintest hint of whisker shadowing on the hollows of his cheeks and on that merest hint of a cleft at his chin. He glanced toward her, and she felt the jolt of his eyes: electric blue, cool, assessing.

And ever so vaguely familiar. Noelle stared at his face, wondering where she had seen him before, and then stunned recognition dawned. Why wouldn't he be confident in himself?

Aidan Phillips was even more of a presence in real life than he was in pictures. And there were plenty of pictures of him.

Less so now than a few years ago, when he and his wife, Sierra, had been unofficially crowned Canadian royalty, he an oil industry magnate, and she a renowned actress. Every public second of their romance and subsequent marriage had been relentlessly documented, photographed and commented on, as if their coming together was Canada's answer to a real-life fairy tale.

Without, sadly, the happy ending.

"Do you know who that is?" she asked her grandfather in an undertone.

He lifted a shoulder.

"He's one of the richest men in Canada."

"I told you," Rufus said, triumphantly. "A typhoon. Though it's a poor man, indeed, who thinks all it takes to be rich is money. Ask her."

"Ask who?"

"Her."

Noelle turned back to see Aidan lifting a little girl out of the helicopter passenger seat. Of course, she knew he was a widower, and she knew there was a child, but he used his substantial influence to protect his daughter from any kind of public exposure.

The little girl was gorgeous—wild black curls springing from under a soft pink, very fuzzy hat that matched her jacket and leggings and snow boots. The cutest little pink furry muff dangled from a string out the sleeve of her jacket. She had the same electric blue eyes as her father. Noelle guessed her to be about five.

Aidan Phillips set the child down in the snow, and she looked around. Smiley ambled over, and the little girl squealed with delight and got down on both chubby knees, throwing her arms around the dog.

"Don't let him lick your face," a shrill voice commanded.

A third passenger was being helped out of the helicopter, an elderly woman with a pinched, forbidding expression.

"Well," Grandpa said, too loudly. "There's a face that would make a train take a dirt road."

"Grandpa!"

But her grandpa had moved forward to greet his guests. After a moment he waved her up, and Noelle went forward, feeling the absolute awkwardness of the situation.

"And this is my granddaughter, Noelle, born on Christmas Day."

Noelle cringed inwardly. Was her grandfather going to reveal her whole history?

"We just call her Ellie, though."

Actually, no one but her grandfather called her Ellie anymore, but she felt it would be churlish to correct him.

"This is Tess and Aidan," her grandfather said, as if he was introducing people he had known for a long time. Despite her feeling of being caught off balance, Noelle smiled at the child, before turning her attention to the man. He extended his hand, and she ripped off her mitten and found her hand enveloped in one that was strong and warm. Ridiculously, she wished she was not in a parka nearly the same shade of pink as the little girl's. She also wished for just the faintest dusting of makeup.

A woman would have to be dead—not merely heartbroken—to not want to make some sort of first impression on Aidan Phillips!

Still, she saw a faint wariness in those intense blue eyes as they narrowed on her face. When his hand enveloped hers it felt as if she had stood too close to lightning. She was tingling!

"A pleasure," he said, but there was something as guarded in his voice as in his eyes, and Noelle was fairly certain he did not think it was a pleasure at all. In fact, his voice was a growl of pure suspicion that sent a shiver up and down her spine. She snatched her hand away from his, put her mitten on and stepped back from him.

"This is quite a surprise," she stammered. "My grandfather only just told me we were having guests for Christmas."

"Nor did he tell me about the lovely granddaughter."

There was something about the way he said *lovely* that was faintly sarcastic, and Noelle felt an embarrassing blush rise up her cheeks. But then she realized Aidan was not commenting on the plainness she had become more painfully aware of since Mitchell's departure, but something else entirely.

Was Aidan Phillips insinuating her grandfather was matchmaking?

How dare he? If ever there was a person incapable of ulterior motives, it was Grandpa.

On the other hand—she slid her grandfather a look from

under her lashes—was there a remote possibility he was meddling in her life? It seemed unlikely. Her grandfather was not a romantic. But he had been unabashed in his disapproval of her relationship with Mitchell, especially when they had moved in together.

Her relationship with Mitchell? Or just Mitchell as a person?

If her grandfather was matchmaking, he seemed rather indifferent to the first encounter of the lovebirds.

Realistically, it simply wasn't Grandpa's style. At all. And yet even as she thought that, she remembered bringing Mitchell to the ranch to meet her grandparents.

What's wrong with him? she had heard Grandpa ask her grandmother. *He doesn't act like he's the luckiest man in the world. He doesn't seem to know how beautiful she is.*

Noelle had heard her grandmother's answer. She knew she had. But every time she tried to recall it, it flitted just beyond where her memory could find it, a wary bird that did not want to be captured.

Her grandfather didn't even know about the final betrayal: that Mitchell had emptied out their joint bank account.

I made it, he'd said, when she had sent him a frantic message through a social media messaging service, asking where the money was.

There had been no acknowledgment that her salary, which had taken care of bills and groceries, had allowed *them* to save quite a substantial nest egg. Toward a wedding. And a house.

What had Grandpa said when she had shown up on his doorstep, her face swollen after a week of solid crying? *It was better in the old days when your family helped you find your partner.*

What was it with her grandfather and this sudden sentimental attachment to how things used to be?

Not that there was anything sentimental on his face at the moment. He was scowling at the older lady, who was wiping frantically at the little girl's dog-kissed face with a linen handkerchief.

"And I ain't had the pleasure?"

"Bertanana Sutton," she said regally, pausing her wiping of the girl's face, but not standing and offering her hand, which Rufus seemed to take as an insult.

"Bertanana?" her grandfather repeated. "That's a mouthful."

"We just call her Nana, though," the little girl said, mischievously.

Grandpa guffawed loudly.

"Excuse me?" Bertanana said imperiously.

"Nana. Just like the Newfoundland dog in *Peter Pan*," Grandpa said.

First of all, Noelle was shocked that her grandfather knew anything about *Peter Pan*, let alone the name and breed of the dog. And second, why was he being so unforgivably rude?

Not that she needed to intervene. Nana was giving her grandfather a look that would have felled a lesser man— or made a train take a dirt road!

"Mrs. Sutton to you," she said.

He flinched and Noelle saw what the problem was. He'd felt judged at Nana's first insinuation that the dog—and its kisses—were dirty. Noelle had a terrible feeling this would not go well.

"Luggage?" Grandpa asked stiffly.

Aidan turned away from them and began to unload the helicopter. For a man who was CEO of a very large company, and moved in the rarefied circles of the very rich and very famous, he seemed every bit as strong as her grandfather. How was that possible when her grandfather was a hardworking man of the land?

With no conversation between them, Aidan and her grandfather filled the back of the side-by-side with quite a large number of suitcases and parcels, and then in went the dog, and Nana and Tess.

"Out of room," Grandpa said, happily, his hurt feelings put aside for now. He took the driver's seat. "You two will have to walk." And then he roared away with a wave of his hand, leaving her standing there in a cloud of snow with Aidan Phillips.

It was obvious there was no room on that vehicle. It made sense that Noelle and Aidan would be left to walk, being neither the youngest nor the oldest of the group.

And yet if someone was looking for evidence of an ulterior motive, it would seem almost embarrassingly obvious that her grandfather had engineered an opportunity to throw them together, alone.

Aidan shoved his hands deep in his pockets and gazed off at the snow-capped mountains, something tight and closed in his face.

She could smell the leather of his jacket in the cold air, and a faint and seductive scent, subtle as only the most expensive of colognes managed to be.

"I'm having a bit of trouble getting my head around all this," she said, her voice strained.

"As am I," he returned coolly.

"I'm not going to pretend I don't know who you are, though I suspect my grandfather doesn't have a clue. I work in Clerical for a small oil company in Calgary, so I know the basics of who is who in the oil industry. I know you are the CEO of the Calgary-based Wrangler Oil."

"And that I was married to Sierra Avanguard?" he asked quietly, his gaze disconcertingly direct on her face.

"Of course, that, too."

"I don't want any pictures of Tess showing up on social media," he said. "Or anywhere else."

It was said formidably, an order.

Really, was it unreasonable? He didn't know her. He was just laying the ground rules. But he was also her grandfather's guest, and it seemed a breach of her grandfather's hospitality for Aidan to feel it was necessary to say this.

"That's fine," she said, matching his cool tone. "I don't want any pictures of my grandfather surfacing, either. I'm sure his privacy is as important to him as yours is to you."

He looked stunned. Obviously, if he had ever been put in his place before, it had been a long time ago.

He tilted his head at her, and looked a little more deeply. Reluctant amusement tickled around the line of that sinfully sensual mouth and sparked in his eyes for a second.

"Maybe he should stay off I-Sell, then," he suggested.

"My grandfather does not have a clue what the repercussions of putting his invitation in a virtual world could be," Noelle said. "I'm afraid I would have dissuaded him, had he confided his Old-Fashioned Country Christmas plans in me."

"Ah."

Noelle wondered if she should tell him there might be others coming. But were there? She decided to take her grandfather aside and find out whether, apart from sending money to strangers, he had any other confirmed guests, before setting off alarm bells. Besides, wasn't there a possibility this was between Aidan and Rufus and she should stay out of it?

Meanwhile she had to satisfy her curiosity about how Aidan Phillips had come to be standing in a field on her grandfather's property! Handsome men did not just fall from the heavens!

"I must say," Noelle said cautiously, "that you hardly seem like the type of man who would be searching an on-line ad site to make your Christmas plans."

"Oh? What type of man do I seem like?"

"The kind who would have a zillion much more glam-orous Christmas options and invitations than this one."

"That's true," he said, with a sigh that could be inter-preted as regretful that he had not accepted one of his many other invitations.

"So what brings you to Rufus McGregor's ranch for Christmas?" she pressed.

Aidan blew out a long breath and ran a gloved hand through his hair, scattering dark wisps that drifted like feathers before they settled obediently back into place. Such a small thing to find so utterly and disconcertingly sexy.

Her ex-fiancé, Mitchell, had been bald as a billiard ball.

It was the novelty of all that silky touchable-looking hair, she told herself firmly. But still, she had *noticed.* Not just noticed. No, noticed *and* found it attractive. This had to be nipped in the bud, of course.

Noelle closed her eyes for a moment. She summoned a picture in her mind of a red dress. It hung in her dark closet at home, its color dulled behind a plastic wrapper. It was the most glorious—and the most expensive—item of clothing she had ever owned.

She had bought it for the engagement party that had never happened. Now, she would never wear it. Or get rid of it, either. It would be defense against such things as this—an odd twinge of longing that had attacked without warning, the first such longing since Mitchell had packed a single bag—he'd only needed shorts and T-shirts for his new life, after all—and bid her adieu with undisguised eagerness to be gone.

"Are you all right?"

She opened her eyes. Aidan was looking at her quizzically.

"Yes, of course. I'm fine. You were going to tell me—"

He looked at her, considering. Something softened marginally in his expression. It was probably very obvious her discomfort was authentic, and that *if* her grandpa had something up his sleeve, she had had no part in it.

"How I came to be here?" he asked, his tone rueful.

She nodded.

"Never tell a five-nearly-six-year-old she can have anything she wants for Christmas."

CHAPTER THREE

"SHE PICKED THIS?" Noelle asked, shocked. "Your daughter, Tess, could have anything she wanted for Christmas
and she picked my grandfather's old place in the middle
of nowhere?"

"Almost anything," Aidan clarified. "No pony."

Uh-oh. Did that explain nasty little Gidget's arrival on
the ranch? Her grandfather *had* said it was the secret he
didn't want let out yet.

"And no puppy," Aidan added after a moment. "I actually was foolish enough to say, in a moment of utter weakness, that she could have anything else."

Noelle suspected he had been momentarily so caught
up in the guilt of refusing Tess a pony or a puppy that he
had caved easily on her request to come here. But why had
she wanted to come here?

"And she picked this?" Noelle asked again.

"I'm as flabbergasted as you are." He regarded her
thoughtfully. "What do you think a little girl who could
have anything would choose?"

Her opinion really seemed to matter to him. He was
looking at her with discomfiting intensity. She hoped he
wouldn't run his hand through his hair again.

"Disneyland?" she hazarded, after a moment's thought.

He looked disappointed in the answer, and she was annoyed with herself for feeling that she had not wanted to let him down.

"Yes, Disneyland. According to my research staff, the number one wish of children around the world is to visit a Disney resort."

She had not only disappointed, she hadn't even been original. Still, if for a moment she didn't make it all about her, what did it say about him that he had set his research staff on the task of discovering what would make his daughter's dreams come true?

"So, you took her?"

"Yes. Tess declared, at the top of her lungs, lying on the walkway in the middle of the park, *It is not Christmas without snow*," he informed Noelle solemnly. "Even though I explained to her the very first Christmas would not have had any snow, we were, at that point, beyond rational explanations.

"I'm lucky I wasn't arrested. Fortunately, four-year-old meltdowns are not the unusual in 'the Happiest Place on Earth.'"

She had to bite back a desire to laugh at the picture forming in her mind of this self-contained man being held hostage by a four-year-old having a tantrum.

He went on, "The holiday transformation of *It's a Small World* failed to impress my daughter, despite the addition of fifty thousand Christmas lights, which is also the number of times I think we went through that particular attraction. For weeks after, I had 'Jingle Bells' and 'Deck the Halls' jangling away inside my head."

"Oh, dear," Noelle murmured. "Would you like me to take those off the caroling list?"

"There's to be caroling?" Aidan asked, horrified.

"All part of an old-fashioned Christmas," she said, deadpan. Of course, she had not planned a single thing for an old-fashioned Christmas. Was it wrong to take such delight in his discomfort? "I think it's a requirement, as well as snow. You can see we have plenty of that."

"The Christmas before Disneyland we had snow," he confessed. "My team found a place in the Finnish Lapland. We stayed in a glass igloo and witnessed the Northern Lights. We rode in a cart pulled by reindeer. We visited Santa's house."

"That sounds absolutely magical." Noelle actually was not sure anything her grandfather could offer would compete with such a Christmas.

"It does, doesn't it?"

"Oh, dear, I can tell by your tone—"

He nodded. "Another Christmas fail. She was three at the time. Santa was not as depicted in her favorite storybook. I think *creepy* is the word she used in reference to him. *Cweepy.* Rhotacism is perfectly normal until age eight."

"Rhotacism?" Noelle asked weakly.

"Trading out the *R* sound for *W*."

Which meant he had checked. Or his research staff had. It was all a bit sad, and somehow made him more dangerous than his wisps of dark hair falling gently back into place after he had raked his hand through them.

Before she could reconjure the red dress, he continued. "And the reindeer were a major letdown. Non-fliers. None with a red nose."

"I guess some elements of Christmas might be best left to the imagination," Noelle said. It seemed to her that Aidan, in his feverish efforts to manufacture the Christmas experience, might have missed the meaning of that first Christmas entirely.

She saw, again, just a hint of vulnerability in him— the single dad trying desperately to make his daughter happy. Especially at Christmas. Desperate enough to join strangers...

Noelle searched her memory. His wife had been a very famous and extraordinarily beautiful actress. Hadn't she died around Christmas? Three years ago? The papers had not been able to get enough of that sad little toddler's face. And then, to his credit, Aidan Phillips had managed to get his daughter out of the limelight and keep her out of it.

She could feel herself softening toward him the tiniest bit.

"And then you would think you could salvage Christmas with lovely gifts, wouldn't you?" He sighed with long-suffering.

Again, she felt he was missing the point, but she went along. "Aren't gifts for little girls easy? Hair ribbons and teddy bears and new pajamas? A jangly bracelet? A miniature oven?"

"Oh, right," Aidan said, as if Noelle was hopelessly naive.

Of course, his little girl probably got those things as a matter of course, so what did Tess then have to look forward to?

"Doesn't she tell you what she wants?"

"Yes, a puppy. And a pony. Every other item on her wish list is reserved for *Santa.* The fat happy Santa at the mall, not the skinny fellow in odd clothes with a real beard in Finland. And it's a secret. If you tell anyone, then Santa won't bring it to you, because the hearty laugh and twinkly eyes are just fronts for a mean-spirited old goat that would punish a little girl for telling her dad what she *really* wants."

Noelle was struck by an irony here. Aidan Phillips, one of the most wealthy and successful men in Canada, if not the world, was in hopelessly over his head when it came to being a daddy at Christmas.

What had her grandfather just said? That a man who

thought money was the only way to be rich was very poor indeed?

Still, it seemed like it should all be fairly easy. Was he the kind of man who could complicate a dot?

"How about that line of dolls that is such a big hit? Millie something?"

"Jilly," he corrected her. "Jilly Jamjar. And her friends. Corrinne Cookiejar. Pauline Picklejar. They all come with the 'jar' they live in."

"Are you making this up?"

"Really? Do I look like the kind of man who could make up a line of dolls who live in jar houses?"

"No," she had to admit, "you do not."

"I wish I was making it up. She already has the first three in the series. But then along came Jerry. Jerry Juicejar."

It was quite funny listening to this extremely sophisticated man discuss the Jar dolls, fluent in their ridiculous names, but she had the feeling it would be a mistake to laugh.

"The Jarheads—my name for the toy manufacturers, not their own—in all their wisdom, made a limited edition of dear Jerry. There's a few thousand of him. Period. For millions of children screaming his name in adulation. I swear the Jarheads are in cahoots with the mean-spirited Santa.

"Which brings us to I-Sell. One momentary lapse on my part. *Okay, go ahead, see if you can find a Jerry Juicejar on there.*"

"You let your five-year-old daughter go on the internet?"

Noelle was treated to a flinty look of pure warning. *Do not judge me.*

"She's not five going on six, she's five going on twenty-one."

Which Noelle found terribly sad. Really, Tess was little

more than a baby, only a year ago being quite capable of throwing a tantrum in the middle of a theme park. Still, she refrained from saying anything. She was beginning to suspect that the do-not-judge-me look she saw in his eyes had something to do with the fact that he had already judged himself with horrendous harshness.

"Plus, she wasn't by herself. Nana was supervising. I've got two acquisitions assistants looking for him full time, and they have not found anyone willing to part with a Jerry. There are some things," Aidan said with a miffed sigh, "that money can't buy."

"There are all kinds of things money can't buy," Noelle said firmly.

He looked dubious about that, even after his failed attempts to purchase Christmas happiness for his daughter with lavish holiday plans, research teams and acquisitions assistants.

"Is it possible Tess would like to just stay home for Christmas?" she suggested softly, as gently as she could. "She just wants what any child wants. To be with you. To be with her family."

"I'm it for family," he said tightly. "Me and Nana. Another fail in the Christmas department, I'm sure. And we don't stay home for Christmas."

A fire, Noelle seemed to remember. In their apartment? Christmas morning? A nation pulled from their Christmas joy to mourn with that very famous family.

"Anyway, she was looking for Jerry Juicejar, and what did she find while her supervisor nodded off on the sofa? An Old-Fashioned Country Christmas."

"You're quite lucky that's all she found," Noelle said.

Again, she got the flinty look, but underneath it she saw just a flicker of the magnitude of his sense of drowning in the sea of parenting requirements.

"You couldn't dissuade her?" She deliberately made her tone neutral, vigilantly nonjudgmental.

Not that he seemed to appreciate her effort! He shot her a look. "You'll soon see how easy it is to dissuade Tess. And I did, very foolishly, promise her she could have anything. A promise is a promise. She'll be the first to let you know that, too. She has a book by that title that she carries in her hip pocket for reference and reminder purposes. So be very careful what you tell her."

"I've made a note," she said seriously, and he shot her a suspicious look to see if she was making light of him.

"I had…er…some of my staff make sure your grandfather was legitimate."

It was faintly insulting, and yet she could hardly blame him.

"And then I spoke to your grandfather on the phone and it all seemed aboveboard. Nice old guy, first Christmas alone. Of course, he neglected to mention Ellie-born-on-Christmas-Day."

"Maybe your research teams just aren't that good," she said drily. "They can't find out what a little girl wants for Christmas and they totally missed me. I go by Noelle, actually, and being born on Christmas Day was not an indictable offense the last time I checked."

"Did I say it like it was?"

"You did."

"It's just so darn…cute. Most people, of course, would hate having their birthday overshadowed by the 'big' day, but I bet you aren't one of them."

She narrowed her eyes at him. "What would make you presume anything about me?"

He lifted a broad shoulder. "Presumptions are a part of life. You made some about me—that I was not the type of man who would need to join strangers for Christmas—and I have made some about you."

"Do tell," she said, though in truth she was bracing herself. She was not sure she wanted him to tell at all.

"There's a look about you. A country girl."

A country girl? She had lived in the city now for nearly five years. She considered herself fairly sophisticated.

Not that you would know it at the moment. She was dressed in a pink parka and her jeans were stuffed into snow boots. On her hurried way out the back door, she had put her grandpa's toque back on. Her cheeks were probably pink, and no doubt her nose was, too.

"Not a touch of makeup. Wholesome," he went on, ignoring the fact that she was looking daggers at him. "Giving. Christmas magic and all that. Hopelessly naive. Probably made a bad choice in a man and Grandpa has stepped in to find you a suitable partner. Right at Christmas. Cue the music."

He began to hum "White Christmas."

She hoped it wouldn't get stuck in her head.

"Are you always so insufferable?" she asked.

"I try…and that's out of character. Not giving at all. Tut-tut."

"Let me tell you my presumptions. You hate Christmas. I can tell by your obnoxious tone." She thought of adding, *No wonder you haven't been able to succeed at giving your daughter a good one*, but stopped herself. It would just be mean. And he was, unfortunately, right about the wholesome and giving part of her nature.

"I wondered about an ulterior motive in getting us here," Aidan said. "Who just invites strangers for Christmas?"

"Well, you can just quit wondering. You will never—never—meet a man with more integrity than my grandfather. He's invited strangers for Christmas because he feels he has something to give, not to take anything."

"Humph," he said with an insulting lack of conviction.

Was Aidan Phillips annoying her on purpose? Surely her face had softened in sympathy at his vulnerable dad side, as he had revealed each of his Christmas failures? Now, he was successfully erasing that. If he was now trying to make her angry—a defense against her unwanted sympathy—it was working all too well!

"My grandfather might be trying to look after me. I hope not, but he's old and his heart is in the right place, which I'm sure you figured out when you accepted his generous invitation to spend Christmas at his home. I may be single, but really, you would both be presuming too much by thinking I would be interested in you!"

Of course, there was the momentary lapse over his hair, but he never had to know.

He stopped. It forced her to stop, too. She tilted her chin and glared at him.

"And you wouldn't be?" he asked, incredulous.

"Oh!" She fought a desire to take off her grandfather's toque and stuff it in her pocket so she wouldn't look quite so *folksy*. "Why would you sound so surprised? Do you have women flinging themselves at you all the time?"

"Yes." He cocked his head at her.

"I am not some country bumpkin who is going to be bowled over by your charm, Mr. Phillips," she said tightly.

"I don't have any charm."

"Agreed."

"You've had a heartbreak, just as I guessed."

The utter audacity of the man. It made her want to pick up a handful of snow and throw it in his face.

"There might be other reasons a woman would not fling

herself at you," she suggested tightly. *Even though that one happened to be true.*

"There might be," he said skeptically.

But, also true, perhaps a woman would recognize instantly that she was not in the same league as you, she thought to herself. *Perhaps she'd recognize she had failed to hang on to a relationship with even a very ordinary guy, so what were her chances of—*

She stopped her train of thought because he was still watching her way too closely and she did not like the uneasy feeling she had that Aidan Phillips, astute businessman, could read her mind.

"It would be very old-fashioned to think a woman's main purpose in life is to find herself a mate," she told him primly.

"And yet here we are at an Old-Fashioned Country Christmas." He tilted his head at her, his eyes narrow and intent again. "Recent?"

"What?"

"The heartbreak?"

"I'm beginning to take a dislike to you."

"It's not my fault."

"That I dislike you?"

"That women fling themselves!"

"You're handsome and you're wealthy and you're extremely successful and perhaps somewhat intelligent, though it's a bit early to tell."

"I used rhotacism in a sentence!"

She ignored him. "Women fling themselves at you. You've become accustomed to it. They probably find the fact that you are a single dad bumbling through Christmas very endearing. Oh, boo-hoo, Mr. Phillips."

It occurred to her that her sarcasm might be coming more from a deep well of resentment that Mitchell was, at this very moment, surrounding himself with bikinis on a beach in Thailand than at Aidan Phillips, but she would take all the protection the shield of sarcasm could give her. Aidan was exactly the kind of man a woman needed to protect herself from. And worse, he knew it.

"Bumbling through Christmas?" he sputtered. "You call Christmas at the Happiest Place on Earth and at Santa's original place of residence bumbling?"

"Failures by your own admission," she said, with a toss of her head, "and should you have doubt, ask your daughter."

Aidan glared at her, though when he spoke, his voice was carefully controlled, milder than his glare. "I think I'm beginning to take a dislike to you, too."

"Good!"

"Good," he agreed. He continued, his voice softly sarcastic, "It's setting up to be a very nice quiet Christmas in the country, after all."

"Emphasis on quiet, since I won't be speaking to you."

"Starting anytime soon?" he asked silkily.

"Right now!"

"Good," he said again.

She couldn't resist. "Good," she said with a curt nod. They strode along the path back to the house in a silence that bristled.

She watched out of the corner of her eye as he yanked his cell phone from his pocket and began scrolling furiously, walking at the same time. It took him a few seconds to realize it wasn't going to work. He stopped.

"Is there cell service?" he asked tightly.

"We're not speaking."

"That's childish."

"You didn't seem to think so a few minutes ago."

"It's just a yes or no," he said.

"No." She should not have felt nearly as gleeful about the look on his face as she did. Clearly the thought of not being joined to his world, where he was in control of everything and everybody—with the possible exception of his daughter—was causing him instant discomfort.

"Will there be cell service at the house?"

"No."

"I'm expecting an important email. I have several calls I have to make."

"Did you get cell service in the Finnish Lapland?"

"Actually, they take pride in their excellent cell service all across Finland."

He managed to make that sound as if they had managed to be more *bumpkin* here than in one of the most remote places in the world.

Noelle had the sudden thought Tess's string of Christmas disappointments might, at a level she would not yet be able to articulate—despite being five going on twenty-one—have had a lot more to do with her father's ability to be absent while he was with her than the inadequacies of Disneyland or the Northern Lights.

"You can make the calls from his landline in the house," she said, maybe more sharply than she intended. "And I guess you could go to the library in the village and check emails. That's what my grandfather does. Mind you, he has to drive. You could take your helicopter. You could be there in minutes. Maybe even seconds! But it would cause a sensation. There would probably be that unwanted publicity involved."

"You're pulling my leg, aren't you?" He sounded hopeful. He was holding his phone out at arm's length, squinting at it, willing service to appear.

"Do I look like the type of person who would pull your leg?"

He regarded her suspiciously, but didn't answer.

It was because he didn't answer that she decided not to tell him there were a few "sweet spots" on the ranch. One was in the hayloft of the barn. You could get the magic bars on your cell phone to light up to two, and sometimes even three precious bars, if you opened the loft door and held your arm out. If the stars were aligned properly and the wind wasn't blowing. You had to lean out dangerously to take advantage of the service. It was a desperate measure to go sit out there in the cold trying to reconnect with the world.

And somehow she knew she'd be out there later tonight, looking at Mitchell's latest posts about his new and exciting life, tormenting herself with all that she wasn't.

She glanced at Aidan. When he felt her eyes on him, he shoved his cell phone in his pocket. His face was set in deep lines of annoyance, as if she had personally arranged the lack of cell service to inconvenience him.

They came over that rise in the road where they could see the house. She wondered if, in his eyes, it looked old and faintly dilapidated instead of homey and charming, especially with the snow, mounded up like whipped cream, around it. He did not even comment on the house at all, or on the breathtaking spectacle of sweeping landscapes and endless blue skies and majestic mountains.

Noelle thought that what she had said earlier in a pique might be coming true.

She disliked Aidan Phillips. A lot.

And that was so much safer than the alternative! She marched on ahead of him, without bothering to see if he followed.

CHAPTER FOUR

AIDAN PHILLIPS WATCHED his hostess move firmly into the lead, her pert nose in the air and her shoulders set with tension.

He'd managed, and very well, too, to annoy her.

That could only be a good thing! He had no idea if the grandfather had ulterior motives in the matchmaking department. And despite Noelle's vehement denial, women did find him irresistible, exactly for one of the reasons she'd stated.

It was the single-dad thing that set women to cooing and setting out to rescue him. It had been most unwise on his part to share his Christmas catastrophes with someone he didn't even know. But there had been something in the wide set of her eyes, in the green depths of them, that had momentarily weakened him, made him want to unburden. But he'd known as soon as he had, by the sudden softness in her face and the that-poor-guy look that he'd come to so heartily resent, that weakness had been—as weakness inevitably was—a terrible mistake.

She'd even articulated his parenting journey. *Bumbling.*

To the best of his abilities, Aidan *was* bumbling through the challenges of being a single parent to a small girl who had lost her mother. It stunned him that his performance would be average at best, or even below average, he suspected, if there was a test available to rate these things.

The truth was, Aidan Phillips was used to being very, very good at things. He had the Midas touch when it came to money, and he had a business acumen that came to him as naturally as breathing. He was considered one of Canada's top business leaders, one to watch. His success was the envy of his colleagues and business competitors. At some instinctive level, he *knew* what to do. He knew when to expand and when to contract, whom to hire, where to experiment. He knew when to be bold. And when to fold.

He'd been called an overachiever most of his life and he considered it the highest form of a compliment.

But then, there was *the secret.*

He sucked at the *R*-word, as in *Relationships.* His marriage, which he had gone into with incredible confidence and high hopes, had been evidence of that. He'd been like an explorer dumped in a foreign land without a map. And instead of finding his way, he had become more and more lost…

His failure in this department made him insecure about his parenting, about his ability to relate to the more sensitive gender of the species, even a pint-size model like Tess.

He could not seem to get the equation right. His business mind needed an equation, but Tess resisted being a solvable puzzle. He loved his daughter beyond reason. From the first moment he'd held her tiny squirming body in his hands, he had been smitten…and yet there was a pervasive feeling of failing, somehow.

If he was looking for a success—and he was—it was Nana. She had come from an agency that specialized in these things, and to him she was like Mary Poppins, albeit without the whimsy.

She loved his daughter—and him—in her own stern

way, and she knew things about children, in the very same way he knew them about business. She knew how to pull uncooperative hair into tight ponytails without creating hysteria. She knew the right bedtime stories, and read them without missing lines as he sometimes did, hoping to get off easy and early to make that important phone call. She knew about playdates with other little creatures who cried too easily, pouted, wanted to play princess and paint their fingernails and generally terrified the hell out of Aidan.

He was guiltily aware Nana's steadying presence allowed him to do what he was best at—work—with less guilt.

And so, Aidan was well aware he was *bumbling* through, doing his best and falling short, winning the unwanted pity and devotion of almost every woman who saw him with his daughter.

It's like they all somehow knew his secret failing, including this one marching ahead of him with her nose in the air.

The truth was, he'd had his reservations about the Old-Fashioned Country Christmas. And so had Nana. For once, he had overruled her, wanting something so desperately and not knowing how to get there.

Wanting his daughter to experience something he'd never had, not even when he had shared the Christmas season with his wife. He wanted her to have that joyous Christmas that was depicted in every carol and every story and every TV show and every movie.

Crazy to still believe in such things.

But the unexpected McGregor granddaughter did. Somehow, he knew Noelle believed. In goodness. And probably miracles. The magic of Christmas and all that rot. He hated it, and was drawn to it at the very same time.

Oh, boy. She was the kind of see-through-to-your-soul

person that a guy like him—who had given up on his soul a long, long time ago—really needed to watch himself around.

If there was a palpable tension between Aidan and herself, Noelle noted things were not going much better in the house.

She dispensed with the toque immediately—she could not help feeling it contributed to the country bumpkin look—but her hair was flyaway and hissing with static underneath it. Aidan looked entertained by her efforts to pat it down, so she stopped, stomped the snow off her feet and left him in the porch.

Nana and her grandfather were having a standoff in the kitchen.

"Surely you don't think these filthy *things* belong on the counter?"

"Don't touch those. There are not filthy, they're greasy. There's a difference. They're engine parts. They're in order!"

"They don't belong in the kitchen!"

"It's my kitchen!"

"But I won't eat food that's been prepared on that." She waved a hand at the mess.

"It looks as if you could stand to miss a few meals."

"Oh! I never!"

"That's obvious, you dried-up old—"

"Grandpa."

In the back of her mind Noelle was thinking, *food*. Had her grandfather laid in enough food for guests? Had he planned for three meals a day for at least five people, plus snacks that would interest a five-year-old? And what about the rooms? Had he freshened them up? Laundered sheets and put out good towels? Most of the rooms in this large house had not been used in years.

The logistics of it, not to mention the squabbling, were beginning to give Noelle an awful headache, which worsened when Aidan came into the kitchen.

Underneath his jacket, he had on an expensive shirt, pure white and possibly silk, not the kind of shirt you generally saw on the ranch. He exuded a presence of good grooming and good taste and subtle wealth that made the room seem too small and somewhat shabby.

This whole idea was so ill conceived, Noelle decided desperately. Couldn't she just announce the Old-Fashioned Country Christmas was a terrible mistake and send them all home? At the moment it seemed everyone, including her grandfather, the instigator, would be more than pleased by such a turn of events!

"She told Tess the stove was dangerous," her grandpa reported furiously. "You know how many kids we've had through this house without a single burn victim?"

Yes, everyone would be more than pleased if an old-fashioned Christmas was canceled, except for Tess. Noelle's eyes were drawn to her stillness.

The little girl, in her candy-floss-pink outfit, with her gorgeous curls and pixie features, was standing off to the side, frozen as a statue, her hand resting on Smiley's head, her wide eyes going back and forth between her Nana and Noelle's grandfather.

"That's quite enough," Noelle said quietly, making a small gesture toward Tess.

All the adults in the room looked at the little girl.

Noelle remembered the orphaned child she had been, and she reminded her grandfather of that with a glance and a loudly cleared throat.

"Sorry," he mumbled in the direction of Nana. "I've become set in my ways."

Nana could have leaped at the opportunity to agree, but in a reasonable tone she said, "I'd be happy to clean up the counters."

"I'll help," Noelle said quickly.

Her grandfather nodded. "But don't touch my engine parts. They're lined up in order. I'll put them away myself. You want to help me put up the outdoor Christmas lights this afternoon?" he asked Aidan, shooting a resentful look at Nana, as if she was displacing him from a house he now couldn't wait to get out of.

"Delighted," Aidan said, his tone cool and not delighted in the least.

Tess broke from her stillness. The tiny worried knot in her brow evaporated. She clapped her hands together. "We're just like a family," she declared.

"Isn't that the truth?" Aidan said pleasantly. Noelle shot him a look. She was almost certain his experiences with family—and with Christmas—had not been good ones. Maybe even before a horrible fire had changed everything?

Could she overcome her initial defensive reaction to him—to his hostility and his dislike of Christmas and his horrible cynicism—and change that?

Really, wasn't that what Christmas was all about? To think about others? Weren't the most meaningful gifts the ones you bestowed upon the strangers that came to your door? Wasn't that in keeping with the spirit of the first Christmas, when the wise men had followed the star to a manger?

Hadn't she been the recipient of amazing gifts from strangers and from family, when, at twelve, she had found herself facing her first Christmas as an orphan?

That was what she had to remember. It wasn't about her.

It was about giving back what had been so freely given. All of them here were going to have to unite in a common goal.

To give motherless Tess—and maybe her daddy, too—a Christmas that would ease some of their painful memories. A Christmas that would be filled with a kind of magic that he had searched for and found all his money could not buy. A Christmas that would be overflowing with the true spirit of the day and the season.

Hopefully, it would make her grandfather's first Christmas without his partner of some fifty-odd years somewhat more bearable, too.

Since these were such happy thoughts, altruistic even, why did Noelle feel as if she was preparing to go into battle?

"Have you ever cut down your own Christmas tree before?" she asked Tess.

The little girl's eyes went very round. She clapped her hands together. A smile lit her face.

"No," she breathed. "We didn't have our own Christmas tree last year. Or the ugly Santa year."

Noelle noticed she had outgrown her rhotacism. Or a therapist had been hired.

Of course they wouldn't have had a tree of their own. Not in a glass igloo and not in the best hotel room money could buy.

Tess frowned with fierce concentration. "Did we before that, Daddy?"

"Of course, we did."

Noelle glanced at Aidan. His face was pained. Obviously, they had had their own Christmas tree once, a memory he was trying to outrun, whether he knew it or not.

"We'll go out and find a Christmas tree," Noelle promised her. "We won't stop looking until we find one that is absolutely right."

"A really big one?" Tess asked.

"Maybe. Or maybe it will be a really small one. We'll know when we see it. It's as if it will whisper to us, *I'm the one.*"

"Really?" Tess asked.

"Really."

"Really?" Aidan said drily.

"I told you it was going to be perfect, Daddy," Tess whispered.

"It sounds dangerous," Nana said.

Grandpa rolled his eyes.

But it was Aidan's face that captivated Noelle. He was, it seemed, trying to contain his cynicism as he looked at his little girl, his handsome face softened with hopefulness.

Despite all his skepticism and suspicion, he just wanted his little girl to be happy.

How hard could it be to put any animosity he had coaxed to the surface aside and make his Christmas wish come true?

Noelle took a deep breath. She knew what would make that little girl happy. The presence of her father. The absolute presence of him, without his emails and his phone calls and all the distractions that he had used to keep from doing the very thing his little girl needed him to do.

Feeling.

Noelle realized she wanted to engineer activities so that Tess spent as much time as possible with her daddy.

"Grandpa, maybe you and Nana could put up the lights this afternoon, after lunch. Aidan and Tess and I will go in search of the perfect tree."

Her grandpa looked as if he intended to protest. Strenuously. As did Nana. Aidan looked none too thrilled, either. He patted his shirt pocket, looking for the reassurance of the cell phone that wasn't there. Her grandfather's mouth opened. Nana lifted her hand as if in class, waiting for permission to register her complaint.

But Tess nearly melted. "Doesn't that sound purr-fect, Daddy?"

Nana's hand drifted down. Grandpa's mouth snapped shut. Aidan gave up his search for his cell phone, squatted in front of his child and let her wrap her arms around his neck.

"It does," he whispered, standing with her in his arms.

Looking at the two of them, an island of desperate need, Noelle felt the enormity of the responsibility she had just shouldered.

She turned her attention away. "Grandpa? Is there, um, a plan for lunch?"

Rufus looked inordinately pleased by the question. "Yes, indeed there is," he said. He pulled a rumpled piece of paper from his pocket. "Today for lunch is pizza!"

"You have that written down?" Noelle asked, astounded.

"For every day," he said. "Finishing with turkey and all the fixin's on Christmas."

He had a meal plan! For heaven's sake, maybe he had given this thing a great deal more thought than Noelle had given him credit for. Maybe her concerns about his mental wellness had been a bit overblown. On the other hand, he'd obviously been in the planning stages for a long time. Why hadn't he shared it with her? She intended to ask him that at the first opportunity!

"I love pizza," Tess said.

"I figured you would," Rufus said, smiling.

Still, even though he hadn't shared his idea with her, Noelle had to admit that maybe, just maybe, Rufus had the right idea, after all. Maybe Christmas should bring strangers together.

"It seems we're a long way from the nearest pizzeria," Aidan said with a certain skepticism.

Then again, maybe not.

Rufus retrieved several frozen pizzas from his chest freezer. While he scooped up engine parts and spirited them away to a new location, Noelle and Nana cleaned behind him. As Noelle watched out of the corner of her eye, Aidan and Tess carefully read the pizza boxes and prepared the pizzas for the oven.

By the time lunch was over, some of the tensions had faded. Immediately following lunch, Rufus directed everyone to their rooms. Noelle had, as surreptitiously as possible, inspected them. Again, her grandfather was prepared.

The rooms were dusted. The linens were clean. The upstairs bathroom was spotless. He'd definitely been preparing for this event for some time.

Probably he had started just about the time that Noelle had started to hear the change in his voice, from defeat to cautious enthusiasm for the season.

Why the secrecy? Why had he not included her in his planning?

Still, despite being a bit hurt by that, there was beginning to be a number of reasons for her to embrace this Christmas plan.

An hour later, she and Aidan had bundled Tess up and headed outside. Tess and Smiley raced ahead of them through the snow, Tess's laughter gurgling out of her as the old dog kept accidentally bumping her legs. Aidan did not look at home carrying an ax, but he had looked offended when Noelle had said she would carry it, along with the saw.

On a high piece of ground, before they entered a grove of trees, he stopped and checked his cell phone.

"Don't even bother," Noelle told him.

He squinted at her, as if realizing for the first time she was there. He put his cell phone away.

"So," Aidan asked, his voice threaded through with cynicism, "why the new plan? You and me looking for a Christmas tree, instead of me putting up lights with your grandfather?"

The nice feeling of this being a good idea that might work out after all shimmered like a mirage about to disappear.

Could he seriously not see how important it was for him to spend quality time with his daughter? Could he not see that it was a gift that he couldn't get cell service?

Still, didn't he have to figure that out for himself?

"You're onto me, Mr. Phillips," she said, blinking at him and smiling sweetly. "Despite me telling you I'm definitely not interested in you, you have seen right through the charade, because what woman couldn't be interested in you, really? So I have engineered this opportunity to spend time with you. I am hoping in the wholesome activity of cutting down a Christmas tree you will see I am excellent with both dogs and children. You will see I am both playful and intelligent, practical and an excellent problem-solver."

His lips were twitching reluctantly. "All that in the cutting down of a tree?"

"It's not simply cutting down a tree. Selection of the tree is important."

"Oh, yes," he said cynically, though his eyes were still sparking with laughter, "the tree is going to speak to us, if I recall."

"That's right. So add 'intuitive' to my checklist as a great mate. Cutting it down and getting it home might be more complicated than you thought. You'll see my strengths. Naturally," she said demurely, "I'll be judging yours, as well. Strength, in particular, is important to a woman searching for a life mate. Possibly more so than intelligence."

"This is the second time you've brought my intelligence up for debate."

"Really? I'll put it in the plus column. That you can count."

"I hardly know what to say."

"Yes, well, that goes in the minus column then. A certain social ineptitude."

He actually laughed. He was trying hard not to, but he did.

His laughter was rich and genuine, and it made him quite extraordinarily handsome. Tess ran back to him, delighted by the sound, wanting to be part of it. Did he really laugh so seldom that it drew his daughter's attention to him?

"What, Daddy, what?" she insisted, tugging on his sleeve.

"Our new friend, Noelle, is very entertaining."

"What does that mean?" Tess asked.

"Playful and intelligent," Noelle supplied helpfully. Was it a weakness to want to make him laugh again and again? And not just for Tess's benefit?

He set down the ax, bent down, scooped up a handful of snow and tossed it at Noelle. It happened so swiftly she didn't have time to get her hands up. The snow hit her toque and drifted down her face.

"I hope," Noelle sputtered, "you didn't consider that a snowball? Definitely in the minus column for you."

She bent, put down the saw, scooped up her own handful of snow and expertly rounded it in her hands, compacting it, firming it up. She inspected it, the perfect ball, hefted it experimentally from hand to hand.

"Wait a minute," he said, holding up his hands, mock surrender.

She pulled her arm back. He gave a shout and raced away from her. The snowball exploded in the middle of his back.

Tess shrieked with laughter. The dog barked.

"Show me how!" Tess insisted.

"Hey, no fair," he yelled. "Two against one."

"Au contraire," Noelle called after him. "All is fair in, well, you know."

She armed Tess with a snowball. Tess chased after her father, who ran away but slowed down enough for her to get him. The little girl was laughing so hard she could barely launch the snowball, let alone land the target. But she had the idea now. She knelt in the snow, giggling fiendishly as she shaped her next snowball.

And while Aidan watched his daughter, amused, Noelle crept forward into range and let loose the four snowballs she had made and cradled in the crook of her arm.

Wham, wham, wham, wham, in quick succession.

"Where on earth did you learn to aim like that?"

"I'm a country girl," she reminded him. "You don't want to let me too near a rifle if you thought that was good."

"Noted," he said. And then he was leaning down, picking up snow, shaping a perfect hard ball between his own gloved hands.

Tess shot forward with her snowball and gave him a good hard shot in the knees.

"Ouch," he yelled with fake pain, while his daughter howled with glee. He came after Noelle.

In minutes the air was filled with laughter, shrieking, the dog barking and snowballs.

Half an hour later, they all lay side by side in the snow, soaked and exhausted from both laughing and playing so hard.

"Did I win, Daddy, did I win the snowball fight?"

"Oh, yeah, not a doubt there."

Aidan turned his head. Noelle could feel him looking at her.

"Off the charts in the playful department," he said. He got to his feet and hovered over her. He held out a gloved hand, and after just a second's hesitation, she took it.

"Oh, well," she said. "When you're not beautiful, you have to make up for it in other ways."

The laughter left his face. He scowled and drew her to her feet, his strength easy. She was standing way too close to him. His scent was heady and crisp. She should have stepped away. He should have let go.

But she did not step away, and he did not let go.

"Not beautiful?" he asked gruffly and then even more strongly. "Not beautiful? What?"

CHAPTER FIVE

NOELLE WAS BEING lifted up by what she saw in Aidan's eyes, lifted up out of her body and delivered to a place where angels gathered.

That place was dangerous, she told herself.

And yet, still, even knowing the danger, it was hard to break the bond between them, between their hands, and their eyes, their bodies so close together, radiating warmth from all their exertions. Even their breath was frosty and tangled, as if they were breathing in the essence of each other.

Noelle yanked her snow-soaked mittens out of his, but somehow she didn't move. Couldn't. He was drinking in her face with a look she could not move away from.

As if he was thirsty and she was a long, cool drink of water. Or maybe she was the thirst and he was the drink of water.

"Not beautiful," she stammered. "I'm not."

"What would make you believe such a thing?"

Her mouth moved to begin reiterating a long list of proofs, but not a single sound came out.

"I knew it," he growled with a fearsome anger. "Some dog in your past—possibly your recent past—has made you believe this thing."

She could still say nothing, stunned by what she saw in his eyes.

He wasn't saying this to make her feel good. It wasn't

some pat line. It came from the deepest part of him, a place where there were no lies or deceptions, only truth.

And if she doubted, Aidan took off his glove. He reached out with a gentleness that almost made her cry for the affirmation of his truth in it. His hand warm, his skin silk over iron, touched her cheek, scraped it, rested there. She could not move away from his touch, captive to his unexpected tenderness.

"You are so beautiful," he said softly. "You may be the most beautiful woman I have ever seen."

Her mouth fell open. She could feel herself leaning toward whatever she saw in his eyes.

"Daddy, are you going to kiss Noelle?"

The little voice, inquisitive, delighted, yanked them apart.

His hand fell down. He shoved it in his pocket. "Of course not!" he said.

"No!" Noelle agreed.

He spun away from her. "I have no idea where that ax is."

She scanned the churned-up snow. "When you find it, the saw should be nearby."

And then some nervous tension broke between them, and the three of them were laughing all over again, kicking up snow until they found the ax and saw.

Back on their journey, after the detour, they entered another grove of trees.

"This is mostly balsam fir," Noelle said. She took a deep breath. "Can you smell them? I think they're the best Christmas trees. They're native to my grandfather's land."

"I can smell them!" Tess said.

They wandered through them, judging this one and that, Tess leaning close to several to smell them and to see if they whispered.

"You might want to explain to her the whispering part is not exactly literal."

"Ah, ye of little faith," Noelle said. "When did you stop believing in magic?"

He didn't answer that, just looked away quickly so that she knew it had been a long, long time ago.

Suddenly Tess, who had been flitting from tree to tree like a bumble bee pollinating flowers, stopped. She stood in front of a tree. She cocked her head. She was utterly still.

And then she turned and looked at them, her face incredulous.

"It whispered!" she said.

Aidan took a surprised step back and looked at Noelle. "Exactly what kind of enchantress are you?" he said.

"Apparently the beautiful kind," she said, laughing.

"But that's the most dangerous kind of all," he said softly, and suddenly that near-miss, near-kiss moment was sizzling in the air between them.

Imagine a man like Aidan Phillips thinking she was dangerous.

Still, she could not linger in the power of that.

"You don't know the meaning of the word *dangerous*," she said. "But chopping down a tree could change that."

"I think there are all kinds of danger, and sometimes the more subtle kinds are way more threatening than the sharp blade of a big ax."

"Is it perfect?" Tess asked. "Is it?"

They all stood looking at the tree. It was about five feet tall, and mounded with snow. Aidan stepped forward and shook it. The snow slid off it and down his back.

"Just taking one for the team," he said. "No need for concern."

The tree, without snow, was nicely filled out on one side and not so much on the other. Though it looked big from Tess's viewpoint, it was obviously very small, maybe a little taller than Noelle was. The branches were too far apart in places. There was another place where a large branch had been damaged and all the needles had turned brown. The top had taken off crazily in a different direction than the bottom, giving the tree quite a crooked lean.

It was, without a doubt, the most perfect Christmas tree any of them had ever seen.

"I'm going to try to break this to you gently," Noelle told Aidan an hour later, "but you are no woodsman."

He had, by now, stripped off his jacket. And his mittens. The sweat was beaded on his brow.

Really? She could have offered to go back to the barn and retrieve the chainsaw. But that would have taken all the fun out of it.

Fun and something else. There was something gloriously breathtaking about seeing the male animal pit his strength against the elements.

Plus, ever since the near kiss, Noelle's senses felt heightened. The light, especially the way it threaded through his coal-dark hair, seemed exquisite. The sharp smell of the tree had intensified as his ax bit into bark and pulp and, finally, sap. Tess's laughter, as she made angels and covered the dog with snow and wrote her name with footprints, filled the glade with fairy music.

Noelle's *you-are-no-woodsman* taunt earned her a good-natured glare, and Aidan renewed his efforts to chop through the trunk of the tree. Finally, it was still upright, but only by the merest of threads of broken wood fiber.

"Move the women, children and dogs to safe ground," he shouted. "Timber."

The tree didn't so much fall, as kind of gently slide down, with a whisper rather than a crash. Several of its branches cracked, making the tree even less perfect than it had been before.

"That was somewhat anticlimactic," Aidan declared, breathing hard.

But Tess was beside herself with excitement. After resting briefly, all of them, ignoring the discomfort of prickly needles and sharp little branches, grabbed on to the tree and began to drag it through the snow.

Night came early at this time of year, and it was nearly dark by the time they got the tree almost back to the house. They were breathless and tired and utterly happy.

They paused for a rest as the house came into view. It was drenched in the dying light of the day, in soft pinks and muted golds and fiery oranges. As the darkness deepened around it, an owl hooted, and in the far distance, a pack of wolves began to sing a haunting and wild song.

"Wolves?" Aidan asked, surprised.

"Yes, relative newcomers to this area."

"Are they on the other side of that field?" he asked.

Noelle smiled at the fierce, protective note in his voice. "The sound really carries on nights like this. I don't think they're close, at all. And that's not a field, though I can see why you would think so when it's covered with snow like that. It's a pond. My grandfather always clears it Christmas Day for skating."

"Oh, too bad, we didn't bring skates. Tess doesn't have any yet. I haven't skated for years. And Nana? Can you imagine?"

They shared a laugh.

A light turned on in the house, throwing a golden glow out the window and lighting up a pathway through the snow. It beckoned them, calling them home, to the promise of warmth against the cooling of the day, a promise of safety against the mysteries of the woods in the night.

And then a door slapped open.

"Are you done yet?" Nana's shrill voice carried across the snow as clearly as the wolf song had.

"Art takes time!" Rufus yelled back. "Where have you been? I needed you to hand me the string of lights marked number fourteen. I had to get down and get it myself. I'm old. I can't be expected to go up and down a ladder a hundred times!"

It was possibly the first time Noelle had ever heard her grandfather refer to himself as old.

"Oh, be quiet, you ancient coot. Do you ever stop complaining? I was helping! I went in to find something for supper."

"Do you think this has been going on since we left?" Aidan asked. He didn't even try to hide his amusement.

"No doubt. I'm not sure what it is. My grandfather never acts the way he does with her."

"You don't know what it is?" Aidan said, looking at her with interest. A smile was tickling his lips.

"No. Do you?"

"It's the age-old game."

She felt shocked. "But my grandmother has only been gone a few months. It wouldn't be right."

"Maybe that's what he thinks, too," Aidan offered softly. "That it needs to be fought. That it isn't right."

"They don't like each other," she insisted, but for some reason she was thinking she had said nearly those same words to Aidan. *I don't like you.*

And he had said them to her.

And then, despite that initial animosity, only hours later, they had come very close to kissing. A shiver went up and down her spine as she contemplated the fact that she might be playing the age-old game with Aidan.

It had to stop. It could only end in pain.

Her grandfather's voice came with clarity through the cold air and across the snow again.

"I hope you didn't meddle with supper."

"It's already in the oven."

"I have a plan I'm following!"

"Oh, well," Nana said, unrepentant. "I think I can figure out how to heat a frozen lasagna."

"That's not for tonight! Tonight was cabbage rolls. It was marked right on the containers. I had Mrs. Bentley mark them."

Noelle smiled. Her grandfather was so organized he'd had one of the neighbors prepare frozen dinners for him and for the company he was expecting. It was just so endearing…and yet again, it nagged at her. Much preparation had gone into this. Why hadn't he told her what he was up to?

Apparently Nana missed the endearing part of an old widower hosting guests for Christmas.

"Oh, don't be so stuck in your ways. The label must have fallen off. Aidan and Tess and Noelle will be home soon, and they'll be hungry. Shouldn't they be home by now? What if Aidan's bleeding to death out there?"

"Maybe all of them got attacked by that wolf pack. Being eaten as we speak."

"What wolf pack?"

"You can't hear them? If you'd stop talking for three seconds… Plug in the lights."

"Wolves?" That shrill note again.

"Plug in the damned lights!"

And into the sudden silence and the gathering darkness, the lights of the house winked on. They were bright primary colors: red and yellow, blue and green. They ran around the roofline, making globes of reflected color in the snow. They marked the gables. They wrapped around the porch pillars and the railings, and they outlined the windows. Noelle could not be sure how two old people had gotten this much done.

Maybe, despite the bickering, there was a certain magic in the air.

Certainly, the house seemed to be saying that. It had transformed from an old ranch house to a gingerbread house, something worthy of a fairy tale, in just an afternoon.

There was something about standing here, with Aidan and Tess, listening to the quarreling of Rufus and Nana in the distance, that made Noelle's heart stand still. And in the silence of her heart not beating, she was sure she heard a little voice.

There *are* other ways that game can end, it said: all good fairy tales end with *and they lived happily-ever-after.*

But Noelle reminded herself firmly of the red dress in her closet, her reminder of broken dreams. This was no fairy tale, she admonished herself sternly. There was no point casting Aidan in the role of a prince, despite his lapse in calling her beautiful and despite the near-miss kiss. He had made it abundantly clear he was not interested in a romance, and that she had better not be, either!

Grabbing the tree again, Noelle moved deliberately away from the lure of the magic in the air and toward the house. Aidan and Tess joined her and they dragged the tree up onto the porch. And then Noelle and Aidan stood, looking at it, while Tess danced around it.

Rufus and Nana admired their find and declared it perfect.

"Are we going to decorate it tonight?" Tess asked. "Please? Please? Please?"

There was something about the hopefulness of a child that made magic very hard to outrun.

CHAPTER SIX

As it turned out there was no tree-decorating that night. Despite a valiant effort to keep her eyes open, Tess went to sleep during dinner. She fell asleep instantly and completely, her hand clutched around her fork. She suddenly just sagged, the fork dropped, and she would have slid to the floor, like a silk dress off a stool, if her father had not risen from his own chair and scooped her up.

Aidan looked down into Tess's sleeping face, and Noelle felt it was a moment worthy of a painting. Not mother and child, but something even more precious, perhaps, for the rarity of its capture.

Father and child.

Strength and vulnerability. Independence and dependence. Largeness and tininess. Worldliness and innocence.

Aidan's face was a study in contrasts: the softness of love, but underneath that a certain fierce protectiveness that she had glimpsed when he'd heard the wolves. This child in his arms? This was what he was willing to die for.

And then he was gone from the dining room, and Noelle felt her own weariness catch up with her. It had been a jam-packed day, full of surprises, physical activity and emotional twists and turns. It had been sometimes exhilarating and sometimes exhausting.

"If you could leave the dishes," she said to Nana and

her grandfather, "I'll look after them in the morning. Good night."

She sought the safety of her room. It was untouched by time. A bed was covered in the pillows, quilt and plush throw—all in shades of pink and white—that she had brought with her when she had moved here at age twelve.

Her grandmother had made the curtains, sheer fabric embossed with pink polka dots, and embellished them with frilly trim. Really, her adult eye could see it was too much, like the room was the unfortunate result of a mating between cotton candy and a tutu. Noelle's teen self was represented by photograph posters on the wall, one of a field of dandelions and one of a rainbow over an old barn. They told her to Dream Big and Never Give Up. The silver-framed picture of her mom and dad was on the dresser.

Except for the addition of the posters when she was around sixteen, Noelle did not change things. She had always loved the room just the way it was, even when she was old enough to want something else. To this day, she loved the remnants of her old life, the bedding she and her mother had chosen together.

The bed was a twin. When she and Mitchell had come to meet her grandparents she had stayed in this room, and he down the hall. Even though her grandparents knew she was living with Mitchell, they had not approved of the arrangement, and Noelle felt it would have been disrespectful to share a room with her boyfriend under her grandparents' roof.

Noelle felt glad of that now. That this room was what it had always been to her, untainted by unhappy memories, a haven in a world that had turned topsy-turvy on her more than once. She got her pajamas out of her suitcase, put them on and flipped out the light. It was usually very dark out here in the country, but tonight brightness from the Christmas lights reflecting off the snow on the roof came through her window and cast her room in muted rainbows. She crawled under her covers, appreciating again the freshly laundered linens, and all her grandfather's hard work to welcome her and others to his home.

She realized she hadn't talked to him as she had intended.

And then she realized she hadn't gone to the barn to check Mitchell's many social media posts for the day, either.

It wasn't too late. It was early. She could get up. She could hear her grandfather and Nana downstairs, the quiet clink of dishes being washed, their voices low and conversational, for once.

A good time to leave them alone and not a good time to find out why she, Noelle, had been excluded from his grand plan for an old-fashioned Christmas.

This would be the perfect time to slip out the door and sneak to the nearest place on the ranch that got cell service.

But her muscles ached pleasantly from chasing through the snow today and from hauling the tree home. She found herself unable to leave the sense of safety and security in her room, unwilling to get out from under her warm down quilt, not wanting to leave the state of languid relaxation both her mind and body were enjoying.

But then she heard sounds and realized Aidan must have tucked Tess into the little bed in the room under the eaves. Now he was in the hall bathroom, brushing his teeth. The water ran for a while longer. Possibly he was shaving. It all seemed very intimate!

Then his footsteps padded by Noelle's door as he went down the hall. She heard him go into the room next to hers, and through the thinness of the old walls she was sure she could hear his clothes coming off and whispering to the floor.

The springs of the bed next door creaked. It seemed to her that he had not had time to put something else on. What would he wear for pajamas? Did he wear pajamas? She had the sudden, totally uninvited thought that he might have slipped in between the sheets naked.

The fact that she would have such a thought made her blush. She wondered if these wayward images in her mind were going to make her blush the next time she saw him.

Her own pajamas now seemed woefully inadequate. She had chosen them for the ranch, for opening presents Christmas morning with her grandfather, not with Aidan Phillips! Red flannel, printed with penguins wearing Santa hats. Was she going to have to change every time she went down the hall to use the bathroom?

Why? To impress Aidan Phillips?

To make him whisper *beautiful* again?

It was all very awkward. It felt suddenly as if the sanctity of her room and her home had been invaded. As if a fine tension had crept into her snug nest. She had never felt this way when Mitchell was down the hall!

Red dress, she whispered to herself, her reminder of the pain of broken dreams, a reminder not to leave herself open to debilitating romantic fantasies.

I'll never be able to sleep now, she thought, watching the gentle play of the Christmas lights on her bedroom ceiling.

And it was the last thought she had before morning.

Aidan lay awake in the unfamiliar bed for a long time, contemplating the day. The room was humble, not what he was used to. A small bed was crowded under a sloped roof that looked as if it had leaked a long time ago. A spring was poking him in his behind. Cheery Christmas lights were shining in the small window, and it was irritating.

But the worst thing was that he, iron man of self-control, had nearly kissed a woman he barely knew. He had told her she was beautiful and watched as the sun rose in her eyes at the compliment, as if Noelle was not used to receiving them.

Aidan considered himself a smart man. And he knew what the smart thing to do would be. It would be to get up in the morning and announce something had come up, that they wouldn't be able to stay for Christmas, after all.

But then he thought of Tess's enjoyment of the day, her deep pleasure in small things: her kinship with the old dog, her glee in the snow, her wonder in finding the perfect tree, her happy exhaustion at the end of the day. He could not remember a day—ever—not even after full agendas in Disneyland, where she had not hauled out her collection of stories to be read as the day died. Tonight, the stories were not even unpacked.

Would he really shatter Tess's Christmas in order to protect himself? No, he wouldn't and he couldn't. But he had to be on guard.

"On guard," he muttered, very softly, so that his voice would not carry through the paper-thin walls. "On guard, on guard, on guard." The chant, unfortunately, seemed to be taking on the tune of "Frosty the Snowman," as if some unwanted magic was worming its way inside of him.

"You can do anything for a few days," Aidan told himself firmly. And he knew, with a touch of satisfaction, that it was true. He would make any sacrifice to allow his daughter happiness.

Maybe he wasn't such a colossal failure as a dad, after all.

Noelle awoke to familiar sounds: her grandfather opening the back door to bring wood in, the sounds of coffee beans being ground, the old iron door on the woodstove creaking open. She glanced at the bedside clock. It was very early.

She got up, and hesitated over the pajamas. It seemed too early to get dressed. It seemed like some kind of concession to *him* that she did not feel comfortable in her own home wearing what she had always worn. So, defiantly, she left them on. In her closet was an old plaid robe, and she put that over the pajamas. And then Noelle determinedly shoved her feet in the only slippers she had brought with her. The old ranch house floors could be like ice in the morning.

She looked down at her feet and warned herself to stop worrying about Aidan Phillips's impressions of her.

Her grandfather was kneeling in front of the stove, blowing lightly, coaxing heat from last night's embers, feeding in little pieces of kindling.

"You're up early," he said. "I'm glad. I got some things to show you."

He pulled a file down off the top of the fridge and presented it to her with shy pride. Noelle opened it.

"You can find so much stuff on the interstate," her grandfather said eagerly, hovering over her shoulder. "The library has a printer you can use for twenty-five cents a sheet."

From the thickness of the file, the library should be able to buy a new printer strictly from the proceeds of her grandfather's printing activities.

In the file were snow activities for children. Coloring snow with spray bottles of water and food coloring. Ice globes made with water frozen in balloons. Creative snowmen. And women. And snow caterpillars. Homemade snow globes. Feeders for birds. Frozen soap bubbles. "Noughts and Crosses" in the snow. Snow forts and snow castles.

"Wow," Noelle said, shutting the file.

"Which one should we do today? With Tess?"

"We could let her choose. I think the morning will probably be used up decorating the tree."

"I've got all the decorations in the attic ready to bring down."

"Grandpa." Noelle tapped the file. "You've been collecting ideas for quite some time."

He nodded happily.

"And you've done a lot of work planning meals. And getting rooms ready."

He seemed to figure out this was going somewhere. He moved over to the counter and his ancient coffee maker. He shot her a look out of the corner of his eye and busied himself measuring his freshly ground beans.

"Why didn't you tell me?" she asked softly. "I'm your family. Why didn't you let me know? Why were you making Christmas plans without me?"

"Without you?" he said. "That's silly. I couldn't have Christmas without you!"

"That's not what I meant. I meant the ad on I-Sell. I meant telling me about Aidan and Tess and the Old-Fashioned Country Christmas. Why did you keep me in the dark?"

"It was a surprise," he said stubbornly.

"You know I don't really like surprises."

"Well, that's just it," he said, his back completely to her now as he fiddled with the coffee maker.

"What's just it?"

His shoulders hunched uncomfortably.

"Tell me."

At that moment an ear-splitting scream came from upstairs. "Stop, stop! You slathering beast!"

Noelle catapulted up the stairs. Her grandfather was already going up them two at a time.

At the top of the stairs, Aidan was coming out of his

room. She nearly collided with him. Despite the fact that the screaming continued, she felt the world go still around her.

His hair was sleep-roughened. There was a shadow of morning whisker on his face.

And he was naked.

Partially naked.

He was wearing pajama bottoms, but his chest and torso were free of clothing. Deliciously so.

There was a carved beauty to his physique that was so compelling Noelle felt completely able to ignore the fact that it sounded as if Nana was being murdered in her bedroom.

His pajama bottoms were plaid, and hung very low on his hips. His feet were bare. How come she had never noticed how incredibly sexy bare feet were before?

"Get off me!" Nana shrieked.

"Oh, stop it," Rufus said. "It's just a dog."

It seemed to Noelle that Aidan's gaze might have rested on what showed of her penguin-pajamas-clad legs jutting out from under the housecoat for just a little too long. Her feet were not sexily bare. They were stuffed into slippers her grandmother and grandfather had given her a long time ago.

"Cookie Monster?" he said, as if he, too, was able to shut out the sounds of Nana screaming.

"Animal." She tilted her chin just to let him know she didn't care what he thought. Though a part of her did. Very much.

"Ah." He turned from her and went down the hallway.

In a daze, Noelle followed Aidan and they both stood in the doorway of Nana's bedroom.

Smiley had invaded. He was on her bed. He had her arms pinned under the covers, his huge paws straddling her, and he was feverishly licking thick gobs of cold cream off her face.

Rufus went and pulled the dog off, barely able to contain his gleeful snickering. Noelle couldn't help feeling he was doubly pleased because he had escaped answering her questions.

But then, terribly, Nana began to cry. "I was dreaming of wolves and—" She buried her poor face, cold cream rearranged unattractively, in her hands. Rufus's delight died on his face. He handed the dog off to Aidan, who looked stunned and uncomfortable, and turned back to Nana.

"There, there," he said, and went and sat on the edge of the bed. He pried a hand away from her face and patted it awkwardly. She turned and buried her face in his shirt. If the cold cream being slathered down the front of him bothered him, it didn't show. His hand slid to her hair.

"There, there," he said again. "You're fine. Everything's okay."

CHAPTER SEVEN

AIDAN BACKED OUT of the room hastily, dog firmly in his grasp He let go of the dog, and actually pulled the door shut behind him as if Nana and Rufus might need a little privacy! Smiley slunk away.

"Is she always…um, like this?" Noelle asked. The hallway felt very narrow. It felt as if his chest was nearly touching her.

She noticed his hair was a little messy. She had to stick her hands in her housecoat pockets to resist the urge to touch it, to smooth it into place.

Red dress, red dress, red dress.

"No," Aidan said, having no idea of the danger his hair was in, or the danger she found herself in. "Never. She's usually very stoic."

"Daddy!"

Another shrill distraction, thank heavens.

"Nice quiet morning at the ranch?" Aidan gave Noelle a wry grin that took the edge off the sarcasm and moved by her to fetch Tess. His naked chest passed within half an inch of her own penguin-pajama-clad one.

"What's wrong with Nana?" she heard Tess ask, and Noelle could hear the fear in her voice.

"She had a bad dream."

"Like I have sometimes?" The fear was already dissipating, her father's calm voice acting like sunshine on fog.

"Yes," he said. "Everything is okay."

He came back into the hallway, the little girl in his arms, nestled securely against the solidness of his chest. Her hair was even messier than his, and again Noelle had an urge to tame those tendrils with her fingertips.

It wasn't just him that had her danger signals blinking on high. It was both of them, this little girl so tugging at her heartstrings. Not as easy to defend against even with her red dress mantra!

"I like your pajamas," Tess told Noelle solemnly. "And your slippers."

"Thank you," Noelle said just as solemnly, and suddenly she was glad she had left on the pajamas and put on the slippers, after all.

"I'm hungry," Tess said, a little girl who had missed her dinner.

"What do you like for breakfast?" Noelle asked.

"Apple Bits." Tess named the popular children's cereal.

"Well, let's see what we have."

Sadly, Aidan put Tess down and went to get dressed.

Tess and Noelle went downstairs and put the dog—who was by the back door making noises like he might be sick—outside. Shockingly her grandfather had Apple Bits. Or maybe it wasn't so shocking. Since he was so organized, he'd probably sent out questionnaires asking what people liked for breakfast.

And so the day began.

Considering its rocky start—with her grandfather evading her questions and Nana being lovingly attacked by Smiley—everything turned good after that.

When Rufus came downstairs he was whistling. When

Nana followed, twenty minutes or so later, she looked relaxed and almost happy.

"I'm making pancakes," Rufus announced.

"We've already had cereal," Noelle said.

He looked crushed until Nana said she'd love pancakes. She added that she loved a man who could cook a good breakfast, and Rufus practically preened as he got his blackened cast-iron pan down off its hook over the woodstove.

Noelle had to race onto the porch before she let the laughter out. Aidan was right behind her. They laughed until their stomachs hurt.

And then with Tess "helping" they wrestled the tree in the door and into the stand, and stood back to admire it. Aidan put the lights on first, avoiding, just barely, words that should not be used around children.

When he was done, Rufus and Nana joined them and boxes of decorations were hauled from the attic. Rufus put on Christmas music and Aidan's groan seemed as if it were mostly for show. Tess was allowed to choose all the decorations. She was in charge of the bottom of the tree and the adults did the top. Smiley was let back in, and he curled up in his basket in the kitchen and refused to join them, though every now and then they would hear a giant wet burp from him that would send them into gales of laughter.

When the tree was done, Nana's objections—which seemed perfunctory, too—that hot chocolate would spoil lunch were quickly dismissed and they all sat in the living room admiring the tree and sipping the beverage.

Though they were near strangers, a sense of knowing each other—of family—was growing between them.

It was because Tess had brought them something they could not have had without her, the magic of making Christmas for a child.

"Oh!" Noelle suddenly remembered. "One last thing. The house isn't ready until the wreath goes on the door."

She got up and hunted through the decoration boxes until she found it. Old roping lariats had been carefully formed into a wreath shape, threaded through with a thick red ribbon that had once been bright but was now faded. Nestled in the curves of the rope and the ribbon were wooden letters—painted bright green by Noelle when she was very young, before her parents had died—that spelled out a single word: *HOPE*.

Aidan was eyeing her find with spectacular distaste, and she supposed it was old and ghastly and hokey. But she loved it. It felt like her grandmother was right here, as if all the love they'd shared was right here.

Noelle took it to the front door and went outside in her socks.

"You want some help?"

She saw Aidan had slipped out with her. "You don't look very impressed with my grandmother's wreath."

"Don't I?"

"No."

"I'm cynical, that's all. It's not the wreath, it's the word."

"Hope?"

"Aw, yes," he said. "What does it mean exactly?"

She gave him a quizzical look. "Isn't it obvious?"

"Tell me," he insisted.

"It's what Christmas is full of—hope. Hope for love. Hope for family. Hope for joy. Hope for a better world. Hope that hardships can be healed. Hope that someday we can think of the ones we have lost with peace instead of grief."

"That's a tall order," he said.

"Well, Christmas is known as a time you can hope for anything at all."

"Hope," he said softly. "Personally, I think that may be the most dangerous thing of all. Maybe it just sets up an expectation that can never be met."

"I'm not sure if that's cynical," Noelle said softly, "or just plain sad. No, I don't need your help. Thanks for offering. I'd rather do it myself."

"As you wish."

And he stepped back inside, leaving her to contemplate that. Who on earth thought hope was the most dangerous thing of all?

Someone who had been hurt very badly. He must have loved his wife very much. Noelle took her time hanging the wreath, and when she went in, lunch was ready.

To her grandfather's chagrin—he had planned soup and buns—Tess had asked for peanut butter and jam sandwiches. Then, when she only ate a quarter of one, Nana muttered about the hot chocolate spoiling lunch.

After lunch, Rufus hauled out his file of activities, but Nana sniffed and suggested gingerbread houses.

"I don't have the stuff to make that," Rufus protested, apparently not liking being thrown off his game plan for the second time in less than an hour.

"You think you're the only one who can have a good idea?" Nana asked, her tone combative. The truce was apparently over between them. "Out. Shoo… I'll get the gingerbread ready."

Grumbling, her grandfather said he had chores to do in the barn.

"Do you need help?" Aidan asked.

"What I need is some alone time!"

Only Noelle knew he was being so rude because he was trying to hide a pony!

"How about a snowman?" she said brightly.

"I think snow person is the current politically correct term," Aidan said.

The snow was all wrong. It was too cold and it made the snow dry and powdery. The snow person collapsed twice before Aidan came up with the idea of adding water to the snow. Even so, he was a terrible snowman: small and lop-sided, and his eyes kept falling out of his head.

Still, Tess loved him and declared him the most perfect snowman ever.

Rufus did not return for making the gingerbread house, which might have been a good thing. Like the snowman, it was a less-than-stellar gingerbread house.

Gumdrops slid haphazardly down the side of it. One of the walls was collapsing under the weight of too much icing. A chunk broke off and Aidan ate it before they could repair it. Then they broke a chunk off for Tess to eat.

All in all, the house was quite ghastly, but Tess declared it the most perfect gingerbread house ever, so they were all happy.

Everyone seemed to have turned in early again tonight, except Noelle's grandfather, who went outdoors to do more chores.

"I'll come," Noelle said. Side by side they fed the horses, Gidget shoving the larger ones out of the way.

"Is the pony for Tess?" Noelle asked with trepidation.

"Yes. She hasn't seen her yet. Just keep her on the other side of the house for as long as you can."

"Her father said she couldn't have one, you know."

"Well, because he doesn't have a place to keep it. I do."

She sighed. That insinuated an ongoing relationship with the Phillipses. She was not sure her grandfather—or, for that matter, herself—should have hopes on that score. And hope was hard, after a day like today, with that growing sense of comfort and safety and family. How did you let that go when it was time?

Noelle was determined to finish the conversation that had started that morning.

"I need to know why you didn't tell me. A pony implies a great deal of before-thought."

"Humph, the pony was easier than trying to think how to feed a crowd for a couple of days. Your grandma looked after all that."

The longing had been in the background all day: as they put up the tree and decorated with her grandmother's collections of ornaments.

"She'd like the house full of people," he said.

"Though if she'd been here, you wouldn't have done it."

"True."

"Tell me why I was kept in the dark."

Her grandfather looked at her. "You don't like surprises. You don't even like changes. You would have tried to talk me out of it. Remember when I did tell you? I got a lecture about the dangers of the interstate."

"*Lecture* is overstating it!"

"The longer you knew about it, the longer you would have worked on me. Maybe you would have even tried to put a stop to it behind my back. For my own good."

Noelle desperately wanted to deny this, but she couldn't.

"You would have said no to the pony, you would have said people weren't really going to come, and that I was being tricked and cheated."

"That makes me sound like an awful wet blanket, but I would have just been trying to protect you, Grandpa."

"I know. But, Ellie, I'm a grown man. It's a bit insulting that you think you have to protect me."

She was silent, surprised by this. "Isn't that what families do?" she asked finally. "Look out for one another?"

"Lookin' out for one another is one thing, but you…" His voice drifted off uncomfortably.

"I what?"

"Never mind."

"No, I want you to tell me."

"Grandma said it was normal, the thing you have, because of what you'd gone through. Because of your mom and dad dying in that accident when you were only twelve."

"What thing do I have?" Noelle asked. "What did Grandma say was normal because of what I'd been through?"

He looked like he regretted saying as much as he had.

"It doesn't matter. Let's just forget it. And have fun."

"I don't think I can forget it now."

Rufus looked apologetic. "You have this thing with control. You think you know what's best for everyone."

"I do?" she asked, appalled.

"Ellie, you don't give yourself over to life. You want all your ducks lined up in a row. You want everything the same all the time. I'm scared if you keep it up, you'll end up just like *her*."

They both knew he was talking about Nana.

"She seems like a very nice lady," Noelle said, hearing the stiffness in her voice.

"Oh, sure. All rigid and shrieking and wanting everyone to obey her rules, and scared of wolves hiding under her bed."

"I am not stuck in a rut," Noelle sputtered.

"Look at your room," he said.

She stared at her grandfather. She wanted so badly for what he was saying not to be true. But she thought of Mitchell leaving, flinging words at her over his shoulder as he shoved his skinny underpacked suitcase through the door.

Nothing's fun with you. Nothing's spontaneous. You can't stand it when I move a chair. We can't go out for dinner without planning for a week. There's no adventure. There's nothing unexpected. I want something else for my life.

"It's normal," her grandfather said softly, "to want the world to be safe. To feel as if you can have control over the things that make it safe. But you pay a price for it, too."

She could feel her eyes welling.

Her grandfather looked at her imploringly. He didn't want her to be upset. He hadn't wanted to say that, at all. She could tell. It was love for her that had made him say it. She felt as if it might have been what she most needed to hear, even though it was painful.

"I'm sorry," Rufus said.

"It's okay," she said quietly. "I'm glad you told me."

"Let's go back to the house."

"I'm going to stay out here for a little while."

"Are you mad at me?"

"No." That was true. She fished her cell phone out of her pocket and wagged it at him. "I get a bit of service up in the loft. I'll just check on the state of the world."

"Probably limping along without you," her grandfather teased, and then pulled her close and kissed the top of her head in a way that made it all okay.

Noelle went up the rickety ladder and crossed the floor. She opened the loft door and sat down in a pile of sweet-smelling hay. For the longest time she didn't look at her phone, but gazed at the stars in an inky night, contemplating what her grandfather had said.

Finally, a chill began to penetrate even her warm jacket.

She clicked her phone on and looked with annoyance at the no-service symbol. She leaned out the hayloft and held the phone at arm's reach. Two bars. Stretching, she hit one of her social media icons. It was already open on Mitchell's page and she saw he had been updating feverishly. She glanced at the most recent post.

Nearly Christmas and snorkeling. That's what I call living life to the fullest.

A girl who looked too young for him was sharing the selfie.

Noelle felt her throat closing, the tears that had threatened earlier were making a reappearance. *Don't cry*, she told herself, but she did.

"Hello."

She whirled and dropped the phone, thankfully inside and not out the open door.

Aidan reached for her quickly, pulled her away from the loft opening and steadied her, his hand warm and strong on her shoulder. "Don't take a tumble out the window. Would put a terrible damper on all the Christmas cheer."

"Don't sneak up on me!" Noelle wiped hastily at her cheeks.

"I wasn't sneaking," he said reasonably. "I saw the light up here and came to investigate. I thought I made quite a bit of noise. Perhaps whatever you were looking at was totally engrossing?"

He seemed to realize his hand was still on her shoulder. He released her and leaned down, and before she could, swooped up the phone. Instead of handing it back to her, he scowled at the screen.

"I thought you said there was no service."

CHAPTER EIGHT

REALLY, AIDAN THOUGHT, the right thing to do at the moment would be to hand Noelle her phone and leave her up here by herself. He had obviously interrupted a very private moment. Had she been crying? It was hard to tell in the dim light.

Still, when Noelle made a grab for the phone, Aidan could clearly see, in its faint glow, that her cheeks had little streaks down them. Definite tear tracks remained despite her efforts to scrub them away with her sleeve. He found himself holding the phone out of her reach, unable to not look at what had caused her such distress.

An ordinary-looking chap was on a beach with a girl who looked way too young for him. He had posted something about snorkeling and living life to the fullest.

"Friend of yours?" He carefully stripped his voice of the anger he was feeling that somehow this man had made her cry.

"Ex. Ex-friend, I mean." The truth rode heavy in her tone. Aidan watched her with narrow eyes as she swallowed hard.

Her ex was putting up a seemingly endless series of posts? Gloating about his new life? He held the phone still out of her reach, continuing to study the picture.

"He wanted adventure," Noelle said faintly, reluctantly, almost apologetically.

Aidan remembered, sickened at himself, how he had needled her—could it possibly be just yesterday—about a recent heartbreak. As if it was somehow all about him.

But in such a short time, he had seen the truth of her. Or maybe it was just this setting, but somehow Noelle seemed pure in a world that was tainted, innocent in a world that was sinfully excessive in every way. It was the very purity of her that had to be guarded against, the part of her that called to some forgotten place in him and tempted him to play, to be carefree, to let go a bit.

He had to protect himself from the unexpected *sizzle* she made him feel, not because of her wholesomeness, but in spite of it. He had to ward that awareness off, not just for his sake, but her own.

He'd already disappointed one woman who was far more worldly than Noelle!

Still, he could not stop himself from trying to say something that would make her feel better. "Well, if you call getting a sunburned head an adventure, I'd say he's got it. That's going to hurt like hell."

"We can only hope," she muttered, and he laughed and handed her her phone, which she turned off and put in her pocket.

"For what it's worth," he said softly, "he's missing the greatest adventure of all."

Now where had that come from? His implication was that sharing a life with her would be the greatest adventure of all.

Her mouth opened. And shut. And opened again. Finally a sound squeaked out.

"I'm apparently a bit of a stick-in-the-mud. A controller." She hiccupped. "Even my grandfather said it was true.

That's why he didn't tell me about anyone else coming for Christmas. Because he thought I would have tried to wreck it before he even got it off the ground."

"Would you have?"

"Yes."

"Just for his own good," he said gently.

"He said if I wasn't careful I'd end up all rigid and shrieking and wanting everyone to follow my rules."

"Ouch."

"I need to quit meddling. I told you there was no cell service here for your own good, too."

"Not just to be mean?" he teased. He realized he liked teasing her. He liked throwing snowballs at her. He liked making gingerbread houses with her.

"I thought I knew what was best for Tess," Noelle said wistfully. "I thought she needed your undivided attention, without distractions from work. None of my business, right? I'm so certain I know what's right for everyone that I'll lie! It's disgusting."

There was a little trickle of tears sliding down her cheeks again. Couldn't she see how much it meant to him that she cared about Tess like that?

He touched her shoulder. It was so slight under his hand. It made her seem exactly as she was—small, vulnerable, needing him in some way.

To validate her, to protect her, to *see* her. "You have a good, good heart, Ellie McGregor."

Embarrassed, she tried to slide out from under his touch. But he would have none of it. Instead of letting her by, he blocked her way.

When she tilted her head up at him, looking askance, he touched her chin with the tip of his pointer finger and looked at her face.

The fight seemed to leave her. She looked back at him.

She looked at him in a way he was not sure he'd ever been looked at before, deeply and intently, as if she was divining secrets about him he did not even know himself.

It felt as if she was turning the tables on him, giving him what he had intended to give her.

He dropped his finger from her chin.

He ordered himself to go, to get away from her. He warned himself he could not be trusted with this kind of innocence, this kind of purity.

But instead of leaving, he put his arms around her and tugged her into his chest, closed his hands on the small of her back and held her tight.

A small mew of protest came from her, followed swiftly by a sigh of surrender. She snuggled into his chest. And then she let go. She wept.

Finally, when the front of his jacket was pretty much soaked, she pulled away from him.

"I'm so sorry. It's been a hard few months. First, my grandfather sold the land. Then my grandmother died. Then Mitchell ended our engagement."

And despite the fact that it had been a hard few months, she had overcome his initial rudeness to her to embrace the needs of his daughter. He thought of how she was working at creating the perfect Christmas, her devotion to it almost fierce.

Aidan Phillips felt something he had not felt for a long, long time. The shame of self-recognition.

He had become a self-centered jerk!

"I should go in," she said uncomfortably, swiping again at her face with her sleeve.

"Don't rush off," he said. "Let's sit for a minute. Look at those stars tonight. I don't remember the last time I paused to look at things. To really see them."

He lowered himself in the hay, and after a moment she

sat down beside him, and they looked out the loft door at the humbling largeness of a star-studded universe.

"It's one of the things I always love about coming here," Noelle said. "Life seems simpler, I feel as if I notice small things more—the smell of wood smoke, the feel of the dog's fur under my fingertips, the stars at night."

The quiet of the night, Noelle at his side, the expanse of the universe all stirred in him a stunning desire.

Just to be a better man. Maybe not forever, but for this moment.

"So," he asked her softly, "what do you think made you want to fix all that is wrong in the world? In my experience, people who are like that usually have a reason."

She hesitated. Aidan could tell she didn't share private things. She was reserved. He was practically a stranger. And yet the invitation of that bejeweled night sky, of a larger world, seemed to be working on her, too.

"My mom and dad died when I was twelve," she said. "That's when I came here to live with Grandma and Grandpa."

"I'm so sorry. How?"

"A car wreck. It was springtime. It seemed as if good weather had come. A freak storm came out of nowhere, and they slid into a truck. They died instantly, which people told me was a blessing.

"And people told me they loved each other so much—which I already knew, of course—and that they had chosen to be together for eternity."

"That's a very thoughtless thing to say," he said gruffly.

She turned to him, her eyes wide.

"Why would you say that?"

"Obviously your mother and father loved you that much, too. They would have never chosen to leave you. What utter clap-trap."

She sighed and leaned into him. "Thank you for saying that."

"I heard it all, too, when Sierra died. People mean well, but honestly, the things they say sometimes! She's in a better place? What better place is there than with your baby? God needed another angel? Her little girl needed a mommy.

"Tess was barely two when her mother died, and I saw how it affected her and still does. The loss of both your parents must have been devastating for you."

"Yes."

Some deep bond of understanding grief connected them.

Then, seemingly randomly, his phone began to ping, as service kicked in and one by one his messages arrived.

He fought a desire to take his phone out of his pocket and hurl it into the night.

"Haven't heard that sound for a while. I can't say I missed it. I thought I would. But I haven't. Amazingly, the world turned without me."

"I think that's what my grandfather was trying to tell me tonight—that life will unfold, whether I have a stranglehold on it or not. Go ahead," she said. "See what's unfolded."

"Not just yet," he said quietly. "Not just yet."

And she leaned her head against his shoulder, and he put his arm around her, and they experienced the glory of the night. But it was cold, and he felt her, after a while, shiver against him.

"Let's go in," he suggested.

"Check your messages first. You never know when you might get another opportunity. The stars have to line up just so."

It seemed to him the stars had lined up just so tonight, and it had nothing to do with receiving cell service. Still, he did have obligations, and people were counting on him to meet those. He pulled his phone out, reluctant to join the world, liking this one, with its quiet and simplicity and connection, just fine. He scanned the messages very quickly, dismissively.

"Work. Work. Work. Christmas Enchantment Ball. Work. Work."

"The Christmas Enchantment Ball?" she asked.

He scrolled back to the annual ball held each year, always the evening before Christmas Eve, to honor those who gave to charities. "Tomorrow night. The theme this year is Silver Bells."

"I think it's still the biggest event on Calgary's social calendar," Noelle said. "My mom and dad were invited once. It was one of the highlights of my mom's life. She got the invitation because she'd been the top fund-raiser for the children's hospital that year. How do you rate a ticket?"

His company was highly philanthropic, and they were always given a block of tickets. There would probably be thirty people from Wrangler there this year.

"Never underestimate the power of charm and good looks," he said, waggling his eyebrows wickedly at her.

That earned him a smack in the arm, which he rubbed dramatically. She shivered again and he got up and extended his hand to her. She took it, and he pulled her to her feet.

He looked at her. She looked back at him. The stars all seemed to be lining up... She leaned in. He leaned in.

And then his phone pinged, a small sound that sounded like an alarm going off. They leaped back from each other as if Tess had happened upon them.

He looked at his phone, an excuse not to look at her, not to wonder what on earth her lips would taste like.

Would they taste as sweet as they looked, like plump dew-encrusted strawberries, fresh from the plant?

He stared intently at the incoming message, at first not even registering what it said. But when it did penetrate, he lifted his shocked eyes to hers.

"Noelle, they found one."

"One what?"

"Guess."

"Jerry?"

"That's it! They found a Jerry Juicejar."

She laughed, sharing his delight and his incredulous disbelief. "It's a Christmas miracle," she teased him. "Of all those messages, even the one about the Christmas Enchantment Ball, that's the one that means the most to you, isn't it?"

"You have no idea," he said, and gave a whoop of pure happiness. "I'll fly in tomorrow and pick him up, then he'll be under the tree waiting for Tess on Christmas morning."

And then it occurred to him. He was being given an opportunity, not just to pick up Jerry Juicejar.

No, maybe it wasn't about that at all.

He was being given an opportunity to be a better man. Not to put his guard up but to let it down, just for a little bit, and just for one shining moment to put her needs ahead of his own. He thought of the wistfulness in her voice when she had mentioned the Christmas Enchantment Ball. He thought of how hard she had been working to make Christmas divine for his thus-far-disappointed-in-the-festivities daughter, despite her own year of losses.

He thought he had just come up with the best Christmas surprise ever. Even the importance of Jerry Juicejar paled in comparison.

"Why don't you come?" he asked softly.

"What? Me?"

He made a point of looking around the empty hayloft and then back at her. "Sure. Don't you have any last-minute Christmas shopping to do? We could pick up Jerry, do a bit of shopping and go for lunch."

Then I can surprise her with the ball.

She was silent, struggling.

"To be honest, I'm a little afraid of the helicopter," Noelle said, finally. "I hope you won't think I'm hopeless, but I've never flown anywhere, never even been on an airplane. I think it's one of those control things. You can probably see why Mitchell left for greener—"

"Stop it," he ordered her firmly, and then more softly, "You can trust me, Noelle."

Her eyes, as green as moss, as soft as a caress, rested on his face.

It felt as if all those stars in the sky, not to mention his heart, stood still, waiting to decide if he was worthy to give the gift he had just offered.

And was he worthy? Could he be trusted with someone like her? Not if he thought lecherous thoughts about pillaging her lips!

CHAPTER NINE

NOELLE STARED AT AIDAN.

She had to say no. She had just revealed her deepest heartaches to him. He felt sorry for her. That was what had prompted this invitation.

But perhaps there was a different way to see it. What if it was an opportunity? This was exactly what her grandfather had wanted her to learn: to say yes to life, instead of no. It was an opportunity to get out of her comfort zone! And she needed to take it.

Plus, ever since the tree had gone up in the living room, she had been aware she had no Christmas gifts to put under it for Tess or Nana or Aidan. And she knew the perfect thing to get them!

If she went to Calgary with Aidan, she could get them each a pair of skates so that they all could skate on the pond Christmas morning, a McGregor tradition.

"You know what?" she said. "Yes, I'll come." It was not as if they were marching off to explore the jungles of South America. They were going to Calgary for an afternoon. In the adventure department it probably barely rated.

Except for the helicopter part.

Except for the Aidan Phillips part.

"Good girl," he said softly.

And just then she realized she did not want him to think

of her as a girl, a heartbroken little waif who had been orphaned at twelve. Who wore pajamas with penguins on them and slippers shaped like hairy monsters, and had hardly changed a thing in the room she had had since she was twelve.

That was not how she wanted Aidan Phillips to see her at all. And she was fairly certain, from the way his eyes had rested on her lips a few minutes ago, that maybe that was not how he saw her. Not completely.

"Of course, I'll ask Nana and Tess to come, too. I wouldn't want to deprive Tess of my undivided attention on our holiday."

Why did she feel disappointed, her own words coming back to bite her?

He cocked his head. "What is that noise? Is somebody there?" He stepped in front of her as if he might have to protect her from marauders.

In some ways, it was a very nice feeling to have someone want to protect her. But she had a feeling that Aidan might be trying to protect her from himself, from the attraction that leaped in the air between them. She realized she had told him quite a bit about herself tonight, but she still virtually knew nothing of him. One more excellent reason to go to Calgary with him!

"It's only horses," she said.

"I didn't know there were horses. How have we managed to keep that from Tess?"

"Good question," she murmured. Should she warn him her grandfather was planning a special Christmas surprise? One that would possibly eclipse even the much-coveted Jerry Juicejar?

It seemed much kinder to just let Aidan enjoy his victory in the Christmas dad department.

Or was it simply duplicitous on her part? Considering

her initial hesitation in accepting his invitation to join him on his trip to Calgary, she now didn't want to do anything to spoil the moment or put her invitation in jeopardy.

The next morning, Tess announced in no uncertain terms she was not leaving the ranch. She was not leaving her new best friend, Smiley. Nana had promised Christmas cookie baking. She wanted to play outside in the snow.

"I agree," Nana said, seeming pleased by the decision. "It will just make everything simpler if we stay. If you could pick me up a few fresh vegetables, that would be great."

"Noelle? I need to talk to you for a minute."

Noelle's grandfather beckoned her to the hall. He handed her a crumpled roll of bills.

"I wasn't 'spectin' Nana. It would just be rude not to have a present for her. Nothing too personal. No jewelry or anything."

"No, I understand perfectly." But looking at how flustered her grandfather was, she was not certain that she did.

"So much for Tess wanting my undivided attention," Aidan said an hour later, after he had filed his flight plan over the phone and they had gone out to the helicopter. He helped Noelle into it. "She's used to me being away for long periods."

"I actually think she's very secure in your love," Noelle said.

"Huh. I actually think my affections have been replaced by those of a dog. Jerry Juicejar will change all that, though. Take that, Smiley!" Despite making light of it, Noelle could tell it mattered to him that she approved of his parenting. Somehow it felt good that her opinion had value with him.

His good humor, his total lack of nervousness as he went through his preflight checks, helped Noelle feel slightly calmer. Still, when he handed her the earphones her heart was beating way too fast, and her palms were sweating as the engines started and the blades slowly, and then rapidly, began to turn.

"Give me your phone," he said.

She found it in her purse.

"Unlock it."

Was this some sort of aviation requirement? She felt so unsophisticated. She unlocked her phone and handed it to him.

He grinned, flipped through it and found the camera. He aimed it at her. "Give me two thumbs up and a big smile," he instructed.

She did and he took the picture, looked at it and handed it back, pleased.

"Post that on a few of your accounts," he told her.

She laughed out loud, and somehow didn't feel as nervous at all.

As they lifted off the ground, the snow kicked up around them in a cloud. The helicopter seemed to be lumbering. Her hands tightened in a knot on her lap.

But when she glanced at his face for reassurance, Aidan was calm and relaxed. Noelle realized that this came to him as naturally as driving a car did to her.

She looked out her window.

Far below them, already, was the ranch house and barn. She was stunned by the beauty of this perspective.

"I feel as if I am looking down on one of those large scenes that model rail enthusiasts build," she said in wonder.

"Are you still scared?"

She liked the way his voice sounded, coming straight into her ear from the headphones. "What makes you think I was scared?"

"The pulse beating in your throat? The white knuckles?"

She laughed and unknotted her hands. It added to her sense of wonder that he had observed her so closely, *cared*. "All over being scared," she said.

"Good. Flying is actually safer than being in your own bathroom."

"What?"

"Statistically you are much safer here than in your own bathroom. You'd be astounded by the number of deaths annually in the powder room."

"How?" she said skeptically.

"I'm assuming wet, slippery surfaces, but I'd have to look at the statistics more closely. You aren't supposed to express doubt! You're just supposed to be reassured."

"Humph! Who studies those kinds of statistics?" she asked.

"Nerds, like me."

He was about the furthest thing from a nerd that she could possibly think of, but glancing at him, she realized he already knew that. He didn't need any reassurances from her. He was teasing her. She loved it!

"Getting ready to land," he said.

"That was unbelievably fast."

"Between the higher speed you can attain and the fact that you can travel in pretty much a straight line, it is really fast. It's a very efficient way for me to visit our job sites."

"And you love to fly," she said.

Aidan smiled.

She loved to make him smile.

"Yes, I do."

He had a vehicle in a parking stall reserved for him at the airport. It was a luxury four-wheel drive with a cute little car seat installed in the second row.

It was the antithesis of her little car, and not like anything her grandfather had ever had at the ranch. Mitchell had always liked sports cars—probably an early warning sign that he was looking for adventure. Still, he had not been able to afford new models, so she had never been in a vehicle with a seat warmer built in.

"This is decadent," she said as her seat began to heat up in the vehicle, chilly from being parked so long. "Helicopters, heated seats." She almost said, *A person could get used to this*, but the very thought drew her up short.

She had said yes unexpectedly to an adventure. There was no sense thinking the course of her whole life was changed. That she was in some way tangling with Aidan Phillips in ways that would last. In fact, it would be downright dangerous to indulge in such thoughts.

On the other hand, didn't she overthink everything?

Couldn't she just enjoy this day for exactly what it was? Wasn't that what *adventure* implied? A delight in the moment, in the unexpected, without trying to read the future, plan ahead, figure out everything into the next millennium?

"Jerry has been delivered to my office, so I thought we'd stop in there, and then maybe head to that new mall. I know you probably have your own things you want to do, but I was hoping you'd help me with something. You mentioned all the small things little girls like. What did you say, hair ribbons and teddy bears. New pajamas? Maybe a bracelet?"

"I'd love to help you with that."

His office was at the heart of the steel-and-glass forest that was downtown Calgary. Noelle worked down here herself, so she knew what a nightmare parking was. She took transit.

But he slipped into an underground spot reserved for him, and they took a posh elevator to the top floor.

His office was stunningly elegant: exotic hardwoods, glass, stylish furniture and great art.

He greeted everyone by name, including the maintenance man. He asked after one employee's child by name, asking how the Christmas concert had gone. Noelle could tell his employees didn't just respect him; they revered him.

It was quite a different picture than what Noelle had imagined when she had first met him—she'd seen him as high-powered and cynical. There was another side to him that he was not quick to let people see. She suspected it was an honor that she was seeing it just days after he'd landed in her life.

They went into his office. It was a corner space with floor-to-ceiling windows looking out over the whole city. Should she take a picture of this to post, too? To show what dizzying heights she was dancing with? But somehow, she seemed to have lost her taste for posting her adventures for the public. Wouldn't everyone just see what she realized herself?

"Spectacular," she whispered, but the truth was she didn't feel all that good about it. Instead, she was feeling totally out of her league. Yes, it was an honor that she was seeing another side of him, but it deepened a sense of inadequacy in her.

He was not the kind of man a girl should fall in love with.

The thought made her heart stand still. Was she falling in love with him? Silly. You could not fall in love in days, could you? In mere hours?

And yet, she felt something for him that was unlike anything she had ever felt before. She had certainly never felt like this with Mitchell—as if her very skin was tingling with aliveness.

"This is what's spectacular!"

He pounced on a package that had been left on his desk.

She looked at the happiness in his face, and again chided herself. Did she always have to be so serious? To the point of being ludicrous?

Of course she was not falling for Aidan Phillips! It was easy to get swept away by helicopters and luxury cars and a fancy office and an entire adoring staff.

"Come look," he said with boyish enthusiasm.

She could not resist. She went over to him and peeked over his shoulder at the package in his hand.

"Oh, my," she said. "Jerry Juicejar is ugly!"

He shouted with laughter, and Noelle looked at his face, luminous with delight, with joy that he was doing something for his daughter.

"This should make up for Disneyland Disaster," he proclaimed.

And she had to nudge away the thought that whatever she was feeling had very little to do with helicopters and luxury vehicles.

It had to do with cutting down trees and sitting in haylofts and seeing the expression on his face whenever he looked at his daughter.

It had to do with recognizing the value of those moments without any need, whatsoever, to put them in a post to share with the world.

He glanced over his shoulder at her. "What?" he asked.

"Nothing," Noelle said and then added brightly, "We better get on with our shopping. Between the two of us we have quite a bit to accomplish yet."

CHAPTER TEN

IF NOELLE HAD hoped shopping would prove a distraction to her sudden, uncomfortable and somewhat exhilarating awareness of Aidan, she was wrong.

It was December 23, and the mall was absolutely thronged.

If this bothered Aidan at all, it did not show. In fact, for a man who had seemed cynical about Christmas not so long ago, he was able to give himself over to the shopping chaos with a certain abandon.

He was the rarest of things—a man who was fun to shop with. She could not help noticing how unfailingly respectful he was to the harried sales staff, teasing smiles out of some of them, always dropping a kind remark about how well they were handling the demands of the crowds.

Their arms were soon laden with parcels: hair bows and the most gorgeous teddy bear Noelle had ever seen. The price of it took her breath away, but Aidan paid for it cheerfully. They bought Tess a set of little bangle bracelets, fuzzy Christmas pajamas, the kind with feet in them, and some new storybooks. Everywhere they went they were mistaken for a couple, for a mommy and daddy doing last-minute shopping, and that overlaid the happiness of the experience with faint wistfulness.

While they were in the bookstore, they came across a photo book of exquisite gingerbread houses.

"Rufus asked me to pick out something for Nana. What do you think?"

"Perfect," he agreed. "Nana, check. Tess, check. Now I just need a bit of private shopping time—"

Noelle realized he intended to get her something. She wanted to protest how unnecessary it was, and at the same time she could not. She wanted to see what he would get her!

And, of course, she still needed to shop for her chosen gift of skates for everyone.

"Why don't we meet at Percival's for lunch?" he said. "It's just a short walk from here."

Noelle gulped. Percival's? "Isn't it, um, kind of hard to get in there?"

"I'll figure it out," he said, and then he cocked his head at her and winked. Winked! They probably knew him by first name at the exclusive eatery, where she had never even attempted a reservation.

She scuttled off to finish her shopping, trying not to be too bowled over by the surprises life could hold if you opened your heart just the tiniest bit.

The skates came in huge boxes. Plus, it was a tradition at the ranch to hang a sock on the mantel on Christmas Eve. The tradition continued no matter how old you were. So she didn't just want to hang a sock for Tess, she wanted one for everyone. Noelle threw her slender budget—already strained by the skates, not to mention Mitchell emptying the account—to the wind and bought stocking stuffers of luxury chocolates, pretty envelopes of hot chocolate, colorful mittens, decks of cards and other Christmassy and cute trinkets.

Aidan had arrived before her for lunch but the maître d' was waiting for her to arrive! He guided her to a private table in a small alcove. She plopped herself down at the table, exhausted but happy.

"What have you there?" he asked, reaching for one of her bags. She slapped his hand away.

He pretended to nurse it and they laughed.

"I hope you don't mind. I ordered. I have a few favorites here."

Of course he had favorites at the most exclusive restaurant in town!

After an absurdly delicious lunch, she said, "I think I'm about finished shopping. How about you? Is there anything else you need to do before we fly back to the ranch?"

She couldn't help smiling at that. Plain old Noelle McGregor was sitting in Percival's, after a lunch of crab-stuffed lobster tails, discussing flying back to the ranch as if it was a normal thing. She seemed to have adjusted to the dizzying heights she was visiting, after all.

"There's going to be a bit of a delay in getting back to the ranch," he said.

"There is? Has something come up for you? At work?"

He passed her a slender box across the table. "Not at work exactly. Here. An early Christmas present."

She picked it up, looked at him quizzically, pulled the gorgeous wrapping from it and opened it.

There was a slim leather necklace box inside, the box tastefully embossed from Calgary's number one jeweler.

Her fingers were trembling as she opened it.

Her mouth fell open.

Inside the box was a delicate necklace, with two tiny jewel-encrusted bells on it. Those jewels couldn't really be diamonds, could they? She couldn't see them being fakes, not from that jeweler.

She lifted her eyes to him. "Aidan, I can't take this. It's too much."

"No, you have to take it. It's a way of thanking you for all you've done to give Tess such a perfect Christmas. I called her before you arrived at the table. They made cookies. She and Nana and your Grandpa. She told me about Smiley knocking the cookies off the counter and eating most of them. She was laughing so hard she could barely get the story out. I have not heard my daughter laugh like that in so long. In way too long."

"I wasn't even there! How can you thank me for that?"

"It's not that, specifically. It's all of it. Snowball fights and cutting down trees."

"I don't know," she said uncertainly. "I don't want gifts for it. It's not as if you have to pay me to make a great Christmas for Tess. I like doing it. I want to."

"I'm not paying you. I'm thanking you. Plus, the necklace goes with the theme."

"What theme?"

"Silver Bells."

She cocked her head at him. "I'm not following. I thought you didn't like Christmas carols."

"Despise them," he agreed. "I'm not talking about the Christmas carol called 'Silver Bells.' I'm talking about the Christmas Enchantment Ball. Tonight."

She gulped. "Are you asking me to go to the ball with you?"

He smiled and nodded.

"Like a date?"

He looked slightly taken aback. "I hadn't thought of it in those terms."

Of course, he hadn't.

"More like I have tickets, we have some time and when it came up the other night, it sounded like something you might enjoy. Like a little Christmas present."

"But you've already given me the necklace. I can't—"

"One for your birthday, one for Christmas. There's no point to the necklace if we don't go to the ball."

"But we're expected back," Noelle said, feeling faintly panicky. "Tess. And Nana. My Grandpa."

"I'm sure Smiley will miss us, too," he said patiently, "but I cleared it with all of them. They were fine with it. Truth to tell, I don't know if they're going to miss us. I'll still get you home tonight. My helicopter turns into a pumpkin at midnight."

She stared at him. She really did feel like Cinderella. What girl didn't want to be Cinderella once in her life? She fought the impulse.

"I don't know what to say. It's impossible, of course. You'd need a special kind of dress for an event like that." Her voice froze, and it felt as if the fight was draining out of her.

Because she thought of the red dress hanging, never unwrapped, in her closet. That dress didn't have to be a caution against hoping for too much. It could be something else entirely. It could be a statement about saying a bold yes to life and to the adventure.

"I can buy you a dress," he said.

"Actually," she said slowly. "I have one that will do nicely."

"Is that a yes, then?"

She stared at him. She couldn't believe the difference a few hours could make in a life.

"It's a yes," she said, and he let out a hoot of delight much as he had done when Jerry Juicejar appeared on his desk. The people at other tables smiled indulgently. She supposed to them it looked like more than it was.

A young couple in love. Maybe it looked as if she had said yes to something else.

He leaned toward her.

"You look beautiful when you blush."

She ducked her head and then looked back at him. Something unfurled inside of her. A great bravery. A wonderful boldness. She felt the shocking jolt of ecstasy from saying yes to the unexpected, to life, to adventure.

Several hours later, she just wasn't as sure. In fact, Noelle felt like she was crumbling like a dried-out Christmas cookie. She had the dress on. Despite the fact that she seemed to have lost some weight, the dress fit like a glove, maybe even better than it had when she first bought it.

The problem was that the dress was shocking.

It was a deep, deep shade of red, like red wine sangria. It was the only designer dress Noelle had ever owned. It was possibly the only dress that had ever taken her breath away. This was the first time she'd put it on since she'd tried it in the store. She remembered the sales lady flitting around her, going into paroxysms of approval.

For your engagement, you say? It is perfect. It's a girl-to-woman dress, yes?

Yes, it was that. There were deep Vs at both the front and the back of the dress that were very daring, and didn't allow for a bra. The dress clung in some places and flared in others, and her near nakedness underneath it heightened that feeling of being sensual and being aware of her sensuality, and of leaving the girl behind.

The paleness of her skin became not a detriment but an asset, as if her body had been cast in the finest Versace porcelain.

She had upswept her hair and dusted her features with makeup. Her eyes didn't look murky. They looked like moss, thick and deep, on a forest floor. There was a calm in them that belied how nervous the dress made her feel.

The dress had a red-carpet-ready feel to it. Oh, dear. Was there a red carpet at the Christmas Enchantment Ball?

She should look it up. If anybody was bound to trip, it would be her, especially in the unfamiliar two-inch stiletto heels.

She picked up the jewelry box he had given her earlier and opened the lid. She looked longingly at the necklace. If she just put it on, the transformation would be complete, just like Cinderella putting on the glass slipper.

She lifted it out of the box and felt the weight of it, the expense of it.

"Oh, God," she whispered. "Miss McGregor, just who do you think you are?"

Instead of putting on the necklace, she put it back in the box and slammed the lid shut.

Noelle reminded herself tautly she was the woman who had been left. Because she was too predictable. And too controlling. Because she never surprised and avoided spontaneity as if it were the plague. Because she was pale and plain, not golden and exotic.

You couldn't change that! You couldn't change by saying yes instead of no. You couldn't change it with a dress. Or a necklace. Had she lost her mind? She couldn't attend a ball with Aidan Phillips! Every single person would look at her and know she was a fraud, an impersonator, an imposter. They would know that she really wasn't sophisticated enough to pull off a dress like this.

It would show, in the barely-there makeup and in fingers that weren't manicured. And everyone would know that despite the fact that she had been in the city for years, she was still just a girl from the country. Aidan had had her totally pegged in the first few minutes of meeting her. She was wholesome and plain. She had a horrible heartbreak, a betrayal, under her belt. A dress couldn't fix that!

She decided to take the dress off. To put on her housecoat and see if she had any chocolate ice cream left. Aidan could go to the ball by himself.

Or she could get dressed in her old blue jeans and her flannel shirt and they could fly home early if he didn't want to attend by himself. She doubted, though, that he would have a normal person's reticence—read her—about entering such a gathering alone.

Suddenly she just wanted to go home to her grandfather's. She wanted to play with the dog and eat cookies and sit by the crackling fire in her pajamas with penguins all over them. She wanted to try to build that snowman again, on a day with stickier snow, and laugh over gingerbread houses. And as night fell, she wanted to go sit in the loft, in a cushion of sweet-smelling hay, with the stars studding the sky outside the open loft door. And not to look at social media postings, either.

Her comfort zone. She wanted back into her comfort zone!

Except Aidan Phillips had invaded her comfort zone, and somehow now, each of those scenarios seemed as if it might feel oddly incomplete if he was not there. If Tess was not there.

There was a knock on the door. There was no doubt it was him. She hadn't ordered pizza. The knock was firm, that of a man sure every door he knocked on would always be opened to him.

She actually looked for a place to hide, but of course, her place was too small to hide anywhere. It was a studio apartment. She'd rented it in a reckless effort to leave behind the space she'd shared with Mitchell. She had been willing to sacrifice size for the awesome central location. The tininess had allowed her to get rid of most of the things they had owned together. Thankfully, selling a few quality pieces had brought her some much-needed funds.

But now she could clearly see—looking around her space with its mishmash of used furniture and mismatched dishes—this was not the type of place a dress like this came out of. It was not the impression you wanted to make with a man like Aidan.

She took a deep breath and marched to the door. On her floor tiles, the shoes made a snappy sound like machine-gun fire. Despite the confidence that should have inspired, once she was at the door, her courage failed her completely. She took another deep breath, and then held her nose closed between her thumb and her pointer.

"Aidan?"

"None other."

"I'm not feeling well. You go."

Silence.

"Without me," she expanded.

Silence.

"To the ball."

Silence.

"Have fun!"

Why didn't he say something? He was probably so used to doors being flung open for him that he was in shock. She waited, holding her breath, like a child playing hide-and-seek, trying to be invisible, trying not to be caught.

Finally, he spoke. His voice was every bit as firm as his knock had been.

"Open the door, Noelle."

She shivered at the calm in his voice, at the expectation of obedience. "I can't. I want you to go without me. You can come get me when it's done. I'm sure I'll be feeling better in a few hours, ready to go home, ready for—"

"Open the door right now, or I'm kicking it in."

She hesitated. "You wouldn't do that." She forgot to plug her nose.

"Try me," he said.

Really? Aidan Phillips did not seem like the kind of guy you wanted to challenge in that particular way. Where did you get a broken door repaired just before Christmas?

She opened the door. Just a crack. She peered out. "I can't," she reiterated, in her best sick voice, a convincing croak. "You need to go away."

"I'm not going away."

CHAPTER ELEVEN

"I'M NOT GOING AWAY."

Noelle shouldn't really feel as if a statement like that was making her bones melt. After all, it was disrespectful of her right to choose.

And she certainly shouldn't feel shaky and confused and as if her world was upside down. But having the most gorgeous man in the universe standing outside her door, threatening to break it down and then saying in that commanding tone that he was not going anywhere, was not exactly what she had bargained for when she'd decided it was harmless to do things a little differently, to let go of a little control.

There was no sense reading too much into it. *I'm not going away* did not mean Aidan would be around for good. There was no kind of promise of permanence in this evening. It wasn't even a date. He'd been hasty in making that abundantly clear! He'd just stay long enough to stir up her nice, quiet life, to plant seeds of discontent, to leave her testing out a new self without the security of the old one to run back to.

This whole evening had been so ill advised. Why had she said yes? Why had she said he could pick her up here? Now Noelle realized she didn't want him to see her modest studio suite, never mind the dress.

She put her shoulder against the door and pushed, trying to get it closed. It was a metaphor for life. Once you had opened certain doors, it was nearly impossible to close them again.

"Move your foot," she told him.

"No. You don't even sound sick. Were you plugging your nose?"

"Don't be ridiculous. Move your foot, or I'll—"

"Get an ax and chop it off? You did warn me axes were dangerous."

He had no right to be making light of this situation. And the ax? Just a reminder of how different their worlds were.

"I'll call the police."

"Sure you will." His tone was ever so faintly mocking, and ever so faintly gentle. "I'll just slip inside while you go get your phone, because it doesn't really look like you have one hidden anywhere in that dress."

So! He could already tell the dress was inappropriately skimpy. She let go of the door and yanked it open so suddenly he stumbled forward.

"There, are you happy?" she asked him.

He regained his balance quickly. His eyes widened. His jaw went slack. He raked an unsteady hand through his amazing hair.

She stood, feeling terribly undressed. The silence stretched. She tilted her chin at him. Naturally, he looked glorious in a beautifully cut formal tux jacket, a brilliant white linen pleated shirt beneath it. The buttons had been replaced with studs, and the cuffs sported diamond jingle-bells cufflinks that matched the ones on the necklace she had not been able to put on. He had on a red bow tie. It was too bad she wasn't going. That shade of red would have looked very nice with her dress.

He was too big and, naturally, it made her place seem small, as if he filled every inch of it. And he was so sophisticated. He must be looking at her shabby collections with judgment.

"Good God," he said huskily. "Happy? Happy doesn't begin to say it."

"I know," she said. "It's not me. That's why—"

"Do you remember that day we threw snowballs and I told you you were the most beautiful woman I had ever seen?"

As if you could forget something like that!

"I was right," he said, his voice a croak.

He didn't appear to be noticing the humbleness of her surroundings at all. But she could not give in to the softness that made her feel toward him, as if she should just lean in and welcome whatever happened next.

"I'm not beautiful," Noelle said. "In fact I feel utterly ridiculous. I feel like a little girl pretending to be a grown-up. I feel like a fraud. Look around. Does a dress like this come from such a place?"

He looked around, a perfunctory glance that did not take in the chipped teapot at the center of her small table, or the handmade curtains, the mismatched kitchen chairs.

His gaze came back to her and something angry and fierce snapped in his eyes. "You know what? He played on all those insecurities of yours. He made you feel less and less and less. For God's sake, take yourself back."

She stared at him.

"Where's the necklace?"

Noelle felt frozen. Impatient, he glanced around, strode over to the table where she had set the box and picked it up. He came back to her.

"I—I—I changed my mind. I can't accept it."

"Turn around," he growled.

She felt surrender shiver along her spine as she turned her back to him and lifted the few tendrils of hair that had escaped down her neck.

He didn't fasten the necklace, not right away. Instead, he slowly scraped the line of her neck with his finger. She quivered from the pure and heated sensuality of his touch. He stroked her again, his palm this time, sliding over the back of her neck, possessively, leashed desire radiating from his touch.

She closed her eyes. She felt herself sink into his hand, her body sway. The necklace settled on her skin, rode slightly above the deep dip of her cleavage. The bells were heated from where his hands had held them.

He turned her around, traced the line of the necklace to the delicate swell of her breast, then let his hand fall away. He combed his hair with it.

She wished he wouldn't do that. It caused inordinate weakness in her. Her knees felt as if they might buckle.

"It's not up to me to make you feel beautiful, Noelle," he said softly, his voice stern, formidable. "It's an inside job. But it starts like this—it starts with you putting your hand through my arm and holding your head up high and recognizing you deserve to feel your own value.

"Beautiful women are a dime a dozen. Women who shine from the inside out, like you do? That's rarer than the blue diamonds in that necklace."

"Blue diamonds," she stammered. "Aidan, I don't think—"

He raised an eyebrow. He crooked his arm to her.

She hesitated, took a deep breath, took that one step toward him and then threaded her arm through his.

She instantly felt his strength. And her own.

"It's a party," he said, tilting his head to gaze at her. "It's a frivolous, fun evening. It's not a panel of judges eyeing your outfit and your performance. Though even if they did, you'd be a perfect ten."

She could feel the steadiness of his arm entwined with

hers. It felt like he was a man you could lean on when your own courage failed.

"That helps put it in perspective," she said, managing a tremulous smile. "It really does. Thanks for talking me back from the edge."

"I didn't talk you back from the edge, Noelle. When you're on the edge, you either turn back or jump."

"I'm not sure I want to jump off any edges!"

"Really? How else do you figure out if you can fly? You might not want to, but you already did tonight."

"Were you really going to kick the door in?"

"Oh, yeah."

"I think I could love it that you're masterful."

"Yeah, at times. It would probably get old after about three seconds."

And then they were both laughing, and she felt giddy, like a child who had jumped off the high diving board for the very first time.

But instead of hitting the water, she had found she had wings. She had found she could fly.

They stepped outside. The cold should have hit her like a brick, but instead she felt warmed through. Besides, she wouldn't be outside for long. She tried not to gape at the vehicle double-parked at the curb.

"A stretch limo?" Noelle asked. "Seriously?"

Her neighbors, in this working-class community of elegant old houses that had been cut up into multiple suites, were sneaking peeks out their windows.

A uniformed chauffeur came and opened the door for her, tipping his cap as she slid by him. Aidan took the seat next to her. He seemed quite at home in the limo. He knew exactly where the chilled champagne was kept!

"You seem to know your way around a limo," Noelle said.

"I guess I do. There won't be any parking for miles

around the venue. And Sierra taught me you can't ask a lady in an extraordinarily sexy dress and high heels to walk ten blocks in the cold."

It was a reminder that he knew a lot about this intimidating world they were headed into. And it was a reminder Aidan Phillips had had another life. He'd landed on her grandfather's ranch with his share of baggage, none of which he had offered to share with Noelle.

It was the first time since the morning they had met that he had mentioned Sierra. Noelle hoped she had an opportunity, and soon, to find out why he and Tess were such an island at Christmas. Surely they had family? If he didn't, Sierra must have? Where were the aunts and uncles, brothers and sisters, cousins?

"When you are in the public eye," Aidan said softly, "someone is always watching. For the mistake. For the misstep. And in this day and age they almost always have a camera."

"Yikes," she said. "I hope I'm not going to prove to be the misstep."

"Relax," he said. "Champagne?"

"Half a flute. Just so I can say I did it. Drank champagne in a limo. Lives of the rich and famous and all that."

He laughed and complied, handing her the glass. The bubbles got in her nose. Her nervousness fled, not because of the champagne, but because he had no nervousness at all. He was going to this event in the same way he flew a helicopter: calm and confident.

"No champagne for you?" she asked.

"Not if I'm going to fly later."

"You remind me of a cat," she said. "Relaxed, but ready, too."

He lifted a wicked eyebrow at her and twirled an imaginary moustache. "You never know when a mouse will come along."

The limo slid into a line at one of Calgary's oldest and poshest downtown hotels. Flashes from cameras were lighting the night. There was a red carpet.

She looked at some of the other people getting out of their vehicles. It wasn't like Hollywood. It wasn't like many of them were recognizable. She had just begun to relax when she noticed something.

People went up the red carpet and then congregated at the huge glass doors of the hotel, greeting friends, exchanging handshakes and super-sophisticated busses on proffered cheeks.

"Oh, my God, Aidan, we have to get out of here."

"We just got here." He followed her gaze. "Don't worry. I won't let anyone kiss you."

"I'm not worried about getting kissed."

"Oh, good," he said. "Still, I think I'll save that pleasure for myself."

She wanted to remind him, a little churlishly, that it wasn't even a date. And she wanted to get out of here. Whatever had possessed her to agree to this?

"What's wrong?" he asked, his voice low, picking up on her distress.

"Look at the dresses."

He peered at them. "Nice. Not one holds a candle to yours, though."

"There's a reason for that. Candle. Think candle."

"I don't follow."

"Candles are red. Flame red."

Aidan looked again. "Oh, I see where you're going with this."

"Everyone is wearing silver. Every. Single. Woman."

"All the better," he said gleefully, not understanding the

enormity of the fashion faux pas at all. "It's like art. It's your turn to be the star. Your turn to do exactly what you've been avoiding your entire life. Your turn to stand out."

Their car stopped. The chauffeur was out, holding open the door for them. Aidan held out his hand.

She looked at it for a long time, and then tentatively she took it.

"Own it," he mouthed at her.

He helped her from the car, and she stood there, feeling the boldness of the color against the silver of the winter night.

Flashes went off.

She set her shoulders and tilted her chin. Aidan put his hand around her waist, possessively.

There was a faint pattering of applause, as if people approved of her breaking the tradition, standing out, being herself.

"Own it," he told her again, his voice husky in her ear, his breath a sensual touch on the nakedness of her neck.

And so she did. With poise she would not have known was part of her, she slipped her one arm through his, raised her other in a friendly wave to those lined up behind the barriers. She tilted her chin and smiled.

Noelle McGregor felt glorious.

Not just because she had on a gorgeous red dress.

Not because she was a light in a sea of silver.

But because she had faced something inside of her. She had faced that little voice that said, *You are not good enough.*

And she had banished it.

And that made her feel worthy of the glorious man who stood beside her.

CHAPTER TWELVE

THE CHRISTMAS ENCHANTMENT BALL had been aptly named. Noelle felt as if she was walking into a fairy tale.

An ordinary, large conference room had been totally transformed into a winter ballroom. An illusion of it being outdoors had been created, with huge Douglas fir trees lining both sides of the room. All ten feet high and identical, as if they had been cloned, they could have been mistaken for artificial trees, except for the heavenly smell in the room. The firs sparkled with millions of tiny white lights and glittering silver ornaments so abundant you could barely tell they had branches.

The lighting was actually causing an optical illusion, as if giant snowflakes were falling inside the room. The dance floor was empty, as of yet, but there were clusters of glamorous people milling about, beginning to find their way to tables nestled amongst the trees.

The women's gowns were jaw-dropping. Expensive— all in theme, all silver—jewelry dripped from fingers and wrists and necks.

A low murmur of chatter, laughter, filled the room.

Aidan was well-known and almost immediately swamped. She would never remember all the names of the people he introduced her to. He snagged another glass of champagne off a passing tray for her, and asked the server to bring him back a juice when it was convenient.

"Noelle?"

It was the last place she expected to see anyone she knew, but there was Gerald Simpson, the owner of the small oil field supply company Mitchell had worked for. Though she and Mitchell had attended a number of company functions she was astounded that he even knew her name. The Alberta oil patch really was a very small interwoven community.

Gerald introduced his wife, but when she went to introduce Aidan, he said, "No introductions necessary. I'd be interested in your take on our provincial government, Mr. Phillips."

Noelle was frankly relieved he said that instead of mentioning Mitchell, but she also wondered if this was how the evening would go: networking, contacts, shoptalk.

But Aidan put a stop to it instantly. "I'd love to discuss that with you sometime, Mr. Simpson, but I hear the band starting and I've been dying to have a dance with Miss McGregor."

Dying? Really?

It was early in the evening. No one was on the dance floor yet. They were milling about in glamorous circles, and three deep at the bar.

"No one's dancing," she whispered as Aidan took her glass from her and set it down on the nearest table.

"I know," he said. "Isn't that great?"

Great? It meant everyone would be watching. It meant that she would be in her least favorite position, the center of attention!

"I like this song," he told her. The band was doing a really good cover of an Adele song. Aidan took her hand and tugged her out to the very middle of the dance floor. He faced her. She faced him. He took one of her hands in his, and tucked it close to his chest. He put his other on her hip.

He never looked away from her.

His hand on her hip, and the way his blue eyes rested on her face—intense, seductive, charmed, captivated—might have been just about the sexiest thing she had ever experienced in her entire life. Until he began to dance, that was.

This was one thing she would not have ever imagined about him. He was a great dancer. If she was out of practice, and not quite so great as him, it never showed. Because he was so graceful and so confident, so comfortable with his body. He was so good at creating an amazing world that held just the two of them. Soon, she totally forgot that others might be watching. They shut out the whole world.

Hips swaying, chests brushing, the distance between them closing and opening up again, the music swirling around them like a wave that they were destined to ride.

"Can I cut in?"

She saw Aidan frown. It was one of the people he had introduced her to when they had first come in. The vice president of his company? Mike Someone?

With ill grace he let her go.

"Where on earth did that lucky dog find you?" Mike asked her.

"Under the Christmas tree," she said with a laugh.

Soon Aidan claimed her back, but then another of his coworkers came and asked to cut in. From these little interchanges she learned a lot about Aidan. It confirmed what she had seen in his office when she had been there briefly with him this afternoon. His people respected him, but they loved him, too. They liked to have fun, and there was lots of good-natured teasing between them. He encouraged that.

And she also had the feeling she was being vetted by them to see if she was worthy of the boss they clearly adored.

The evening was exhilarating. Noelle had never felt so beautiful, so much like a princess. She could not believe how quickly the time flew. Suddenly, it was midnight—hadn't he promised to get her home before midnight, lest his means of transport turned into a pumpkin—and the last dance was being announced.

"May I have the last dance?" he said, bowing to her. It was courtly and old-world and charming, and he didn't seem to care who was watching.

"You may," she whispered.

Aidan took Noelle's hand. He had thought, from the moment he first entertained the notion, that the Christmas Enchantment Ball was a gift to Noelle.

But from the moment she had opened the door of her tiny studio suite, he had known that was not the case at all.

Bringing Noelle to the ball was a gift to himself.

It was the first time he'd taken a woman out since the death of his wife.

And what a woman he had chosen! Being with Noelle was like watching a bud of a rose unfurling to its full glory. He'd watched her go from being shy and awkward in that dress, which was a different color than everyone else's, to owning the dress, and her own beauty, completely. It was an astonishing metamorphosis.

Noelle was each of the things he had always known her to be: wholesome, giving, pure somehow. But now he could clearly see that there was a hidden layer, a depth of passion that was her secret, and which she had saved for just the right man.

And tonight, it was her gift to him, to Aidan, that he

was the right man, the one who was there when she awakened fully to her power and beauty and sensuality. The one who was there when she owned all the sides of herself.

Every man in the room saw it in her, her confidence and her hunger, and they were drawn to her like bees to the opened flower that she was.

And yet, as he took her hand for the last dance, he felt her giving this gift into his keeping exclusively. Something tried to nudge him, to warn him to keep a distance, but he chased all the voices away.

He had always been ruled by reason, and he could see the delicious irony that it was this wholesome woman from the country who was making him just embrace the moment, in all its exquisite glory. And its exquisite glory was awareness of her, so sharp it was almost painful, so heady it was more intoxicating than champagne, so complete it made him feel as if he was full to the top and then overflowing.

He took her hand and led her right to the middle of the dance floor again, just as he had for the first dance.

He knew they were both exhilarated and exhausted by the evening, that neither of them could believe how quickly it had gone by or what a wonderful time they had had.

They waited, gazing at each other for the music to start.

The song that began to play was Canadian music icon Anne Murray's "Could I Have This Dance."

"Could I?" Aidan asked gruffly.

She mock-curtsied to him and took his proffered hand. He drew her close, closer than he had for any other dance. He rested his chin on top of her head, and they swayed together to the beautiful song. He was suddenly aware of how little she had on under the dress, and that rather than making her feel self-conscious, it made her feel all grown-up, sexy, desirable.

It felt as if the song was being sung just for them, as if each question was being asked of them, as if each observation was being made by them.

The music ended.

Still they stood, looking at one another. Aidan dropped his head over hers and claimed her mouth.

His lips were tender on hers. The world faded. It was just the two of them, in a winter fairy tale. He could tell she loved his taste, his scent, his touch as much as he loved hers. Her lips parted even more...

And then he broke away, and felt the shock of it. In his well-planned life, this was an unplanned moment, in the middle of a crowded room. He had not expected this.

To feel so alive again, after such a long time of allowing himself only one feeling: the victory of success in his chosen field.

It took them a long time to leave, saying goodbye to everyone, getting stopped by so many people along the way.

But finally they were outside.

To find a complete enchantment. Snowflakes as big as feathers were falling from the sky.

A complete enchantment unless, of course, you had been planning on flying a helicopter.

It seemed to him the fates had chosen to laugh at him when he most needed control.

Noelle watched as Aidan whipped his phone out of his pocket before taking off his jacket and settling it around her shoulders.

It was still warm from him as if it had been heated in an oven. Noelle wondered if she should object, but then she snuggled in his jacket and the old-fashioned concept of chivalry.

"My grandmother used to say snowflakes were angel kisses."

"Where did this come from?" He scowled as he glared at his phone. He didn't appear to have heard her remark. He flicked to the weather. "It's not even showing it snowing."

She lifted her face and felt the kisses land, wet and delightful on her cheeks. Her sense of magic in the air increased. Apparently his did not. She watched him run a hand through his hair, sending snowflakes flying.

She reached up and tucked a stray strand back into place. It felt exactly as she had known it would from the very first moment she had dreamed of doing it. Just right.

"We can't fly in this," he said. "We'll have to wait and see if it clears."

They were so, so different. She saw angel kisses; he saw obstacles getting in the way of what he wanted.

And yet, maybe because of the magic they had just shared, she saw their differences could be good things. Life was about balance, wasn't it?

Her elbow firmly in his hand, she began to navigate the steps that had not been snow-covered when they came up them. Unfortunately, her shoes were not intended for slippery conditions. Her foot slipped out from under her and her ankle twisted.

She probably would have tumbled right down the steps if his reflexes had not been so swift, his hold on her elbow so strong.

"Lean on me," he said. And then he practically carried her to the waiting limo. She was not even sure how he knew which one it was; there were so many limos here.

But he didn't give her address to the driver, he gave his own.

"Did you want to drop me at home?" she asked, thinking he must have overlooked the fact that she needed to go home.

"Why don't we go to my place? I don't want to leave you on your own with a possible twist to your ankle. As soon as it clears, we'll make a run to your place and pick up what you need to go back to the ranch. I'm afraid—" he squinted out his window "—it may be morning before we can go."

He was inviting her to his place. The circumstances were hardly romantic. She should insist she would be fine on her own.

But the temptation to see where he lived—and how—was just too great. She settled back in the deep luxury of the limo cushions and watched as they sped through a night that was turning from magically snow-filled to a full-blown blizzard.

Aidan lived on the top floor of one of Calgary's premier downtown condominiums. Though it was only blocks from her own apartment, it was a different world entirely. Noelle had read the starting price to get into one of these units was over three million dollars.

It was wonderful to ride up a private elevator, to exit into a plush living room with floor-to-ceiling windows that looked out on the Calgary downtown skyline and the dark ribbon of water that was the Bow River.

The decor was like something out of a magazine: low-slung white leather furniture, shaggy area carpets, an open concept plan with a huge granite island with stools around it, a high-tech kitchen beyond that.

But the space seemed so very sophisticated, adult. Christmas had been ignored. There was no tree, and no decorations up. A single childish drawing of Santa had been attached to the stainless steel fridge with a magnet.

"No wonder you can't have a puppy," Noelle murmured. "Where on earth does Tess play?"

Even before Noelle spoke, Aidan felt as if he was looking at his space with vision altered by his few days on the ranch.

It didn't seem friendly, at all, never mind child-friendly.

"Tess plays wherever she wants," he said, and heard a bit of a defensive note in his voice. "The housekeeper has been in. That's why there are no toys about."

"The housekeeper," Noelle echoed.

"You've gotten wet," he said. "You're shivering. It's late. Do you want me to show you a room? Are you tired?"

"Not really. I feel a little wound up still. What a wonderful evening. I can't thank you enough. I should call Grandpa, though, and let him know we will be delayed."

"You're not concerned about waking him?"

"I'm more concerned about him worrying."

It had been a wonderful evening. He felt reluctant to let it go. Did she, too? Somehow this *feeling* he had wasn't part of what he'd bargained for when he'd thought of giving her this gift.

The feeling of being aware of her. That dress had taken his awareness to a new level, and then dancing with her, touching her, watching her awaken to her own glorious sensuality and power had intensified it even further. He was totally bewitched. He had to get her out of that dress, and not in the way a man would normally be thinking of doing with a beautiful woman!

"Why don't I find you some dry clothes, and we'll have a hot chocolate before we turn in. I need to check weather forecasts."

He found her one of his T-shirts and a pair of his pajama bottoms and showed her the guestroom. He noticed she was still limping slightly as she went to put them on.

When she emerged again, he realized getting her out of the red dress had not accomplished what he wanted. At all. Who could have anticipated that she would look more beautiful in an oversize T-shirt than she had in that stunningly spectacular dress?

After she made her phone call, she sat down on his sofa, curled her feet under her and took a sip of her cocoa. There was a little dot of cream on her lip. He hurried off to find ice for her ankle and made her set it on it. She glanced around and blew on the hot chocolate.

"What?" he asked.

"This space doesn't seem like you," she said, after a moment's hesitation. "Or Tess."

He debated sitting on the couch beside her, but opted for the much safer chair across from her. "I lived here before I met Sierra. When we were married, she brought in a designer. After the fire, I had the option of moving, or doing things differently, but it was suggested to me that Tess needed to come back to familiar surroundings, not something brand-new. I didn't want to feel as if I was erasing her mother from her life."

He could see the way Noelle was looking at him. Though he had kept his tone neutral and tried to strip his words of emotion, something had betrayed him. He'd given away one of his secrets. He had a feeling that Noelle McGregor could divine secrets the way a water witcher could find water. She was looking at him now as if she *knew* he'd been unhappy, as if she knew something had not been quite right in a relationship that had been so carefully and consistently portrayed as perfect.

Or perhaps it was the decor that had given away something. It was so unlike the ranch, so unlike Noelle's own cluttered, but friendly, little apartment.

This space struck him as being like the movie sets his

wife was so familiar with. It created an illusion of a home, without quite ever being a home.

"I don't understand why there are no decorations up," Noelle said, probing the secret.

"We're never here at Christmas." Aidan made his voice cool, uninviting.

But Noelle was looking at him with a softness that threatened his every hard edge, that shone like a beacon beckoning him home from stormy seas.

"Why are you and Tess so alone at Christmas? Where's your family? Where's Sierra's family?"

"It's been such a good night," he said. "Maybe we shouldn't—"

"You know how you told me I could trust you in the helicopter? I did, and I don't regret it. I discovered I'm braver than I think."

She gazed at him, not saying the obvious. She was requiring bravery and trust from him, also. A different kind of bravery and trust. She looked adorable in his T-shirt, the pajama pants swimming on her, her feet tucked up under her, the ice pack sliding off her slightly swollen ankle.

She had washed off her makeup and let her hair down.

Her eyes were as deeply green as a shaded place in the forest. He hadn't known her very long. And yet, he felt as if he could trust her as much as he had ever trusted anyone. Had he ever told anyone of these dark secrets in his heart?

No.

And suddenly, looking at her, he felt a terrible weakness. To tell someone. To trust someone with it. To not be so alone in the whole world. He had always felt alone. Even when he was with Sierra. Even though he had hoped for something different.

"You know that day you put up the wreath, and I saw

that word? *Hope?* I told you that hope was the most dangerous thing of all?"

"Yes, I've had trouble forgetting that."

"I'm not saying this because I want your pity, or *Oh, poor you,* but I was an only child, an accident, I suspect."

She gasped, and he smiled wearily at her.

"My mom and dad never stopped fighting. Christmas would come, and every single gift I asked for would be given—bicycles or expensive game consoles, the best clothes, the greatest sports shoes. Our whole living room would be filled with gifts. It *looked* like the perfect Christmas.

"But I only wanted one thing—please, stop fighting. That's what I hoped for. Prayed for, even. I'd watch all the Christmas movies and listen to the songs, and they all promised the same thing. It was practically a guarantee that everything that was wrong would somehow become right at Christmas. Even cannons would stop firing and men at war would put down their guns and go meet one another.

"But the war in our house never stopped. My parents finally divorced—thank God—when I was eight. My memories of family were of fighting, and then after the divorce, being used as a club for my mother and father to smack each other with.

"And so, when I met Sierra and we loved each other so fiercely, I thought we could do it differently. Looking back with a tiny bit of the maturity that I wish I'd had then, I realize neither of us came from happy families. Sierra wouldn't even talk about hers. She made up her name to cut any link with them."

Her eyes followed his hand as he raked his hair. He remembered her fingertips in it earlier. He wanted to stop talking, but for some reason he could not explain, the memory of her fingertips in his hair kept him speaking.

"Looking back, what chance could two people coming from histories like that have? We had a whirlwind romance. From the moment I met her, I felt bowled over. When we discovered she was pregnant, just weeks after we met, we were excited. We wanted to get married. We *hoped* we would become the family we dreamed of. Maybe we were even frantic to be that family. Had we waited, we might have discovered we simply didn't have what it took."

"I'm sorry."

"Don't get me wrong. She was a beautiful, vivacious woman. But complicated, in the way highly gifted people sometimes are. I felt like I stole her life force from her, without knowing how I was doing it. I couldn't seem to make her happy. I started spending more time away from her. She felt lonely, I guess, and misunderstood. She started drinking…and worse. We began having fights that could rival anything my parents had ever had. We managed to keep our deep dysfunction secret from the press—never underestimate the power of a good press secretary. The night of the fire—Christmas Eve—we'd had a tremendous row.

"Tess woke up crying. All I could think was *We're doing to this poor kid what was done to us.* I couldn't make Sierra calm down. So I took Tess and I left.

"Sierra didn't normally smoke, never in public. But if she felt stressed, or started drinking, she smoked. The fire investigation said it was a cigarette.

"It never got out to the public that Tess and I weren't there. The public perception of us as the perfect fairy-tale couple remained intact. It makes all of it, somehow, even harder to bear."

"I'm so sorry." Her voice was soft, a caress of pure compassion.

He lifted a shoulder. He wanted to stop, but somehow

he could not, as if he was a train running down a track with no one in control. He hated that the most, being out of control.

"I never even heard from her family, not even when she died. I had a private detective track them down. I wasn't sure if they should know about Tess or not."

"And?"

"Not," he said wearily.

"And your own mother and father? They don't see Tess?"

"My father died before she was born. My mother married a man who lives in Australia. She sends a card and a gift. Now and then she calls. She told me she's way too young to have someone call her Grandma. Tess calls her Peggy."

"Now I know why you think hope is the most dangerous thing," she said. Her eyes were sparkling, as if she was holding back unshed tears. It did not feel like she pitied him. It felt like the truest empathy he had ever experienced.

The train running down the track did not result in a wreck, but in something else entirely unexpected. His heart felt open in a way he was fairly certain it never had been before.

Maybe it was like some kind of a Christmas miracle.

CHAPTER THIRTEEN

"You're the only person I've ever said that to," Aidan heard himself admit slowly. "I don't know if I should have."

But there was something about her, from the green of her eyes to her belief in angel kisses, that invited confidences. Or weakness, depending how you looked at it.

"Why?" Noelle's voice was as soft as the relentless snowflakes drifting down outside his window.

"It feels like a betrayal of Sierra. Of her memory. Tess doesn't really remember her, so I've kind of created this perfect Mommy for her to remember."

"That doesn't sound like something a true cynic would do."

"Sometimes I even surprise myself," he admitted. "Like sharing this tonight. That's a surprise."

"Maybe it's just a weight you've carried by yourself for too long."

He waited to feel the shame of having let his guard down, of having let out secrets that he should not have, the guilt at his loss of control.

Instead, looking at Noelle, he felt she was right. He felt a new lightness, as if he had carried a burden for too long.

And he also felt exhausted.

"I'll show you where you're going to sleep tonight."

"Not just yet," she said softly. She patted the sofa beside her.

He knew he should resist this. He knew it. And yet he was not that strong. He got up from his own chair and went and sat beside her.

"Closer," she said, her voice soft but firm.

He moved toward her, until his leg was touching her leg, until the length of his side was pressed against the length of her side, fused. Her hand took his.

She lifted it to her lips and then lowered it to her lap, stroking it, all the while saying nothing. She did not try to fix or pry.

And yet he felt her tenderness, her compassion, the purity of her beautiful spirit in that featherlight touch on his hand.

"Thank you," he said gruffly.

He did not resist when she guided his head to her shoulder, when she traced the plains of his face with her fingertips, healing in her touch.

Something in him that he did not know he held in constant tension unraveled. Her breath deepened, and so did his. He marveled that he felt as deeply relaxed as he had ever felt.

No, something more than relaxed.

He felt safe.

In Noelle's touch, in her total and unconditional acceptance of him, Aidan felt as if he had finally, finally found his way back to a place he had never really been: home.

He wasn't sure how long he was there, but her voice came to him through a thick haze.

"Aidan, you are going to get a sore neck. Go to bed."

He rose and stared down at her, and then held out his hand. She took it, and he pulled her gently to her feet. The bag of partially melted ice that had been on her ankle splatted to the floor.

She went to pick it up, but he did not want such a mundane thing to break the magic between them.

"Leave it," he insisted.

He led her down the hall to his bedroom, through the door, to the luxurious largeness of his bed. He pulled back the sheets with one hand, holding her hand tight with the other.

Then he turned and looked at her. Faint light was washing through the window, washing her in the silver enchantment that had shivered through the whole evening. She looked at him, wide-eyed, willing for whatever came next in a way that made him slightly ashamed, that called on him to be the better man.

"Let me just hold you," he said gruffly.

Her expression relaxed into a mixture of disappointment and relief that made him feel, with abundant clarity, it had been the right decision.

Slipping into the bed beside her, pulling her fully clothed body against his own. Feeling her breath on his chest and her hair tickle his chin, her scent waft up to his nostrils, her softness filling all his emptiness, Aidan felt like for once he was the man he had always wanted to be.

Noelle woke to soft light, muted gray falling across her face. For a moment she felt disoriented, but then she felt Aidan's arm over her midriff, heavy and possessive, in a way that made her heart feel full. His scent filled her with euphoria like a forbidden drug, one that once you had it, you could never ever get enough.

She took advantage of the fact that he still slept to study his face, dark whiskers, his hair falling over his brow.

After a while, she became aware of other things. The

massive bed they shared could easily be a single size, they were cuddled so close together. The room was as beautiful as the rest of his space, but as beautiful as it was, it was impersonal, like a hotel room. Where were the photos and the socks on the floor? Where was Aunt Bessie's old wardrobe, the framed art of a child? Somehow there was no history here, and none of his dynamic personality. It made her acutely aware that all his success was driven by a need to outrun the loneliness of his own heart.

Out the window the huge snowflakes still fell. Her sense of well-being left her. It was still snowing. And it was Christmas Eve. She touched his shoulder, and he pressed against her hand, buried his face in her neck. She took a deep breath and nudged more firmly.

His eyes flashed open. So blue. Full of tenderness. Welcome.

"Noelle," he said, his voice a purr of pure seduction.

Easy to want to follow it to wherever temptation led, but no. It was Christmas Eve. They had responsibilities.

"Look at the weather," she said to him.

His eyes narrowed on her face, and then he looked over her shoulder. He rolled away from her, was out of the bed in one lithe move, and went to the window. He opened the curtain fully.

And said a word she had not heard him use before.

It was when he turned back to her that she knew, somehow, someway, that without her permission, following the trail of breadcrumbs life had put out for her, she had come to this.

She loved this man. It was crazy. And stupid. Their worlds were a million miles apart. It was too fast. She had no idea where this was all going. Just like in the story of Cinderella, midnight loomed. Only their midnight was

Christmas. He was sharing his life with her until just after Christmas. Then what?

And even with all these rational thoughts crowding around her, Noelle loved him for the panic on his face that she read correctly even before he spoke it.

"It's Christmas Eve. Tess needs me to be with her."

"I know," she said softly.

"Believe it or not," he said, "I am my little girl's Santa Claus and despite my hard-earned cynicism about everything Christmas, I take that responsibility very seriously. I don't ever want Tess to be as cynical about the season as I am. Jerry Juicejar has to have magically appeared under the Christmas tree tomorrow."

"I know," Noelle said.

"I'll drive."

"Of course," she said. She saw it. The fierceness in him. The warrior. With the tender heart. That he would do whatever it took to be with his daughter on this day, especially, that held so many bad memories for them.

"Look, it might be tense," he said. "I'm sure driving conditions will be abysmal."

"I know."

"You don't have to come."

But, of course, she did. The option of spending Christmas Eve, and no doubt Christmas, by herself was untenable.

"This has got to bring up painful fears for you," he said.

"It does. I have avoided bad roads ever since my parents' accident."

He nodded.

"I've avoided a lot of things. I'm not going to let fear rule me anymore," she said. And she meant it.

And so, when they headed out an hour later, she had a sense, not of being afraid, but of tackling a great adventure with a man she trusted. After his confidences last night she trusted him more than ever. And she had admitted her secret love for him. Once again, doubts crowded. But she shoved them away, determined to cherish these moments.

Telling herself that love made everything possible. Even the impossible.

The vehicle was a good one, a heavy-duty four-wheel drive, the kind that had been invented for the military but adapted to civilian use.

They piled all their gifts in it. And a thermos of coffee. Snacks. Extra clothing. A car blanket. An emergency kit with a flashlight and a candle, matches and first-aid equipment.

The primary highway south of Calgary, while not in the best of condition, was passable. The plows and sanding trucks were working full force to help keep the roads safe for people anxious, as Noelle and Aidan were, to be with loved ones for Christmas.

The vehicle felt solid and safe, but Noelle was aware her sense of safety came as much from Aidan as from the vehicle. Aidan drove the same way he flew a helicopter, with the great calm and confidence of a man certain of his own strengths and abilities.

They listened to music and chatted easily. He made her laugh out loud with stories of Tess and his own bumbling through single parenthood. She told him of coming, as a child of the city, to live with her grandmother and grandfather on their ranch, and how she had come to love it. They argued playfully about music choices and favorite movies and TV shows.

She felt so relaxed—and truthfully, nursing her secret love for him, happy to have this time alone with him—that she could scarcely believe a storm raged outside the capsule of warmth and laughter and safety that they shared.

It was when they turned off the main road and onto the secondary highway that conditions deteriorated. The road crews were not giving the secondary roads the same priority, and the storm seemed to thicken around them. The little traffic there was crawled along, back tires slithering.

And then in the line of cars in front of them, the brake lights of a small blue car flashed red in the storm. Noelle and Aidan watched helplessly as a deer, followed by another, darted out in front of it. The car avoided the deer, but lost control and swung around in several looping circles before going off the road, its snub nose buried in a snowdrift. The cars behind it avoided collision, but once they regained traction, they kept going.

Only Aidan pulled well off the road. "Stay here," he told her.

Watching him push his way to the car and lean in to talk to the driver, she was overcome with a sense of admiration for him. Despite all he had been through—a terrible childhood and a disappointing marriage and the death of his partner—this was still who he really was. Decent and honorable. The one who could be counted on to stop, even in the middle of a storm, and do the right thing.

He claimed cynicism, but underneath that was the heart of a good man, and a strong one. One able, in challenging circumstances, to make the right decision, to be better for the things he had faced and overcome, not bitter.

A young man, the driver, got out of the car. And then the other door opened, and a young woman climbed out. She reached into the back seat and retrieved a baby!

It was obvious the young woman had had a terrible fright, and Noelle got out of the vehicle and went to her. She held out her arms to the baby, and found it snuggled against her.

They went and sat in Aidan's warm vehicle while the

two men figured it out. Aidan had a towrope in their vehicle, and he soon had the blue car back on the road. They determined it was safe to drive and the little family was back on their way.

Noelle sighed contentedly, as they too got back on their way. "Did that feel like the perfect Christmas moment to you?"

Aidan cocked his head and squinted, thinking about it.

And then he turned to her, and gave her perhaps the most radiant smile she had ever seen.

"Perfect," he agreed.

Again the storm deepened around them. When they turned off the secondary highway to the country lane that eventually would lead to Rufus's ranch, there had been no plows. The snow was unbelievably deep and the going was slow. Still, there was that feeling of being in a capsule with him, warm and safe, a wonderful intimacy blossoming between them.

Normally the drive from Calgary to her grandfather's took a little over two hours. They had been on the road for eight when they finally turned at the wooden gate that marked the beginning of his road. The last light was leeching from the short winter day. They were less than six kilometers from Christmas! From lights and egg nog and singing around the tree, from Tess's excitement and wonder, from a fire in the living room stone fireplace that was lit only once or twice every year.

Her grandfather had obviously been out on the tractor, clearing the road. His road appeared to be in better shape than the lane had been.

But then, without warning, a huge snow-laden tree crashed across the road in front of them. The sudden cloud of snow that enveloped them was dramatic and oddly silent.

Aidan stomped on the brakes and the big sturdy vehicle

shuddered to a halt, its windshield wipers clearing away the sudden onslaught of yet more snow, the bumper practically resting on the branches of the fallen tree.

Aidan leaned back, closed his eyes, and then turned and looked at her. "A few seconds later…"

"I know." Her heart was thudding crazily.

They both let that sink in. That life could change that quickly in a few seconds.

After getting over the initial shock, she reached for her phone.

"I'll just call Grandpa. He'll come for us in the tractor."

She glared at her phone.

"Let me guess," Aidan said quietly. "We're already in the twilight zone of no service."

"He's going to be so worried. Should we walk?"

Aidan squinted out into the snow. "No, I don't think so. It's getting dark, the storm is making visibility really poor. The road is going to disappear again fairly shortly. There are just too many stories of people getting lost in stuff like this. I'd rather sit tight until morning."

"My grandfather will be worried about us."

"You know, your grandfather strikes me as a guy who has dealt with a lot of stuff in his time. He's used to this country, to bad weather, and poor roads and nonexistent communication, and nature throwing a kink in the best-laid plans. I think he'll be okay, and I think he'll make it okay for Tess and Nana."

And then something else sank in, at least for her.

That a person could do whatever they wanted, have any plan they wanted, but there were bigger forces to contend with.

Sometimes, no matter how badly you wanted to be home for Christmas, it just was not going to happen.

"What is that over there?"

Noelle followed his gaze. A shape was barely visible through the blowing, thick snow.

"Oh!" she said. "We're at the old honeymoon cabin."

He turned and gave her a look. "You're kidding, right?"

"No," she said. "I'm not kidding at all."

CHAPTER FOURTEEN

NOELLE ACTUALLY FELT herself blushing under his incredulous gaze. It wasn't as if she had planned for them to happen upon the honeymoon cabin!

"A honeymoon cabin in the middle of nowhere," he said, his voice threaded through with disbelief.

"It's not really in the middle of nowhere," Noelle said. "All this land used to be McGregor land. My grandfather sold it this year. There's no one left to ranch it."

He reached out and squeezed her hand at the emotion in her voice.

"Anyway, we're quite close to the old property boundary. My great-great-great-grandfather built the first cabin right there to bring his new bride home. If legend is correct, he'd talked his old sweetheart into coming from Scotland to join him. Later, they built the bigger house in a place closer to water and more protected from the wind."

"Well, let's go see if it's habitable. It would probably be a more comfortable place to spend the night than the truck."

But when she got out of the truck, her weak ankle turned again. She tried to muffle her little cry of pain, but Aidan, who had gone ahead, came back immediately. "Wait here a sec. I'll go see if it's locked."

"No one around here would lock a cabin. For the very reason we find ourselves in now. Somebody might need it."

"In that case..."

He swooped her up in his arms and plowed through the snow, holding her tight to his chest. He made her feel light as a feather, protected, cared for.

He went up the snow-clogged steps, managed to wrestle the door handle open while juggling her in his arms, and then—

"Don't!" she said.

But it was too late. He had carried her over the threshold of the Honeymoon Cabin.

She giggled and buried her head in his shoulder. It was too easy to imagine being carried over this threshold by him in different circumstances.

He gave her a wry look, and then set her down at a chair at the sturdy table by the woodstove. He went back to the vehicle and retrieved the emergency kit, which had a flashlight in it. He shone the beam around.

Noelle hugged herself against the deep chill permeating the cabin. Despite the cold in the room a certain warmth shone through.

It was just one simple room, but it was lovely. She was surprised to see the red plaid curtains over the one window looked new. They were so homey. There was a matching tablecloth on the table. She lifted a corner. Hand-sewn.

A large, colorful rag rug, the kind her grandmother had made, covered the main area, but she had never seen one quite this large before.

Over in one corner was a bed hewn from logs, the mattress and bedding rolled tight and wrapped in plastic against invading rodents.

In the opposite corner was the kitchen—a few shelves with crockery and pots and pans, a counter, an old enamel bowl.

"It became a tradition," Noelle said slowly. "Everyone had their honeymoon here. My parents were probably the last ones."

She looked again at the new window coverings and at the tablecloth. She stared at the rug. She noticed, even in the dark, that there were framed embroideries on the walls.

It wasn't even on her grandparents' land anymore, but somehow she knew. Her grandmother, thinking Noelle was going to marry Mitchell, had asked to use it, and had gotten it ready for them. It had probably been one of the last things she'd done.

Noelle began to cry. Aidan came and put his arms around her, held her tight.

"Hey," he said. "It's okay. It's been a long day."

"A long, good day," she said, forcing her voice past the tightness in her throat. "I was crying because I think my Grandma McGregor got this ready for me, before she died. For my honeymoon."

"If I ever find that guy," he promised fiercely, "I'm going to smack him right on his sunburned bald head."

She hiccupped through tears and laughter. "No, don't do that. I'm not sorry I'm not marrying Mitchell. Not anymore."

She contemplated that for a second. When *exactly* had she begun to understand it was a blessing that he had gone? When had she begun to see that, in settling for an imitation, she could have missed the real thing?

For the first time, she felt forgiveness for Mitchell. Something in him had *known* it wasn't quite right.

It was still lousy that he had cleared the bank account, but in retrospect, it had been a small price to pay for an extremely valuable lesson.

"I'm beginning to see that it was not going to be right for me. They're not sad tears," she finally managed to hiccup. "I just, for a moment there, felt so close to them. I can feel their love in the room."

"I can feel it, too," he said softly, coming and standing behind her, draping himself over her chair to hold her.

She reared her head back to look at him. "What? You can? Aidan Phillips? Mr. Cynic?"

"Maybe it's a Christmas thing," he said, smiling. "Okay, let's get some heat happening."

He let her go and went to investigate the wood heater. "There's kindling," he said, surprised. "And some wood, enough to get us started, anyway."

"These cabins are always left ready to use. You just never know when a stranger might need shelter."

He turned and looked at her. "It's kind of like finding a manger, isn't it?"

The skeptic in him seemed to be completely gone. Gone since he had shared his secrets last night. "Yes," she whispered. "It is."

They were silent, both of them feeling the sacredness, a connection to each other and to a shared moment of finding shelter in an unexpected place on a night when it was so needed.

Aidan got the fire started, and soon the flames were crackling. The heat in the small space was instant.

"Don't look so surprised," he said. "I was a Boy Scout, you know."

That must be where he had learned the value of good deeds! He went back into the storm and soon was back in the cabin, arms laden with supplies from the vehicle.

Then Aidan found an ax and went outside. While she listened to the steady rhythm of him chopping wood, Noelle got up from the chair and limped around the small space. She found oil for the lamps and lit them. She looked through the cupboards. Tinned goods were never left, because they could freeze and explode. A mouse had been in the boxed soups and biscuit mix.

"Aidan?" She limped out to the porch. There was already wood stacked neatly there. What was he doing? Over the ferocious howl of the wind, she could hear him chopping away in the darkness.

He must not have seen the wood stacked on the porch. Despite being a Boy Scout, he was a city guy—he wouldn't know you couldn't burn a freshly cut tree.

Favoring her leg with the twisted ankle, Noelle went into the storm herself, filling several buckets with snow. Then she began the task of melting it into water on the stove. While that was happening, she got the mattress out of the wrapping and made the bed. It was a lovely feeling, making the cabin homey for Christmas Eve.

Still. One bed. Again. She was not sure tonight would end the same as last night had. Noelle was not at all sure she could any longer keep from loving him in every sense of that word. She ached for him. She ached for the taste of his lips and the feel of his hands, and for the steadiness of his eyes on her. She ached for a completeness between them.

She heard him on the porch.

The door flew open, and Noelle saw that Aidan had not been chopping firewood in the forest. Not at all.

He had found them the perfect Christmas tree and he wrestled it in the door, leaving puddles of snow as he crossed the floor.

"For you," he said. He dropped the tree and went back to shut the door against the storm screaming in through it.

Noelle was glad he had turned his back for a moment. She had to compose herself. Somehow, Aidan going out into the storm to get this tree, for her, meant more than the necklace she still wore around her neck.

Aidan went back to the tree. Because of the unevenness of how the trunk had been cut, standing it up proved a near impossible task, but created waves of laughter between the two of them. As they contemplated their options, together, Noelle could feel the bonds deepening between them.

Finally, with one of the tree's branches nailed to the wall to keep it from falling over, it was ready for decorations. They made decorations out of anything they could find. There was a ball of string on one of the lower kitchen shelves and so they strung pine cones they found close to the cabin. They made snowballs out of napkins and garlands out of toilet tissue. They cut angels and snowmen and stars from a stack of bright green paper plates they found.

When they couldn't fit one more thing on their beautiful tree, they pulled the table close and sat down admiring it. They drank hot chocolate and ate all her stocking stuffers for supper.

On one of the shelves they found a deck of cards, and he showed her how to play some poker hands. And then she showed him how to play Ninety-Nine. And then, in honor of Tess, they played Go Fish and Crazy Eights.

It was the best Christmas Eve she had ever had. As the wind shrieked outside and snow pelted the windows, here inside the cabin there was a richness in the air itself. It was cozy. There were no distractions, no cell phone service, no need to "check" the constant incoming media. There was no TV and no computers. There was simplicity. Warmth. Food. Each other.

They laughed until they hurt as they played the card games, and made up new rules, and said silly things, and playfully cheated, and made up excuses to touch each other's hands.

But then the laughter died.

And was replaced by something else when his hand

lingered on hers just a little too long. Their eyes met and held. A sizzling awareness leaped up between them, like embers that had smoldered harmlessly and suddenly burst into flame.

Noelle could barely breathe as desire chased every other thing from her mind: every worry, every past heartache, every thought for the future, gone. Obliterated in the need to strengthen the connection between them.

He put pressure on her hand, increasing it until she followed its command, out of her own chair and onto his lap. She raked his beautiful hair with her hands, loving the silken feel of it. He touched the tendrils of hers with a certain gentle reverence.

But then the gentleness—if not the reverence—was gone. Replaced by heat. And hunger.

He placed his hand on the back of her neck and pulled her mouth to his.

Sweet, sweet welcome. At first, it was tenderness and joyous exploration. It was taste and scent and sensory overload. When it felt as if she might explode for the sensation, it intensified again, becoming something more, more urgent, more compelling, uncontrollable and unstoppable.

A command as ancient as time.

Noelle felt a primal need burning within her, to know him in every way it was possible for a woman to know a man. The Christmas cottage faded. The tree and the warm glow of the oil lamps disappeared from her consciousness. All that existed in her world was Aidan.

Aidan and his chocolate-flavored kisses. Aidan and his deep blue eyes. Aidan and the scrape of his whiskers across her sensitive skin. Aidan and the fresh-cut pine smell that clung to him. Aidan and the way his hands felt as they brailled her face and her earlobes and her neck and the dip between her breasts.

Her hands went under his shirt and touched his naked flesh. His skin was molten and silky. His muscles were enticingly hard beneath her fingertips.

He stood up from the chair, with her in his arms, and carried her to the bed. He set her down on it with exquisite tenderness, and then he stood staring at her, the brightness of his eyes clouded with desire. She held out her arms to him, and with a groan of pure surrender, he came down, lowering himself on top of her.

She felt the full length of him, his sinewy strength. She shuddered with wanting.

He plundered her then with his tongue. He plundered the insides of her ears and the hollow of her collarbone. He ran his tongue down the length of her neck and lower.

And then his lips found hers again.

And all innocence was lost.

This was a man. Pure, 100 percent, unadulterated man. He was a warrior. And a prince. He was unleashed, barely tamed. He was a man who knew what he wanted.

She welcomed this side of him.

She welcomed him to lose his legendary control. She reveled in the fact that she was the one who had made it happen. But just as she felt victory close, he pulled away from her. Panting, he sat on the edge of the bed.

"I can't," he said.

"Yes, you can," she whispered, her voice raw with need.

"No, I can't."

"Why?" she asked devastated. "Why?"

Why? Aidan looked at her beautiful face, flushed with longing. For *him*. But it was wrong on so many levels.

She did not even know this about herself, but Noelle McGregor was not this kind of woman. At all. She was the kind of woman that asked more of a man. Demanded more of a man. That a man with any moral fiber at all had to ask himself very hard questions before he took it to the next level.

She'd already been with one man who was completely unworthy of her. Who had not asked the hard questions.

Where was it going? What could he offer? Did he have honorable intentions for the future?

Aidan had to look at this realistically. They had known each other days, not weeks, not months. It seemed impossible to feel this strongly about her, to have her feel this strongly about him. Was the intensity of this experience, of being snowbound together in this little cabin, creating illusions that could not stand up to the test of reality?

And yet, when he looked at her, that word, *forever*, seemed for the first time in a long time like something he could actually hope for.

And if he was prepared to offer forever, in what way was it honorable to do this first? She was a woman who deserved a slow courtship. Who deserved to be cherished and honored and respected. Who deserved *I do*.

And before that, even, who deserved to be buried under gifts that caused her wonder. She deserved to be courted: to be taken dancing. And for candlelit dinners. And for long walks. And on journeys of delight.

Perhaps it was being a single dad to a daughter that made him so aware of the right way to do things. He wanted to give Noelle everything he hoped a worthy suitor would someday give Tess.

When he looked into her face, Aidan knew he'd been given the best Christmas gift of all. The one he had always hoped for and had come, over time, not to believe in.

He had fallen in love with Noelle McGregor.

Or it felt as if he had.

But if it was true, it needed to survive the intensity of what they had experienced over the last few days.

He could not hold out that hope to her until he was 100 percent certain it was true.

"What?" she whispered, reading every thought that crossed his face with consternation.

"Merry Christmas," he said to her softly, giving her the best present he knew. Honoring her.

He moved away from her slowly. He knew he dared not look back at her, lying on that bed, her eyes imploring him. Aidan put on his jacket and his boots. He opened the door to the scream of the wind and the relentless pelting of snow.

The best thing for both of them would be if it cooled down between them, if they made no decisions while in this fever of wanting.

"I'm going to sleep in the truck," he told her.

Walking away from her willingness was just about the hardest thing Aidan Phillips had ever done.

CHAPTER FIFTEEN

CHRISTMAS. AIDAN WAS astounded that that was his first thought. His neck hurt from sleeping in the truck, and he was cold. He had turned the engine on and off through the night, but it was currently off.

Then he knew why it had been his first thought.

Impossibly, he could hear the sharp jangle of bells. He sat up on the seat and peered out the windshield, but it was covered in a thick layer of snow. The sound of bells grew louder, and then a little girl's laugh.

Aidan tumbled out of the truck. The sun had come out and nearly blinded him with its brilliance, the fresh, deep snow sparkling with a million blue lights.

A horse-drawn sleigh was coming toward him, huge gray horses throwing up clouds of snow, a sleigh skimming along behind them.

And in that sleigh was Rufus and Nana and Tess, Smiley packed onto the front seat with them.

The sleigh pulled up beside him, the huge horses blowing warm steam out their noses. Tess, radiant, held out her arms and he picked her off the seat, kissed her cheek, held her close.

"Merry Christmas, Daddy!"

"Merry Christmas, Tess."

He scanned her face. If she had experienced a moment's

concern about her father not arriving for Christmas Eve, it did not show in her sparkling eyes now.

"Guess what?" Tess breathed. "Santa didn't come. Rufus said it's the first time, ever, that a snowstorm has stopped Santa." Tess sighed with contentment, somehow thrilled to have been a part of this historic event.

Aidan sought Rufus's eyes over Tess's shoulder, thanking him for managing to twist it in such a way that it deepened the magic for Tess instead of destroying it.

"Santa will come tomorrow, instead," Tess said officiously. "He will need extra cookies and the reindeer will need extra carrots."

A Christmas disaster transformed. A little girl thinking not of her own disappointment but of poor Santa's discomfort.

"We didn't open any presents," Tess said.

"Why not?" Aidan asked her, ruffling her hair.

"Daddy! Silly! It's not Christmas without you."

He looked into her sparkling eyes and felt deep gratitude for the amazing gift of his little girl. He felt the love between them that he had so often witnessed between Noelle and her grandfather. He felt grateful that, despite all his doubts about his parenting abilities, despite his bumbling, Tess seemed to be turning out just fine.

"How did you find us?" Aidan asked Rufus.

Rufus looked…different. And so did Nana. They both looked younger, brimming over with *something* that had nothing to do with the crisp morning sleigh ride.

"I figured you'd get as far as the lane. A tree fell outside the house last night, too. Wiped out the power. And then I just kind of went *Ah, I bet they're at the cabin.* Where's Noelle? How come you're in the truck when there's a perfectly good cabin right there?"

Aidan shuffled uncomfortably and Rufus gave a snort of knowing laughter.

"Protecting my granddaughter's virtue, were you?" And then softly, and with utter sincerity, "Good man."

For some reason, the older man's approval and praise meant a great deal to him. It made the sacrifice he had made last night worth it. Aidan met his eyes with a sheepish smile.

And then the door of the cabin opened and Noelle came out.

Aidan watched her and felt his heart swell. She was beautiful. With no makeup and her hair flying every which way, and her crumpled clothes from yesterday, she was beautiful. As beautiful as she had been in that extraordinary red dress. He had done the right thing. There was no way he could have shared a bed with her two nights in a row with nothing happening.

She started to come toward them smiling, an endearing shyness in her smile, just a hint of uncertainty as her eyes met his and then skittered away.

Aidan noticed she was still limping ever so slightly, and he went to her. She gazed up at him, asking, imploring. He smiled reassuringly, touched her cheek. "Happy Birthday," he said softly.

"Merry Christmas, Aidan."

"Happy Birthday, my little Christmas star!" Rufus got down off the sleigh with a vigor that belied his age. He went to Noelle and picked her up and swung her around. She laughed out loud and kissed her grandfather's weathered cheek.

Aidan felt it right then. Something stinging behind his eyes as he watched them. He felt the longing he had been outrunning since he was a little boy.

It was in the very air between Noelle and her grandfather. The love. The sense of family. The deep knowing that they would always have a place to come home to.

Could he have that, too? What a gift it would be to give his daughter such a thing. It would require the bravest thing of all: to hope again, to say yes.

Greetings dispensed with, Rufus went and surveyed the tree that had fallen in front of the truck.

"Should be able to move that with the tractor. I had to cancel, though, Old-fashioned Country Christmas. I didn't want anyone risking life and limb to get here. Plus, there's no power. Pretty hard to cook a turkey dinner without that. Good thing I still have that old rotary phone that you young people think is so funny. You don't need power to make a few calls. And we got the woodstove. You can cook a few rudimentary things on that."

"Aw, Grandpa," Noelle said. "I'm sorry about your Christmas plans."

"Ha." Rufus lifted a shoulder. "You get to be my age and you figure it all out—there's a greater plan. It's probably better than anything I could ever plan for myself, anyway."

Those words seemed to fill every space in Aidan's head as they began loading gifts out of the truck and into the sleigh. Tess wanted to sit in the front with Nana and Rufus, and Aidan found himself under a shared blanket with Noelle. He took her hand and squeezed it gently.

He thought of the strange set of events that had brought them together. He thought of playing in the snow with her, and her eyes on him as he had cut down the tree. He thought of her laughing as he bungled gingerbread decorating. He thought of them sitting in the cold in the hayloft looking at stars. He thought of the new lightness in her spirit as she had owned that red dress and owned the Enchantment Ball. He thought of how he'd confided his broken dreams to her and how it had felt—not like a weakness, but like an invitation to wake up, to live again. He thought of driving with her through the storm, and her incredible calm and bravery. He thought of decorating that funny little tree with her last night, and playing cards, and laughing until his stomach hurt.

It seemed as if it could be true. All part of a greater plan.

Noelle gave him her full attention, scanning his face. And whatever she found there reassured her, because she broke out in a smile.

Aidan felt himself reach for what he saw in Noelle's eyes. He watched his daughter wrap her arms around the dog as the sleigh lurched forward, and he saw Nana slip her arm around Rufus's waist. He saw the old man's smile as he turned his head to look at Nana.

Love. It was in the air. Was it possible that was what was really part of a greater plan? It all boiled down to that, didn't it? That simple instruction, the one the seed had been planted for on a Christmas Day a long, long time ago.

Love one another.

Love the strangers you met along the way. And the family you'd been given, even with their flaws.

Love one another.

Every single time that magnificent force—love—came to you, say *yes* instead of no.

Aidan felt that question intensify within himself. Could he say yes to what he had waited his entire life to feel?

A sense of being part of something larger than himself?

He struggled for a moment. It seemed overwhelming. The cynic in him tried to rise up, one last time. But then he felt even that part of him surrender to it, that larger force, which sparkled in the air on this snowy Christmas morning.

Inwardly, he heard a whisper. Yes. And then louder, a celebration, yes.

* * *

Noelle felt his surrender. She had not been aware that some heaviness remained in Aidan, until it was gone, until she saw a new sparkle in his eyes when he looked at her.

Her grandfather wheeled the horses around and they headed back across the fluffy banks of sparkling snow, toward the distant home place. The horses' manes lifted, and their footsteps beat a muffled tattoo in the snow. Their bells could have been church bells; they rang across the crisp air with such purity.

"Gee up," her grandfather said, slapping the reins. The horses changed gait easily, pulling forward powerfully, the sleigh skimming along behind them. Tess laughed out loud, and, if Noelle was not mistaken, Nana tucked herself against Rufus just a little more tightly. It was cold, and yet the sun, the blanket and most especially Aidan's hand in hers made it seem bright and warm.

It was Aidan's voice that lifted in song. "Jingle bells, jingle bells, jingle all the way…"

His voice was beautiful, strong and steady, a pure tenor. Tess clapped her pink-mittened hands with delight and looked at her father's face with pure wonder, the wonder of a child who still believed in the magic and the miracles of Christmas.

Her voice, innocent and bold, joined her father's. And then they were all singing, and the dog was howling along, and it was, possibly, the best Christmas moment Noelle had ever experienced. When that song died, another one rose to take its place. They sang all the way back to the house.

While Rufus looked after the horses, Nana herded them all inside and managed to do quite nicely, putting together a Christmas breakfast on the woodstove.

After they had eaten, Tess was not waiting one more second for her presents. Aidan managed to spirit Jerry

Juicejar away for delivery by Santa the next day, but aside from that, the living room was soon filled with torn wrapping paper and her squeals of delight.

Tess presented Noelle with a gift. She was being unusually shy.

"I didn't have anything for you, so I made it."

Noelle unwrapped her gift to find a carefully illustrated and printed book. It was a story about a girl whose birthday fell on Christmas. "This is amazing. I can't believe you could make such a thing. You're only five."

"Nearly six," Tess said, beaming nonetheless. "Nana had to help me with some of it."

Noelle stared at the painstaking printing and knew she would cherish the handmade book forever.

The skates were the biggest hit, and Tess insisted they must go to the pond immediately.

They all piled outside, skates strung over their shoulders. The pond was covered in nearly a foot of snow, so after testing the thickness of the ice, Rufus fired up the tractor and cleared the whole thing. After that, he invited Nana up into the crowded cab with him, and they headed off to clear the road and move the tree. He waved off Aidan's offer of help.

Noelle watched, delighted, as Aidan coached Tess through her first time on skates. She had seen glimpses of it all along, but he seemed newly relaxed, some guard completely down, and it was heart-warming to see what a good dad he was, patient, firm, funny.

Nana and Rufus returned, Nana driving Aidan's vehicle back down the cleared road. And then the elderly couple put on skates, too. They took over Tess's coaching, and the beautiful little girl skated off between Rufus and Nana, holding both their hands.

And then Aidan held out his hand to Noelle. And they

skated until their legs hurt and laughed until they could laugh no more. He hummed "Could I Have This Dance," and they tried dancing together on skates, ending up in a tangled heap, Noelle beneath him, looking up into his sapphire eyes with wonder.

Could this really be happening to her?

It was Christmas Day and it was her birthday and she was in love, and it was the best day she had ever had. But in the back of her mind she heard a whisper, *Tomorrow is Boxing Day.* She shoved the thought away. Surely, everything had changed...

When exhaustion and cold finally set in, a huge bonfire was lit and a kettle of hot chocolate placed beside it. They roasted wieners for Christmas lunch, and then, when the power did not come back on, again for dinner.

"The best Christmas ever," Tess mumbled, with little smudges of mustard and ketchup smeared around the bow of her mouth.

"Yes," Aidan agreed, his eyes meeting Noelle's. "The best Christmas ever."

"And Santa is still going to come tomorrow, isn't he? I have to put out cookies. I have to put out—"

But Tess fell asleep in her father's arms before these important errands could be completed. The bonfire light was casting her face in gold and Aidan's, too, and the stars winked on in an ink-dark sky. They finally retreated to the house, Tess nestled into Aidan's shoulder.

Aidan and Noelle put the sleepy girl in her pajamas and tucked her into her bed together. She didn't even wake up. By the time they were done, Rufus and Nana had also disappeared. So the two of them put out milk and cookies for Santa, and retrieved Jerry Juicejar from his hiding place and put him under the tree. Then they hung the socks, one for each member of the household, and filled them with what was left of the Christmas treats.

They were small things. And yet they filled Noelle's heart with a sense of how it would be to be together, as a couple, as a family, as a mom and dad to Tess.

Was that where all this was going? When she looked into his eyes, her breath nearly stopped for the truth she saw there.

She touched his cheek.

He touched hers.

And the words found their way to her mouth.

"I love you."

She stood on her tiptoes and took his mouth.

"Hey," he protested, though the protest was weak, "there's no mistletoe."

She felt disappointed. Once again, he was the one backing away. Did it mean he did not feel the same way? Had she embarrassed herself? Was it ridiculous to make such a declaration after such a short time?

He stood there, utterly still, looking at her.

And then he spoke the words.

"I love you, too."

His voice was gruff with emotion. The words seemed to stun him. His moved his hand away from her cheek and stroked it over the swollen plumpness of her lip. Her tongue reached out and touched it, and he gasped with longing, but swiftly took his hand away. He looked at it, and then at her.

He wheeled away from her, and she heard his soft tread on the stairs, and then moments later, she heard his bedroom door softly, but firmly, close.

"The best Christmas ever," Noelle whispered, hugging herself tightly.

CHAPTER SIXTEEN

"NOELLE, WAKE UP! Wake up." Tess was shaking her urgently. "We have to go downstairs and see if Santa came."

She opened her eyes slowly, loving this moment, and loving this little girl, loving the man who stood in the doorway of her room.

"I'm awake," she said. "Go get Nana and Rufus."

"They're up already. Come on. Come on."

Noelle got out of bed, self-conscious in the penguin jammies. She quickly put her housecoat on over the top, and followed Tess and Aidan down the stairs.

Tess stopped at the door of the living room. She shrieked and ran in. "It's Jerry!"

Noelle and Aidan came in behind her. Nana was in the room, but not Rufus. Noelle felt a moment's regret that her grandfather had missed this delightful moment.

But then Aidan put his hand around her shoulder and they exchanged a smile, bathed in the little girl's joy. Aidan kissed Noelle casually, on the mouth.

At that exact moment, Tess turned from Jerry. Her eyes went wide.

"Daddy?" she asked softly. "Is Noelle going to be my mommy?"

Aidan felt himself go still. He felt the shock of Tess's question wash over him. This was how poor a parent he had been. It was beyond bumbling. He'd been thinking of himself. He'd immersed himself in the joy of Noelle loving him.

He'd allowed himself to believe in miracles.

But he, of all people, should know better than that. What, in his world, in his experience, had given him the skill to make a relationship work? Hadn't he thought, once, filled with hope and dreams, that he could write his own story? That he could learn? That he could overcome the lack of love in his childhood?

His marriage had proved him so wrong. One thing about being good at business? You knew never to repeat the same mistake twice.

And not just for him. How could he drag his daughter down this road? How could he hold out to her a shining promise of a family? A mommy? Only to have her in the front row to view his failings when it all began to fall apart? Hadn't Tess been damaged enough?

And what of Noelle?

Could he do that to her? Could he take that offering of her sweet love and watch it turn to dust and ash? Could he be the one who put out the light he had seen in her eyes this morning when she had told him she loved him?

Had he really answered her? Had he really given her false hope? Had he really allowed temporary good feelings to sway his judgment for the future?

As a businessman he knew you could not do that. You had to rely on instincts, yes, but then you had to do the hard work, the research, the plausibility studies to back up those instincts. Just jumping in on a hunch, basing your move on a feeling, was catastrophic in business.

The plausibility study, he realized, had already been done. He had not passed the litmus test with Sierra. He could not drag his daughter through another failure.

As a shocked stillness came over the room, Aidan moved

a step away from Noelle. She looked as if she was holding her breath, waiting to hear how he would respond to that innocent question.

But he was saved from answering.

"What?" Nana was at the window, and she had looked out, possibly to give the couple at least an illusion of privacy as they contemplated the enormity of the question that had just been asked. "What has that old fool gone and done now?"

Aidan, looking for respite from the awkwardness of the question, went and stood at the window beside Nana.

He felt his heart break in two. Rufus was shuffling across the yard with a pony. There was a red ribbon around its neck.

It wasn't just Tess. And Noelle. It was Rufus, too. And Nana. All hoping for love to win.

Maybe Rufus had been matchmaking from the start. Maybe he'd gotten a pony for Tess in the hope of keeping all their lives tangled together once Christmas was over. The old guy probably knew any man with a brain was going to fall in love with Noelle given time and the right circumstances. Rufus, with that pony, was setting things up so that nature could take its course.

Aidan felt a crushing responsibility to stop this train before it got too out of control, before it caused a wreck that took everyone down with it.

"Did you know about this?" he asked Noelle. The heartbreak had been stripped from his voice, and in its place was the pure ice of a man who knew he had to be cold enough to save everyone around him who was foolish enough to give him one more chance to get it right.

Noelle joined him at the window. Here came Rufus and Smiley through the snow, leading Gidget, who had a bow around her neck. It did not look like the little horse had cooperated with the bow-tying exercise, as it was hanging crookedly.

Noelle scanned Aidan's face. He looked so very cold, his beloved features cast in stone. She didn't want to admit she'd known, but she couldn't just throw her grandfather under the bus, either.

She nodded, and something hardened in Aidan's face.

"Please keep Tess away from the window," Aidan said tersely. And then without even putting on a jacket he slipped into shoes by the door and went out into the cold.

Noelle could not bear to watch what happened. She got down on the floor with Tess, who was busy taking Jerry out of his wrapper and exploring the Juicejar house.

It seemed like a long time later that Aidan came back, followed by her grandfather, who gave her a baffled look and lifted his shoulder. Neither man said anything about the pony.

"Time for us to pack our bags," Aidan said, knocking the snow off his boots, refusing to look at Noelle.

So, he was on his original schedule, after all.

"I'm not leaving!" Tess screamed. "I'm not leaving Smiley. I'm not leaving Noelle and Rufus. We're building a snowman today. We're making cookies. We're—" her voice dissolved into a sob.

Noelle went and gathered the little girl in her arms. What could she say? She could not make her any promises. When she glanced at Aidan's face, she did not see any hope for a future there. How had it all fallen apart so quickly?

But for now, it was not her heartbreak she needed to focus on. It was Tess. "It's all right, sweetheart," she whispered to the little girl, feeling her chest get wet with tears. She stroked her hair. "Everything will be all right," she said. As she glanced again at Aidan, it didn't feel that way. It felt like nothing could ever be right again.

"Can I see you outside?" Aidan asked Noelle. The coldness in his tone chilled her to the bone.

Noelle, with a final kiss on Tess's silky hair, put the little girl away from her. "Go gather up your things," she said softly.

She put on her coat and went outside. He already had his vehicle warming up. She hugged herself, quite a different hug than the one last night.

"What happened?" she asked, scanning his features so closed to her.

"I've had a wonderful time," he said formally. "As has Tess. I can't thank you enough for the Christmas you have given my daughter and myself."

Who was this cool stranger?

"I won't be seeing you again, Noelle."

Even though she had already sensed it, this announcement was like being hit with a pail of cold water. Her mouth fell open. Her voice was trembling. "W-w-what? W-w-why?"

"I can't do it to Tess," he said softly. "I can't hold out all this hope to her, and then watch her world come tumbling down around her again."

"Does it have to? Come tumbling down?"

"I trusted you. I told you the only rule for Christmas was no pony, and you knew. Can you see how that would have forced us to keep coming back here? Forced us to tangle our lives more and more with yours? And your grandfather's? It was extremely manipulative."

"You pompous ass! My grandfather was trying to make a little girl happy. How dare you make that about you? How dare you make those judgments of him when he has been nothing but generous to you? That speaks to you. Not to him."

"Yes," Aidan said sadly. "It does. It speaks to me. Goodbye, Noelle."

She stood there quivering with fury and shock. She would not give him the satisfaction of crying in front of him. She whirled and went back in the house.

She hugged Tess and Nana, who were both coming down the stairs with their packed things, looking shocked.

And then, as quickly as their guests had come, they were gone, and Noelle was there alone with her grandfather.

"I'm sorry," he said. "I didn't think through the pony thing."

"Oh, Grandpa," Noelle said, and went and put a reassuring arm around his shoulders. "You have the best heart of any man I know. Don't ever doubt that."

"Why did they leave then?" her grandfather asked grumpily.

She thought of Tess's innocent question, and she thought of that word poking out from under the Christmas wreath on the front door. Hope.

"It has to do with the most dangerous thing of all," she said softly.

"Ah," Rufus said. "Love. He'll come around."

But Noelle thought of the stony look on Aidan's face, and somehow she doubted that he would, even as she nursed the most dangerous thing of all.

Hope.

For some reason, Noelle finally remembered what her grandmother had said, that night she had overheard her grandparents talking during her and Mitchell's visit to the ranch.

What's wrong with him? her grandfather had asked of Mitchell.

For the longest time, Noelle had not remembered her grandmother's answer. But now she did, so clearly she wondered how she could have ever thought she'd forgotten.

It's not what's wrong with him, her grandmother had said. *It's what's wrong with her to accept that kind of treatment.*

That was why it had flitted around the edges of her mind, like a wily cat that did not want to be caught. Because she could not bear it that her beloved grandmother had thought there was something wrong with her.

Now, the entire conversation came pouring back.

She longs to be loved, Rufus had said. *He doesn't deserve that.*

And her grandmother had said, *You don't choose a man like that if you long to be loved. I think you choose a man like that if you are scared to death of being loved. It has already hurt you so badly, you can't do it again.*

Right there, on Boxing Day, Noelle stood in the wisdom and light and truth of her grandmother's words. She had chosen Mitchell because he would require less of her heart, not more.

She was aware she was not that woman anymore.

Noelle was aware she had spent too much of her life already waiting for a man to come to his senses. She was done with that. She would not demean herself in that way again.

She loved Aidan, but it occurred to her, after she had left her grandfather's and gone back to work, that love didn't weaken people. It made them stronger.

And so she vowed to be stronger for loving Aidan. She vowed not to be a woman scared to death of being loved.

She refused to sit around eating ice cream for supper

and sulking. She fought the temptation to weep and wring her hands, and ask what might have been. Instead, she decided to become the woman in the red dress, to own her own life.

She quit all her social media outlets. She did not miss them. She didn't want to live vicariously. She wanted to live! And so she became a volunteer who read to children at the library. If it made her yearn for Tess, that was part of the price of loving. She took a ballroom dancing class, and loved that so much she signed up for a jazz class, too.

Still, every time the phone rang, she hoped.

Every time she saw a dark head moving through a crowd on a downtown street, she hoped.

Every time she heard "Could I Have This Dance," she hoped.

Because now she knew something she had not known before: that life could change in a second, that good things and miraculous things could come to you as quickly and as shockingly as loss.

One night, her phone rang as she was leaving her dance class, which had run quite late. Her grandfather would not call at this time of the night unless there was a problem. She answered the phone with a faint fear beating in her heart.

Silence.

And then a whisper. "Noelle?"

It was not her grandfather. The hair stood up on the back of her neck as she recognized that childish, sweet voice. "Tess?"

"We need you."

"What?"

"You said everything would be all right! You promised."

Noelle knew she had not promised, but she also knew

the little girl had heard a promise, of sorts, and she felt the agony of missing them. "What's wrong, Tess?"

"My daddy was happy. He was happy when we were with you. I miss him being like that. I miss you." She started to cry. "He's so grumpy. He says he's not mad, but he acts like he is. He's on his phone all the time. I need you to come make my daddy happy again."

"Where are you?" Noelle asked, worried. Why was Tess whispering? Where was Aidan? She could not imagine he had allowed Tess to make this call.

"Daddy went in the shower so I took his phone. Because I hate his phone. I was going to hide it, but then I found your name. *N-o-e-l-l-e*."

Noelle tried to think why her number would be in his phone. Then, vaguely she recalled he had taken it when they were Christmas shopping, in case they lost track of each other in the busy mall.

"Did you remember I know my alphabet?"

"I remember everything about you, sweetheart."

"Before I hid it, I pushed your name. And you answered! I have the best hiding place for the phone. He'll never find it here. He won't even hear it ring. You want to guess?"

"The fridge?"

Tess laughed happily. "Farther away than that."

"Umm, the coat closet?"

"Nope, farther, even. You probably can't guess how far."

"You didn't go out of your apartment, did you?" Noelle asked, alarmed.

"I ran away," she said stubbornly.

"Are you in your apartment?"

Silence.

"Are you in the building?"

"Maybe," Tess said coyly.

"No one's with you? Where is Nana?"

"Nana's gone."

"Gone where?"

"To be with Rufus and Smiley."

Beneath her alarm, Noelle contemplated that. Not a word from her grandfather. How recent was this development?

"When did she go?" Noelle asked, trying to get some idea of how long Tess had been off on her adventure.

"I want to be with Rufus and Smiley, too."

"Are you by yourself right now, Tess?"

"Jerry is with me. I'm in a room with brooms. And shovels. It smells funny, but I don't care."

For a moment Noelle panicked. Jerry? Who was Jerry? Some creep who had found Tess and led her to the broom closet that smelled funny?

Oh! Jerry! Jerry Juicejar.

Noelle's mind raced. She could not hang up and call Aidan. She didn't even think she had Nana's number. Both must be frantic. Or did Nana even know? Did Aidan know? Or was he still in the shower?

"How long have you and Jerry been in the broom closet?" Not in their suite, Noelle deduced. They wouldn't need snow shovels in their suite. Tess was in the building. In some kind of janitorial room in the building.

"A long time," Tess said with a sigh. "I ate my chocolate candy already."

Noelle could tell Tess firmly to get out of the closet and go home. But the child was five! What if she took a wrong turn? Or met the wrong person?

Noelle oriented to where she was. She had walked to her dance class. She began to run toward Aidan's condo complex. Five minutes? Ten? She could not let Tess hear her panic.

Trying to keep the breathlessness out of her tone, she said, calmly and conversationally, "How is Jerry?"

"He's not as much fun as Smiley."

"Smiley misses you."

A little hiccupped sob. "I know. I miss him, too."

"Did I ever tell you about the dog I had when I was a little girl?"

"No." Reluctant curiosity.

"His name was Puddles."

"That's a good name!"

"Yes, it was, because at the beginning he made puddles all over the place. That's what puppies do."

Tess giggled.

"When he stopped making puddles, he got into other mischief. Once, when we were sleeping, he went into the bathroom and grabbed the end of the toilet paper roll in his teeth and ran all through the house with it. There was toilet paper everywhere."

Tess laughed. And Noelle kept talking. Five blocks.

"Once, my mom had made roast beef, and it was on the counter. She just left it for a minute, and when she came back in the room it was gone. And Puddles licked his lips and then he burped."

Four.

"Noelle! Dogs don't have lips."

"Don't they?"

"Smiley burped after he licked Nana's face."

Three.

"Yes, he did."

Two. She could see his condo complex. There were police cars in front of it! Noelle put on a burst of speed, grateful for those jazz classes improving her lung capacity. She raced in the door.

Aidan was standing in the lobby in the middle of a knot of policeman. He was in his robe.

In a split second Noelle saw everything there was to see about him. She saw how deeply and completely he loved.

How deeply and completely he wanted to protect what he loved.

How deeply and completely he felt loss.

He saw her come in the doors. At first, it barely pierced his distress. But then, before his guard came up, she saw it.

The relief that she was here. The love—his love—that he had tried to protect her from, somehow seeing it as imperfect. Flawed. Doomed to failure.

She took the phone from her ear and pressed it to her chest, put a finger to her lips. The lobby went silent.

She went to him and stood on tiptoe.

"Maintenance room?" she whispered.

And he was racing down the hall with her behind him, and the police behind them both. He went down an emergency exit to the basement, raced down a dark hallway and threw open a door.

The ribbon of light that went in the door revealed Tess, Jerry pressed tight against chest, her mouth smeared with chocolate. She dropped the phone she had pressed to her ear.

Her father scooped her up and held her so tight it was a wonder the little girl could breathe.

"Daddy," Tess whispered, touching his cheek. "Are you crying?"

CHAPTER SEVENTEEN

IT SEEMED IT was hours later that Tess was safely tucked into her own bed, ugly Jerry lodged comfortably beside her. The police were finally gone. Aidan sat on the sofa, his elbows on his knees, his head cradled in his hands.

Noelle brought him tea. He took it, and she sank down on the couch beside him.

His eyes met hers, the longing undisguised, before he looked quickly away. It was the face of a man tormented.

And Noelle knew why she had not allowed herself to sink into despair after his departure on the day after Christmas. She knew why, instead of taking to her bed and a bucket of ice cream, she had learned to dance and gone to read to children at the library.

Because love required her to find herself.

Love required her to be strong enough, sure enough in her own being, to go into the darkness he had wrapped himself in and bring him back out. To be brave enough to rescue this lonely, strong man who was determined to use his strength for all the wrong things. To keep love at bay, instead of to embrace it.

"I understand it now," she said softly. "You didn't leave because of a pony."

He was stubbornly silence.

"You used that as an excuse."

"What are you talking about?"

"I'm talking about you loving me."

He drew his breath in sharply. His mouth moved, but no sound came out. The fact that he seemed incapable of denying it gave her the courage to go on.

"You love me so much," Noelle told him softly, "that you thought you had to protect me. You couldn't possibly see yourself succeeding in this arena. How could you succeed at love?"

"Precisely," he said.

"You had no models for a good relationship. You saw that when you married Sierra. That you didn't have the tools to make it work."

He nodded.

"And yet your love for Tess is the model for all love," she told him softly.

"It's not. Look at what just happened. She ran away from me."

"Did she? Or did she know in her heart what needed to happen? Did she sense somehow that you needed me?"

He looked as if he intended to protest. His mouth opened. But again, not a single sound came out.

"You were trying to protect both of us, Tess and me, weren't you, from what you saw as your inevitable failure?"

"Look, this conversation is pointless—"

"I agree," she said. "The time for talking is done."

He actually looked relieved. Until she leaned toward him. He could have gotten away, but he was paralyzed. She took his lips with her own. Tenderly. She let the touch of her lips tell him what he would not allow himself to hear in words.

That she was strong enough to face the storms.

That when his strength failed, hers would take over.

That she carried within her a legacy of such enormous love that the light of it would guide them both through the uncertain waters of a life together.

At first, his lips remained closed against hers. And yet, he did not push her away. She sensed he wanted to, but could not. And so she deepened her kiss until she felt the tiniest give in him, the tiniest of surrenders.

And into that gap, she poured everything she was, and it was like sunlight pouring over snow, turning what was hard and cold into something silver and liquid.

He broke free of her lips, but he did not get up and leave. Or throw her out. Instead, he seemed to be eyeing the life rope she was throwing him.

"What if I hurt you?" Aidan whispered. "And in hurting you, hurt my daughter? She wants you as a mommy so desperately. I'm going to blow it."

"Are you?" Even though he had said that, she could see him reaching out for that rope.

"Yes," he said.

"Just trust it a little bit," Noelle told him. "Just trust love a little tiny bit, and see what it can do. Let's see what happens next."

For a long time, he said nothing. But then he took the rope she offered, Noelle saw the answer in his eyes, she saw in them that little flicker of light that was at the heart of the human spirit, and that was at the core of all human strength.

The ability, in the face of overwhelming evidence that it might be heartbreaking to do so, to still say yes to hope.

"All right," he said. "Let's see what happens next."

Over the next few months, Noelle discovered that Aidan was not a man who did anything by half measures, including seeing what happened next, including falling in love.

He courted her with an intensity, an attention to detail, a fierceness, a tenderness that made her feel as if she was the most loved woman in the world.

He wined her. He dined her. He showered her with gifts. They hiked the trails of Banff National Park and rode the gondola to the top of the world. They rode a different kind of gondola in Venice and snorkeled off the coast of Kona in Hawaii. They went to visit the wineries of the Sonoma Valley. They rode in a hot air balloon. They took a road trip and found each of the hidden hot springs of the Kootenays. They embraced adventures: rock climbing and kayaking and white water rafting. They took cooking classes and ballroom dancing classes.

They discovered what it meant for them to be a couple. Rufus and Nana, who had gotten married a scant two months after Christmas, happily took Tess when they went away.

And they discovered what it meant for them to be a family. They took Tess to Disney World in Florida, and the fabulous Atlantis resort in the Bahamas. They took in children's theaters and themed playgroups.

And for all this, Noelle's favorite moments with Aidan and Tess remained the simplest ones. Walking hand in hand along the Bow River as pussy willow buds burst in the trees. The three of them going together to story time at the library, or sprawled out on the floor of the children's section of the bookstore. Sitting on a bench and eating hotdogs at the truck downtown at lunch hour. All of them crowded into Tess's bed reading stories at night.

Best of all was when they went to the ranch together. Watching the quiet love grow between Nana and Rufus, and watching Tess learn to ride Gidget, playing board games at night and sitting in the hayloft together after everyone else had gone to bed.

The ranch was "their" place somehow, the place where, entirely free of distractions, something bolder and more beautiful than they had ever imagined for their lives had taken root.

They were at the ranch one summer evening when Aidan asked her to go for a walk with him.

They found themselves at the Honeymoon Cabin.

"I have a gift for you," he said quietly.

Noelle laughed. She had tried so hard to dissuade him from gifts, but there was no point. She took the envelope he held out to her. "What is it?"

"Open it."

Noelle opened it and found a sheaf of legal-looking papers.

"I don't understand what this is."

"Your grandfather took me aside a few weeks ago and gave me a talking-to."

"Really? What did he say?"

"He said he understood I was trying to do the honorable thing. He said he understood that it was important for a man to make the woman he loved feel as if she was a princess. He said he understood the value of an old-fashioned courtship. But he said enough was enough. He told me to get on with it."

Aidan was looking at her with a quiet intensity that made her heart stand still. That thing he did to her heart never seemed to change.

"He said time was shorter than a person could ever imagine. He said that's why he and Nana did things so quickly. Because they have both experienced losses and they have the maturity to understand that time runs out.

"He told me to marry you and have some babies, already."

"Aidan Phillips! Are you asking me to marry you?"

He was silent.

Even as her heart soared, Noelle could not resist teasing him. "Because my grandfather told you to?"

"Actually, he said all that after."

"After?"

"After I asked his permission. Quit rushing me!"

"His permission?"

"To marry his granddaughter."

Suddenly, Noelle didn't feel like teasing him anymore. This was real. This was what it all had been building toward: the time together, the increasingly heated looks and kisses. She loved spending time with him. She would not give up a moment of their romance.

But she was with her grandfather on this one.

She needed Aidan at a different level now. She needed to touch him in places where no one else touched him, and she needed to let the heat of his kisses spread until they were both weak with it. She needed there to be no more reasons to say no.

Aidan got down on one knee before her. She resisted the impulse to touch his hair.

He reached into his pocket and pulled out a velvet box. He snapped open the lid. The band within, studded with perfect diamonds, winked with astonishing blue lights. He cleared his throat.

"Noelle McGregor, I am so in love with you I can barely think for it. I am so in love with you I can barely breathe for it. You have taken a landscape that was bleak and dark and brought it to color and life. You have shown me the meaning of my life. You have become the role model for my daughter.

"I cannot imagine my life without you. I want to spend the rest of my days with you. I want to have children. I want to love you until you are breathless with my love.

"Will you marry me?"

Noelle was crying shamelessly. She dropped the papers he had given her and they scattered in the wind. She let her hands roam in his hair, relishing it, delighting in it. This incredible man was asking her to join lives with his. For the rest of their lives. Forever.

"Yes," she whispered. "Yes."

He rose to his feet and gathered her in his arms, and then shouted so loud the mountains sent an echo back to them.

"Thank you," he whispered. "Thank you for giving me something to hope for."

It was a long time before they came up for air.

"I guess we should find all those papers," he said reluctantly.

"What are they?"

"The deed for all this land. We're going to build our house here one day. And raise our children here."

"You bought back the McGregor land?"

"Every inch of it."

"But you're not a rancher!"

"I can learn. Plus, I figured you probably won't be able to keep your hands off me if I'm wearing a cowboy hat and riding a horse."

"I can barely keep my hands off you now," she said wryly.

"Oh, in that case, maybe I'll just lease the grazing rights."

It was her turn. "Thank you."

Not just for the land. In fact that seemed like the least of it. For all of it. For teaching her what love was. For giving her back her sense of family. For renewing her trust in life. For giving her a sense of herself, for allowing her to evolve into a woman worthy of love.

Worthy of him.

They turned, and hand in hand, they chased down all those papers that were scattering in the wind. It seemed those papers were playing with them, leading them on a path that pointed straight to the future.

EPILOGUE

"I THINK WE should paint a hippopotamus on the wall," Tess said, her voice full of authority. At seven, she knew everything, including, apparently, what a new baby brother would require in his nursery.

"A hippopotamus?" Aidan repeated, trying to buy time. He wasn't quite sure that would fit with the nursery theme that he and Noelle had decided on—blue, jauntily nautical—to welcome their first child together, a boy, to the world. He didn't have a whole bunch of time for this, and a hippopotamus seemed like a rather large design change.

He gulped, trying not to think about the lack of time. In less than a week their baby was due.

"Maybe you should ask Mama," he suggested.

Tess had started calling Noelle Mama within a week of the wedding. Neither Noelle nor Aidan had suggested it; she had apparently come up with it on her own. Not Mommy, not a replacement for her mother who had died, but a new name.

"Ask me what?"

Aidan turned, paintbrush in hand, and looked at his wife.

She was exactly what he had recognized, what his heart had recognized—from the first moment she had thrown a snowball at him.

The most beautiful woman in the world. The woman who could change everything. The woman who was brave enough to come and rescue him from his lonely world.

"Can we have a hippopotamus in here?" Tess asked.

Noelle pretended to consider it. "Aren't they awfully big?" she asked, seriously. "Do you know what they eat?"

Tess's laughter, so frequent, so joyous, pealed through the room. "Painted on the wall, Mama. Not a real one."

Noelle contemplated the blank, pale blue wall. "I think that would be perfect," she said.

Aidan suppressed his groan.

Tess sighed with contentment, and went and cupped her hands on Noelle's tummy. "Hello, in there," she called loudly, "Hello, Ben."

And then she put her ear to Noelle's stomach. "I hear him," she decided. "Oh! He kicked me. Daddy! Come feel him."

And so he went and laid his hand over the tautness of Noelle's belly. Their eyes met as the baby seemed to do a somersault inside of her.

"Is it time?" he asked, stunned by the violent activity. "I'll get the car. I'll call Nana. I'll—"

Noelle was smiling at him, indulgently. She, and she alone, was entrusted with this truth. If he ran his billion-dollar company the way he awaited the birth of their baby—nervous, impulsive, jumping at every shadow—Wrangler would be broke.

Noelle, on the other hand, didn't seem the least bit worried about whether or not it was time. He had suggested they move back to his condo in the city until the baby arrived. When Noelle said no, he woke in the night, scanning the sky for storms. Even though it was fall—no chance of being snowed in, at all—he contemplated possible disasters. Trees falling. Water rising. Vehicles not starting.

Noelle had gotten up one night to find him coming in from outside.

"It's the middle of the night," she told him.

"I was just checking."

"Checking what?"

"It's windy."

She had cocked her head at him.

"A tree could come down over the driveway!"

"You could bring the helicopter out here," she said. "A straight run to the hospital. Most of them even have landing pads right on the property."

He was actually thinking how brilliant she was, until he caught on that she was teasing him.

"A baby is nothing new here," she told him gently, when she saw the worry furrow his brow. You'd almost think she was planning on having it at home.

Home.

They had built the house last year, in a clearing not too far from the Honeymoon Cabin. He could actually see the old cabin from their master bedroom window upstairs.

They had, of course, had their honeymoon there. They'd married at the ranch just a few days before Christmas, a year to the day since they met.

Noelle could have had the wedding anywhere. She could have had a ball that would have matched the Christmas Enchantment Ball. She could have chosen a beach somewhere. She could have had a live band and dancing deep into the night.

Instead, they had exchanged their vows on the porch of the old ranch house. Tess had scattered snowflakes made out of paper instead of flower petals.

Noelle had said no to a white dress. She didn't think it was the color of celebration. She thought it would just blend with all that snow.

Instead, she had looked gorgeous in a red gown, sure of herself, a woman confident enough to fly joyously in the face of tradition.

They could have had a feast catered by the best chef in Calgary. But Noelle had laughed that off. Instead, they had cleared the barn and plank tables had been set up that groaned under the weight of all the neighborhood women bringing their favorite dishes. After supper the tables had been cleared away, and the fiddles had come out. They had danced until dawn.

They could have had a honeymoon anywhere in the world. They could have left the ranch behind and flown to Tuscany, or to a private island a friend of his owned.

No. Instead, when the party was over, Rufus had hitched up the sleigh and delivered them to the Honeymoon Cabin.

They had spent five glorious days of exquisite time in that snowbound little cabin, with nothing but each other.

By then they had traveled much of the world together, witnessed marvels and discovered treasures beyond imagining.

And yet, in that cabin, there had been a sense of having everything they would ever need.

Each other.

He could not think of that time without his mouth going dry with wanting her. He could feel that desire build within him.

Not just to touch her, not just for the incredible intensity of them together, physically, but for the intimacy of that time in the cabin.

Aidan realized he was a man who had been given a gift worth cherishing. He had a sense of knowing where home was.

Not really in a cabin, or on a ranch. Not really in this brand-new home that they had designed and built together.

As beautiful as it was, this building was just a house. Home was where she was, where Noelle was. It was that place of safety where they laughed and cried and celebrated and felt sorrow together.

His home, forever, was nestled in the heart of the woman he loved.

"A purple one?" Tess asked.

"A purple what?"

He got *the* look.

"A purple hippopotamus, of course," Tess said.

"Yes, I think a purple hippopotamus would be perfect," Noelle agreed. He frowned at the wall. There were all kinds of logistics to consider. What size should it be? And who had the skill to paint a hippopotamus? It could just end up looking like a giant purple blob on the wall. Even if it turned out okay, did a hippopotamus of any color go with the carefully chosen nautical theme of the baby room at all?

But looking at his wife and his daughter, he knew none of that mattered. They weren't, either of them, about things looking perfect.

His daughter had tried so desperately to tell him that, when he had been busy giving her Christmases that looked so right, and felt so wrong.

Tess and Noelle were all about how things *felt*. Even if that was messy and chaotic and threw the best-laid plans to the wind.

He sighed, and decided not to weigh in on the hippopotamus. It was an argument he was bound to lose.

At that moment, the puppy, who was not allowed in here, pushed through the door. He was a black Lab, and he looked a lot like his namesake, Smiley, had.

Aidan had thought a puppy right now was the worst possible idea. But when Noelle and Tess were onside for something, they were a formidable pair.

The puppy, Smiley, too, thumped his tail, pleading to join them. Then in the excitement of having broken into the forbidden sanctum, Smiley gave them an apologetic look and piddled on the floor.

And their laughter rang out and filled the room, and danced out the open windows and sparkled in the surrounding forest, like fairy dust.

Aidan, that most pragmatic of men, could picture that laughter taking on a life of its own, and going out and out and out from them. He could picture it threading its way around a Christmas wreath where he had seen the word *HOPE* and then soaring on, past the forest, over the glades, and beyond what he could see, and even beyond what he could imagine.

He could picture that laughter joining the rushing rivers and the shooting stars, joining the great mystery that had given birth to it in the first place.

Aidan, that most pragmatic of men, could picture the laughter holding a force within it as brilliant as sunlight, a force that radiated outward, the only force that had ever really changed the world.

Love.

Their laughter held the magnificent healing power of love.

* * * * *

SAME TIME, NEXT CHRISTMAS

CHRISTINE RIMMER

For MSR, always.

Chapter One

December 23, four years ago...

Even with the rain coming down so hard he could barely make out the twisting gravel road ahead of him, Matthias Bravo spotted the light shining through the trees.

The Jeep lurched around another twist in the road. For a few seconds before the trees obscured his view, Matt could see his getaway cabin in the clearing up ahead. Yep. The light was coming from the two windows that flanked the front door.

Some idiot had broken in.

Swearing under his breath, Matt steered his Jeep to the almost nonexistent side of the road and switched off the engine and lights.

The rain poured down harder, pounding the roof,

roaring so loud he couldn't hear himself think. Out the windshield, the trees with their moss-covered trunks were a blur through the rippling curtain made of water.

Should he have just stayed home in Valentine Bay for Christmas?

Probably. His injured leg throbbed and he was increasingly certain he'd caught that weird bug his brothers had warned him about. He had a mother of a headache and even though he'd turned the heater off several miles back, he was sweating.

"Buck up, buddy." He slapped his own cheek just to remind himself that torrential rain, a sliced-up leg, a headache and a fever were not the worst things he'd ever lived through.

And at the moment, he had a mission. The SOB in his cabin needed taking down—or at the very least, roughing up a tad and kicking out on his ass.

Matt kept his rifle in a hidden safe at the back of the Jeep. Unfortunately, the safe was accessed through the rear door.

"No time like the present to do what needs doing."

Yeah. He was talking to himself. Kind of a bad sign.

Was he having a resurgence of the PTSD he'd been managing so well for over a year now?

No. Uh-uh. Zero symptoms of a recurrence. No more guilt than usual. He wasn't drunk and hadn't been in a long time. No sleep problems, depression or increased anxiety.

Simply a break-in he needed to handle.

And going in without a weapon? How stupid would that be?

He put on his field jacket, pulled up the hood, shoved open his door and jumped out, biting back a groan when his hurt leg took his weight.

The good news: it wasn't that far to the rear door. In no time, he was back inside the vehicle, sweating profusely, dripping rain all over the seat, with the rifle in one hand and a box of shells in the other.

Two minutes later, rifle loaded and ready for action, he was limping through the downpour toward the cabin. Keeping to the cover of the trees, he worked his way around the clearing, doing a full three-sixty, checking for vehicles and anyone lurking outside, finding nothing that shouldn't be there.

Recon accomplished, he approached the building from the side. Dropping to the wet ground, he crawled to the steps, staying low as he climbed them. His leg hurt like hell, shards of pain stabbing him with every move he made. It was bleeding again right through the thick makeshift bandage he'd tied on the wound.

Too bad. For now, he needed to block the pain and focus.

As he rolled up onto the covered porch, he swiped back his dripping hood and crawled over beneath the front window.

With slow care, he eased up just enough to peer over the sill.

He got an eyeful.

A good-looking brunette—midtwenties, he would guess—sat on the hearth, warming herself at a blazing fire. She wore only a bra and panties. Articles of clothing lay spread out around her, steaming as they dried.

Was she alone? He didn't see anyone else in there. The cabin was essentially one big room, with bath and sleeping loft. From his crouch at the window, he could see the bathroom, its door wide open. Nobody in there. And he had a straight visual shot right through to the back door. Nada. Just the pretty, half-naked brunette.

She looked totally harmless.

Still, he should check the situation out from every possible angle before making his move.

Was he maybe being a little bit paranoid? Yeah, possibly.

But better safe than sorry.

He dragged himself over beneath the other front window. The view from there was pretty much the same. The woman looked so innocent, leaning back on her hands now, long, smooth legs stretched out and crossed at the ankles. She raised a slim hand and forked her fingers through her thick, dark hair.

Grimly, he pulled up his hood and crawled down the steps into the deluge again. Circling the cabin once more, close-in this time, he ducked to peer into each window as he passed.

Every view revealed the leggy brunette, alone, drying off by the fire.

By the time he limped back to the front of the building and crept up onto the porch again, he was all but certain the woman was on her own.

Still, she could be dangerous. Maybe. And dangerous or not, she *had* broken in and helped herself to his firewood. Not to mention he still couldn't completely discount the possibility that there was someone upstairs.

He'd just have to get the jump on her, hope she really was alone and that no damn fool hid in the loft, ready to make trouble.

Sliding to the side, Matt came upright flush against the front door. Slowly and silently, he turned the knob. The knob had no lock, but he needed to see if the dead bolt was still engaged. It was. He took the keys from his pocket. At the speed of a lazy snail, in order not to alert the trespasser within, he unlocked the dead bolt.

That accomplished, he put the keys away and turned the knob with agonizing slowness until the door was open barely a crack. Stepping back, he kicked the door wide. It slammed against the inside wall as he leveled the barrel of his rifle on the saucer-eyed girl.

"Freeze!" he shouted. "Do it now!"

Sabra Bond gaped at the armed man who filled the wide-open doorway.

He was a very big guy, dressed for action in camo pants, heavy boots and a hooded canvas coat. And she wore nothing but old cotton panties and a sports bra.

No doubt about it. Her life was a mess—and getting worse by the second.

Sheepishly, she put her hands up.

The man glared down the barrel of that rifle at her. "What do you think you're doing in my cabin?"

"I, um, I was on my way back to Portland from my father's farm," she babbled. "I parked at the fish hatchery and started hiking along the creek toward the falls. The rain came. It got so bad that I—"

"Stop." He swung the business end of his rifle upward toward the loft. "Anyone upstairs? Do not lie to me."

"No one." He leveled the weapon on her again. "Just me!" she squeaked. "I swear it." She waited for him to lower the gun. No such luck. The barrel remained pointed right at her. And, for some incomprehensible reason, she couldn't quit explaining herself. "I was hiking and thinking, you know? The time got away from me. I'd gone miles before the rain started. It kept getting worse, which led me to the unpleasant discovery that my waterproof jacket is only water resistant. Then I found your cabin..."

"And you broke in," he snarled.

Had she ever felt more naked? Highly unlikely. "I was just going to stand on the porch and wait for the rain to stop. But it only came down harder and I kept getting colder."

"So you broke in," he accused again, one side of his full mouth curling in a sneer.

Okay, he had a point. She *had* broken in. "I jimmied a window and climbed through," she admitted with a heavy sigh.

Still drawing a bead on her, water dripping from his coat, he stepped beyond the threshold and kicked the door shut. Then he pointed the gun at her pack. "Empty that. Just turn it over and dump everything out."

Eager to prove how totally unthreatening she was, Sabra grabbed the pack, unzipped it, took it by the bottom seam and gave it a good shake. A first-aid kit, an empty water bottle, a UC Santa Cruz Slugs hat and sweatshirt, and a bottle of sunscreen dropped out.

"Pockets and compartments, too," he commanded.

She unhooked the front flap and shook it some more. Her phone, a tube of lip balm, a comb and a couple of hair elastics tumbled to the floor. "That's it." She dropped the empty pack. "That's all of it." When he continued to glare at her, she added, "Dude. It was only a day hike."

"No gun." He paced from one side of the cabin to the other. She realized he was scoping out the upstairs, getting a good look at whatever might be up there.

Apparently satisfied at last that she really was alone, he pointed the gun her way all over again and squinted at her as though trying to peer into her brain and see what mayhem she might be contemplating.

Hands still raised, she shook her head. "I'm alone. No gun, no knives, no nothing. Just me in my underwear and a bunch of soggy clothes—and listen. I'm sorry I broke in. It was a bad choice on my part." *And not the only one I've made lately.* "How 'bout if I just get dressed and go?"

He studied her some more, all squinty-eyed and suspicious. Then, at last, he seemed to accept the fact that she was harmless. He lowered the rifle. "Sorry," he grumbled. "I'm overcautious sometimes."

"Apology accepted," she replied without a single trace of the anger and outrage the big man deserved— because no longer having to stare down the dark barrel of that gun?

Just about the greatest thing that had ever happened to her.

As she experienced the beautiful sensation of pure relief, he emptied the shells from his rifle, stuffed them in a pocket and turned to hang the weapon on the rack above the door. The moment he turned his back to her, she grabbed her Slugs sweatshirt and yanked it on over her head.

When he faced her again, he demanded, "You got anyone you can call to come get you?" She was flipping her still-damp hair out from under the neck of the sweatshirt as he added, "Someone with four-wheel drive. They'll probably need chains or snow tires, too." When she just stared in disbelief, he said, "That frog strangler out there? Supposed to turn to snow. Soon."

A snowstorm? Seriously? "It is?"

He gave a snort of pure derision. "Oughtta check the weather report before you go wandering off into the woods."

Okay, not cool. First, he points a gun at her and then he insults her common sense. The guy was really beginning to annoy her. Sabra had lived not fifteen miles from this cabin of his for most of her life. Sometimes you couldn't count on the weather report and he ought to know that. "I did check the weather. This morning, before I left on my way to Portland. Light rain possible, it said."

"It's Oregon. The weather can change."

His condescending response didn't call for an answer, so she didn't give him one. Instead, she grabbed her still-soggy pants and put them on, too, wishing she'd had sense enough to keep driving right past the sign for the fish hatchery. A hike along the creek to the falls had seemed like a good idea at the time, a way to lift her spirits a little, to clear her troubled mind before going on back to Portland to face finding a new apartment during the remaining two weeks and two days of her vacation from work—a vacation that was supposed to have been her honeymoon.

The big guy grunted. "And you didn't answer my question. Got anyone you can call?"

"Well, let me see…" Her mom had been dead for six years now. Her dad was three hours away in Eu-

gene until New Year's. Five days ago, on the day before she was supposed to have gotten married, she
and her ex-fiancé had called it quits for reasons too
upsetting to even think about at the moment. And she
just wasn't ready to ask any of her Portland friends to
drive eighty miles through a blizzard on the day before Christmas Eve to save her from a stranger with
a bad attitude in an isolated cabin in the middle of the
forest. "No. I don't have anyone to call."

The big guy did some swearing. Finally, he muttered, "Let me get my tree in here and I'll drive you
wherever you need to go."

Get outta town. Mr. Grouchy Pants had a *tree*? She
was almost as surprised as when he'd kicked open the
door. "Uh, you mean *you* have a Christmas tree?"

His scowl deepened. "It's Christmas, isn't it?"

She put up both hands again. "It's just, well, you
don't seem like the Christmas-tree type."

"I like Christmas." He narrowed his blue eyes at
her. "I like it *alone.*"

"Gotcha. And thank you—for the offer of a ride, I
mean. If you can get me to my car at the fish hatchery, I can take it from there just fine. As for the tree,
I'll help you bring it in."

"You stay here. I don't need you."

"Good to know." She tugged on her socks and boots
and not-quite-waterproof jacket as he pulled a tree
stand out from under the sink, filled it with water and
put it down near the door—and now that she wasn't
terrified half out of her wits, she noticed that he was
limping.

His right pants leg was torn up, hanging in tatters
to the knee. Beneath the tatters, she could see a bit

of bloody bandage—a very bloody bandage, actually, bright red and wet. It looked like he was bleeding into his boot.

He straightened from positioning the tree stand and took the three steps to the door.

She got up. "Do you know that you're bleeding?" He didn't bother to answer. She followed him outside. "Listen. Slow down. Let me help you."

"Stay on the porch." He growled the command as he flipped up the hood of his jacket and stepped out into the driving rain again. "I'll bring my Jeep to the steps."

She waited—because, hey. If he didn't want her help, he wasn't going to get it. Still, she felt marginally guilty for just standing there with a porch roof over her head as she watched him limp off into the downpour.

He vanished around the first turn in the road. It was getting dark. She wrapped her arms across her middle and refused to worry about that bloody bandage on his leg and the way he walked with a limp—not to mention he'd looked kind of flushed, hadn't he? Like maybe he had a fever in addition to whatever was going on with that leg…

Faintly, she heard a vehicle start up. A moment later, a camo-green Jeep Rubicon rolled into sight. It eased to a stop a few feet from the steps and the big guy got out. She pulled up her hood and ran down to join him as he began untying the tree lashed to the rack on the roof.

He didn't argue when she took the top end. "I'll lead," was all he said.

Oh, no kidding—and not only because he was so damn bossy. It was a thick noble fir with a wide circle of bottom branches that wouldn't make it through the door any other way.

He assumed the forward position and she trotted after him, back up the steps and into the warmth of the cabin. At the tree stand, he got hold of the trunk in the middle, raising it to an upright position.

She crouched down to guide it into place and tighten the screws, sitting back on her heels when the job was done. "Okay. You can let it go." He eyed her warily from above, his giant arm engulfed by the thick branches as he gripped the trunk. His face was still flushed and there were beads of moisture at his hairline—sweat, not rain, she would take a bet on that. "It's in and it's stable, I promise you," she said.

With a shrug, he let go.

The tree stood tall. It was glorious, blue-green and well shaped, the branches emerging in perfectly balanced tiers, just right for displaying strings of lights and a treasure trove of ornaments. Best of all, it smelled of her sweetest memories, of Christmases past, when her mom was still alive. Ruth Bond had loved Christmas. Every December, she would fill their house at Berry Bog Farm with all the best Christmas smells—evergreen, peppermint, cinnamon, vanilla…

"Not bad," he muttered.

She put away her memories. They only made her sad, anyway. "It's a beauty, all right."

He aimed another scowl at her. "Good, then. Get your gear and let's go." Was he swaying on his feet?

She rose to her height. "I don't know what's wrong

with your leg, but you don't look well. You'd better sit down and let me see what I can do for you."

"I'm fine."

"Get real. You are not fine and you are getting worse."

He only grew more mulish. "We're leaving."

"I'm not getting in that Jeep with you behind the wheel." She braced her hands on her hips. He just went on glaring, swaying gently on his feet like a giant tree in a high wind. She quelled her aggravation at his pig-headedness and got busy convincing him he should trust her to handle whatever was wrong with him. "I was raised on a farm not far from here. My mom was a nurse. She taught me how to treat any number of nasty injuries. Just let me take a look at your leg."

"I'll deal with that later."

"You are wobbling on your feet and your face is red. You're sweating. I believe you have a fever."

"Did I ask for your opinion?"

"It's not safe for you to be—"

"I'm fine."

"You're not."

"Just get your stuff, okay?"

"No. Not okay." She made a show of taking off her jacket and hanging it by the door. "I'm not leaving this cabin until we've dealt with whatever's going on with your leg."

There was a long string of silent seconds—a battle of wills. He swayed and scowled. She did nothing except stand there and wait for the big lug to give in and be reasonable.

In the end, reason won. "All right," he said. He shrugged out of his coat and hung it up next to hers.

And then, at last, he limped to the Navajo-print sofa in the center of the room and sat down. He bent to his injured leg—and paused to glance up at her. "When I take off this dressing, it's probably going to be messy. We'll need towels. There's a stack of old ones in the bathroom, upper left in the wooden cabinet."

She went in there and got them.

When she handed them over, he said, "And a first-aid backpack, same cabinet, lower right." He set the stack of towels on the sofa beside him.

"I've got a first-aid kit." It was still on the floor by the hearth where she'd dumped it when he'd ordered her to shake out her pack. She started for it.

"I saw your kit," he said. She paused to glance back at him as he bent to rip his pants leg wider, revealing an impressively muscular, bloodstained, hairy leg. "Mine's bigger."

She almost laughed as she turned for the bathroom again. "Well, of course it is."

His kit had everything in it but an operating table.

She brought it into the main room and set it down on the plank floor at the end of the sofa. He'd already pushed the pine coffee table to the side, spread towels on the floor in front of him and rolled his tattered pants leg to midthigh, tying the torn ends together to keep them out of the way.

She watched as he unlaced his boot. A bead of sweat dripped down his face and plopped to his thigh. "Here." She knelt. "I'll ease it off for you."

"I've got it." With a grunt, he removed the boot. A few drops of blood fell to the towels. His sock was soggy with it, the blood soaking into the terrycloth when he put his foot back down.

"Interesting field dressing." She indicated the article of clothing tied around his lower leg.

One thick shoulder lifted in a half shrug. "Another T-shirt bites the dust."

"Is it stuck to the wound?"

"Naw. Wound's too wet." He untied the knots that held the T-shirt in place.

When he took the bloody rag away, she got a good look at the job ahead of her. The wound was an eight-inch crescent-shaped gash on the outside of his calf. It was deep. With the makeshift bandage gone, the flap of sliced flesh flopped down. At least it didn't appear to go all the way through to the bone. Blood dripped from it sluggishly.

"Let me see…" Cautiously, so as not to spook him, she placed her index and middle fingers on his knee and gave a gentle push. He accepted her guidance, dipping the knee inward so she could get a closer look at the injury. "Butterfly bandages won't hold that together," she said. "Neither will glue. It's going to need stitches."

For the first time since he'd kicked open the door, one side of his mouth hitched up in a hint of a smile. "I had a feeling you were going to say that." His blue eyes held hers. "You sure you're up for this?"

"Absolutely."

"You really know what to do?"

"Yes. I've sewn up a number of injured farm animals and once my dad got gored by a mean bull when my mom wasn't home. I stitched him right up."

He studied her face for a good five seconds. Then he offered a hand. "Matthias Bravo."

She took it. "Sabra Bond."

Chapter Two

Sabra washed up at the kitchen-area sink, turning and leaning against the counter as she dried her hands. "Got a plastic tub?"

"Under the sink." He seemed so calm now, so accepting. "Look. I'm sorry if I scared you, okay?" His eyes were different, kinder.

She nodded. "I broke in."

"I overreacted."

She gazed at him steadily. "We're good."

A slow breath escaped him. "Thanks."

For an odd, extended moment, they simply stared at each other. "Okay, then," she said finally. "Let's get this over with."

Grabbing the tub from under the sink, she filled it with warm water and carried it over to him. As he washed his blood-caked foot and lower leg, she laid out the tools and supplies she would need. His first-aid pack really did have everything, including inject-able lidocaine.

"Lucky man," she said. "You get to be numb for this."

"Life is good," he answered lazily, leaning against the cushions, letting his big head fall back and staring kind of vacantly at the crisscrossing beams overhead.

Wearing nitrile gloves from his fancy kit, she mopped up blood from around the injury and then injected the painkiller. Next, she irrigated the wound just the way her mom had taught her to do.

As she worked, he took his own temperature. "Hundred and two," he muttered unhappily.

She tipped her head at the acetaminophen and the tall glass of water she'd set out for him. "Take the pills and drink the water."

He obeyed. When he set the empty glass back down, he admitted, "This bug's been going around. Two of my brothers had it. Laid them out pretty good. At least it didn't last long. I was feeling punk this morning. I told myself it was nothing to worry about…"

"Focus on the good news," she advised.

"Right." He gave her a wry look. "I'm sick, but if I'm lucky, I won't be sick for long."

She carried the tub to the bathroom, dumped it, rinsed it and left it there. When she returned to him, she repositioned the coffee table, sat on the end of it and covered her thighs with a towel. "Let's see that leg." She tapped her knees with her palms, and he stretched the injured leg across them.

"Can you turn your leg so the wound is up and keep it in that position?"

"No problem." He rolled his foot inward, turning his outer calf up.

She put on a fresh pair of gloves and got to work.

It took a lot of stitches to do the job. He seemed content to just sprawl there, staring at the ceiling as she sewed him up.

But, now she had him at her mercy, there were a few questions she wanted to ask. "Did somebody come after you with an ax?" He lifted his head and mustered a steely stare. She grinned in response. It was so strange. Not long ago, he'd scared the crap out of her. Yet now he didn't frighten her in the least. She actually felt completely comfortable kidding him a little. "Do not make me hurt you."

He snorted. "It's embarrassing."

"I'll never tell a soul."

"It was raining when I cut down that tree. I forgot to bring gloves and my hands were soaking wet. Plus, I was feeling pretty bad from this damn bug I seem to have caught."

She tied off a stitch. "So then, what you're telling me is you almost chopped off your own leg?"

He let his head fall back again. "I come from a long line of woodsmen on my mother's side," he said wearily. "No self-respecting member of my family ever got hurt while cutting down an eight-foot tree."

"Until you."

"Go ahead, Sabra Bond, rub it in."

"Where'd you get that tree?" She tied off another stitch. "I didn't see a tag on it. Have you been poaching, Matthias?"

"You can call me Matt." He said it in a lovely, low rumble that made her think of a purring cat—a very large one. The kind that could easily turn dangerous. "Everyone calls me Matt."

"I kind of like Matthias."

"Suit yourself."

"I'll ask again. Did you steal that gorgeous tree from the people of Oregon?"

He grunted. "I'll have you know I'm a game warden, a Fish and Wildlife state trooper. I *catch* the poachers—so no, I didn't steal that tree. I took it from property that belongs to my family."

"Ah. All right, then. I guess I won't have to turn you in."

"You can't imagine my relief."

"I have another question."

"Why am I not surprised?"

"Didn't it occur to you to head for a hospital or an urgent care after you took that ax to your leg?"

He didn't answer immediately. She was considering how much to goad him when he muttered, "Pride and denial are powerful things."

By the time she'd smoothed antibiotic ointment over the stitched-up wound and covered it with a bandage, he was sweating more heavily than ever. She helped him off with his other boot. "Come on," she coaxed. "Stretch out on the sofa, why don't you?"

"Just for a few minutes," he mumbled, but remained sitting up. He started emptying his pockets, dragging out his phone, keys and wallet, dropping them next to the lamp on the little table at the end of the sofa. From another pocket, he took the shells from his rifle. He put them on the little table, too, and then leaned back against the cushions again.

She asked, "Do you have another sock to keep that bare foot warm?"

"You don't have to—"

"Just tell me where it is."

He swiped sweat from his brow. "In the dresser upstairs, top drawer, left."

Sabra ran up there and came down with a pillow from the bed and a clean pair of socks. She propped the pillow against one arm of the sofa and knelt to put on the socks for him. By then, he wasn't even bothering to argue that she didn't need to help him. He looked exhausted, his skin a little gray beneath the flush of fever.

She plumped the pillow she'd taken from the bed upstairs. "Lie down, Matthias." He gave in and stretched out, so tall that his feet hung off the end. "Here you go." She settled an afghan over him and tucked it in around him. "Okay, I'll be right back." And she hustled over to the sink to run cold water on a cloth.

"Feels good," he said, when she gently rubbed the wet cloth across his forehead and over his cheeks. "So nice and cool. Thank you…" Under the blanket, his injured leg jerked. He winced and stifled a groan. The lidocaine was probably wearing off. But the acetaminophen should be cutting the pain a little— and lowering his fever.

"Just rest," she said softly.

"All right. For few minutes, maybe. Not long. I'll be fine and I'll take you where you need to go."

She made a sound of agreement low in her throat, though she knew he wasn't going anywhere for at least a day or two.

Within ten minutes, he was asleep.

Quietly, so as not to wake him, she cleaned up after the impromptu medical procedure. She even rinsed out his bloody boot and put it near the hearth to dry.

Two hours later, at a little after eight in the evening, Matthias was still on the couch. He kept fading in and out of a fevered sleep. There wasn't much Sabra could do for him but bathe his sweaty face to cool him off a little and retuck the blanket around him whenever he kicked it off.

She put another log on the fire and went through the cupboards and the small fridge in the kitchen area. He had plenty of food, the nonperishable kind. Beans. Rice. Flour. Pasta. Cans of condensed milk, of vegetables and fruit. She opened some chili and ate it straight from the can, washing it down with a glass of cold water.

Matthias slept on, stirring fitfully, muttering to himself. Now and then he called out the names of men, "Mark, no!" and "Nelson, don't do it!" and "Finn, where are you?" as if in warning or despair. He also muttered a woman's name, "Christy," more than once and vowed in a low, ragged rumble, "Never again."

He woke around nine. "Sabra?" he asked, his voice dry. Hoarse.

"Right here."

"Water?"

She brought him a tall glassful. "Don't get up. Let me help." She slipped her free hand under his big, sweaty head and held the glass to his mouth as he drained it.

With a whispered "Thank you" and a weary sigh, he settled against the pillow again.

She moistened another cloth in the icy water from the sink and bathed his face for him. "You know what, Matthias?"

"Ungh?"

"I'm going to go ahead and unload your Jeep for you."

He made another low sound in his throat. She decided to take that sound for agreement.

"Well, great." She patted his shoulder. "I'll just get after that, then. Go back to sleep." Scooping his keys off the side table, she put on her jacket and quietly tiptoed out to the porch.

The gorgeous sight that greeted her stole her breath and stopped her in her tracks.

Just as Matthias had predicted, the rain had turned to snow. She gazed at a world gone glittering white.

In the golden light that spilled out the cabin windows, the fat flakes fell thick and heavy. They'd piled up on the ground and decorated the branches of the western hemlock and Sitka spruce trees. There was a good three inches already.

"So beautiful," she whispered aloud and all of her worries just fell away, both at the mess that currently added up to her life and the challenges she'd faced in the past few hours.

How could she be anything but happy in this moment? Christmas was falling from the sky.

She knew what was coming. She would be staying in this cabin for at least a few days with the man who'd introduced himself by pointing his rifle at her. Should she be more upset about that?

Probably.

But after they'd gotten past those terrifying first

minutes when she'd feared he might shoot her, things had definitely started looking up. He was a good patient, and he seemed kindhearted beneath that gruff exterior.

And this situation? It felt less like an ordeal and more like an adventure. As if she'd fallen out of her own thoroughly depressing life—and into a weird and wonderful Christmassy escapade.

Stuck in a one-room cabin with a big, buff injured stranger for Christmas?

She'd take that over her real life any day of the week.

As it turned out, she didn't need the car key. Matthias had left the Jeep unlocked.

And there were treasures in there—three large boxes of groceries. Fresh stuff, greens and tomatoes. Apples. Bananas. Eggs, milk and cheese. A gorgeous rib roast, a fat chicken and some really pretty pork chops.

It was a good thing she'd decided to bring it all in, too. By morning everything would have been frozen.

She carried the food in first, then his laptop, a box of brightly wrapped Christmas gifts probably from his family and another boxful of books, as well.

After the boxes, she brought in three duffel bags containing men's clothes and fresh linens. Detouring to the bathroom, she stacked the linens in the cabinet. She carried the bags of clothes up to the loft, leaving them near the top of the stairs for him to deal with when he felt better.

Her sick, surly stranger definitely needed some chicken soup. She hacked up the chicken. She put the pieces on to simmer in a pot of water with onions and garlic, a little celery and some spices from the cute little spice rack mounted on the side of a cabinet.

The night wore on. She fished the cooked chicken from the pot. Once it was cool enough to handle, she got rid of the bones, chopped the meat and returned it to the pot, along with some potatoes and carrots.

On the sofa, Matthias tossed and turned, sometimes muttering to the guys named Nelson and Mark, even crying out once or twice. She soothed him when he startled awake and stroked his sweaty face with a cold cloth.

When the soup was ready, she fed it to him. He ate a whole bowlful, looking up at her through only slightly dazed blue eyes as she spooned it into his mouth. Once he'd taken the last spoonful, he said, "I've changed my mind. You can stay."

"Good. Because no one's leaving this cabin for at least a couple of days. It's seriously snowing."

"Didn't I warn you?"

"Yes, you did. And it's piling up fast, too. You're gonna be stuck with me through Christmas, anyway."

"It's all right. I can deal with you." He sat up suddenly. Before she could order him to lie back down, he said, "I really need to take a whiz—get me the cane from that basket by the door, would you?"

"You need more than a cane right now. You can lean on me."

His expression turned mulish. "You're amazing and I'm really glad you broke into my cabin. But as for staggering to the head, I can do it on my own. Get me the damn cane."

"If you tear any of your stitches falling on your ass—"

"I won't. The cane."

She gave in. *He* wasn't going to. The cane was handmade of some hard, dark wood, with a rough-hewn bear head carved into the handle. She carried it back to him. "Still here and happy to help," she suggested.

"I can manage." He winced as he swung his feet to the floor and then he looked up at her, waiting.

She got the message loud and clear. Pausing only to push the coffee table well out of his way, she stepped aside.

He braced one hand on the cane and the other on the sofa arm and dragged himself upright. It took him a while and he leaned heavily on the cane, but he made it to the bathroom and back on his own.

Once he was prone on the couch again, he allowed her to tuck the afghan in around him. She gave him more painkillers. Fifteen minutes later, he was sound asleep.

By then, it was past three in the morning. She checked her phone and found text messages—from her dad and also from Iris and Peyton, her best friends in Portland. They all three knew that it had ended with her fiancé, James. She hadn't shared the gory details with her dad, but she'd told her BFFs everything. The texts asked how she was doing, if she was managing all right?

They—her friends and her dad—believed she was spending the holiday on her own at the farm. However, with no one there but her, the farmhouse had seemed to echo with loneliness, so she'd told Nils and Marjorie Wilson, who worked and lived on the property, that she was leaving. She'd thrown her stuff in her Subaru and headed back to Portland, stopping off at the fish hatchery on the spur of the moment.

And ending up stranded in a cabin in the woods with a stranger named Matthias.

Really, it was all too much to get into via text. She was safe and warm with plenty of food—and having a much better time than she'd had alone at the farmhouse. There was nothing anyone could do for her right now. They would only freak out if she tried to explain where she was and how she'd gotten there.

Sabra wished them each a merry Christmas. She mentioned that it was snowing heavily and implied to her girlfriends that she was still at the farm and might be out of touch for a few days due to the storm. To her dad, she wrote that she'd gone back to Portland—it wasn't a lie, exactly. She *had* gone. She just hadn't gotten there yet.

Though cell service in the forest was spotty at best, a minor miracle occurred and all three texts went through instantly—after which she second-guessed herself. Because she probably ought to tell someone that she was alone with a stranger in the middle of the woods.

But who? And to what real purpose? What would she even say?

Okay, I'm not exactly where I said I was. I'm actually snowed in at an isolated cabin surrounded by the Clatsop State Forest with some guy named Matthias Bravo, who's passed out on the sofa due to illness and injury...

No. Uh-uh. She'd made the right decision in the

first place. Why worry them when there was nothing they could do?

She powered off the phone to save the battery and wandered upstairs, where she turned on the lamps on either side of the bed and went looking for the Christmas decorations Matthias had to have somewhere.

Score! There were several plastic tubs of them stuck in a nook under the eaves. She carried them downstairs and stacked them next to that gorgeous tree.

By then, she was yawning. All of a sudden, the energy had drained right out of her. She went back to the loft and fell across the bed fully clothed.

Sabra woke to gray daylight coming in the one tiny window over the bed—and to the heavenly smell of fresh coffee.

With a grunt, she pushed herself to her feet and followed her nose down to the main floor and the coffee maker on the counter. A clean mug waited beside it. Matthias must have set it out for her, which almost made her smile.

And Sabra Bond never smiled before at least one cup of morning coffee.

Once the mug was full, she turned and leaned against the counter to enjoy that first, all-important sip.

Matthias was sitting up on the sofa, his bad leg stretched out across the cushions, holding a mug of his own, watching her. "Rough night, huh?"

She gave him her sternest frown. "You should not have been up and you are not allowed to speak to me until I finish at least one full cup of coffee."

He shrugged. But she could tell that he was trying not to grin.

She took another big gulp. "Your face is still flushed. That means you still have a fever."

He sipped his coffee and did not say a word. Which was good. Great. Exactly what she'd asked for.

She knocked back another mouthful. "At least you're not sweating anymore. Have you taken more acetaminophen since last night?"

He regarded her with mock gravity and slowly shook his head in the negative.

She set down her mug, grabbed a glass, filled it with water and carried it over to him. "There you go. Take your pills. I'll need to check your bandage and then I'll cook us some breakfast."

He tipped his golden head down and looked at her from under thick, burnished eyebrows. His mouth kept twitching. Apparently, he was finding her extremely amusing.

"What?" she demanded.

He only shook his head again.

She marched back to the counter, leaned against it once more and enjoyed the rest of her coffee in blessed silence.

"You don't happen to have an extra toothbrush, by any chance?" she asked once she'd drained the last drop from the mug. He just gave her more silent smirking. "Oh, stop it. You may speak."

"You're such a charmer in the morning."

She grunted. "Toothbrush?"

"Under the bathroom sink. Small plastic tub. There should be a couple of them still in the wrappers and some of those sample-sized tubes of toothpaste."

"Thank you—need more coffee before I go in there? Because I am completely serious. For today at least, you're not getting up unless you really need to."

He set his mug on the coffee table and reached for the bottle of painkillers. "No more coffee right now. I'll have another cup with breakfast."

The fire was all but out. She added a little kindling and another log. As soon as the flames licked up, she faced him. "Do not get up from that couch while I'm in there."

He was stretched out on his back again, adjusting the afghan, but he dropped it to make a show of putting his hands up in surrender. "I will not move from this spot until you give me permission."

She grabbed her pack. "That's what I wanted to hear."

In the bathroom, she didn't even glance at the mirror. Not at first. The coffee had gone right to her bladder, so she took care of that. It wasn't until she stood at the sink to wash her hands that she saw what Matthias had been trying not to laugh about.

She had three deep sleep wrinkles on the left side of her face and her hair was smashed flat on that side, with another ratty-looking section of it standing straight up from the top of her head.

A little grooming was definitely in order. She took off her clothes and gave herself a quick sponge bath, after which she brushed her teeth, put her clothes back on and combed her hair, weaving it into a single braid down her back.

By then, she almost looked human.

Snow had piled up on the sill outside the tiny bathroom window. She went on tiptoe to peer through the clear part of the glass.

A blanket of unbroken white extended, smooth and sparkly, to the tree line. The trees themselves were more white than green. And it was still coming down.

Everything out that window looked brand-new. And she felt…gleeful.

She had someone to spend her Christmas with. And a gorgeous tree to decorate.

So what if that someone was a stranger and the tree wasn't hers? This totally unexpected interlude in the forest was just fine with her. She felt energized, very close to happy. And ready for anything.

For the first time in a long time, she looked forward with real anticipation to whatever was going to happen next.

Chapter Three

Matt was feeling almost human again. Yeah, his leg ached a little. But he'd taken his temperature before he made the coffee. It was down two degrees. His headache was gone.

Sabra came out of the bathroom looking a lot more pulled together than when she'd gone in. Though really, she'd been damn cute with her hair sticking up every which way, giving him the evil eye, ordering him to keep his mouth shut until she'd had her coffee.

"How about some oatmeal?" she asked as she refilled his coffee mug. "Think you could keep that down?"

He had zero desire to eat mush. "Did I dream it or did you haul everything in from the Jeep last night?"

"No dream. I brought the food and your other things inside."

"And you made soup."

"Yes, I did."

"It was delicious. I can't tell you how much I appreciate everything you've done and I would like eggs, bacon and toast. Please."

She handed him the mug and then stood above him, holding the coffee carafe, her head tipped to the side as she studied him. "I'm not going to be happy with you if it all comes right back up." She put on her don't-mess-with-me look, just to let him know who was boss.

Damn. The woman had attitude. And she took care of business. She was tough and resourceful and pretty much unflappable—with a dry sense of humor.

Not to mention she looked amazing in panties and a sports bra.

Matt liked her. A lot. He was a little blown away at how much. As a rule, he was cautious around new people. But for her, he would definitely make an exception. He said what he was thinking. "I could have done a lot worse than to get snowed in with you."

For that, he got a small nod and a hint of a smile. "I'm glad you're feeling better. I just want you to be careful not to overdo it."

"Eggs," he said longingly. "Toast. Bacon."

She made a disapproving face, but then she cooked him the breakfast he asked for. He did his part and kept the food down. After the meal, she changed his bandage. His leg wasn't pretty, but there was no sign of infection.

Once she'd changed the dressing, she got him some sweats and clean underwear from the duffel bags she'd brought in from the car. She even allowed him to hobble into the bathroom on his own steam.

He brushed his teeth, cleaned himself up a little and changed into the stuff she'd brought downstairs for him. When he emerged into the main room, she said he looked a little green and ordered him to lie down.

"I have a request," she said as she tucked the old afghan in around him.

"My Jeep? My bank account number? The deed to this cabin? Whatever you want from me, it's yours."

She laughed. The sound was low and a little bit husky. Every time she bent close, he could smell her. She'd used the Ivory soap in the bathroom, yeah, but beneath that, her body itself smelled clean and sweet, like fresh-baked bread or maybe sugar cookies. Sugar cookies and woman.

A knockout combination.

Really, she had it all going on. He'd never realized before that he might have a type. *Hi, I'm Matt Bravo and I like my women hot, smart, competent and bossy.* As soon as he was capable of washing up in the bathroom without needing a nap afterward, it was going to get really difficult not to put a move on her.

Now, though? He was weak as a baby and fading fast, making her one-hundred-percent safe from his bad intentions.

"Keep your bank account," she said with a grin. "It's your tree I'm after."

He imagined reaching up, running a finger down the velvety skin of her neck, maybe tugging on that thick braid down her back—and what was this he was feeling? Like he had a crush on her or something.

Matt didn't do crushes. He'd been in love once and

it had all gone to hell like everything else in his life at that time. Nowadays, he went out occasionally with women who wanted the same thing he did—satisfying sex. And no sleeping over.

Although, in all honesty, if he was going to crush on a woman, it would have to be this one.

"Matthias? You okay?"

He picked up the conversation where he'd dropped it. "I noticed you found the decorations and brought them down."

She grinned. "It's Christmas Eve. You're in no condition to decorate that tree and it's not going to decorate itself. Is it all right with you if I do it?"

She was way too much fun to tease. "You sure you don't want the Jeep? It's a Rubicon. Super fancy. You can go off-road in it, take a seventy-degree downhill grade on rugged terrain without even stopping to consider the risks—because there are none."

A sound escaped her, a snappy little "Ffft." She gave him a light slap on the shoulder with the back of her hand. "Stop messing with me. Say yes."

He stared up into those beautiful brown eyes. "Yes."

"Well, all right." She retucked a bit of his blanket. "That wasn't so hard, was it?"

He reached back and punched his pillow a little, all for show. "Have fun."

"I will."

"And try to keep the noise down. I need my sleep." He turned his head toward the back of the sofa and closed his eyes.

But not two minutes later, he rolled his head back the other way so he could watch her work.

Methodical and exacting, that was her tree-decorating style. She found the lights, plugging in each string first, replacing the few bulbs that had gone out. There weren't many bad bulbs because Matt took care of his gear. Also, the lights weren't that old.

This was his third Christmas at the cabin. His great-uncle Percy Valentine had given the place to him when Matt was discharged from the service. *A few wooded acres and a one-room cabin, Matthias,* Uncle Percy had said. *I'm thinking it will be a quiet place just for you, a place where you can find your-self again.*

Matt wasn't all that sure he'd found himself yet, but he liked having his own place not far from home to go when he needed it. He had a large family and they kept after him to start showing up for Christmas, which had always been a big deal for all of them.

His mom had loved Christmas and she used to do it up right. She and his dad had died when Matt was sixteen, but his older brother Daniel had stepped up, taken custody of all of them and continued all the family Christmas traditions.

He loved them, every one of them. He would do just about anything for them. But for Christmas, he liked the cabin better. He liked going off into a world of his own now and then, needed it even. Especially for the holidays. There was something about this time of the year that made the ghosts of his past most likely to haunt him.

Through half-closed eyes, he watched as Sabra strung the lights. She tucked them in among the thick branches just so, making sure there were no bare spaces, the same way he would have done. When she neared the top, she found the folding footstool in the closet under the stairs and used it to string those lights all the way up.

She had the lights on and was starting to hang ornaments when his eyes got too heavy to keep open even partway. Feeling peaceful and damn close to happy, he drifted off to sleep.

When he woke again, Sabra was curled in a ball in the old brown armchair across from the sofa, asleep. She'd found a book, no doubt from the bookcase on the side wall. It lay open across her drawn-up thighs, her dark head drooping over it.

The tree was finished. She'd done a great job of it. He just lay there on the sofa and admired it for a few minutes, tall and proud, shining so bright. She'd even put his presents from the family under it.

But he was thirsty and his water glass was empty. He sat up and reached for the cane that he'd propped at the end of the sofa.

That small movement woke her. "Wha...?" She blinked at him owlishly. "Hey. You're awake." She rubbed the back of her neck.

He pushed back the afghan and brought his legs to the floor. "The tree is gorgeous."

She smiled, a secret, pleased little smile. "Thanks. How're you feeling?"

"Better." He pushed himself upright and she didn't even try to stop him.

"You look better. Your color's good. Want some soup?"

"If I can sit at the table to eat it."

"You think you're up for that?"

"I know I am."

* * *

Matthias *was* better. Lots better.

So much better that, after dinner that night, when he wanted to go out on the porch, she agreed without even a word of protest.

"You'll need a warmer coat," he said, and sent her upstairs to get one of his.

The coat dwarfed her smaller frame. On her, it came to midthigh and the arms covered her hands. She loved it. It would keep her toasty warm even out in the frozen night air—and it smelled like him, of cedar and something kind of minty.

On the porch, there were two rustic-looking log chairs. Sabra pushed the chairs closer together and they sat down.

The snow had finally stopped. They'd gotten several feet of the stuff, which meant they would definitely be stuck here for at least the next few days.

Sabra didn't mind. She felt far away from her real life, off in this silent, frozen world with a man who'd been a stranger to her only the day before.

He said, "My mom used to love the snow. It doesn't snow that often in Valentine Bay, but when it did she would get us all out into the yard to make snowmen. There was never that much of it, so our snowmen were wimpy ones. They melted fast."

"You're from Valentine Bay, then?" Valentine Bay was on the coast, a little south of Warrenton, which was at the mouth of the Columbia River.

He turned to look at her, brow furrowing. "Didn't I tell you I'm from Valentine Bay?"

"You've told me now—and you said your mom *used* to love the snow?"

"That's right. She died eleven years ago. My dad, too. In a tsunami in Thailand, of all the crazy ways to go."

"You've lost both of them? That had to be hard." She wanted to reach out and hug him. But that would be weird, wouldn't it? She felt like she knew him. But she didn't, not really. She needed to try to remember to respect the guy's space.

"It was a long time ago. My oldest brother Daniel took over and raised us the rest of the way. He and his wife Lillie just continued right on, everything essentially the way it used be, including the usual Christmas traditions. Even now, they all spend Christmas day at the house where we grew up. They open their presents together, share breakfast and cook a big Christmas dinner."

"But you want to spend your Christmas alone."

"That's right."

A minute ago, she'd been warning herself to respect the man's space. Too bad. Right now, she couldn't resist trying to find out more. "Last night, you were talking in your sleep."

He gave her a long look. It wasn't an encouraging one. "Notice the way I'm not asking what I said?"

"Don't want to talk about Mark and Nelson and Finn?"

He didn't. And he made that perfectly clear—by changing the subject. "You said you grew up on a farm?"

"Yes, I did."

"Near here, you said?"

"Yeah. Near Svensen."

"That's in Astoria."

"Yeah, pretty much."

"But you were headed for Portland when you suddenly decided on a hike to the falls?"

"I live in Portland now. I manage the front of the house at a restaurant in the Pearl." The Pearl District was the right place to open an upscale, farm-to-table restaurant. Delia Mae's was one of those.

"Got tired of farming?" His breath came out as fog.

She gathered his giant coat a little closer around her against the cold. "Not really. I'm a farmer by birth, vocation and education. I've got a bachelor's degree in environmental studies with an emphasis in agroecology."

"From UC Santa Cruz, am I right?"

"The Slugs hat and sweatshirt?"

"Dead giveaway." He smiled, slow and sexy, his white, even teeth gleaming in the porch light's glow. She stared at him, thinking that he really was a hot-looking guy, with those killer blue eyes, a shadow of beard scruff on his sculpted jaw and that thick, unruly dark blond hair.

And what were they talking about?

Farming. Right. "Our farm has been in the Bond family for generations. My dad and mom were a true love match, mutually dedicated to each other, the farm and to me, their only child. All my growing-up years, the plan was for me to work right along with them, and to take the reins when the time came. But then, when I was nineteen and in my first year at Santa Cruz, my mom died while driving home from a quick shopping trip into downtown Astoria on a gray day in February. Her pickup lost traction on the icy road. The truck spun out and crashed into the guardrail."

Matthias didn't even hesitate. He reached out between their two chairs, clasped her shoulder with his large, strong hand and gave a nice, firm squeeze. They shared a glance, a long one that made her feel completely understood.

His reassuring touch made it all the easier to confess, "I have a hard time now, at the farm. It's been six years since my mom died, but my dad has never really recovered from the loss. I guess, to be honest, neither have I. After college, I just wanted something completely different."

"And now you run a restaurant."

"The chef would disagree. But yeah. I manage the waitstaff, the hiring, supervising and scheduling, all that."

He shifted in the hard chair, wincing a little.

"Your leg is bothering you," she said. "We should go in."

"I like it out here." He seemed to be studying her face.

"What?"

"I like *you*, Sabra." From the snow-covered trees, an owl hooted. "I like you very much, as a matter of fact."

A little thrill shivered through her. She relished it. And then she thought about James. She'd almost married him less than a week ago. It was turning out to be much too easy to forget him.

"What'd I say?" Matthias looked worried.

"Something nice. Too bad I'm not looking for anything remotely resembling romance."

"It's not a problem," he said in that matter-of-fact way of his. "Neither am I."

She felt a flash of disappointment, and quickly banished it. "Excellent. No romance. No…fooling around. None of that. We have a deal."

He nodded. "Agreed. And I sense a story here. You should tell it to me."

"Though you won't tell me yours?"

"I'm sure yours is more interesting than mine." Again, he shifted. His leg hurt. He just refused to admit it.

"I'm braver than you, Matthias."

He didn't even try to argue the point. "I have no doubt that you are."

"I'll put it right out there, tell you all about my failures in love."

He looked at her sideways. "You're after something. What?"

She laughed. "I'm not telling you anything until you come back inside."

In the cabin, they hung their coats by the door. Matt took off his boots and settled on the sofa with his bad leg stretched out.

"You want some hot chocolate or something?" she offered.

Was she stalling? He wanted that story. He gestured at the armchair. "Sit. Start talking."

She laughed that husky laugh of hers. The sound made a lightness inside him. She was something special, all right. And this was suddenly turning out to be his favorite Christmas ever.

She took off her own boots, filled his water glass for him and put another log on the fire.

Finally, she dropped into the brown chair across the coffee table from him. "Okay. It's like this. I've been engaged twice. The first time was at Santa Cruz. I fell hard for a bass-playing philosophy major named Stan."

"I already hate him."

"Why?"

"Was he your first lover?" As soon as he asked, he wished he hadn't. A question like that could be considered to be crossing a certain line.

But she didn't seem turned off by it. "How did you know?"

"Just a guess—and I'm not sure yet why I hate him. Because I like *you*, I think, and I know it didn't last with him. I'm guessing that was all his fault."

"I don't want to be unfair to Stan."

Matt laughed. It came out sounding rusty. He wasn't a big laugher, as a rule. "Go ahead. Be unfair to Stan. There's only you and me here. And I'm on *your* side."

"All right, fine." She gave a single, definitive nod. "Please feel free to hate him. He claimed to love me madly. He asked me to marry him."

"Let me guess. You said yes."

"Hey. I was twenty-one. Even though losing my mom had rocked the foundations of my world, I still had hopes and dreams back then."

"Did you move in together?"

"We did. We had this cute apartment not far from the ocean and we were planning an earthcentric wedding on a mountaintop."

"But the wedding never happened."

"No, it did not. Because one morning, I woke up alone. Stan had left me a note."

"Don't tell me the note was on his pillow."

Stifling a giggle, she nodded.

"Okay, Sabra. Hit me with it. What did the note say?"

"That he couldn't do it, couldn't marry me. Marriage was just too bougie, he wrote."

"*Bougie?* He wrote that exact word?" At her nod, he said, "And you wondered why I hate Stan."

"He also wrote that I was a good person, but I didn't really crank his chain. He had to follow his bliss to Austin and become a rock star."

"What a complete douchebasket."

"Yeah, I guess he was, kind of."

"*Kind* of? People shouldn't make promises they don't mean to keep."

Sabra sat forward in the big brown armchair.

Was he speaking from painful experience? She really wanted to know. But he didn't want to talk about himself—not as of now, anyway. And those deep blue eyes had turned wary, as though he guessed she was tempted to ask him a question he wouldn't answer.

"Keep talking," he commanded. "What happened after Stan?"

"After Stan, I decided that my judgment about men was out of whack and I swore to myself I wouldn't get serious with a guy until I was at least thirty."

Now he was looking at her sideways, a skeptical sort of look. "Thirty, huh?"

"That's right."

"And as of today, you are…?"

"Twenty-five," she gave out grudgingly.

"And why am I thinking you've broken your own rule and gotten serious since Stan?"

"Don't gloat, Matthias. It's not attractive—and you know, I kind of can't believe I'm telling you all this. I think I've said enough."

"No. Uh-uh. You have to tell me the rest."

"Why?"

"Uh." His wide brow wrinkled up. "Because I'm an invalid and you are helping me through this difficult time."

She couldn't hold back a snort of laughter. "I really think you're going to survive whether I tell you about James or not."

"So. The next guy's name is James?"

She groaned. "The *next* guy? Like there've been a hundred of them?"

He sat very still. She could practically see the wheels turning inside his big head. "Wait. I think that came out wrong."

"No, it didn't. Not at all. I'm just messing with you."

"You're probably thinking I'm a jerk just like Stan." He looked so worried about that. She wanted to grab him and hug him and tell him everything was fine—and that was at least the second time tonight she'd considered putting her hands on him for other than purely medical reasons.

It had to stop.

"No," she said. "I honestly don't think you're a jerk—and look, Matthias, I've been meaning to ask you…"

* * *

Matthias *felt* like a jerk, whether or not Sabra considered him one. He'd been having a great time with her, like they'd known each other forever.

Until he went and put his foot in it. As a rule, he was careful around women. He wasn't ready for anything serious, so he watched himself, made sure he didn't give off the wrong signals.

But Sabra. Well, already she was kind of getting under his skin. There was so damn much to admire about her—*and* she was fun. And hot.

But they'd agreed that the man/woman thing wasn't happening. He was friend-zoned and he could live with that. Anything more, well…

It would be too easy to fall for her. And he didn't want to fall for anyone. Not yet. Maybe never. The last year or so, he'd finally started to feel like his life was back on track. True, getting something going with a woman could turn out to be the best thing that ever happened to him.

But it might send him spinning off the rails.

He just wasn't ready to find out which.

"Do you maybe have some sweats I could wear?" she asked. "Something soft to sleep in would be great…"

She was going to bed now? It wasn't much past nine.

No doubt about it. He'd definitely screwed up.

"Uh, sure," he said, and tried not to let his disappointment show. "Take anything you want from whatever's upstairs."

"I was thinking I might even have a bath, if that's all right with you?"

"Now?"

"Well, I mean, no time like the present, right?"

"Absolutely. Go ahead."

She got up. "Can I get you anything before I—?"

"No. Really. I'm good."

She took off up the stairs. Not five minutes later, she came running back down with an armful of his clothes and disappeared into the bathroom.

He sat there and stared at the tree and tried not to imagine what she was doing behind that shut door. Really, he must be getting better fast—he had the erection to prove it.

Friend-zoned, you idiot. And that's how you want it.

He needed to take his mind off his exceptionally clear mental image of Sabra, naked in the tub, her almost-black hair piled up on her head, random strands curling in the steam rising from the water, clinging to the silky skin of her neck as she raised one of those gorgeous long legs of hers and braced her foot on the side of the tub.

Lazily, humming a holiday tune under her breath, she would begin to work up a lather. Soap bubbles would dribble slowly along her inner thigh…

Matt swore, a graphic string of bad words.

And then he grabbed his cane and shot to his feet, only swaying a little as his bad leg took his weight— yeah, he'd promised her he would stay on the sofa unless he had a good reason to get up.

Well, clearing his mind of certain way-too-tempting images was a good enough reason for him.

He limped over to the bookcase. She'd set the box

of books he'd brought from home right there in the corner on the floor.

Might as well shelve them. He got to work, his leg complaining a little when he bent down to grab the next volume. But it wasn't that painful and it kept his mind from wandering to places it had no business going.

He was three-quarters of the way through the box when the bathroom door opened.

"Matthias. What the—? You promised you'd stay off your feet."

Yep. He could already smell the steaminess from across the room—soap and wet and heat and woman.

"Matthias?"

Slowly, so as not to make a fool of himself lurching on his bad leg and proving how right she was that he shouldn't be on his feet, he turned to her.

Cutest damn thing he ever saw.

She was covered head to toe, dwarfed by his Clatsop Community College sweatshirt and a pair of his sweatpants she must have rolled at the waist, his red-toed work socks like clown shoes on her narrow feet.

Damn it to hell, she looked amazing, all rosy and soft, swimming in his clothes—and she'd washed her hair, too. It was still wet, curling sweetly on her shoulders.

His throat felt like it had a log stuck in it. He gave a quick cough to clear it. "I, um, just thought I might as well get these books out of the box."

She simply looked at him, shaking her head.

"C'mon," he coaxed. "I'm doing fine. It's not that big a deal."

She pressed her soft lips together—hiding a smile

or holding back more scolding words? He couldn't tell which. But then she said, "I washed out my things. They're hanging over the tub and the shower bar. Hope that's okay."

"You don't even need to ask."

"All right, then."

A silence. Not an awkward one, surprisingly. She regarded him almost fondly—or was that pure wishful thinking on his part?

She spoke first. "Thought I would grab a book or two, read myself to sleep."

He wanted to beg, *Stay. Talk to me some more.* But all he said was, "Help yourself."

Big socks flapping, she crossed the room to him and made her choices as he just stood there between the box and the bookcase, breathing in the steamy scent of her, wishing she would move closer so he could smell her better.

She chose a thriller and a love story set in the Second World War that had won a bunch of literary awards a few years ago. "Okay, then," she said finally. "Anything else I can do before I go? Shall I unplug the tree?"

"Nope. I'm almost done here. Then I'll lie down, I promise."

"Fair enough." Both books tucked under one arm, she turned for the stairs.

He bent to grab another volume, shelved it, bent to grab the next.

"Matthias?" He straightened and turned. She'd made it to the top. "Merry Christmas."

He stared up at her, aching for something he didn't

want to name, feeling equal parts longing and gladness—longing for what he knew he wouldn't have.

Gladness just to be here in his cabin in the forest, stranded. With her.

"Merry Christmas, Sabra."

She granted him a smile, a slow one. And then she turned and vanished from his sight.

Chapter Four

Christmas day, Sabra woke to morning light streaming in the loft window. She could smell coffee, which meant that Matthias had been on his feet again.

She went downstairs scowling. But that was more her natural precoffee face than disapproval. The tree was lit up, looking fabulous. He was sitting on the sofa, his laptop across his stretched-out legs, apparently not in pain, his color excellent.

He'd left a mug waiting for her by the coffee maker, same as yesterday. She filled it and drank it just the way she liked it, without a word spoken.

Once it was empty, she set the mug on the counter. "Did you happen to take your temperature?"

He ran his thumb over the touch pad. "Normal."

"You have internet on that laptop?"

He tipped his head toward his phone on the coffee

table. "Not using it now—but yeah, when I need it. Mobile data through my cell. It's a little spotty here in the middle of nowhere, but it works well enough." He looked up and smiled at her. Bam! The gray winter morning just got a whole lot brighter. "I also have a speaker. We can have Christmas music."

"How wonderful is that?" She wandered over to see what game he was playing. "Solitaire?"

"It's mindless. I find it calming." He won a game and the cards flew around and settled to start over.

She went on into the bathroom, where her clothes weren't quite dry yet and her hair looked almost as bad as it had the morning before.

After breakfast, Matthias said he wanted a real bath. She went into the bathroom first, gathered up her things and took them upstairs, after which she found a roll of plastic wrap and waterproofed his bandaged lower leg.

He hobbled into the bathroom and didn't come out for an hour. When he finally emerged smelling of toothpaste and shampoo, she checked his stitches. There was no swelling and less redness than the day before.

"Lookin' good," she said.

"Great. I'm putting on the tunes." He used a cable to hook up his speaker to his phone. Christmas music filled the cabin.

She insisted that he open his presents. "Just sit there," she said, "nice and comfy on the couch. I'll bring them to you."

"That doesn't seem fair."

"If I'm happy doing it, it's fair enough."

His presents were the stuff guys get from their families at Christmas. Shirts and socks and a nice heavy jacket. A humorous coffee mug. Gift cards. More books.

Sabra enjoyed the process. For the first time since her mom died, she was loving every minute of Christmas. Sitting out on the porch in the freezing cold, coming downstairs in the morning to the coffee Matthias had already made though she'd ordered him not to—everything, all of it, seemed sparkly and fresh, entertaining and baggage-free.

When the last gift card had been stripped of its shiny wrapper and pretty ribbons, he said, "There's one more under there somewhere."

"You sure? I think that's all."

"I'll find it." He reached for his bear-headed cane.

"Nope. Sit." She got down on hands and knees and peered through the thick tiers of branches. "I see it." It was tucked in close to the trunk. Pulling it free, she sat back on her heels. The snowman wrapping paper was wrinkled and the bow was made of household twine. "I don't remember this one."

"I had to make do with what I found in the kitchen drawers."

"It's for me?" Her throat kind of clutched. Maybe. A little.

"Yeah—and don't make a big deal of it or start in on how I shouldn't have been on my feet."

She slanted him a sideways look. "Lotta rules you got when it comes to giving someone a present, Matthias."

"It's Christmas. I wanted you to have *something*, okay?"

"Um. Okay." She gazed at him steadily, thinking what a great guy he was under the gruffness and self-protective, macho-man bluster.

"It's nothing," he mumbled. "Just open it."

Oh, she definitely was tempted to dish out a little lecture about how a guy should never call any gift "nothing." But then he would consider that making a "big deal." Better not to even get started. She untied the twine bow and tore off the wrinkled paper.

Inside was a See's Candy box and inside that, a folded piece of paper bag and a small, roughly carved wooden animal. "It's so cute." She held it up. "A hedgehog?"

"Close. A porcupine. I made it last night, sitting out on the porch after you went to bed."

She started to chide him for not going to sleep early as he'd promised—but then pressed her lips together before any words escaped. His gift touched her heart and being out on the porch for a while didn't seem to have hurt him any.

He said, "Me and my Swiss Army knife, we have a great time together."

She turned the little carving in her hands, admiring his work. "I love it. Truly. Thank you."

He gave a one-shouldered shrug. "I thought you might want a souvenir, something to remind you of all that can happen if you go wandering into the woods at Christmastime. You could end up facing down a crazy man with a gun and then having to perform emergency surgery." He grinned.

She felt an answering smile lift the corners of her mouth. "Why a porcupine?"

"No reason, really. I got out my knife and a nice bit of wood that was just the right shape to become a porcupine."

"Great choice. I'm a porcupine sort of girl—kinda prickly."

"But cute."

Was she blushing? God. Probably. "Did you make your cane?" She tipped her head toward where it leaned against the end of the sofa.

"Yes, I did."

She had that urge again—to jump up and hug him. Again, she resisted it. But her defenses were weakening. The more time she spent with him, the more she wanted to touch him, to have him touch her.

Shifting her legs out from under her, she sat cross-legged on the floor, set the sweet little porcupine beside her and unfolded the paper-bag note.

Merry Christmas, Sabra,

I'll make your coffee whether you allow me to or not. And I'll shut up while you drink it. Feel free to break into my cabin anytime.

Matthias

She glanced up to find him watching her. "You realize you just gave me an open invitation to invade your forest retreat whenever the mood strikes."

He gazed at her so steadily. "Anytime. I mean that."

Did she believe him? Not really. But still, it pleased her no end that he seemed to like having her around.

* * *

It was a great Christmas, Matt thought, easy and lazy. No tension, zero drama.

They roasted the prime rib he'd brought and sat down to dinner in the early afternoon. There was time on the porch to enjoy the snowy clearing and the tall white-mantled trees. He had board games and they played them. She won at Scrabble. He kicked her pretty butt at Risk.

Not long after dark, as they were considering a game of cribbage, the power went out. She got the footstool from under the stairs and handed him down the two boxes of candles he kept ready and waiting on top of the kitchen cabinets. They lit the candles, set them around the room and ended up abandoning the cribbage board, gravitating to their usual places instead—Matt on the sofa, Sabra curled up in the brown easy chair.

He felt comfortable enough with her to bring up the awkwardness the night before. "I really didn't mean to insult you last night—you know, what I said about you and that guy named James…"

She gave him a look he was already coming to recognize, sort of patient. And tender. "I told you that I wasn't insulted."

"But then you jumped to your feet and ran and hid in the bathroom."

"Did not," she said sharply. "I took a *bath*." She huffed out a breath. "Please."

He said nothing. He was getting to know her well enough to have a general idea of when to keep his mouth shut around her, let her come to the truth at her own speed.

And she did, first shifting in the chair, drawing her legs up the other way, wrapping her slim arms around them. "I thought maybe I was getting too personal, I guess."

"You weren't. If you want to tell it, I'm listening."

Her sleek eyebrows drew together as she thought it over. "It *is* helpful, to have someone to talk to. You're a good listener and this is just the right situation, you know? You and me alone in this cabin, away from the rest of the world. I think it shocked me last night, how easy it was to say hard stuff to you. You're the stranger I'll probably never see again once the roads are clear and we can go our separate ways." She swiped a hand down her shining dark hair and flicked her braid back over her shoulder.

He could sit here forever, just looking at her.

She had it right, though—yeah, he ached to kiss her. To touch her. To see where this attraction he felt for her might go.

But at the same time, he'd been careful not to tell her too much about himself, about his life. He'd come a long way in the past few years. But not far enough. He still wasn't ready to jump off into the deep end with a woman again.

And Sabra Bond? She was the kind a guy should be ready to go deep with.

Sabra hugged her knees a little closer, thinking how the man across the coffee table from her reminded her of her dad a little—her dad the way he used to be, back in the old days, before they'd lost her mom. Like her father, Matthias was self-contained. He really listened. He took her seriously but he knew how to kid around, too. He also seemed the sort of man who would tell the truth even when it hurt.

"So, where was I?" she asked.

He tipped his dark gold head to the side, considering, for several long seconds before replying. "You told me about Stan, who left in the middle of the night to move to Austin and become a rock star, the lousy bastard. What about James?"

"James. Right. After Stan, I swore off men."

"How'd that work out?"

"For a while, I had no romantic relationships of any kind. Then, in my last year at Santa Cruz, I met James Wise. James is from a wealthy Monterey family and he was studying computer game design—not really seriously, though, as it turned out."

"Right. Because…trust fund?"

"A giant one. He was fooling around with game design and his parents were constantly pressuring him to join the family real estate development firm."

"So you two were a thing, you and James?"

She nodded. "We were. He was fun and he didn't seem to take things too seriously. I was so proud of myself for finally having a no-strings sexual relationship."

"But then…?"

"After we dated for a month or two, James started pushing for marriage."

Matthias made a low, knowing sort of sound. "And you explained that you planned to be single for years yet."

"I did, yes. We split up at graduation. I moved to Portland."

"A fresh start."

"That's right. I got my own place and a job at that restaurant I told you about, where I met Iris and Peyton, who became my best friends. I kept promising my friends I would enjoy my freedom, get out and experience a few hot and sexy nights with men I never intended to spend forever with. Somehow, that never happened. And then James showed up in Portland."

"Because he couldn't live without you."

"That is exactly what he said." She turned sideways and hung her legs over the chair arm, using the other arm as a backrest, shoving a throw pillow behind her for extra support. "And how'd you know that?"

"Lucky guess. Continue."

"Well, I really had missed him. Yeah, I knew he was a little…irresponsible, maybe. But he was so romantic and sweet—and lighthearted, you know? Since my mom's death, a little lightheartedness means a lot. He kind of swept me off my feet. We got a place together and he kept pushing for marriage…"

"And you finally said yes."

"Nailed it."

"But what about those no-strings flings you promised your girlfriends you'd be having?"

"Never got around to them. And I know, the plan was I would wait till I was thirty to even get serious. Yet, somehow, there I was, saying yes to James—also, full disclosure? I'd never actually met his family or taken him to meet my dad."

"Uh-oh."

"Tell me about it." She groaned. "I ask you, could there have *been* more red flags?"

"Don't beat yourself up. It's all in the past, right?"

A little shudder went through her. "Right. The very

recent past, unfortunately—but anyhow, we agreed we'd skip the fancy wedding. I'd never wanted one of those and he could not have cared less either way. We set a date for a quickie Vegas ceremony, which was to have taken place exactly six days ago today. Then after the wedding, the plan was that James would sweep me off for a Christmas vacation-slash-honeymoon in the Seychelles."

"Christmas in the tropics. That does sound romantic. Ten points for James."

"I thought so, too. And I did insist he had to at least meet my dad first, so we went to the farm for Thanksgiving."

"Did you have a nice visit?"

She narrowed her eyes at him. "Go ahead, Matthias. Pour on the irony."

"Sorry." He didn't look the least regretful.

"You're enjoying this far too much."

"I'm only teasing you—you know, being *lighthearted*?"

She pulled the pillow out from behind her back and threw it at him.

He caught it. "Whoa. Just missed the candle."

"Watch out. I'll do worse than knock over a candle."

He put the pillow under his injured leg. "So? The visit to the farm…?"

"It was bad. My dad was polite to James, but two days in, Dad got me alone and asked me if I was really sure about marrying the guy."

"Ouch. That's tough."

"And I reacted with anger. I said some mean things about how, since we'd lost Mom, he didn't care about anything—but now, all of a sudden, he's got a negative opinion he just has to share concerning my choice of a life mate."

"Admit it," Matthias interjected in that rough, matter-of-fact tone she already knew so well. "You were worried that your dad might be right."

She decided his remark didn't require a response. "After the awfulness with my dad, James and I went back to Portland."

"Your dad was right, though—am I right?"

She wished she had another pillow to throw at him. "Seven days ago, the day before we were supposed to head for Vegas, James's parents arrived out of nowhere at our apartment."

"Not good?"

"Horrible. They'd come to collect their errant son before he made the biggest mistake of his life— marrying some nobody farmer's daughter when the woman he grew up with, a woman from an excellent family, a woman who loved him with all her heart, was waiting for him in Monterey—with their little boy who needed his daddy."

"What the—? James had a kid?"

She nodded. "One he'd never said a word to me about."

"Okay, now I want to kick his snotty little rich-guy ass."

"Thank you. Anyway, James asks his parents to leave. They go. At this point, I'm reeling. I demand an explanation—and James just blurts out the truth he never bothered to share with me before. He says yes, there's a little boy. That in the year between graduation and when he showed up in Portland, he'd gotten back with his childhood sweetheart and she'd had his baby. He says he hates that maybe his parents are right. Monica—his baby mama—really does need him and so does his son. He says he's sorry, but he can't marry me and he's leaving for Monterey right away."

"Sabra."

She glared across the coffee table at him to keep from getting weepy over her terrible life choices. "What?"

"This all happened a week ago?"

"James went back to Monterey exactly one week ago today, yes."

Matthias took the pillow out from under his leg, plopped it on the coffee table and scooted around so he could rest his leg on it again. Then he patted the space beside him. "Come here."

"Why?"

He only patted the empty cushion some more.

"Fine." She got up and sat next to him.

And he hooked his giant arm around her and pulled her close. "Lean on me. It's not going to kill you."

She let her head drop to his enormous shoulder, breathed in his minty, manly evergreen scent—and felt comforted. "Thanks."

His breath brushed the crown of her head. He might even have pressed a kiss there, though she couldn't be sure. "Continue."

"What else is there to say? I gave him back his ring and he packed a suitcase and left. I told myself to look on the bright side. I had three weeks off work for the honeymoon that wasn't happening, time off from the daily grind to pull it together, find a new place and sublet the apartment I can't afford to keep by myself."

"Plus, you'd dodged a major bullet not marrying a cheating, dumb-ass rich kid from Monterey."

"Yay, me." It felt good to be held by him. She snuggled in a little closer. When she tipped her head back to glance up at him, he bent close and touched his nose to hers, causing a sweet little shiver to radiate out from that small point of contact.

"You okay?" he asked, blue eyes narrowed with concern.

"I am," she replied, resting her head on his shoulder. "I threw some clothes in a bag and went to the farm, where my dad was still wandering around like a ghost of himself. But at least he hugged me and said he loved me and he was glad I hadn't married the wrong man. He wanted me to come with him for Christmas with my mom's side of the family, but I wasn't up for it. After Dad left, it got really lonely at the farm, so I started back to Portland—and the rest, you know."

"Luckily for me, you ended up here in time to save my sorry ass from my own hopeless pigheadedness."

"You're welcome." She eased free of his hold to bring a knee up on the sofa cushion and turn toward him. "And at least I've learned something from the disaster that was James."

"What's that?"

"For the next five years, minimum, the only relationships I'm having are the casual kind."

He scratched his chin, pretending to think deeply about what she'd just said. "I don't know, Sabra. Isn't that what you promised yourself after things went south with Stan? You seem to be kind of a sucker for a marriage proposal."

She was tempted to fake outrage. But really, why

bother? He was absolutely right on both counts. "Yeah, I do have that teensy problem of being monogamous to the core." A sad little laugh escaped her. "It's bred in the bone with me, I guess."

"Why's that?"

"My parents fell in love when they were kids—and their dedication to each other? Absolute. I just want what they had, but so far it's not happening." Matthias was watching her with a kind of musing expression. And she felt…bold. And maybe a little bit giddy. She took it further. "I'm probably never trying love again. And I'm incapable of having casual sex with men I don't know. That means I'm doomed to spend my life only having sex with myself—and I know, I know. TMI in a big way." Matthias chuckled. It was a rough sound, that chuckle. And very attractive. She felt strangely proud every time she made him laugh. "And now that I've totally overshared the story of my pitiful love life, you sure you don't want to do a little sharing, too?"

He grunted. "Do I look like the sharing type to you?"

She didn't back down. "Yeah. You do. Talk to me about the things you said in your sleep the other night."

He went straight to tough-guy denial. "No idea what you're talking about."

"The name Nelson doesn't even ring a bell?"

"Who?" he sneered—but in a teasing kind of way that seemed to give her permission to keep pushing.

Sabra pushed. "So…you don't want to talk about Mark or Finn, either, or the woman you mentioned. Christy, I think her name was…"

He squinted at her, as though he was trying to see inside her head. "You really want to hear this crap?"

"I'm sure it's *not* crap. And yes, I really do."

"All right, then." And just like that, he gave it up. "Christy was my high school sweetheart. We were still together after a couple of years of community college. I was messing up all over the place back then, drinking, exploring the effects of a number of rec-reational drugs and playing video games instead of taking care of business. My issues had issues, I guess you could say. But at least I knew Christy was the love of my life."

"That's sweet."

He snorted derisively. "Wait for the rest of it. At twenty, after squeaking through my sophomore year with a C-minus average, my older brother Daniel gave me a good talking-to—a few blows were thrown. But he did get through to me. I decided to enlist, to serve my country and get my act together.

"Before I left for boot camp, I proposed and Christy said yes. We agreed to a two-year engagement so that she could finish college before the wedding. A year later, while I was overseas, she Dear Johned me via email and then married the guy she'd been cheating on me with."

"Oh, dear God, Matthias. That's bad."

"What happened with Christy was by no means the worst of it." His eyes were flat now, far away.

She felt terrible for him and almost let him off the hook. But he fascinated her. She wanted to know his story, to understand what had shaped the man he was now.

"Nelson and Mark were good men," he continued

in a monotone. "We served together in the Middle East. They didn't make it home. I got discharged due to injury. I was a mess. There were surgeries and lots of therapy—both kinds, physical and for my screwed-up head. Finn was my brother."

"Was?" she asked in a small voice, stunned by this litany of tragedy.

"It's possible he's still alive. He disappeared when he was only eight. That was my fault. I was six years older and I was supposed to be watching him. We still have investigators looking for him."

"I'm so sorry," she said, aching for him and for those he'd lost. "I really don't know what to say…"

"Don't worry about it. Can we talk about something else now, you think?"

"Absolutely."

And just like that, he shook it off and teased her, "I guess, with you being incapable of casual sex, I don't have to wonder if you took advantage of me that first night when I was at my weakest."

She followed his lead and teased him right back. "Don't look so hopeful."

"Damn. It was only a dream, then?"

"All right, I admit it." She fluttered her eyelashes madly. "For you, I have made a monogamy exception. You loved it—actually, it was good for both of us."

"I kind of figured it would be." He said that with way more sincerity than the joking moment called for.

And all of a sudden, the warm, candlelit cabin was charged with a whole new kind of heat.

Okay, yeah. The guy was super hot in his big, buff, ex-military kind of way. Plus, they'd forged a sort of instant intimacy, two strangers alone in the middle of the woods.

But getting into anything *really* intimate with him would be a bad idea. After all, she'd just gotten messed over by her second fiancé.

Having sex with Matthias would only be asking for trouble.

Wouldn't it?

Or would it be wonderful? Passionate and sweet and magical. And right.

Chemistry-wise, he really did it for her—at least, as far as she could tell without even having kissed him yet.

Why should she run from that, from the possibility of that? Maybe they could have something beautiful.

Something for right now. Just between the two of them.

Maybe, for the first time, she, Sabra Bond, could actually have a fling. That would be progress for someone like her.

They stared at each other in the flickering candlelight.

Was he just possibly thinking the same thing she was?

Sex.

Matt was definitely thinking about sex. About how much he wanted it. With the woman sitting next to him. "Sabra."

Her big eyes got bigger. "Um, yeah?"

"Whatever I say now is just going to sound like so much bull—"

She whipped up a hand. "No. No, it's not. I get you,

Matthias. I do. I think, you and me, we're on the same page about this whole relationship thing. It hasn't even been a full week since I almost married a man who'd failed to tell me he had a child. I'm not ready for anything serious, not in the least. I need about a decade to figure myself out first."

"Yeah. I get that." He gave it to her straight out. "I'm not ready, either."

"But I, well, I *have* been thinking about it," she confessed. "About the two of us, here, alone. Like strangers. And yet somehow, at the same time, not strangers at all."

Were they moving too far, too fast? Yeah, probably.

He tried to lighten things up a little. "It's all the excitement and glamour, right? I mean, I know we're having a wild old time here, playing board games, sitting out on the porch watching the snow melt."

She laughed. He really liked her laugh, all husky and musical at once. But then she answered with complete sincerity. "I'm having the best time. I really am."

And what could he do but reply honestly, in kind? "Me, too." He wanted to kiss her. What man wouldn't? And as their hours together drifted by, it kept getting harder to remember why kissing her wouldn't be wise.

She got up and went back to her chair. He wanted to reach out, catch her hand, beg her to stay there on the sofa beside him. But he had no right to do any such thing.

She settled in across the coffee table, gathering her knees up against her chest, resting her pretty chin on them. "I have a proposition for you."

His heart rate picked up. "Hit me with it."

"What if we both agreed that this, right now, in this

cabin at Christmas, just you and me—this is it? This is all. When it's over and we go our separate ways, that's the last we'll ever see of each other."

He felt regret, that it was going nowhere between the two of them—regret and relief in equal measure. A man needed to be realistic about what he was capable of. And what he wasn't. As for Sabra, well, she'd just gotten free of one romantic mess. A new one was the last thing she needed. "You're saying we won't be exchanging numbers?"

"That's right. No details about how to get in touch later. And no looking each other up on social media, no trying to track each other down."

"We say goodbye and walk away."

"Yes." She sat a little straighter in the chair. "What do you think?"

He stuck out his hand across the coffee table. She shifted, tucking her legs to the side, leaning forward in the chair and then reaching out to meet him.

"Deal," he said as he wrapped his fingers around hers.

Chapter Five

The second Matt released her hand, the power popped back on.

The lights flickered, and then steadied. The tree came alive, blazing bright.

"You think it'll go out again?" she asked in a whisper.

"Hell if I know." He shifted his bad leg back onto the sofa, stretching it out as before.

They sat there, waiting, for a good count of twenty. When the lights stayed on, she bent forward to blow out the candle between them.

"Leave it for a little while, just in case," he suggested.

"Sure." She gazed across the coffee table at him—and started backing off the plan. "I, well, I just realized…" Her cheeks were bright red. She was absolutely adorable.

"Realized what?" he asked, keeping his expression serious, though inside he was grinning. Yeah, he wanted to do her ten ways to Sunday.

But if it never happened, he would still have so much—the memory of her smile, the clever bite of her sharp words. The way she only got calmer when things got scary. And how, even after he'd introduced himself by threatening her with a rifle, she'd stepped right up to do what needed doing, not only patching him up, but also taking good care of him while he was out of it.

No matter how it all turned out, this was a Christmas he wouldn't forget. Even if he never so much as kissed her, he felt a definite connection to her and he was one of those guys who didn't make connections easily.

She did some throat clearing. "It just occurred to me…"

"Yeah?"

"I don't have condoms. I'm going to take a wild guess and say you don't, either."

Wrong. Last summer he'd let Jerry Davidson, a lifelong friend, fellow game warden and self-styled player, use the cabin as a romantic getaway. Jerry had left a box of them upstairs.

"Are you getting cold feet?" he asked gently.

She scowled. "Matthias, just tell me. Do you have condoms or not?"

"I do, yeah. Upstairs in the dresser, top drawer on the right."

She blinked. "Oh. Well, okay, then—and what about your leg?"

He gave a shrug. "It could cramp my style a little, I have to admit."

"Do you want, um, to back out, then?"

He grinned. She did that to him, made him grin. Made him see the world as a better place. Made him feel comfortable in his own skin, somehow. "Not a chance."

She answered his grin with one of her own. "Then you're only saying that we should be careful, take it slow?"

"Yeah. Slow. Slow is good." He gestured at his stretched-out leg. "Slow also happens to be just about all I can manage at this point."

She leaned in a little closer. "You think you could make it up the stairs?"

"Baby, I know I could."

Her grin turned to a soft little smile. "Slowly, right?"

"That's right."

All of a sudden, she was a ball of nervous energy. She shot out of the chair. "How about some hot chocolate?"

"Sounds good." He started to get up.

"No. You stay right there. I'll get it." And she bolted for the kitchen area, where she began rattling pans. He considered following her over there for no other reason than that he liked being near her—plus, he wanted to be sure she wasn't suddenly freaking out over the plans they'd just made.

But maybe she needed a few minutes to herself. Maybe she was going to tell him that, on second thought, getting into bed with him was a bad idea.

Well, if she'd changed her mind, she would say so.

No need to go looking for disappointment. If it was coming, it would find him soon enough.

He picked up his phone and got the music started again, choosing slower songs this time, Christmas ballads and easy-listening jazz.

When she returned with two mugs, she set one in front of her chair and then edged around the coffee table to put his down where he could reach it comfortably. "Here you go."

"Thanks." Before she could retreat to the other side of the table, he caught her arm in an easily breakable grip.

Her eyes widened and her mouth looked so soft and full. He couldn't wait to kiss her. "I gave you marshmallows," she said softly, like it was their secret that no one else could know.

"I love marshmallows."

"Excellent," she replied in a breathless whisper.

He exerted a gentle pressure on her arm, pulling her down a little closer, so he could smell the clean sweetness of her skin, feel the warmth of her, imagine the beauty hidden under his baggy sweatshirt and track pants.

She didn't resist him, though she gulped hard and her breathing had grown erratic. Another quivery little smile pulled at the corners of her mouth.

One more tug was all it took. Those soft lips touched his. She sighed. The sound flowed through him. It was a happy sort of sound, warm.

Welcoming, even.

He smiled against her lips, letting go of her arm as he claimed her mouth, being careful to give her every opportunity to pull away or call a halt.

She did neither.

And he went on kissing her, keeping it light and tentative at first, brushing his lips across hers. He caught her pillowy lower lip between his teeth, biting down just enough to make her give him a little moan as he eased his fingers up over the slim curve of her shoulder.

Taking hold of her thick braid, he wrapped it around his hand, a rope of silk. She hummed into his mouth, her lips softening, giving to him, letting him in to explore the smooth, wet surfaces beyond her parted lips.

"Sabra," he whispered.

She murmured his name, "Matthias," in return.

He liked that, the way she always used his full name. Other people rarely did.

Slowly, he let the wrapped braid uncoil. That freed his hand to slip under it and clasp her nape. Her skin was warm satin, so smooth against his roughened palm. He ran his thumb and forefinger down the sides of her neck, relishing the feel of her. The fine hairs at her nape brushed at him, tickling a little in a way that both aroused him and made him smile.

He needed her closer.

Exerting gentle pressure with his hand on her nape, he guided her down to sit across his thighs.

She broke the kiss to ask, "Your leg?"

"It's fine." He caught her mouth again. She opened with a yearning little moan.

The kiss continued as he clasped her braid once more and ran his hand slowly down it. He tugged the elastic free, tossed it in the general direction of the coffee table, and then set about working his fingers through the long strands until they fell loose down her back and across her shoulders. The dark waves felt good between his fingers. They clung to his hand as he continued to kiss her slowly and thoroughly.

Letting her know that there was no rush.

That it was just the two of them, alone, together, for at least the next couple of days.

Plenty of time to explore each other, *know* each other in the best sort of way.

She pulled back, the black fans of her eyelashes lifting slowly. Her pupils had widened. She looked dazed. He probably did, too.

He leaned in to take her mouth again, a quick, hard kiss. "I can't wait to get my clothes off you."

She laughed—and then whispered, "We get to *unwrap* each other."

"Exactly."

"We are each other's Christmas present."

He pressed his forehead to hers as he ran the backs of his fingers up and down the side of her throat. "Best. Present. Ever."

She caught his jaw and held his gaze. "I love your eyes. They are the deepest, truest blue—kiss me again."

He did. She opened for him instantly and he took what she offered him, tasting her deeply, running his hands up and down her slim back, gathering her closer, so he could feel her breasts, their softness pressing against his chest.

That time, when she lifted her mouth from his, she got up. He didn't try to stop her. The whole point was not to rush.

She went and sat across the coffee table. "Drink your cocoa while it's still hot."

* * *

An hour later, the lights were still on.

He turned off the music. She blew out the candles and unplugged the tree. He grabbed the pillow she'd brought down for him that first night and followed her up the stairs.

Halfway up, she paused and glanced back at him over her shoulder. "You doing all right?"

His leg? He'd forgotten all about it. He had more important things on his mind. "Yeah. I'm good."

She gave him a little nod and they continued on up into the loft. Through the single window, the full moon was visible, a ghostly silver disc obscured by a thin curtain of clouds.

At the bed, she flipped on one of the lamps. He passed her his pillow. She set it next to hers and turned back the blankets. He went to the dresser for the box of condoms, taking out a few, carrying them back to the far side of the bed, setting them on the nightstand.

Though she'd teased him about unwrapping each other, they didn't linger over getting their clothes off, but got right after it, tossing track pants and sweatshirts in a pile on a chair.

She was so damn pretty, slim and tight and strong, her dark hair in loose, messy curls on her shoulders.

He reached for her. She came into his arms and she fit there just right, her skin so smooth, her eyes wide and hopeful, fluttering shut as he lowered his mouth to hers.

She tasted of hope—the kind of hope he rarely allowed himself anymore, hope for a future that included more than himself, alone, getting by. She made him feel close to her, intimate in the deepest way.

Even if it was only for right now.

Those quick, clever hands of hers caressed him, gliding up his chest, exploring, her fingers pausing to stroke their way out along his shoulders and then back in to link around his neck. "So good to kiss you," she whispered against his mouth.

"The best," he agreed. He wanted to taste every inch of her and now was his chance.

Working his way downward, he dropped nipping kisses in a trail along the side of her neck, and then in a looping pattern across her upper chest.

She murmured encouragements, her hands first cradling his face and then slipping up into his hair.

Her breasts were so beautiful, small and high, full on the underside, the nipples already hard. He tasted them, drawing them in deep as she grasped his hair tighter, holding him there, at her heart.

But there was so much more woman he needed to kiss. He kept moving, kissing on downward, dropping to his knees, not giving a damn if he split a stitch or two.

"You okay?" she asked, her head bent down to him, her hair brushing the side of his face.

"Never better." He kissed her smooth, pretty belly and then dropped more kisses around to the side of her, where he nipped at the sweetly curved bones beneath the silky flesh, feeling lost in the best kind of way—lost to the taste and smell of her.

She must have been lost, as well. Dropping her head back, she moaned at the shadowed rafters above.

"So pretty." He blew a teasing breath into the neatly trimmed sable hair at her mound, bringing his hands up to pet her a little.

"Oh!" she said. "Oh, my!" And she giggled, reaching for him, cradling his face again. She was swaying on her feet.

He caught her by the side of her hip to steady her. She felt so good, he couldn't resist sliding his hand around her, getting a big handful of her smooth round backside.

She looked down at him then, her eyes deep and dark, beckoning him. Their gazes locked. "Kiss me," she whispered. "Right there."

And he did, using his tongue, his teeth, everything, then bringing his eager hands back to the center of her, parting her for his mouth.

Already, she was slick and wet. He made her more so, darting his tongue in, licking her, then holding her still, spreading her wider with his fingers, so he could get in close and tight.

By then, she was whimpering, muttering excited encouragements. "Yes!" and "Please!" and "That! More. Oh, that…"

He gave her what she asked for, staying with her all the way, using his fingers to stroke into her. Using his tongue, too, until she went over with a low, keening cry.

He could have stayed right there on his knees forever, touching her, kissing her, petting her, whispering dark promises of all he would do to her.

But then, with a happy sigh, she dropped back away from him onto the bed, her slim arms spread wide.

"I think I just died." She lifted her head and watched him as he braced his hands on either side of her fine thighs. "Your stitches!" she cried, that mouth he couldn't wait to kiss again forming a worried frown as he pushed himself upright.

"My stitches are just fine," he promised. "It's my knees that are shaking."

She reached up slim arms as he rose above her. "Come down here. Please. I need you close."

He went down, falling across the bed with her, catching himself on his forearms in order not to crush her completely. "I'm right here."

"And I am so glad." She touched him, learning him, her palms smoothing over his back, his shoulders, along his arms. Her fingers lingered on the ridges of scar tissue that marred his chest, neck and arms. She didn't remark on them, though.

He appreciated that.

There was nothing to say about them. He was one of the lucky ones. He'd come back from the Middle East damaged, battered—but all in one piece, after all.

He dipped close to capture her mouth again as her quick hand eased between them and encircled his hardness. When she did that, he couldn't hold back a groan.

Tightening her grip on him, she gave a little tug, bringing another rough sound from him as she pushed him onto his back and rose above him. Curving down over him, she claimed him with her mouth.

Lightning flashed along his nerve endings and the blood pumped hot and fast through his veins. She drove him just to the edge and then slacked off to tease and flick him with her tongue as she continued to work him over with those talented hands—both hands, together.

Somehow, he lasted for several minutes of that glorious torture.

But there did come a point where he had to stop her. Catching hold of her wrist, tipping up her chin with the other hand, he warned in a growl, "I'm about to go over."

She grinned, a saucy little grin. "Please do."

"Not till I'm inside you."

"But I like it. I want you to—"

"Come up here." He took her under the arms and pulled her up on top of him, so they were face-to-face, her long legs folded on either side of his body. "You are so beautiful." And then he speared his fingers into her hair, pulling it maybe a little harder than he should have. But she didn't complain.

Not Sabra. She only gave a sweet little moan and opened for his kiss.

Those idiots who'd left her?

What the hell was the matter with those two?

If she was his, he would keep her forever, keep her happy, keep her satisfied. He would never be the chump who let her go.

But she *wasn't* his.

And he needed to remember that.

Remember that neither of them was ready for anything life changing, and that was all right.

They had tonight, the next day, maybe a few days after that. They had this Christmastime with just the two of them, Sabra and Matthias, alone in his cabin in the forest.

He went on kissing her, deep and hard and endlessly, reaching out a hand for the night table and a condom. With a groan, she broke their kiss and gazed down at him through wide, wondering eyes as she lifted her slim body away from him enough for him to deal with the business of protection.

"I'll stay on top." She bent close again and scraped his scruffy jaw with her teeth. He breathed in the scent of her, so sweet, musky now. "Okay?" she asked.

"Best offer I've had in years." He groaned as she wrapped her hand around him and guided him into place. "Look at me," he whispered, as he slipped an inch inside.

She met his eyes, held them, and lowered slowly down. "Yes. Oh, yes..."

It hurt so good, her body all around him, wet and hot and so damn tight. "Sabra."

"Yes..."

She let out a sharp, pleasured cry as she took him all the way.

There was a moment of complete stillness between them. They waited, breath held. And then she moaned. She curved her body over him, her hair falling forward to caress his cheek and rub against his neck.

Then they were moving together. He pushed up into her, matching her rhythm as she picked up speed.

The way she rode him? Nothing like it. Sweet and slow and long.

Hard and fast and mercilessly. He could go forever, be with her forever, lost inside her sweetness.

Held.

Known.

Cherished.

He wanted it to last and last. Was that really so much to ask?

She seemed to understand his wish, to want it, too.

For a while, they played with each other, slowing when one of them got too close to the edge, then getting swept up in the hungry glory of it all over again, going frantic and fast. She rode him so hard. He would never get enough of her, of being inside her.

Too bad they really couldn't hold out indefinitely.

He felt her climax take her, the walls of her sex clutching around him. He gritted his teeth, clasping the fine, firm curves of her hips, holding on more tightly than he should have, trying to outlast her.

By some miracle he managed it, lived through the wonder of her pulsing hard and fast around him.

When she collapsed on his chest with a sigh of happy surrender, he let go, let his finish roll through him—burning, breathtaking, overpowering. He gave himself up to it with a triumphant shout.

The snow started to melt the next day.

Sabra wished it would freeze again and stay that way. She fantasized about being stuck in the cabin forever, just her and Matthias in a world all their own.

But the snow kept melting. By the twenty-eighth, there was nothing left of it beyond a few dirty patches dotting the clearing and the dirt road leading out. Matthias drove her to the fish hatchery, where she got in her little blue Subaru Outback and followed him back to the cabin.

They stayed on.

To sit on the porch as the night fell, to wander into the forest hand in hand, laughing together under the tall trees, sharing stories of their families, of their lives up till now.

They spent a lot of time naked upstairs in the bed

under the eaves. And downstairs, on the couch, in the big brown chair, wherever and whenever the mood struck—which was often.

And every time was better than the time before.

On New Year's Eve, they didn't bother to get dressed the whole day. They made love and napped all wrapped up together and toasted in the New Year with whiskey from a dusty bottle Matthias pulled from the back of a cupboard.

And then, all of a sudden, totally out of nowhere, it was New Year's Day.

She didn't want to go.

But that was the thing. She *had* to go. She had her life to cobble back together. She had her promise to herself, to *get* a life, a full and happy life, on her own.

And they had a deal. It was a good deal. Christmas together.

And nothing more.

He helped her carry her stuff to her Outback. It only took one trip. And then he held her in his arms and kissed her, a kiss so right and so consuming, she had no idea how she was going to make herself get in the car and drive away.

He cradled her face in those big, wonderful hands and his blue eyes held hers. "God. I don't want to say goodbye."

Her eyes burned with tears she wouldn't let fall. "Me neither." It came out in a ragged whisper because her throat had clutched with sadness and yearning for what would never be. She lifted up and brushed her lips to his once more, breathing in the evergreen scent of him. *I will never forget*, she promised in her heart. Overhead, a bird cried, a long, keening sound. "Goodbye, Matthias."

"Wait." He pulled something from his jacket pocket. "Give me your hand."

She held it out. He took it, turned it palm up and set a key there, then gently folded her fingers over the cool metal. She looked up at him, confused, searching his face that she'd already come to love—just a little. "What's this?"

"A key to the cabin."

"But—"

He stopped her with a finger against her lips. "So here's my offer. I work flexible hours, fill in for everyone else all year long. Except at Christmas, when they give me first crack at the schedule. I'll be right here, same time, next year, from the twenty-third till New Year's Day. Alone. If you maybe find that you wouldn't mind spending another Christmas with me, just the two of us, just for Christmastime, well then, you have the key."

"Matthias, I—"

"Uh-uh." He brushed his thumb across her mouth. She felt that slight touch all the way down to the core of her. His eyes were oceans she wanted to drown in, an endless sky in which she longed to take flight. "Don't decide now. A lot can happen in a year."

She threw her arms around him and buried her face against his shoulder. "I miss you already."

He said her name, low. Rough. They held each other hard and tight.

And then, by silent mutual agreement, they both let go and staggered back from each other. She stuck the key in her pocket to join the wooden porcupine he'd given her.

He pulled open her door for her and shut it once she was behind the wheel, tapping the door in a final salute.

She watched him turn and go up the steps.

That was as much as she could take of him walking away. She started the engine, put it in Drive and headed for Portland.

Chapter Six

Matt, the following June...

It was Friday night at Beach Street Brews in Valentine Bay. The music was too loud and the acoustics were terrible. The barnlike brew pub was wall-to-wall bodies, everybody laughing, shouting, meeting up, partying down.

Matt nursed a beer and wished he hadn't come.

Jerry Davidson, his friend since first grade, pulled out the chair next to him and dropped into it. "C'mon!" Jerry shouted in Matt's ear. "I met a girl. She's at the bar. And she's got a good-looking friend."

Matt raised his mug and took another sip. "Have fun."

The band crashed through the final bars of Kongos' "Come with Me Now." The applause was thunderous. "We'll be back," growled the front man into the mic.

When the clapping faded down, Matt enjoyed the relative silence.

Until Jerry leaned close and started talking again. "It's that girl, isn't it? The one from the cabin? You're thinking about her, aren't you?"

He was, yeah. But no way was he getting into that with Jerry. He never should have told his friend about Sabra. Sabra was *his*. A perfect memory to treasure. He didn't have a whole hell of a lot of those and Jerry needed to quit telling him to move on.

"Leave it alone," Matt said. "I told you. It's not going anywhere. It was great and now it's over." *Unless she shows up again at Christmas.*

God. He hoped she would.

But too much could happen in the space of a year. Sabra was hot and smart, kind and funny and easy to talk to. In spite of her vow to stay single for years, by Christmas, some lucky bastard would coax her into giving love another try. Matt hated that guy with a pure, cold fury. Whoever the hell he might turn out to be.

At least once a week he almost convinced himself it would be okay to look her up online. He never did it, though. And he *wouldn't* do it. They had an agreement and he would keep the promise he'd made to her.

Jerry clapped him on the shoulder. "You need to relax and have a good time."

"Jer. How many years you been giving me that advice?"

"Hmm." Jerry stroked his short, thick ginger beard. "Several."

"Do I ever listen?"

"Before last Christmas, you used to. Now and then."

"I'm not in the mood." Matt tipped his head toward the bar. "And a pretty woman is waiting on you."

Jerry glanced up to give his latest conquest a quick wave. "You're insane not to come with me."

"Go."

Jerry gave it up and headed back to the bar.

Matt nursed his beer and wished it was Christmas.

Sabra, that September...

"More wine?" Iris held up the excellent bottle of Oregon pinot noir. At Sabra's nod, her friend refilled her glass.

It was girl's night in at Iris and Peyton's apartment in downtown Portland—just the three of them. Sabra could safely afford to indulge in the wine. Back in January, she'd rented a one-bedroom in this same building, so home was two flights of stairs or a very short elevator ride away.

Peyton, her caramel-colored hair piled in a messy bun on the top of her head, turned from the stir-fry she was cooking and asked Sabra, "So can I tell him to give you a call?"

"He's a hottie." Iris did a little cha-cha-cha with her shoulders, her hair, which she wore in natural corkscrew curls, bouncing in time with the movement. "And no drama, which we all love."

He was Jack Kellan, the new sous chef at Delia Mae's, where they all worked.

"Jack is a great guy," Sabra said, thinking of Matthias as she did every time her friends got after her to get out and mix it up—and no, she hadn't told anyone about what had happened at Christmas. It was her secret pleasure, having known him, everything they'd shared. Often, she found herself wondering where he was and what he might be doing right now.

But no, she wasn't getting attached, wasn't pining for her Christmas lover. Uh-uh. No way.

Iris scoffed. "Could you *be* any less enthusiastic?" Iris had that Tyra-Banks-meets-Wendy-Williams thing going on. All power, smarts and sass. Nobody messed with Iris. "This swearing-off-men thing? Sabra, honey, it's not a good look on you."

Totally out of nowhere, emotion made her eyes burn and her throat clutch. "I'm just not ready yet, you know?"

Iris set down the bottle of pinot and peered at her more closely across the kitchen island. "Something's really got you bothered. What?"

"Come on, now." Peyton turned off the heat under the stir-fry and she and Iris converged on either side of Sabra. "You'll feel better if you talk about it."

"Is it your dad?" Iris ventured gently.

Sabra drooped on her stool as her friends shared a knowing look.

"It's her dad," confirmed Peyton.

Sabra had been up to the farm a few days before. As usual, she'd come home earlier than planned. "He's just worse every time I see him. He's thinner, more withdrawn than ever. I want to be there for him, but he won't talk about it, about Mom. It's like there's a brick wall between him and the rest of the world. Nobody gets in, not even me."

"Oh, honey…" Iris grabbed her in a hug and Peyton wrapped her arms around both of them.

Sabra leaned her head on Iris's shoulder. "I keep telling myself he'll get better. But the years keep going by and he only seems sadder and further away, like he's slowly fading down to nothing. It scares me, it does. And I don't know what to do about it."

Her friends rubbed her back and hugged her some more. They offered a number of suggestions and Sabra thanked them and promised to try to get her dad to maybe join a men's group or see a therapist. They all agreed that Adam Bond had been a prisoner of his grief for much too long.

There was more wine and Peyton's delicious stir-fry. Iris talked about the guy she'd just broken up with and Peyton was all dewy-eyed over the new man in her life. By midnight, Sabra was feeling the wine. She looked from one dear friend's face to the other—and she just couldn't hold back any longer.

"Ahem. There is something else I keep meaning to tell you guys…"

"Hmm," said Peyton thoughtfully. She and Iris exchanged yet another speaking glance.

Iris nodded. "We knew it."

"Spill," commanded Peyton.

Sabra set down her empty glass. "It's like this. Last Christmas, when I was supposedly snowed in at the farm?"

"Supposedly?" Iris scowled. "Meaning you weren't?"

Sabra busted to it. "I wasn't at the farm and I wasn't alone."

"A man," said Peyton. It wasn't a question.

"That's right. I stopped off on the way back here to Portland for a hike—you know, trying to get out of my own head a little. I started walking and it started raining. I took shelter at this empty cabin. And then the owner arrived…"

They listened without interrupting as she told them about Matthias, about her Christmas at the cabin, about pretty much all of it, including how he'd given her a key as she was leaving, just in case she might want to spend another Christmas with him.

Iris screeched in delight and Peyton declared, "Now, that's what I'm talking about. James the jerk? He couldn't keep you down. He goes back to the baby mama he'd forgotten to mention and what do you do? Head out for some hot, sexy times with a hermit in the forest."

Sabra whacked her friend lightly with the back of her hand. "Matthias is not a hermit. He has a real job and a big family in Valentine Bay."

"He just hides out alone in an isolated cabin for Christmas," teased her friend.

"Not last Christmas, he didn't," Sabra said smugly. Her friends high-fived her for that and she added more seriously, "He's had some rough times in his life and he likes to get off by himself now and then, that's all."

Peyton scolded, "You took way too long to tell us, you know. It's been months and months. It's almost the holidays all over again."

"Yeah, well. Sorry. But I wasn't going to tell *any-one*, ever. Overall, it was a beautiful time, the *best* time. And after I got back to Portland, well, I kind of thought of it as our secret, Matthias's and mine."

"We get it," said Iris.

"But we're still glad you finally told us," Peyton chimed in.

Iris nodded. "It's a yummy story, you and the cabin guy."

Peyton was watching Sabra a little too closely. "Look at me," she commanded. When Sabra met her gaze, Peyton shook her head. "I knew it. You're in love with him, aren't you?"

No way. "Nope. Not a chance. I'm immune to love now, not going there again."

"Of course you will go there again," argued Iris.

"Well, if I do, it won't be for years. And anyway, how could I possibly be in love with him? I knew him for ten days."

"You should just call him," Iris advised.

"I told you. I don't have his number and I'm not tracking him down online because getting in touch wasn't part of the deal—and yeah, I still have the key to the cabin. But that doesn't mean I'll be meeting him in December."

Her friends didn't argue with her, but she saw the speaking glance that passed between them.

Matt, December 1...

The three-legged Siberian husky Matt had named Zoya followed him into his bedroom.

He'd found her hobbling along the highway on his way home from Warrenton, four months ago now. No collar, no tags. He'd coaxed her to come to him and, after some hesitation, she did, so he'd driven her to the shelter here in Valentine Bay. They'd checked for an ID chip. She didn't have one.

Two weeks later, he stopped by the shelter to see if her former owner had come for her.

Hadn't happened. No one had adopted her, either.

The vet who helped out at the shelter said the husky was just full-grown, two or three years old and in excellent health. Her left front leg had been amputated, probably while she was still a puppy. She was well trained, happy natured and responded to all the basic commands.

Matt had done some research and then had a long talk with the vet about caring for a tripod dog. By then, he was pretty much all in on Zoya.

He brought her home. It was a little like having a kid, a well-behaved kid who wanted to please. He took her to doggy day care every workday, where she got lots of attention and pack time with other dogs.

Him. With a dog.

Matt wasn't sure what exactly had gotten into him to take her. But when she looked at him with those unearthly blue eyes, well, he could relate, that was all. She needed a human of her own. And he'd been available. Plus, it was time he stepped up, made a commitment to another creature even if he wasn't ready to give love with a woman any kind of a chance.

His four sisters all adored her. He'd taken her to a couple of family gatherings. The first time he showed up with Zoya, the oldest of his sisters, Aislinn, had pulled him aside...

"I have to ask." Aislinn gazed at him piercingly. "A *Siberian* husky?"

He understood her implication. "Yeah, well. I probably would have adopted her anyway, but it seemed more than right, you know? I only have to hear the word *Siberian* and I think of Finn. It's good to be reminded, to never forget."

Ais's dark eyes welled with moisture. "Nobody blames you."

"I know. But I do blame myself because I am culpable. If I'd behaved differently that day, Finn might be here with us now."

"Mom blamed *herself*."

"Yeah, well, there's plenty of blame to go around."

"Matt. Mom gave you permission to go off on your own—and then she told Finn that it was fine if he went with you."

"It is what it is, that's all. Now, stop looking so sad and let's hug it out."

With a cry, Ais threw herself at him. He wrapped his arms around her and held on tight, feeling grateful.

For his family, who had never given up on him no matter how messed up he got. For Zoya, who seemed more than happy to have him as her human.

And also for Sabra Bond, who had managed to show him in the short ten days he'd spent with her that maybe someday he might be capable of making a good life with the right woman, of starting a family of his own.

"How 'bout a walk, girl?"

Zoya gave an eager little whine and dropped to her haunches.

Matt crouched to give her a good scratch around the ruff. "All right, then. Let me get changed and we're on it."

He took off his uniform, pausing when he stepped

out of his pants for a look at the crescent-shaped scar from that little run-in with his own ax last Christmas. It was no more than a thin, curved line now. Sabra had patched him up good as new. The older scar on his other leg was much worse, with explosions of white scar tissue and a trench-like indentation in the flesh along the inside of his shin. There were pins and bolts in there holding everything together. He'd almost lost that leg below the knee.

But almost only counts in horseshoes. And now, that leg worked fine, except for some occasional stiffness and intermittent pain, especially in cold weather when it could ache like a sonofagun.

In his socks and boxer briefs, he grabbed a red Sharpie from a cup on the dresser and went to the closet. Sticking the Sharpie between his teeth to free both hands, he hung up his uniform. Once that was done, he shoved everything to the side, the hangers rattling as they slid along the rod.

The calendar was waiting, tacked to the wall. It was a large, themed calendar he'd found at Freddy's—Wild and Scenic Oregon. He'd bought it for what could only be called sentimental reasons. Bought it because he couldn't stop thinking of Sabra.

Sappy or not, marking off the days till Christmas had made him feel closer to a woman he hadn't seen in months, a woman he'd actually known for one week and three days.

For November, the calendar offered a spectacular photo of the Three Sisters, a trio of volcanic peaks in Oregon's section of the Cascade Range. Below the Three Sisters, he'd x-ed out each of November's days in red.

Lifting the calendar off the tack, he turned it to December and a picture of Fort Clatsop in the snow. He hooked it back in place and pulled the top off the Sharpie. With a lot more satisfaction than the simple action should have inspired, he x-ed off December 1.

Already, there was a big red circle around the ten days from December 23 to New Year's.

Satisfaction turned to real excitement.

Only twenty-one days to go.

December 23, three years ago...

It was late afternoon when Matt turned onto the dirt road that would take him to the cabin.

He had a fine-looking tree roped to the roof rack and the back seat packed with food, Christmas presents, and the usual duffel bags of clothes and gear. The weather was milder this year, real Western Oregon weather—cloudy with a constant threat of rain, no snow in the forecast.

Zoya, in her crate, had the rear of the vehicle. He would have loved having her in the passenger seat next to him, but with only one front leg, a sudden lurch or a fast stop could too easily send her pitching to the floor.

He was nervous, crazy nervous—nervous enough to be embarrassed at himself. The eager drumming of his pulse only got more so as he neared the clearing. He came around the second-to-last turn where he'd seen the lights in the windows the year before, hope rising...

Nothing.

Maybe she was waiting on the front porch.

He took the final turn.

Nobody there.

The nervous jitters fled. Now his whole body felt heavy, weighed down at the center with disappointment, as he pulled to a stop in front of the porch.

She hadn't come—not yet, anyway.

And he really had no right to expect that she would. He'd offered. It was her move.

And maybe she'd simply decided that one Christmas alone with him had been plenty. She was smart and beautiful and so much fun to be with. She'd probably found someone else.

He had to face the likelihood that she wouldn't show.

That she'd moved on.

That he would never see her face again.

He could accept that. He would *have* to accept it, his own crazy longing and the carefully marked calendar in his bedroom closet aside.

Reality was a bitch sometimes and that wasn't news.

He got out, opened the hatch in back, let Zoya out of her crate and helped her down to the ground. "Come on, girl. Let's get everything inside."

An hour later, he had the fire going, the Jeep unpacked, the groceries put away, and Zoya all set with food and water by her open crate. The tree stood proud in the stand by the window, not far from the front door. It was bigger and thicker than last year, filling the cabin with its Christmassy evergreen scent. A box of presents waited beside it. He'd even carried all his gear upstairs.

The disappointment?

Worse by the minute.

But he wasn't going to let it get him down. "Okay, sweetheart," he said to his dog. "I'm going to bring down the decorations and we'll get this party started."

Zoya made a happy sound, followed by a wide yawn. She rolled over and offered her belly to scratch, her pink tongue lolling out the side of her mouth, making her look adorably eager and also slightly demented.

"Goofy girl." He crouched to give her some attention. But before he got all the way down, she rolled back over and sat up, ears perking.

And then he heard the sound he'd been yearning for: tires crunching gravel.

His heart suddenly booming like it would beat its way right out of his chest, he straightened. Out the front windows, he watched as the familiar blue Subaru Outback pulled to a stop.

Chapter Seven

By a supreme effort of will, Matt managed not to race out there, throw open her car door, drag her into his arms, toss her over his shoulder and carry her straight up the stairs.

His tread measured, with Zoya at his heels, he crossed the cabin floor, opened the door and stepped out into the cold, gray afternoon. The dog whined, a worried sort of sound. She liked people, but new ones made her nervous—at first, anyway.

"Sit."

Zoya dropped to her haunches on the porch, still whining, tail twitching.

Sabra. Just the sight of her filled him with more powerful emotions than he knew how to name.

She got out of the car.

Hot damn, she looked amazing in tight jeans, lace-up boots and a big sweater printed with Christmas trees.

"You cut your hair." It came to just below her chin now.

Standing there by her car, looking shy and so damn pretty, she reached up and fiddled with her bangs. Her gorgeous face was flushed, her deep brown eyes even bigger than he remembered. "I don't know. I just wanted a change."

"It looks good on you."

A secret smile flashed across those lips he couldn't wait to taste again. She gave a tiny nod in acknowledgment of the compliment, her gaze shifting to Zoya. "You have a dog?"

Zoya knew when someone was talking about her. She quivered harder and whined hopefully. "More like she has me. I found her on the highway, dropped her off at the animal shelter—and then couldn't stop thinking about her."

Sabra laughed. God, what a beautiful sound. "Can't resist a pretty stray, huh? Such gorgeous blue eyes she's got. What's her name?"

"Zoya."

"I like it. Is it Polish, or...?"

"Russian." He gave a shrug. "She's a Siberian husky. It seemed to fit."

"Is it okay if I introduce myself?"

"Sure."

She clicked her tongue and called the dog.

When Zoya hesitated, he encouraged her. "It's all right, girl. Go." And she went, tail wagging, hopping down the steps to greet the woman Matt couldn't wait to kiss.

He followed the husky down to the ground and gave the woman and the dog a minute to get to know each other. By the time Sabra rose from giving Zoya the attention she craved, he couldn't wait any longer.

He caught her arm, heat zapping through him just to have his hand on her, even with the thick sweater keeping him from getting skin to skin. "Hey."

"Hey."

"I'm really glad to see you." It came out in a low growl.

She giggled, the cutest, happiest little sound. "Prove it."

"Excellent suggestion." He pulled her in close, wrapping both arms around her. And then he kissed her.

Zap. Like an electric charge flashing from her lips to his. Her mouth tasted better than he remembered, which couldn't be possible. Could it? He framed her face with his two hands and kissed her some more.

It wasn't enough. He needed her inside, up the stairs, out of her clothes…

She let out a little cry as he broke the kiss—but only to get one arm beneath her knees. With the other at her back, he scooped her high against his chest.

"I'm taking you inside," he announced.

"Yes," she replied, right before he crashed his mouth down on hers again.

He groaned in pure happiness, breathing in the scent of her, so fresh, with a hint of oranges, probably from her shampoo. Whatever. She smelled amazing. She smelled like everything he'd been longing for, everything he'd feared he would never touch or smell or taste again.

Kissing her as he went, he strode up the steps, across the porch and on inside, pausing only to wait for Zoya to come in after them before kicking the door shut with his foot.

Sabra broke the kiss to look around, her hands clasped behind his neck, fingers stroking his nape like she couldn't get enough of the feel of his skin. "The tree looks so good, even better than last year. And it smells like heaven." She pressed her nose against his throat. "It smells like you…"

"We'll decorate it," he said gruffly when she tipped her head away enough to meet his eyes again. "Later." He nuzzled her cool, velvety cheek, brushed a couple of quick kisses across her lips.

"You're so handsome. So big. So…" She laughed, a carefree sort of sound. "I am *so* glad to see you."

"Likewise, only double that—wait. Make that quintuple."

She stroked a hand at his temple, combing her fingers back into his hair. "I have stuff to bring in."

"Later." Zoya stood on her three legs looking up at them, tipping her head from side to side, not quite sure what the hell was going on. "Stay," he commanded, as he headed for the stairs.

"Your leg seems better."

"Good as new."

"I can walk, you know," she chided.

"Yeah. But I don't know if I can let go of you." He took her mouth again. Desire sparked and sizzled through his veins. Already, he was so hard it hurt.

"I've missed you, too," she whispered into the kiss.

"Not as much as I've missed you." He took the stairs two at a time and carried her straight to the bed, setting her down on it, grabbing the hem of her big sweater. "I like this sweater."

"Thanks."

"Let's get it off you." He pulled it up.

She raised her arms and he took it away, tossing it in the general direction of a nearby chair. She dropped back on her hands. He drank in the sight of her, in her skinny jeans and a lacy red bra, the kind a woman wears when a man might be likely to see it, to take it off her.

"So pretty." He eased his index finger between one silky strap and her skin and rubbed it up and down, from the slight swell of her breast to her shoulder and back again. Happiness filled him, bright and hot, to go with the pleasure-pain of his powerful desire. He bent closer, right over her, planting both fists on the mattress to either side of her. "I have an idea."

Her eyes went wide. "Yeah?"

"Let's get *everything* off you. Let's do that now."

A slow smile was her answer.

He dropped to his knees at her feet and untied her boots, pulling them off and her snowflake-patterned socks right after them. She shoved down her jeans. He dragged them free and tossed them aside.

In her red bra and a lacy little thong to match, she reached for him, pulling him up beside her—and then slipping over the edge of the bed to kneel and get to work on *his* boots.

He helped her, bending down and untying one as she untied the other. They paused only long enough to share a quick, rough kiss and in no time, he was out of his boots and socks. The rest of his clothes followed quickly. He ripped them off as she climbed back on the bed and sat on folded knees.

Resting her long-fingered hands on her smooth thighs, breathing fast, she stared at him through eyes gone black with longing. Reaching behind her, she started to unclasp her bra.

"No." He bent across the bed to still her arms. "Let me do that." *Or not.* He allowed himself a slow smile. "And on second thought, this bra and that thong might be too pretty to take off."

She caught the corner of her mouth with her teeth, her eyes promising him everything as she brought her hands to rest on her thighs again.

He took her by the wrists and tugged. She knelt up. Scooping an arm around her, he hauled her to the edge of the bed and tight against him. "It's been too long," he muttered, dipping his head to kiss that sweet spot where her neck met her shoulder.

The scent of her filled him—oranges, flowers, that beautiful sweetness, the essence of her, going musky now with her arousal.

He kissed her, another deep one, running his tongue over hers, gliding it against the ridges of her pretty teeth.

So many perfect places to put his mouth.

He got to work on that, leaving her lips with some reluctance, but consoling himself with the taste of her skin, licking the clean, gorgeous line of her jaw, moving on down to bite the tight flesh over her collarbone. She moaned when he did that and tried to pull him closer. He resisted. He had plans of his own.

Slowly, he lowered her bra straps with his teeth, using a finger to ease the lacy cups of the bra under her breasts so he could kiss those pretty, puckered nipples. She looked so amazing, with her face flushed, her eyes enormous, pure black, hazy with need, and her breasts overflowing the cups of that red bra.

He backed up again. When she moaned in protest and grabbed for him, he commanded, "Stretch out your legs."

She scooted back to the middle of the bed and stuck her feet out in front of her. "Like this?"

"Just like that." He grabbed her ankles and pulled. With a surprised laugh, she braced her hands behind her as he hauled her to the edge of the bed again.

"Lie back," he instructed as he went to his knees, pushing her smooth thighs apart to get in close and tight.

As he kissed her through the lace of that teeny-tiny thong, she moaned and fisted her fingers in his hair. "Matthias, please!" He glanced up at her sharp cry. "It's been a year. Come up here, right now. Come here to me."

He couldn't argue—didn't want to argue. He needed to be joined with her. He needed that right now.

And the gorgeous, soaking-wet thong? In the way.

He hooked his fingers in at both sides of it, pulled it down and tossed it halfway across the room. She undid the pretty bra and dropped it to the floor as he rose to yank open the bedside drawer. He had the condom out and on in record time.

"Come down here." She grabbed hold of his arm and pulled him on top of her, opening for him, wrapping those strong legs around him. Holding him hard and tight with one arm, she wriggled the other between them, took him in hand and guided him right to where they both wanted him.

"At last," she whispered, pushing her beautiful body up hard against him, wrapping her legs around him even tighter than before.

He was wild for her, too. With a surge of his hips, he was deep inside.

She cried out as he filled her.

"Too fast?" He groaned the words. "Did I hurt you?"

"No way." She grabbed on with both hands, yanking him in even tighter. "Oh, I have missed you."

"Missed you, too," he echoed. "So much…"

And he lost himself in her. There was only Sabra, the feel of her beautiful body around him, taking him deep.

They rolled and she was above him. That was so right, just what he needed—until they were rolling again, sharing a laugh that turned into rough moans as they arrived on their sides, facing each other, her leg thrown across him, pulling him so close. She urged him on with her eager cries.

He didn't want it to end. She pulled him on top again. Somehow, he held out through her first climax, gritting his teeth a little, groaning at the splendid agony of it as she pulsed around him. It was like nothing else, ever—to feel her giving way, giving it up, losing herself in his arms.

When she went limp beneath him, he sank into her, kissing her, stroking her tangled hair, waiting for the moment when she began to move again.

He didn't have to wait long.

Hooking her legs around him once more, she

surged up against him. With a deep groan, he joined her in the rhythm she set as she chased her second finish all the way to the top and over into free fall.

That time, he gave it up, too, driving deep within her as the pleasure rolled through him, rocketing down his spine, opening him up and sending him soaring.

Leaving him breathless, stunned—and deeply happy in a way he couldn't remember ever being before.

By the time Matthias let her out of bed an hour later, Sabra was starving.

Luckily, she'd brought fresh sourdough bread and a variety of sandwich fixings. They carried the food in from the Subaru and she made sandwiches while he unloaded the rest of her things.

Once they'd filled their growling bellies, he put on the Christmas tunes and they decorated the tree—working together this year, which meant the whole process was a whole lot more fun and took half the time it had the year before.

She'd brought ornaments. "You need at least one new ornament every year," she explained.

"I do?" He got that look guys get when women tell them how it ought to be, that *Huh?* kind of look that said women's logic really didn't compute.

"I brought three." She grabbed her pack from its hook on the far side of the door and pulled them out, each in its own small box. "Open them."

He obeyed, taking them from the boxes and hanging them on the tree. They included a porcupine carved from a pinecone, a crystal snowflake—and a blown glass pickle.

"Each has an important sentimental meaning…" She let the words trail off significantly.

He was up for the game. "Let me guess. The porcupine because I gave you one last year. And the snowflake to remind me that being snowed in can be the best time a guy ever had—he just needs to be snowed in with you."

She nodded approvingly. "What about the pickle?"

He turned to study the ornament in question, which he'd hung on a high branch. It was nubby and dark green, dusted with glitter, twinkling in the light. "It's a very handsome pickle, I have to say."

"You're stalling."

"Hmm." He pretended to be deep in thought over the possible significance of a pickle.

She scoffed at him. "You haven't got a clue."

"Wait." He put up a hand. "It's all coming back to me now."

"Yeah, right."

"Didn't I read somewhere that you hide a pickle ornament on the tree and the kid who finds it gets something special? Also, I think I remember hearing that pickle ornaments bring good luck."

"You're actually smirking," she accused.

"Me? No way. I never smirk."

"You knew all along."

He caught her hand and pulled her in close. "Do you think I'll get lucky?" He kissed her. "Never mind. I already have."

"Oh, yeah," she answered softly. "Pickle or no pickle, from now until New Year's, I'm your sure thing."

* * *

Later, they had hot chocolate on the front porch, with Zoya stretched out at their feet and gnawing enthusiastically on a rawhide bone.

Sabra had barely emptied her mug and set it down on the porch beside her chair when Matthias held out his hand to her.

The second she laid her fingers in his, he was pulling her up and out of the chair, over onto his lap.

Things got steamy fast. In no time, she was topless, with her pants undone.

She loved every minute of it, out there in the cold December night, with the hottest man she'd ever met to keep her toasty warm.

The next morning, he snuck down the stairs while she was still drowsing. When she followed the smell of fresh coffee down to the main floor, he didn't say a word until she'd savored that first cup.

"I have a Christmas Eve request," she said over breakfast.

He rose from his chair to bend close and kiss her, a kiss that tasted of coffee and cinnamon rolls and the promise of more kisses to come. "Anything. Name it."

"I want to finish the hike to the falls that I started last year."

He sank back to his chair. "It's rough going. Lots of brush and then several stretches over heavily logged country, where it's nothing but dirt and giant tree stumps, most of them out of the ground, gnarly with huge roots."

She gave him her sweetest smile. "You said 'anything.' And I still want to go."

They set out half an hour later.

Matthias kept Zoya on a leash most of the way. They wound through barren stretches of rough, logged terrain, eventually entering the forest again, where the trail was so completely overgrown, it grew difficult to make out the path.

They bushwhacked their way through it. At one point, Sabra turned to look back for no particular reason—and saw snowcapped Mt. Rainier in the distance. She got out her phone and snapped a picture of it.

They went on to the top of the falls. It wasn't much to look at. The trees grew close and bushy, obscuring the view. They drank from their water bottles and he poured some into a collapsible bowl for Zoya.

"It's beautiful from below." He pointed into the steep canyon. "I mean, if you're up for beating your way down through the bushes."

"Yes!" She said it with feeling, to bolster her own flagging enthusiasm for the task. The overcast sky seemed to be getting darker. "No rain in the forecast, right?"

He gave her his smug look. "Or so all the weather services have predicted."

"We should get back, huh?"

He pretended to consider her question. "I thought you wanted to get a good view of the falls."

She leaned his way and bumped him with her shoulder. "That sounds like a challenge."

He gave a lazy shrug. "It's no problem if you think it's too much for you."

She popped the plug back into her water bottle. "That does it. We are going down."

And down they went.

Zoya was amazing, effortlessly balanced on only three legs. She bounced along through the underbrush, never flagging. Sabra and Matthias had a little more difficulty, but they kept after it—and were rewarded at the bottom by the gorgeous sight of the tumbling white water from down below.

"Worth it?" he asked.

"Definitely." She got a bunch of pictures on her phone.

"Come here." He hooked his giant arm around her waist and hauled her close, claiming her lips in a long, deliciously dizzying kiss. She got lost in that kiss—lost in *him*, in Matthias, in the miracle of this thing between them that was still so compelling after a whole year apart.

Twice in her life, she'd almost said *I do*, but she'd never felt anything like this before. She loved just being with him, making love for hours, laughing together, sharing the most basic, simple pleasures, the two of them and Zoya, in a one-room cabin.

Or out in the wild at the foot of a waterfall.

A drop of rain plopped on her forehead. Then another, then a whole bunch of them.

It was like someone up there had turned on a faucet. The sky just opened wide and the water poured down.

They both tipped their faces up to it, laughing.

"Why am I not the least bit surprised?" she asked.

He kissed her again, quick and hard, as the water ran down her face and trickled between their fused lips.

"Come on." He pulled up her hood and snapped

the closure at her throat. "Let's find shelter. We can wait out the worst of it."

"What shelter?" She scoffed at him. "I haven't seen any shelter."

"Follow me." He pulled up his own hood. "Zoya, heel." He set off, the dog looping immediately into position on his left side. "Good girl." He pulled a treat from his pocket. Zoya took it from his hand as he started back up the hillside. Sabra fell in behind them.

When they got to the trail, it was still coming down, every bit as thick and hard as the day they'd met. They set off back the way they'd come. She had waterproof gear this time, so most of her stayed dry. It could have been worse.

About a mile or so later, Matthias veered from the path they'd taken originally. The brush grew denser and the rain came down harder, if that was even possible.

"Did you say there would be shelter?" she asked hopefully from behind him.

Just as the question escaped her lips, a shelflike rock formation came into view ahead. She spotted the darkened space between the stones. He ducked into the shadows, Zoya right behind him.

Sabra followed. It was a shallow depression in the rock, not quite a cave, but deep enough to get them out of the deluge.

"Get comfortable." He slid off his pack and sat with his back to the inner wall. Zoya shook herself, sending muddy water flying, and then flopped down beside him as Sabra set her pack with his. "It could be a while." He reached up a hand to her.

She took it, dropping to his other side, pulling on

his hand so that she could settle his arm across her shoulders. "Cozy."

"Ignore the muddy dog smell."

She pushed back her hood and sniffed the air. "Heaven." And it kind of was, just to be with him. A world apart, only the two of them and Zoya and the roar of the rain outside their rocky shelter. She asked, "What's your deepest fear?"

"Getting serious, are we?" He pressed his cold lips to the wet hair at her temple.

"Too grim? Don't answer."

"No, it's good. I can go there. A desk job would be pretty terrifying."

"You're right." She leaned her head on his shoulder. "All that sitting. Very scary."

"I like to keep moving."

"Me, too."

"What are *you* afraid of?" he asked.

She didn't even need to think about it. "That I'll never be able to make myself go back and live at our farm."

He waited until she looked up into his waiting eyes. "It's that bad?"

"Yeah. Because it was so good once. I have too many beautiful memories there, you know? The farm was always my future, always what I wanted to do with my life. And now it's just a sad place to me. I go for a visit, and all I want is to leave again."

He tipped up her chin with the back of his hand. "How's your dad doing?"

She gazed up into those deep blue eyes and felt *seen*, somehow. Cherished. Protected. Completely accepted. "He's thin, my dad. It's like he's slowly disappearing. I need to spend more time with him. But I can't bear to be there. Still, I *need* to be there. I told him at Thanksgiving that I would move home, work the farm with him, the way we always planned. I said I wanted to spend more time with him."

"You sound doubtful."

"I guess he noticed that, too. He said that he was doing fine and he knew that coming home wasn't going to work for me. He said that I had my own life and I should do what *I* wanted."

"He's a good guy, huh?"

"My dad? The best—just, you know, sad. The lights are on but he's not really home." She laid her head on his shoulder again. They watched the rain together.

She must have dozed off, because she suddenly became aware that the rain had subsided to a light drizzle. Zoya's tags jingled as she gave herself a scratch.

And suddenly, Sabra wanted to get up, move on. "Let's hit the trail, huh?"

"Sure."

They shouldered their packs and set out again.

Matt really wouldn't have minded at all if this holiday season never came to an end. It was so easy and natural with Sabra. They could talk or not talk. Tell each other painful truths, or hike for an hour without a word spoken. Didn't matter. It was all good.

Back at the cabin, they gave Zoya a bath.

Then they rinsed the mud out of the tub and took a long bath together. That led to some good times on the sofa and then later upstairs.

They came down to eat and to play Scrabble naked.

She beat the pants off him—or she would've, if he'd had pants on.

By midnight, she was yawning. She went on upstairs alone. He put his clothes back on. Then he and Zoya, some nice blocks of basswood and his Swiss Army knife spent a couple of quality hours out on the porch.

He climbed the stairs to the loft smiling.

When he slid under the covers with her, she shivered and complained that his feet were freezing. But when he pulled her close and wrapped himself around her, she gave a happy sigh and went right back to sleep.

Christmas morning zipped past in a haze of holiday tunes, kisses and laughter.

Matt had left the gifts from his family at home to open later and they gave each other simple things, silly things. He'd carved her another porcupine, a bigger one, for a doorstop. She had two gifts for him: a giant coffee mug with the woodsman's coat of arms, which included crossed axes and a sustainable forestry slogan; and a grenade-size wilderness survival kit that contained everything from safety pins to fish hooks and lines, water bags, candles and a knife.

The afternoon was clear and they went for another hike.

On the twenty-sixth, they drove down the coast to the pretty town of Manzanita and had dinner at a great seafood place there. He'd almost suggested they try a restaurant he liked in Astoria, but then decided against it. They had an agreement, after all, to keep their real lives separate. She'd told him last year that her farm was near Svensen, which was technically in Astoria. He kind of thought it might be pushing things, to take her too close to home.

And he *wasn't* pushing, he kept reminding himself. She'd said she wasn't ready for anything more than the great time they were having. And he wasn't ready for a relationship, either.

Or he hadn't been.

Until a certain fine brunette broke into his cabin and made him start thinking impossible things. Like how well they fit together.

Like how maybe he *was* ready to talk about trying again with a woman—with *her*.

He kept a damn calendar in his closet, didn't he? A paper one. Who even used paper calendars anymore?

Just lovesick guys like him, schmaltzy guys who had to literally count the days, mark them off with big red x'es, until he could finally see her again.

But how to have the taking-it-to-the-next-level conversation?

He felt like he could say anything to her—except for the thing he most wanted to say.

Sabra, I want more with you. More than Christmas and New Year's. I want the rest of the winter.

And the spring and the summer. And the fall?

I want that, too.

I want it all, Sabra. I want it all with you.

But the days zipped by and he said nothing.

And then the more he thought about it, well, maybe he really wasn't ready. If he was ready, he would open his mouth and say so, now wouldn't he?

* * *

The only problem with this Christmastime as far as Sabra was concerned?

It was all flying by too fast.

Phone numbers, she kept thinking.

Maybe they could just do that, exchange phone numbers. Really, they were so close now, a deep sort of closeness, sometimes easy. Sometimes deliciously intense.

She couldn't bear to just drive away and not see him until next year—or maybe never, if he found someone else while they were apart. If he...

Well, who knew what might happen in the space of twelve months? They hadn't even talked about whether or not they would meet up again next year.

She needed his phone number. She needed to be able to call him and text him and send him pictures. Of her. In a pink lace bra and an itty-bitty thong.

Seriously, the great sex aside, it was going to be tough for her, when she left him this year. She felt so close to him. It would be like ripping off a body part to say goodbye.

But then, that was her problem, wasn't it?

She got so attached. There was no in-between with her. She fell for a guy and started picking out the china patterns.

This, with Matthias, was supposed to be different. It was supposed to be a way to have it all with this amazing man, but in a Christmas-sized package. With a date-certain goodbye.

Exchanging numbers was a slippery slope and she was not going down it. She was enjoying every minute with him.

And then, on the first of January, she was letting go.

* * *

All of a sudden, it was New Year's Eve.

Matt and Sabra stayed in bed, as they had the year before, only getting up for food and bathroom breaks and to take a shower together—and twice, to take Zoya out for a little exercise.

Matt willed the hours to pass slowly—which only made them whiz by all the faster.

Sabra dropped off to sleep at a little after midnight. He lay there beside her, watching her beautiful face, wanting to wake her up just to have her big eyes to look into, just to whisper with her, have her touch him, have her truly *with* him for every moment he could steal.

Man, he was gone on her.

It was powerful, what he felt for her. Too powerful, maybe.

Dangerous to him, even. To his hard-earned equilibrium.

He'd lived through a boatload of loss and guilt. The guilt over Finn had almost destroyed him before he was even old enough to legally order a beer.

Sometimes he still dreamed about it, about that moment when he turned around in the snowy, silent Siberian wilderness, and his annoying eight-year-old brother wasn't there.

He'd been angry that day—for the whole, endless trip up till then—angry at his parents, at the crap that they put him through, with their damn love of traveling, of seeing the world. That year, it was Russia. They saw Moscow and Saint Petersburg—and of course, they had to visit the Siberian wilderness.

Daniel, the oldest, had somehow gotten out of that

trip. That made Matt the main babysitter of his seven younger siblings.

It had happened on a day trip from Irkutsk. They'd stopped for lunch somewhere snowy and endless; off in the distance, a stand of tall, bare-looking trees. Matt just had to get away. He decided on a walk across the flat snow-covered land, out into the tall trees. He told his parents he was going.

"Alone," he said, scowling.

His mom had waved a hand. "Don't be such a grouch, Matt. Have your walk. We'll keep the other kids here."

He set out.

And Finn, always adventurous, never one to do what he was told to do, had tagged along behind him.

Matt ordered him to go back to the others.

Finn just insisted, *Mom said I could come with you*, and kept following. And then he started chattering, about how he thought the huskies that pulled their sled were so cool, with their weird, bright blue eyes, how he wanted a husky, and he was going to ask Mom for one.

Matt still remembered turning on him, glaring. *"Just shut up, will you, Finnegan? Just. Please. Stop. Talking."*

Finn had stared up at him, wide-eyed. Hurt. Proud. And now silent.

He never said another word.

Five minutes later, Matt turned around again and Finn was gone.

That really was his fault, losing Finn. The guilt that ate at him from the inside was guilt he had earned with his own harsh words, with the ensuing silence that he'd let go on too long.

His parents died two years later, on the first trip they'd taken since Finn disappeared. That trip was just the two of them, Marie and George Bravo, a little getaway to Thailand, to try to recapture the magic they found in traveling after the tragic loss of their youngest son. They'd checked in to the resort just in time for the arrival of the tsunami that killed them.

To Matt, the Thailand getaway had seemed a direct result of his losing Finn in Russia. He'd been sure in his guilty heart that his parents would never have been in Thailand if not for him.

After his parents died, Matt was constantly in trouble. And if you could drink it, snort it or smoke it, Matt was up for it in high school and during those two years at CCC. The only good thing in his life then had been Christy, his girl.

He told Christy everything, all of his many sins. She loved him and forgave him and made him feel better. Until she grew tired of waiting for him to come home from the other side of the world, dumped him and married someone else.

As for Mark and Nelson, well, at least he didn't actively blame himself for their deaths in Iraq. All he'd done in that case was to survive—which had brought its own kind of guilt.

Survivor guilt, he'd learned through living it, was just as bad as the guilt you felt for losing your own brother. It had taken a whole lot of counseling to get on with his life after Iraq.

But he *had* gotten on with it. He was doing all

right now, with a good life and work that he loved. He'd even taken a big step and gotten himself a dog.

And now there was Sabra. And he couldn't help wanting more than Christmas with her.

Just ask for her number. How dangerous can that be?

Damn dangerous, you long-gone fool.

When a man finally finds a certain equilibrium in his life, he's reluctant to rock the boat—even for a chance to take things further with someone like Sabra.

Morning came way too soon. He made her coffee and she drank it in the usual shared silence.

Then he dragged her upstairs again, where they made love once more.

They came down and had breakfast, went outside and sat out on the porch for a while.

And then, around noon, Sabra said she had to get going.

Matt helped her load her stuff into the Subaru. It took no time at all, the minutes zipping by when all he wanted was to grab onto them, make them stand still.

Too soon, they were saying their goodbyes, just like last year, but with Zoya beside them.

Sabra knelt to give his dog a last hug.

When she rose again, she said, "I don't have the words." She gazed up at him through those deep brown eyes that he knew he'd be seeing in his dreams all year long. "It's been pretty much perfect and I hate to go."

Don't, then. Stay. "I hate to *see* you go."

She eased her hand into a pocket and came out with the key.

No way. He caught her wrist and wrapped her fingers tight around it. "Next year. Same time. I'll be here. I hope you will, too."

"Matthias." Those big eyes were even brighter with the shine of barely held-back tears. "Oh, I will miss you…"

Stay.

But he didn't say it. Instead, he reached out and took her by the shoulders, pulling her in close, burying his nose against her hair, which smelled of sunshine and oranges. She wrapped her arms around him, too. He never wanted to let her go.

But it had to be done.

Slowly, she lifted her head. He watched a tear get away from her. It gleamed as it slid down her cheek. Bending close, he pressed his mouth to the salty wetness.

She turned her head just enough so their lips could meet. He gathered her even tighter in his arms, claiming her mouth, tasting her deeply.

The kiss went on for a very long time. He wished it might last forever, that some miracle might happen to make it so she wouldn't go.

But she hadn't said a word about taking it further— and neither had he.

Her arms loosened around him. He made himself take his hands off her and reached for the door handle, pulling it wide.

She got in and he shut it.

With a last wave through the glass of the window, she started the engine.

He stepped back. Zoya gave a whine.

"Sit," he commanded.

The husky dropped to her haunches beside him. He watched Sabra go, not turning for the porch steps until the blue Subaru disappeared around the first bend in the twisting dirt road.

Chapter Eight

The following May...

Sabra stood by the empty hospital bed her father didn't need anymore. She held a plastic bag full of clothes and other personal belongings that Adam Bond wouldn't ever wear again.

Really, there was nothing more to do here at Peaceful Rest Hospice Care. She should go.

But still, she just stood there, her dad's last words to her whispering through her head. *Don't cry, sweetheart. I love you and I hate to leave you, but I'm ready to go. You see, it's not really cancer. It's just my broken heart...*

"There you are." Peyton stood in the open door to the hallway.

Iris, who stood behind her, asked, "Have you got everything?"

Words had somehow deserted her. Sabra hard-swallowed a pointless sob and held up the bag of useless clothing.

"Oh, honey," said Peyton, and came for her, Iris right behind her.

They put their arms around her, Iris on one side and Peyton on the other. She let herself lean on them and felt a deep gratitude that they were there with her.

"Come on," whispered Iris, giving her shoulders a comforting squeeze. "It's time to go."

That June...

At Berry Bog Farm, the office was the large extra room at the rear of the house, between the kitchen and the laundry room, just off the narrow hallway that opened onto a screened-in porch.

Sabra sat at the old oak desk that had been her father's and his father's before him. She scrolled through the spreadsheet showing income and expenses as she waited for Nils Wilson, her father's longtime friend and top farmhand.

The back door to the screen porch gave a little screech as it opened.

She called out, "In the office, Nils!" and listened to the sound of his footfalls on the wide-plank floor as he approached.

He appeared in the doorway to the back hall, tall and skinny as ever, with a long face to match the rest of him. Deep grooves had etched themselves on either side of his mouth and across his high, narrow forehead. "Hey, pumpkin." He'd always called her pumpkin, for as long as she could remember.

She got up and went to him for a hug. He enfolded her in his long arms. She breathed in the smell of cut grass and dirt that always seemed to cling to him, a scent she found infinitely comforting, a scent to soothe her troubled soul. She asked after his wife of thirty-two years. "How's Marjorie?"

"About the same." Twenty-four years ago, when Sabra was still toddling around in diapers, Nils and Marjorie had put up a manufactured home across the front yard from the farmhouse. Marjorie worked wherever she was needed. She raised goats and chickens and she ran the farm's fresh flower business. She sold gorgeous bunches of them at local markets and also to several florist shops in the area. "She runs me ragged." Nils put on a long-suffering look.

Sabra smiled at that. "And you wouldn't have it any other way."

"Humph," said Nils, meaning yes. He liked to play it grumpy sometimes, but everyone knew how much he loved his wife.

"I missed her this morning when I drove in." Sabra gestured toward the two guest chairs opposite the desk. Nils followed her over there and they sat down.

"You know how she is," said Nils. "Up with the roosters, ready to work."

"I know. I'll catch her this evening."

"Come for dinner?"

"I'll be there."

He reached across the short distance between them to put his wrinkled, work-roughened hand over hers. "How're you holdin' up?"

Her throat ached, suddenly, the ache of tears. She gulped them down. "All right."

He shook his head. "Pumpkin, you were his shining light."

She sniffed and sat up straighter. "No. Mom was that. But he was a good dad. The best." *And I should have been here for him.*

Nils gave her hand a squeeze before pulling back. "So. We're gonna talk business now, is that it?"

"Yes, we are."

"Good. When are you coming home to stay?"

That lump in her throat? It was bigger than ever. "Well, I, um…"

Nils got the message. "You're not coming home." He said it flatly, his disappointment clear.

"I just, well, I hope you and Marjorie will stay on."

"Of course we will."

"We'll change our arrangement. I will drive up every couple of weeks, to keep on top of things. But you'll be running the place. Both you and Marjorie will be getting more money."

"Pumpkin, I got no doubt you will be fair with us. That's not the question. It's about you."

"Nils, I—"

"No. Now, you hear me out. You are a Bond, a farmer to the core. You were born to run Berry Bog Farm. I just want you to think on it. You belong here with us. Won't you come home at last?"

"I'm just, well, I'm not ready to do that and I don't know when I will be ready."

What she didn't tell him was that she was considering putting the farm up for sale. She *would* tell him, of course, as soon as she'd made up her mind.

Right now, though?

She felt she ought to sell, that she would never be able to come back and live here, that just showing up every few weeks to go over the books and handle any necessary business was almost more than she could bear. There were far too many memories here, from happy through bittersweet all the way to devastating.

So yeah. She ought to sell. If she did, she would see to it that Nils and Marjorie were provided for. But no matter how much she settled on them, they wouldn't be happy if she sold the place. The farm was their home.

And really, she couldn't stand the thought of that, either, of letting the land that was her heritage go.

Which left her in a bleak limbo of grief and indecision.

Later, in the evening, after dinner with the Wilsons, she trudged upstairs to her dad's room and tackled packing up his things. As she cleaned out his closet, her thoughts turned to Matthias. She missed him. She ached to have a long talk with him, to feel his muscled arms around her. Life would be so much more bearable if she could have him near.

She paused, her head in the closet, one of her dad's plaid jackets in her hands—a Pendleton, red and black. Adam Bond had always been a sucker for a nice Pendleton. Shirts, jackets, coats, you name it. He had a lot of them. They were excellent quality. People knew he liked them and gave them to him for Christmas and his birthday.

A sob stuck in her throat because he would never wear his Pendletons again.

Backing out of the closet with the jacket in her

hand, she sank to the edge of the bed, putting her palm down flat on the wedding ring quilt her mom had made before Sabra was even a twinkle in her dad's eye.

Idly, she traced the circular stitching in the quilt, thinking of Matthias—his blue, blue eyes, his beautiful, reluctant smile. The way he held her, sometimes hard and tight, like he wanted to absorb her body into his. And sometimes so tenderly, with a deep, true sort of care.

Really, it wouldn't be difficult at all to track him down. He worked for the Department of Fish and Wildlife locally and he had a big family in Valentine Bay.

Would he be angry with her for breaking their rules?

Or would he hold out his arms to her and gather her close? Would he say how happy he was that she'd come to find him? Would he promise her that eventually this grayness would pass, that things would get better and life would make sense again?

She laughed out loud to the empty room, a hard, unhappy sound.

Because she was being sloppy and sentimental. She wasn't going to contact him. She and Matthias had what they had. It was tenuous and magical and only for Christmas.

No way would she ruin it by trying to make it more.

That July...

Matt had two remaining relatives on his mother's side of the family—Great-Uncle Percy Valentine, who'd given him the cabin, and Percy's sister, Great-Aunt Daffodil Valentine.

In their eighties, the never-married brother and sister lived at Valentine House on the edge of Valentine City Park. Matt found his great-aunt and uncle charming and eccentric, sharp-witted and no-nonsense. Daffy and Percy came to all the big family gatherings. But Matt made it a point to drop by and see them at home now and then, too.

He always brought takeout when he came. This time, Daffy had requested "Bacon cheeseburgers with the works, young man."

Matt knew how to take an order and arrived bearing grease-spotted white bags from a Valentine Bay landmark, Raeleen's Roadside Grill. He'd brought the cheeseburgers, fries, onion rings and milkshakes—chocolate for him and Daffy, vanilla for Uncle Percy.

Letha March, who'd been cooking and cleaning at Valentine House for as long as Matt could remember, answered the door and ushered him and Zoya into the formal parlor, which contained too much antique furniture, an ugly floral-pattered rug, and his great-aunt and uncle.

"You got Raeleen's!" Daffy clapped her wrinkled hands in delight. "You always were my favorite great-nephew."

"Aunt Daffy, I know you say that to all of us."

Daffy patted his cheek and smiled up at him fondly as Percy bent to greet Zoya. Letha got out the TV trays so they could chow down right there in the parlor the way they always did.

As they ate, Uncle Percy reported on his progress with the search for Finn. Percy, who often referred to himself as "the family sleuth," had been in charge of the search from the beginning. He worked with private investigators, a series of them. Each PI would find out what he or she could and turn in a report. And then Percy would hire someone else to try again. Each investigator got the benefit of the information his predecessors had uncovered. For all the years of searching, they hadn't found much.

But Percy would never give up. And he and Matt had agreed that when, for whatever reason, Percy could no longer run the search, Matt would step up.

"So there you have it," Percy concluded. "As usual, it's not a lot."

Matt thanked him and they made encouraging noises at each other in order not to get too discouraged. No matter how hopeless it seemed sometimes, the worst thing would be to give up and stop looking.

Daffy slipped Zoya a French fry. "Now tell us what is happening in your life, Matthias." She and Percy always called him by his full name.

Same as Sabra did.

Sabra.

He'd been thinking of her constantly. He wanted more time with her, wanted to take it beyond the cabin, make it real between them. They could go slow. She was in Portland, after all. They would have to make some effort to be together.

But he was willing. He wanted to be with her. Whatever it took.

"What is that faraway look in your eye?" asked Uncle Percy.

Matt shocked the hell out of himself by telling them the truth. "I've met someone. Her name is Sabra Bond.

Born and raised on a farm near Astoria. Now she manages a restaurant in Portland. She has dark hair and big brown eyes and she's smart and funny and tough and beautiful. I'm crazy about her."

He told them how and when he'd met her and about the two Christmases they'd spent together at the cabin. He even explained about the agreement—just the two of them, just for Christmas, no contact otherwise.

"But you want more," said Aunt Daffy.

"I do, yeah."

"It does my old heart good," said Uncle Percy, "to see you coming back from all you've been through."

Daffy gave a slow nod. "You are truly healing, Matthias, and that is a beautiful thing to see."

Uncle Percy reached over and clapped a hand on his arm. "Finding yourself, that's what you're doing. Didn't I tell you that you would?"

"Yes, you did."

"We're so happy for you," cried Daffy.

"I just… I'm not sure how to try for more with her, not sure how to ask her, not sure what to say."

"Just speak from your heart," advised Daffy. "The specific words will come to you, as long as you show your true self and tell her clearly what you want."

Percy added, "Be honest and forthright and it will all work out."

Later that night, at home, Matt considered taking Percy's advice to heart immediately. How hard could it be to find her, really? Online searches aside, there were only so many farms on the outskirts of Astoria.

But then, well, no.

Stalking the woman wasn't part of their deal.

Being patient wouldn't kill him. He would wait for Christmas and pray she showed up this year, too.

Matt marked another X on his calendar, bringing him one day closer to seeing her again.

That September...

"Come on, man." Jerry tipped his head toward the dark-haired woman three tables over. "She's a knock-out and she likes you. What are you saving it for, I'd just like to know?" It was yet another Friday night at Beach Street Brews and as always, Jerry was after him to hook up with someone.

Matt wondered why he'd come. "Cut it out, Jer. Let me enjoy my beer." Matt needed that beer. He also needed not to be hassled while drinking it.

A week before, his brother Daniel's wife Lillie had given birth to twins, Jake and Frannie. The twins were fine, but two days after the birth, Lillie had died from complications mostly due to lupus. It was a tough time in the Bravo family.

And the last thing Matt needed right now was a night with a stranger.

Jerry poured himself another glass from the pitcher on the table between them. "This is getting ridiculous. I've gotta meet your holiday hookup, see what's so special you're willing to go all year without—"

"Drop it, Jerry." Matt turned and looked his ag-gravating friend squarely in the eye. "Just let it go."

"I don't get it. That's all I'm sayin'."

"Yeah, well. You've said it. Repeatedly. I heard you. Stop."

"It's not healthy to—"

"That does it." Matt shoved back his chair. "I'm outta here."

"Aw, c'mon, man. Don't get mad."

"You have fun, Jerry." Matt threw some bills on the table.

Jerry looked kind of crestfallen. "Listen. I'm sorry. I've got a big mouth, I know. I should try to keep a lid on it."

"Yeah, you should—and you're forgiven."

"Great. C'mon, stay."

He clapped his friend on the shoulder. "Gotta go."

"So…maybe *I* should make a move on her?" Jerry gave the dark-haired woman a wave.

Matt just shook his head and made for the door.

Three months left until Christmas at the cabin. Losing Lillie really had him thinking that life flew by way too fast, that everything could change when you least expected it and a man needed to grab what he wanted and hold on tight.

This year, if Sabra showed up, he was not letting her go without asking for more.

December 23, two years ago…

She was already there!

Matt saw the lights gleaming from the cabin windows at the same turn where he'd spotted them two years before. His heart seemed to leap upward in his chest and lodge squarely in his throat. His pulse raced, gladness burning along every nerve in his body as he rounded the next turn and the turn after that.

The front door swung open as he rolled into the yard and pulled to a stop behind the Subaru.

Sabra emerged dressed in a long black sweater and leggings printed with reindeer and snowflakes, knee-high boots on her feet. Her hair was longer this time, the dark curls loose on her shoulders. He couldn't wait to get his hands in them.

Shoving the car into Park, he turned off the engine, threw the door wide and jumped out to catch her as she hurled herself into his outstretched arms.

"At last," they whispered in unison.

And then he was kissing her, breathing in her sweet, incomparable scent, going deep, hard and hungry. She laughed as he angled his mouth the other way and she jumped up, lifting those fine legs and wrapping them good and tight around him, her arms twined behind his neck.

He was halfway up the steps, devouring her mouth as he went, before she broke their lip-lock and started to speak. "I'm so—"

"Get back here." He cradled her head, holding her still so he could claim those beautiful lips again.

Before he crashed into her that time, she got a single word out. "Zoya?"

He groaned, gentled his hold and pressed his forehead to hers. "See what you do to me? I almost forgot my own dog."

She took his face between her hands and offered eagerly, "One more kiss?"

He gave it to her, long and deep, turning as he kissed her, heading back down the steps. She dropped her feet to the ground at the back of the vehicle. He let her go reluctantly and opened the hatch. Zoya rose in her crate, stretching and yawning. "Sorry, girl," he muttered. Behind him, he heard Sabra chuckle.

"C'mon out." He opened the crate and helped the husky down to the ground.

"Zoya! It's so good to see you." Sabra knelt to greet her, scratching her ruff, giving her long strokes down her back as Zoya whined and wriggled with happiness. "I've missed you so much…"

Matt waited impatiently for her to finish her reunion with his dog. When she finally rose, he reached for her again.

She danced away, laughing, her gaze on the tree tied to the roof rack. "I swear, you found a thicker tree than last year. So gorgeous…"

"Just beautiful," he agreed. He wasn't referring to the tree. Catching her elbow, he pulled her close again. "So then. Where were we?"

Those dark eyes held a teasing light. "We should bring it in, put it in water and—"

With a growl, he covered her sweet mouth with his, taking her by the waist and then lifting her. She got the hint, surrendering her mouth to him as she wrapped her legs and arms around him again.

He carried her up the steps and in the door without stopping that time, counting on Zoya to stick close behind. As soon as they cleared the threshold, Sabra stuck out a hand and shoved the door shut.

Reluctantly, he lifted his mouth from hers, noting that not only had she gotten the fire going, she'd set out water for Zoya. The dog was already lapping it up.

"Oh, I cannot believe you're actually here." Her smile could light up the darkest corner of the blackest night.

"It's been too long," he grumbled.

"Oh, yes it has." She caught his lower lip between

her pretty teeth and bit down lightly, sending heat and need flaring even higher within him.

"That does it," he muttered. "We're going upstairs."

"Yes," she replied, suddenly earnest. "*Now*, Matthias. Please."

He told Zoya to stay and started walking, carrying her up there, kissing her the whole way.

At the bed, she clung to him. He started undressing her anyway, pulling her long sweater up and away, not even pausing to give her lacy purple bra the attention it deserved, just unhooking it, ripping the straps down and whipping it off her, revealing those beautiful high pink-tipped breasts. "Everything. Off," he commanded, peeling her legs from around him, setting her down on the mattress.

She didn't argue. He stripped and she stripped. In a short chain of heated seconds, they were both naked. He went down to the bed with her, grabbing for her, gathering her close.

This was no time to play.

It had been way too long and he couldn't wait. Lucky for him, she seemed to feel the same.

"Hurry," she egged him on. "I have missed you so much…"

He touched the heart of her: soaking wet, so ready.

"Yes," she begged him. "Please. I want you now."

With a groan, he stuck out a hand for the bedside drawer.

She curled her fingers tightly around him, bringing a rough moan of pure need from him as she held his aching length in place. He rolled the condom halfway on and she took over, snugging it all the way down.

That did it. He was not waiting for one second longer.

Taking her by the shoulders, he rolled her under him, easing his thigh between hers and coming into her with a single deep thrust.

She moaned his name and wrapped her legs and arms around him, pulling him in so tight against her, as though she couldn't bear to leave an inch of empty space between her body and his.

They moved together, hard and fast. There was nothing but the feel of her, the taste of her mouth, the scent of her silky hair tangling around him, the heat of her claiming him, taking him down.

He gave himself up to it—to her, to this magic between them, to the longing that never left him in the whole year without her.

"Yes!" she cried, and then crooned his name, "Matthias, missed you. Missed you so much…"

Just barely, he held himself back from the brink, waiting for her, drawing it out into sweet, endless agony.

And then, at last, she cried out and he felt her pulsing around him. Through a monumental effort of will, he stayed with her as she came apart in his arms. Finally, with a shout of pure triumph, he gave in and let his finish take him down.

So tightly, he held her, never wanting to let go.

But when he finally loosened his hold on her, she gave a gentle push to his shoulders. He took the hint and braced up on his arms to grin down at her.

But his grin didn't last.

She met his gaze, her eyes haunted looking in her

flushed face. Her soft mouth trembled. "Oh, Matthias."

"What? Sabra, what's the matter?"

Her face crumpled and she burst into tears.

Chapter Nine

"Sabra—sweetheart, talk to me. Come on, what is it?" Matthias was staring down at her, golden eyebrows drawn together, clearly stunned at this out-of-nowhere crying jag.

The tears poured from her, blurring her vision. "Sorry. So sorry. I can't… I don't…" Apparently, complete sentences were not available to her right now. She sniffled loudly and swiped at her nose.

"Stay right there," he instructed, easing his body off hers. She squinted through her blurry eyes, trying to contain her sobs as he removed the condom and tied it off. The tears wouldn't stop falling.

Miserable, she turned away from him. Curling herself in a ball, she tried to get control of herself, but for some reason, that only made the tears come faster.

The bed shifted as he rose.

A minute later, he touched her shoulder, the gentlest, kindest sort of touch. "Hey. Here you go…"

With a watery little sob, she rolled back to face him. "Just ignore me. That's what you should do. Just go on downstairs and—"

"I'm going nowhere. Here. Take these." He handed her a couple of tissues.

"Oh, Matthias." She swiped at her nose and her cheeks. "This, um, isn't about you. I hope you know that. I'm so glad to see you. So glad to be with you. But this…" She gestured with the tissues at the whole of herself. "I don't know why I'm doing this. I don't know…what's the matter with me, to be such a big crybaby right now." She sniffled and stared up at him, *willing* him to understand, though she'd said nothing coherent so far, nothing to help him figure out what was bothering her. "I don't know what I'm saying, even. Because, what *am* I saying? I have no idea."

"It's okay."

"No, it is not."

"Well, I can see that. But I mean, between me and you, everything is okay. I'm right here and whatever you need, I'll do whatever it takes to make sure you get it." He got back on the bed with her. "Now, come here." He took her shoulders gently. She scrambled into his lap like an overgrown child and buried her face against his broad, warm chest. "You're safe," he soothed. "I'm right here." He stroked her hair, petted her shoulder, rubbed his big hand up and down her back.

She huddled against him, relishing the comfort he offered, matching her breaths to his in order to calm herself, endlessly grateful to have his steady strength to cling to.

For several minutes, neither of them spoke. He held her and she was held by him. Finally, she looked up to find his eyes waiting.

"What is it?" he asked. "Talk to me."

She sniffled and wiped more tears away. "My dad died."

His forehead scrunched up. "Oh, Sabra." He ran his hand down her hair, brushed a kiss against her still-wet cheek. "When?"

"In the spring. He, um, it was cancer, non-Hodgkin's lymphoma. He didn't get treatment. Not for years, I found out later. And by the time he did, it was too late. He, well, he wanted to die. He told me so, right there at the end—not that he *had* to tell me. I knew. He never got over my mom's death. He just, well, he didn't want to be in this world without her."

Matthias pulled her close again. She felt his warm breath brush the crown of her head. "I'm so sorry…"

She wiped her nose with the wadded-up tissues. "I should feel better about it. I mean, he got what he wanted, right?"

He kissed her temple. "That doesn't mean you can't miss him and want him back with you."

"He was ready. He said so."

"But *you* weren't ready to lose him."

She tipped her face up to meet his clear blue eyes again. "You're right. I wasn't ready. I also wasn't *there* when he needed me. He would always say he was fine and he understood that I needed to get out, make my own way, move to Portland, all that." Another hard sob escaped her. She dabbed her eyes and shook her head. "I should have tried harder, should have kept after him, gotten him to a doctor sooner. When he said he was all right, I just accepted it, took his word for it. And now, well, he's gone and I've got more regrets than I can name. I can't bear to sell the farm, but I couldn't stand to live there, either. It's like I'm being torn in different directions and I can't make up my mind, can't decide which way to go."

"So don't decide."

She blinked at him, surprised. "*Don't* decide?"

"Do you have someone you trust taking care of the farm?"

"Yeah, but—"

"If you don't *have* to decide right now, don't. Wait."

"Wait for…?"

"Until you're ready."

"But I'm a mess. How am I supposed to know when I'm ready?"

He looked at her so tenderly, not smiling, very serious. But there was a smile lurking in his eyes, a smile that reassured her, that seemed to promise everything would somehow work out right in the end. "The question is, do you think you're ready to decide about the farm right now?"

"God, no."

"Well, there you go. Take it from someone who's had a whole hell of a lot of therapy. When you're grieving, it's not a good time to have to make big choices. Sometimes life doesn't cooperate and a choice *has* to be made anyway. Then you do the best you can and hope it all works out. But you just said you don't have to decide right this minute. So don't. Procrastination isn't always a bad thing."

She turned the idea over in her mind. "Don't decide…"

"Not until you either *have* to decide, or you're sure of what you want."

What he said made a lot of sense. "Okay then. I will seriously consider procrastination." She giggled at the absurdity of it—and realized she felt better. She really did. Sometimes a girl just needed a long, ugly cry and some excellent advice.

She snuggled in close, enjoying his body heat. For a little while, they simply sat there in the middle of the rumpled bed, holding each other.

"What about you?" she asked softly. "Any big changes in your life since last Christmas?"

He told her of his sister-in-law, who'd died in early September after giving birth to twins. "Her name was Lillie. She was only a year older than me, but still, she was kind of a second mother to all of us after our parents died, so losing her is a little like losing our mom all over again."

She lifted up enough to kiss his cheek. "That's so sad."

"Yeah. We all miss her. And my brother Daniel, her husband, has always been one of those too-serious kind of guys. Since Lillie died, I don't think anyone has seen Daniel crack a smile."

"Give him time."

"Hey. What else can we do?"

"Life is just so *hard* sometimes…" She tucked her head beneath his chin and he idly stroked her hair.

Downstairs, she heard Zoya's claws tapping the wood floor. The husky gave a hopeful little whine.

Sabra stirred. "We should get moving. Your dog is lonely and your Jeep is not going to unload itself."

The next day, Christmas Eve, they decorated the tree and Matt took her out to dinner at that seafood place in Manzanita. When they got back to the cabin, they sat out on the porch until after midnight, laughing together, holding hands between their separate chairs until he coaxed her over onto his lap. It started snowing.

"It's beautiful," she said as they watched the delicate flakes drifting down.

"And the best kind, too," he agreed.

She chuckled and leaned her head against his shoulder. "Yeah. The kind that doesn't stick."

By Christmas morning, the snow had turned to rain.

All Christmas day and the day after, Matt tried to find the right moment to talk about the future. That moment hadn't come yet, though. But he was waiting for it, certain he would know when the time was right.

It was a bittersweet sort of Christmas. Sabra had lost her dad and Lillie was gone from the Bravo family much too soon. Still, Matt was hopeful. He felt close to Sabra—closer than ever, really.

Every hour with her was a gift, fleeting, gone too soon. But exactly what he needed, nonetheless. She was everything he wanted, everything he'd almost given up hope of having in his life.

Like last year, they went hiking together. He loved that she enjoyed a good, sweaty hike, that she didn't mind slogging through the rain on rough, overgrown terrain for the simple satisfaction of doing it, of catching sight of a hawk high in the sky or a misty waterfall from deep in some forgotten ravine.

He wanted her, *all* of her. He wanted her exclusively and forever. They were meant to be together. He just knew it was time for them to make it *more*.

Too bad that the right moment to ask for her phone number never quite seemed to come.

And the days? They were going by much too fast.

Five days after Christmas, they got up nice and early. Matt made the coffee and was silent while Sabra had her first cup. They ate breakfast and took Zoya for a walk.

Back in the cabin, Sabra grabbed his hand and led him upstairs. They peeled off their clothes and climbed into bed. The lovemaking was slow and lazy and so good. It only got really intense toward the end.

They'd just fallen away from each other, laughing and panting, when Zoya started whining downstairs.

Sabra sat up, listening. "Is that a car outside?"

Zoya barked then, three warning barks in succession.

By then, Matt was out of the bed and pulling on his jeans. "I'll see what's up." He zipped up his pants and ran down the stairs barefoot, buttoning up his flannel shirt as he went.

The knock on the door came just as he reached the main floor. From the foot of the stairs, he could see out the front windows.

Parked behind his Jeep and Sabra's Outback was a

Silverado 4x4 with the Oregon State Police logo on the door and State Trooper printed over the front wheel.

Matt instructed Zoya to sit and opened the door. "Jerry," he said wearily.

Jerry grinned. "Hey, buddy. Hope I didn't interrupt anything. I was in the area and I thought, why not stop in and say hi?"

As if he didn't know what his old friend was up to. "You should call first."

Jerry got that busted look. "Yeah, well I…" He swiped off his hat and leaned around him. "Hey!"

"Hello," Sabra said as she came up beside him wearing the sweater and jeans he'd taken off her a half hour before.

Matt introduced them.

Sabra seemed okay with Jerry dropping in. Matt had mentioned his friend to her in passing more than once. She was aware that Jerry and Matt had known each other most of their lives.

Really, it shouldn't be a big deal, but it pissed Matt off that Jerry had dropped in without checking first, mostly because of what Jer had said that night in September, about how he *had* to meet Sabra, had to see what was so special about her.

"You want some coffee?" Matt asked grudgingly, causing Sabra to shoot him a questioning frown. She'd guessed from his tone that he wasn't happy.

Jerry gave a forced laugh. He knew he was out of bounds. "Coffee would be great."

They had coffee and some Christmas cookies Sabra had brought. They made casual conversation. Jerry said the tree was beautiful and too bad the snow hadn't stuck at least through Christmas day and blah-

blah-blah. At least he was charming and friendly with Sabra.

"I'll walk you out," Matt said when Jerry got up to go.

"Uh, sure." Jerry said how great it was to have met Sabra and she made the same noises back at him.

"I'll be right back," Matt promised.

She gave him a nod, and he followed Jerry out to his patrol truck.

"Okay, what?" mumbled Jerry when they reached the driver's door. "Just say it."

"You got a phone. I got a phone. Why didn't you call first?"

Jerry put his hat back on. "I wanted to meet her, okay? I was afraid you'd say no." Matt just looked at him, dead-on. Jerry stuck his hands in his pockets. "All right, yeah. I should have called. And I'm sorry." He looked kind of sad.

And why was it always damn-near impossible to stay pissed off at Jerry? "I told you the situation. As of now, friends and family don't enter into what I have with her."

"I get it. My bad."

"Don't pull anything like that again."

"Never." Jerry looked appropriately chastised—but then he slanted Matt a hopeful glance. "She's hot and I like her—and you said 'as of now'? You're planning to take it to the next level, then? Because really, man, I only want you to get whatever makes you happy."

Matt kind of wanted to grab his friend and hug him. But he needed to be sure that Jerry got the message. "Stay out of it, Jer."

"Yeah. I hear you, man. Loud and clear." He climbed in behind the wheel. "Happy New Year, buddy."

"Happy New Year."

"I liked your friend," Sabra said when Matt got back inside the cabin.

"Everybody likes Jer. He told me he thinks you're hot."

One side of her gorgeous mouth quirked up in a reluctant smile. "I'm flattered—I think." She caught the corner of her lip between her teeth, hesitating.

"Go ahead and say it."

"Well, is everything okay with you and him? You seemed kind of annoyed with him."

His heart rate accelerated and his skin felt too hot. He wanted to tell her, right then, how he felt, what he longed for with her.

Was this it, the right time, finally? He stared at her unforgettable face that he missed the whole year long and ached to go for it, this very minute, to finally ask her to consider giving him more than the holidays.

Staring at her, though? It never was enough. He reached out and slipped his hand under the silky fall of her hair. Curling his rough fingers around her smooth nape, he pulled her nice and close. She tipped up her chin and he claimed a kiss.

And when he lifted his head, somehow the moment to ask the big question had passed.

"Well?" she prompted.

"I wasn't happy that he just dropped in without calling, that's all."

"Isn't that kind of what friends do?"

"Sure, mostly. But Jerry *knows*."

"About us, you mean?"

He nodded. "I told him that I'm crazy about you."

She smiled then, a full-out smile. "You did?"

He wished she would smile at him like that every day. Every day, all year round. "Absolutely. Jerry knows we just have Christmastime, that it's just you and me, away from our real lives."

"So, if he'd asked first, you would have told him to stay away?"

"I don't know. I would've asked you. Found out how you felt about his coming by. We would have decided together." And now he *had* to know. "How *do* you feel about it?"

She was biting the corner of her lip again. "I guess you're right. It's supposed to be just us, just for the holidays. Inviting our friends in isn't part of the deal."

Ouch. That wasn't at all what he'd hoped she might say.

Tell her. Ask her. Do it now.

But he hesitated a moment too long.

And she asked, "When you went out to the truck with him, did you make it up with him?"

He let the main issue go to answer her question. "I did. I can never stay mad at Jerry."

"Well, good." She stepped in close again, put her slim hands on his chest and slid them up to link around his neck. "What do you say we take Zoya for a nice long walk?" At their feet, the husky whined her approval of that suggestion. "The weather's just right for it."

He grunted. "Yeah, cloudy with a chance of rain."

"Welcome to Oregon." She kissed him, after which they put on their boots and took the dog outside.

* * *

The rest of that day was gone in an instant and the night that followed raced by even faster.

All of a sudden, it was New Year's Eve. Time for naked Scrabble and naked Clue—naked everything, really. Matt and Sabra only got dressed to take the dog outside.

At midnight, they toasted in the New Year with a nice a bottle of champagne courtesy of Sabra. Upstairs, they made love again. And again after that.

She drifted off to sleep around two in the morning.

Matt stayed awake, planning what he would say before she left tomorrow, trying to think of just the right words that would make her agree they were ready for more than the holidays together.

By noon New Year's Day, he still hadn't said anything. Apparently, he was a complete wimp when it came to asking for what he wanted the most.

At a little after one in the afternoon, she said she had to get her stuff together and get on the road. He helped her load up the Outback, as he had the year before and the year before that.

And then, way too soon, long before he was ready, they were standing by her driver's door and she was saying goodbye. She knelt and made a fuss over Zoya, and then she rose and moved in close, sliding her hands up over his chest slowly, the way she loved to do, hooking them at the back of his neck.

"I hate to leave." She kissed him, a quick brush of those soft lips across his.

He stared down at her, aching inside. She was getting away from him and if she left now without him opening his damn mouth and saying what he needed to say, he would have to break their agreement and track her down in Portland. Either that, or he wouldn't set eyes on her for another damn year—maybe never if something happened and one of them didn't show up next December.

He'd been waiting for the right moment, the right moment that somehow never came. And now here they were and she was going and it was *this* moment.

Or never.

"Matthias?" Her sleek eyebrows drew together in concern. "What's the matter? What's happened?"

He clasped her shoulders—too hard, enough that she winced. "Sorry." He forced himself to loosen his grip. "I…" The words tried to stick in his throat. He pushed them out. "Sabra, I want more."

She stared up at him, her eyes growing wider. "Um, you want…?" He waited. But that was it. That was all she got out.

He tried again. "*This*, you and me for Christmas. It's beautiful. Perfect. Except that it's not enough for me, not anymore. I want to be with you, spend time with you when it's not Christmas. I want to see you in February, in June and in the fall. I want, well, I was thinking we could just start with phone numbers, maybe? Just exchange numbers and then try getting together soon, see how it goes."

She only stared up at him, eyes enormous in her suddenly pale face.

Was this going all wrong?

He kind of thought it might be.

Should he back off?

Probably.

But he'd been such a damn coward for the last ten days. He needed to go for it. Now that he'd finally opened his mouth and said what he wanted, he needed to take it all the way. "Sabra, I—"

She silenced him by putting up her hand between them, pressing her fingers to his lips. "Oh, I just, well, I thought we understood each other, we agreed that we—"

"Stop." He caught her wrist. "Let me finish."

With a shaky sigh, she nodded, carefully pulling free of his grip, stepping back from him—one step. Two.

He got on with it, because no way could he wait another year to tell her what was in his heart. "I'm in love with you, Sabra." A tiny cry escaped her, but she caught herself, pressing her hand to her mouth, swallowing down whatever she might have said next. He barreled on. "I want the rest of my life with you. But I know I'm never going to get it if I don't tell you how much I want you, want *us*, you and me, together. In the real world. I want to meet your friends and introduce you to my family. I want to show you my hometown and get the tour of your farm. I don't want to push you, I—"

"That's not fair." She spoke in an angry whisper.

He blinked down at her. "Excuse me?"

"You *are* pushing me, Matthias. You're asking me for things that I don't know how to give."

Okay, now. That kind of bugged him. That made him mad. He said, way too quietly, "How am I going to have a prayer of getting more from you if I don't ask for it?"

"Well, it's just that we have an agreement. And yet, all of a sudden, you're all about forever."

"Sabra, it's been two years—two years and three Christmases. That is hardly 'all of a sudden.'"

Her soft mouth twisted. "You know what I mean."

"Uh, no. I guess I don't."

"Well, um, last year, for instance?"

"What about it?"

"Last year, I was kind of thinking the same thing."

Hope exploded in his chest. "You were? Because so was I. I wanted to ask you then, for more time, for a chance, but I didn't know where to start."

"Yes, well, it was the same for me." She didn't look happy. Shouldn't she look happy, now they'd both confessed that they wanted the same thing?

He didn't get it. "Well, then?" he prodded. "Sabra, what is the problem? You want more, you just said so. You want more and so do I." He dared a step closer.

She jerked back, whipping up a hand. "You don't understand. That was last year. Everything's different now."

"Why? I don't get it. We're still the same people."

"No. No, we're not." She shook her head wildly. "Everything's changed for me, since my dad died."

"Sabra…"

"No. Wait. Listen, please. I see things so differently. I understand now that I've been kidding myself, thinking someday I would find love and happiness with someone, with *you*."

"But you have it. You have me. I love you."

"Oh, please," she scoffed. "Love and happiness? They just end, Matthias. They end and they leave you alone, with nothing. They leave you a shell of who you were, leave you just getting through the endless days, waiting for the time when it doesn't hurt anymore. And I, well, I can't. I just can't."

"But you said—"

"This." She talked right over him, lifting both hands out to her sides in an encompassing gesture, one that seemed to include him and the cabin, the clearing, the forest, the whole of the small world they shared over Christmas. *"This* is all I have in me. This is all it will ever be. I can never give you anything more and if you need something more, well, then you need to go out and get it."

Sabra glared at Matthias. And he just stared at her—a hurt look, and angry, too.

Well, fine. Let him stare. Let him be angry, as angry as she was—that he'd done this, that he'd sprung this on her. She couldn't take this. She didn't know how to deal.

At the same time, deep within her, a small voice chided that she was way overreacting, that her emotions were knocked all out of whack by her grief over her dad.

She felt so much for the man standing in front of her, felt desire and affection, felt *love.* Yeah. She did. She felt love, deep and strong. She didn't want to lose him.

But she *was* losing him. She *would* lose him. That was how life was—shining moments of joy and beauty, followed by a loneliness that killed.

Considering a future with him right now? It was like trying to decide what to do about the farm. She couldn't go back there and she couldn't let go of it.

It was all mixed up together—the farm, Matthias, her dad.

Her dad, who was gone now. She missed him so much and she despised herself for that, for daring to miss him, when she hadn't been there for him during the last, lonely years of his life.

She'd left him to waste away on his own when he needed her most.

And this, with Matthias, well, what more was there to say? "I really do have to go."

Matt got the message. He got it loud and clear.

She'd cut him off at the knees, wrecked him but good. She had to go?

Terrific. He wanted her out of there, wanted *not* to be looking into those big, wounded eyes.

He reached out and pulled open the door to the Subaru. "Drive safe, Sabra." The words tasted like sawdust in his mouth. Still, he did wish her well. "You take care of yourself."

She stared at him, her eyes bigger than ever, her face much too pale. And then, slowly, she nodded. "You, too." She got in behind the wheel.

This is how it ends, he thought. No goodbye kiss, no hope that there ever might be more.

Not so much as a mention of next year.

There probably wouldn't be a next year—not for the two of them, together. Somehow, he was going to have to learn to accept that.

After this, well, what was there to come back for?

He wanted more and she didn't. Really, where did they go from here?

He shut the door, called to his dog and went up the steps to the cabin without once looking back.

Chapter Ten

Sabra, the following March...

She didn't know what had come over her, really.

A...lightening. A strange sense of promise where for months there had been nothing but despair.

On the spur of the moment, she took four days off work in the middle of the month and drove up to the farm. Nils and Marjorie were at their house when she pulled into the yard. They ran out to greet her, grabbing her in tight hugs, saying what a nice surprise it was to see her. Meaning it, too.

Marjorie took her out to see the lambs. She also met with Nils for a couple of hours. They went over the books, discussed the upcoming market season. Soon, they would be planting blueberries, raspberries, blackberries and strawberries. They talked about the huge number of turkey orders for Thanksgiving—so many, in fact, that they'd already had to stop taking them. Next year, Nils planned to raise more birds.

Sabra joined Marjorie and Nils for dinner. Later, alone in the main house, she wandered the rooms. A cleaning team came in every three weeks to keep things tidy, so the place was in okay shape. But the greenhouse window in the kitchen needed someone to put a few potted plants in there and then take care of them.

And really, when you came right down to it, a kitchen remodel wouldn't hurt, either. In time. And a paint job, definitely. The old homestead could do with a general freshening-up if she ever intended to live here again.

Live here again?

Where had that idea come from?

She shook her head and put the thought from her mind.

That night, she slept in her old room, a dreamless, peaceful sort of sleep—or mostly dreamless, anyway.

Just before dawn she woke and realized she'd been dreaming of Matthias, a simple dream. They were here, in the farmhouse, together. In her dream, they went out to the front porch and sat in the twin rockers her dad had found years ago at a yard sale and refinished himself. Zoya snoozed at their feet.

Sabra sat up in bed, stretched, yawned and looked out the window where the pink fingers of morning light inched across the horizon. Shoving back the covers, she ran over there, pushed the window up and breathed in the cool morning smell of new grass and damp earth.

Spring was here. Already. And leaning on the sill she felt…close. To her mother and her father, to all the generations of Bonds before her.

The idea dawned like the new morning.

She didn't want to sell the farm.

She wanted to move home to stay.

Sabra, that July…

"So just track him down," insisted Iris. "You blew it and you need to reach out, tell him you messed up, that your head was all turned around over your dad dying. You need to beg him for another chance."

"I can't." Sabra dropped a stack of folded clothes into an open box.

"Can't?" Iris scoffed. "Won't. That's what you really mean."

"It wouldn't be right to him," said Sabra.

"Oh, yeah, it would. It's the rightest thing in the world, telling a man who loves you that you love him, too, and want to be with him."

They were at Sabra's apartment—Sabra, Iris and Peyton, too. Sabra was moving home to the farm and her friends were pitching in, helping her pack up to go.

She tried to make Iris understand. "It wasn't our deal to go looking for each other, to go butting into each other's regular lives. If I want to change the agreement, I need to do it when I see him, at Christmas."

"Who says you'll see him at Christmas?"

"Well, what I mean is that next Christmas would be the time to try again, if that's even possible anymore."

Iris shook her head. "Uh-uh. Not buying. You're just making excuses not to step up right now and get straight with the man you love."

Peyton emerged from the closet, her arms full of clothes. "Honey, I'm with Iris on this one." She dropped the clothes on the bed for Sabra to box up. "You screwed up. You need to fix it."

"And I will. At Christmas. I still have the key. I'll show up, as always, and I'll pray that he does, too."

Iris put both hands to her head and made an exploding gesture. "Wrong. Bad. You need to act now. He could find someone else in the next five months."

"He could have found someone else already," Sabra said, something inside of her dying a little at the very thought. "I *told* him to find someone else. I can't go breaking our rules and chasing after him now. If he's found someone new, I've got no right to try to get in the middle of that. I've got no right and I *won't*."

Iris opened her mouth to argue some more, but Peyton caught her eye and shook her head. "It's your call," Iris conceded at last. "But just for the record, I think you're making a big mistake."

Matt, early August...

Friday night at Beach Street Brews was as crowded and loud as ever. Matt was glad to be out, though. Sometimes a guy needed a beer, a bar full of people, and some mediocre rock and roll played at earsplitting levels.

The noise and party atmosphere distracted him, kept him from brooding over Sabra. It had been seven months since she'd made it painfully clear that they were going nowhere. Not ever. He needed to get over her, to get over *himself*.

It was past time for him to stop being an emo idiot and move the hell on. Life was too damn short to spend it longing for a woman who would never give him more than a holiday hookup. He was ready, after all these years, for a real relationship.

And damn it, he was through letting the important things pass him by.

Jerry, across the table from him, leaned in. "Someone's been asking to meet you." Jerry tipped his red head at two pretty women, a blonde and a brunette, as they approached their booth. "The blonde," said Jerry. "Mary's her name…"

The two women reached the booth. Jerry scooted over and patted the empty space next to him. The brunette sat down.

The blonde smiled shyly at Matt. "Matt Bravo," he said.

Her smile got brighter. "Mary Westbrook."

He moved over toward the wall and Mary slid in beside him.

They started talking, Matt and Mary. She'd gone to Valentine Bay High, graduated the same year as his sister Aislinn. Now Mary worked as a physical therapist at a local clinic. She had sky-blue eyes, a great laugh and an easy, friendly way about her.

No, she wasn't Sabra.

But Matt liked her. He liked her a lot.

Early November...

Matt sat on the sofa in his brother Daniel's study at the Bravo family house on Rhinehart Hill. Across the room, beyond his brother's big desk, the window that looked out over the front porch framed a portrait in fall colors, the maples deep red, the oaks gone to gold. Daniel's fourteen-month-old twins, Jake and Frannie, were upstairs with their latest nanny. Sometimes it was hard to believe how big those kids were now, and that it had been over a year since they lost Lillie.

A glass of scotch in each hand, Daniel came and sat in the armchair across the low table from Matt. He handed Matt a glass and offered a toast. "To you, Matt. And to the new woman in your life."

"Thanks." Matt touched his glass to his brother's and sipped. The scotch was excellent, smoky and hot going down.

Daniel took a slow sip, too. "I've been instructed to inform you that we all expect to be meeting Mary at Thanksgiving."

Matt chuckled. "Instructed, huh?"

Daniel didn't crack a smile. But then, he rarely did. "We have four sisters, in case you've forgotten."

"Sisters," Matt kidded back. "Right. I vaguely remember them, yeah."

"They're all pleased to learn you've met someone special. They want to get to know her. Connor and Liam do, too." Connor and Liam were third- and fourth-born in the family, respectively. "And so do I."

"Well, Aislinn has already been after me to bring Mary." The truth was, he'd hesitated over inviting

Mary. "I was kind of thinking it was too soon, you know?"

Daniel said, "It's never too soon if you really like someone."

An image took shape in his mind. It wasn't of Mary and he ordered it gone. "Well, good. I did invite her. She said yes. Mary's looking forward to meeting the family."

"I'm glad. And I'm happy for you…"

Two days later…

Unbuttoning his uniform shirt as he went, Matt led the way into his bedroom, Zoya hopping along behind. She stretched out on the rug by the bed and panted up at him contentedly as he finished getting out of his work clothes and stuffed them in the hamper.

That night, he was taking Mary out to eat and then to a stand-up comedy show at the Valentine Bay Theatre. He grabbed a pair of jeans from a drawer, tossed them across the bed and went to the closet for a shirt to wear under his jacket.

When he grabbed the blue button-down off the rod, he caught sight of a corner of this year's Wild and Scenic Oregon calendar still tacked to the wall. The hangers clattered loudly along the rod as he shoved them back, hard.

Why had he even bought the damn thing this year—and not only bought it, but for several months, continued crossing off the days?

Apparently, for some men, being told to forget it was just never enough.

The calendar was turned to October, with a view

of the Deschutes National Forest in fall. Below the beautiful picture of trees in autumn, the calendar page itself showed not a single red X. He'd stopped marking the days the month before.

And why was he keeping it? The calendar was of zero use or interest to him now.

He yanked it off the wall. The tack went flying. He heard it bounce on the closet floor, somewhere he'd probably step on it in bare feet one day soon.

Too bad. He didn't have time to crawl around looking for it now. Carrying the shirt in one hand and the calendar in the other, he ducked out of the closet. Marching straight to the dresser, he tossed the calendar in the wastebasket there. Then he dropped the shirt on the bed with his jeans and turned for the bathroom to grab a quick shower.

Sabra, early December...

In downtown Astoria, the shop windows and the streets were all decked out for Christmas. Acres of lighted garland bedecked with shiny ornaments and bells looped between the streetlights. Live trees in pots lined the sidewalk, each one lit up and hung with bright decorations.

At the corner, a lone musician played "White Christmas" on a xylophone. Sabra paused with a few other bundled-up shoppers to listen to the tune. When the song came to an end, she tossed a dollar in the open case at the musician's feet. Pulling her heavy jacket a little closer against the winter chill, she crossed the street and continued on to midway along the next block.

The store she sought was called Sugar and Spice. Like every other shop on the street, it had Christmas displays in the front windows, scenes of festively dressed mannequins, ones that were definitely more spicy than sweet. One mannequin wore a sexy elf costume and another, a red thong sewn with tiny, winking party lights. One had her hands bound behind her back with handcuffs, a Santa hat slipping sexily over one eye while a male mannequin in a leather jockstrap and policeman's hat tickled her with a giant green feather.

Inside, the girl behind the counter wore a skimpy Mrs. Santa Claus costume and a gray wig topped by a crown of Christmas tree lights. "Hey. What can I help you with?"

"Just looking…" Sabra headed for the racks of revealing lingerie.

Sexy Mrs. Claus followed her over there. "Are you wanting anything in particular?"

Help from an expert?

Really, what could it hurt? "It's like this," Sabra said as she checked through the bra-and-panty sets. "I'm in—or at least, I've *been* in—this wonderful relationship. But we aren't together all the time. We meet up for several days, once a year."

Mrs. Claus looked confused. "What's the kink?"

Sabra laughed. "It's just once a year, over Christmas, no contact otherwise. Is that a kink?"

Mrs. Claus let that question go. "Let me try again. So…there's a problem in this relationship?"

"Well, the thing is, last year it ended badly and it was all my fault."

Mrs. Claus made a soft, sympathetic sound. "Oh, no."

"Yeah. And, see, I don't want to break our rules.

I'm not going to stalk the guy. But this year, I'll be there at the usual place and time in case he does show. I'm going to knock myself out to make things right, make it..."

"More?" suggested Mrs. Claus.

Sabra paused in her impatient flicking from one panty set to the next. "More. Yes. That's it. I want more with him. Last year, he was already there in the *more* department. He wanted to take the biggest chance of all with me. But I wasn't ready. I said some things that I wish I hadn't. It's very likely he took what I said to mean it was over between us. And now, I only want a prayer that he might be willing to give me another shot. I don't need handcuffs or a latex suit. I just want to feel confident. If he shows up and I get lucky enough to make it as far as taking off my clothes..."

"You want him wowed." Mrs. Claus had that look, the one a sales professional gets when she finally understands exactly what her customer is shopping for. "You don't want to role-play or try something new. You just want to be you, the sexiest possible you."

Sabra grabbed an itty-bitty black satin number, held it up and joked, "You don't happen to have this in camo?"

Mrs. Claus's smile was slow and also triumphant. "As a matter of fact, we do."

Sabra bought the sexy camo undies and several other seductive bits of lace and satin. She knew that cute underwear wasn't the answer to anything, really. If Matthias was through with her, a see-through bra wouldn't change his mind.

And yet, she felt hopeful and excited.

She was ready to go all in with him, at last. All he had to do was show up this year and she would pull out all the stops to get just one more chance with him.

December 23, last year...

Sabra's heart just about detonated in her chest when she turned the last corner and rolled into the clearing. Matthias, in a uniform that looked identical to the one his friend Jerry had been wearing when he stopped by the year before, leaned back against the tailgate of a state trooper patrol truck.

He's here! He came!

For a few glorious, too-brief seconds, she knew she was getting the second chance she'd longed for, that this year, she was going to make everything come out right.

She pulled her car to a stop several feet back from the man and the truck.

About then, in the silence that followed turning off the engine, she started putting it together.

This was all wrong.

No lights in the cabin, Matthias in his uniform, with a mud-splattered state police vehicle behind him. No Zoya. No gorgeous Christmas tree tied to a rack on the roof.

And he hadn't moved yet. He remained at the tailgate, big arms across his chest, his hat shading his eyes.

Her hands shook and her stomach pitched and rolled. She sat there in the driver's seat, her heart hurling itself madly against the wall of her chest, unable to move for a good count of ten.

But this was her show, now wasn't it? She could already see that he wasn't planning a tender reunion. If she didn't want to talk to him, she ought to start the engine again and drive away.

That seemed the less painful option in the short run—and also the one that would always leave her wondering, leave her hanging. Leave her wishing she'd asked him straight out for another chance.

If he said no, well, *Goodbye* was an actual word. And she needed to hear him say it out loud.

First step: get out of the damn car.

But still she didn't move. Her mind sparked wildly, impulses firing madly, going off like bottle rockets in her brain, shooting along the endless network of nerves in her body, leading her exactly nowhere.

Grabbing the latch with shaking fingers, she gave it a yank.

The door opened and she swung her legs out, rising without pausing to steady herself. Surprisingly, she didn't go pitching over facedown in the dirt.

She was on her feet and moving toward him. A couple of yards away from him, she stopped. He swiped off his hat. The pain in her chest was damn near unbearable.

His blue eyes told her nothing. They *gave* her nothing.

The sun was out, of all things. It brought out the silvery threads in his dark blond hair. He was so beautiful, all square-jawed and uncompromising, with that broad chest and those big arms she wanted wrapped good and hard around her.

Not mine. The two words ripped through her brain

like a buzz saw. Whatever they'd had, it was gone now. He was not hers and he never would be.

She'd had her chance and she hadn't been ready. It was no one's fault, really. Timing did matter and hers had been seriously bad. "I take it you're not staying."

Matt had dreaded this moment.

He'd known that whatever happened—if she showed, if she didn't—it was going to be bad.

But this—the very sight of her, the stricken look on her face—it was worse than he'd ever imagined it could be.

"I didn't really expect you to show," he said. The words felt cruel as they fell from his lips. He'd driven out here feeling angry and wronged, self-righteous. Ready to lay it on her that he'd taken her advice and found someone new, willing her to be here so he could have the final say.

But now, having simply watched her get out of her car and walk over to him, having looked her square in her beautiful face, all that sanctimonious fury had drained out of him. He had no anger left to sustain him.

"I'm on duty," he said.

"Uh, yeah. I kind of figured that."

"But I came by just in case you showed up, so you wouldn't wonder—I mean, you know. Be left hanging."

"Thank you." The skin was too pale around her soft lips. He needed to reach for her, hold her, soothe her.

He wrapped both arms across his chest good and tight, the hat dangling from between the fingers of his right hand. It was the only way to keep himself from grabbing her close.

Spit it out, you SOB. Just say it. "I've met someone."

"Ah." The sound was so soft. Full of pain. And understanding. Two bright spots of color flamed high on her cheeks. He was hurting her, hurting her so bad.

What she'd done to him last year? It was nothing compared to what he was putting her through now.

He needed to explain himself, he realized, needed to say something *real* to her, something true, from his heart. "Sabra, I swear to you, I never would have moved on."

She swallowed convulsively and gave him a sharp nod. "Yeah." It came out a ragged little whisper. "I know that. I do."

"You were so insistent. So sure."

"Yes. You're right. I was."

"You *told* me to find someone else."

"And you did." She smiled. It seemed to take a lot of effort. "I'm, um, glad for you. I want you to be happy, Matthias, I honestly do."

"You have meant so much to me," he said, striving for the right words, the true words, from his heart. "More than I seem to know how to say."

Kind, Sabra thought. *He's trying so hard to be kind.*

So why did it feel like he was ripping her heart out?

Worst of all, she got it. She saw it so clearly. What he was doing to her now was essentially what she'd done to him a year ago.

She'd hurt him, told him outright he would never have what he longed for from her. He'd done what he had to do to get over her. She knew she had no one to blame but herself.

Now she just needed to hold it together, get through this with some small shred of dignity intact.

She was about to open her mouth and wish him well with his new love—and the words got clogged in her throat.

Because she just couldn't.

If another woman loved him now and did it well and fully, well, all right then. He should be with that woman.

But to completely give up, right here and now?

She just wasn't that good of a person. "I have a request."

"Name it."

"I have the key and I'll give it to you if that's how you want it. But I'm asking you to let me keep it for one more year. Let me keep it and I will be here, same time as always, next year. If you're still with your new love, just stay away till the sun is down. If you don't show by dark, that will be all I need to know. I'll lock up and push the key under the door. You'll never see me again."

There was more. So much more she needed to say, including the most important words…

I love you, Matthias. I love you and I should have said so last year.

But she hadn't. Instead, she'd told him to find someone else. And now they were here, in the cold December sunlight, saying goodbye. And she had no right at all to speak her love out loud.

She shut her mouth and waited, certain he would

say that he wanted his key back and he wanted it right now.

But he only stood there, holding his hat, arms folded hard against her, his expression blank, those beautiful eyes of his so guarded.

Time stretched out on a razor's edge of loss and misery. She tried to reassure herself.

He wasn't asking for the key back, was he? That was a good sign.

Wasn't it?

She almost let herself feel the faintest glimmer of hope.

But then he broke the awful silence. "Goodbye, Sabra."

And with that, he put his hat back on and turned on his heel, heading for the driver's side of the pickup. She just stood there, afraid to move for fear she would shatter.

He got in, turned the engine on, circled the cabin and disappeared down the twisting dirt road.

She held it together, barely, until the sound of his engine faded away in the distance.

Then her knees stopped working. With a strangled cry, she sank to a crouch. "Get up," she muttered, disgusted with herself.

But it was no good. Her heart was aching so bad and there was really no alternative but to give herself up to the pain.

At least he was gone. He wouldn't have to see this.

It was just her and her broken heart, the bitter taste of regret on her tongue.

Wrapping her arms around herself, Sabra gave in

completely. Slowly, she toppled onto her side. Curling up into herself on the cold winter ground, she let her tears fall.

Chapter Eleven

Sabra, the following March...

"This kitchen is gorgeous," Peyton declared from her favorite spot at Sabra's new chef-quality stove. "You did it all. The farm sink, these quartz counters. Clean white cabinets with all the storage options and inner drawers. I'm so jealous."

Sabra, sitting at the island next to Iris, sipped her wine. "You saw it before. A bad memory from the early '80s. Uh-uh. It was crying out for an update and we've been doing better than ever since I finally moved home and started tackling my job here, day-to-day. I've hooked us up with two new restaurants, big accounts. It all helps—and you, my dear Peyton, are invited to make your magic in my new kitchen anytime." The wonderful smell of Peyton's special pasta sauce graced the air. "You, too." Sabra elbowed Iris playfully and then raised her wineglass. "Just bring more of this wine with you when you come."

An hour later, they sat on the long benches at the harvest table her great-grandfather had built and shared the meal Peyton had cooked for them. It wasn't until they'd taken their coffee into the living room that Sabra's friends started in on her about the "cabin guy" and how she needed to get over him.

Iris insisted, "You can't spend the whole year just sitting around waiting on a guy who's with someone else and only showed up last year to say goodbye."

Pain, fresh and sharp, stabbed through her at the thought of that too-bright December day. "Who says I'm just sitting around? I've got a farm to run."

"Please, girlfriend. We're not talking about work and you know we're not. We're talking about your social life, which is essentially nonexistent."

"Wait a minute. I have *you* guys. I have other friends, too, longtime friends I grew up with. We've reconnected since I moved home and we get together now and then, meet up for a show or lunch, or whatever."

"You do hear yourself," Peyton chimed in. "*Friends*, you said."

"We are talking *men*," said Iris. "And not men *friends*. Uh-uh. You owe yourself at least a few hot nights, some seriously sexy times."

"That's not going to happen. It's not who I am and I'm fine with that."

"Just download a few dating apps," Peyton pleaded.

"FarmersOnly.com, for crying out loud," moaned Iris.

"But I—"

"No." Iris shook a finger at her. "No excuses. Even if everything goes the way you hope it will next Christmas, even if it's over with the other woman, if he drops to his knees and begs for one more chance with you—that changes nothing. You *owe* that man nothing. From now until then is a long time. You owe it to *yourself* to make good use of that time."

"Make *use* of it?" Sabra scoffed. "What does that even mean?"

"It means that you went from Stan the Swine to James the Jerk to once a year with the cabin guy. It's not going to kill you to step out of your comfort zone and see what's out there. You need to mix it up a little. You just might find a man who's as ready for you as you are for him."

"But I *told* you. Matthias *was* ready. *I* messed it up."

"Don't you dare blame yourself." Iris was nothing if not loyal. "You'd lost your *dad*. That man you're pining for now could have been a *little* more understanding."

"And you've already boxed yourself in," Peyton chided. "You won't contact the guy before Christmas."

"I told you, that's our agreement and—"

"Understood." Peyton cut her off, but in a gentle tone. "My point is, there's nothing more you can do for now in terms of Matthias."

"So?"

"So, it's a lot of months until December. Make those months count, that's all we're saying."

"It's a numbers game," declared Iris. "You've got

to get out there and kiss a lot of toads before you're ever going to meet the right guy for you."

"I've already met the right guy," Sabra said quietly, knowing in her deepest heart that it was true. "I've met the right guy—and he's with someone else now."

Her friends shook their heads.

They sipped their coffee in silence for a few seconds.

"Just try," Peyton urged softly at last. "A few dates, that's all. Give some other guy a shot."

Sabra wasn't exactly sure how they'd done it. But Peyton and Iris had prevailed. She had three dating apps on her phone now.

And she made an effort. She truly did. She filled out her profile information in detail, honestly. And she asked Marjorie, who had a certain aptitude with a digital camera, to take some good pictures of her which she posted with her profiles.

And then she started interacting, reaching out to guys whose profiles and pictures looked interesting, responding when someone reached out to her. She went with her instincts. If a guy seemed creepy or catfishy, she let him know she wasn't interested and moved on.

Truth to tell, none of them *really* interested her. Because she wanted Matthias and she just plain *wasn't* interested.

When she'd failed to so much as meet a guy for coffee by the end of April, Iris gave her a pep talk about not trying hard enough, about the need to get out there, in real life.

Sabra knew her friend had a point. There was trying—and there was *really* trying. Yeah, she'd put up the profiles and interacted a little online, but nothing more.

And that made her kind of an internet dating jerk, now didn't it? She wasn't benching or breadcrumbing anyone. She was simply wasting the time of the men she right-swiped. She needed to do better, make a real effort, if only to prove to herself that there wasn't some unknown guy waiting out there who was just right for her, a guy who could have her asking, *Matthias Bravo, who?*

Could that ever actually happen?

No. Uh-uh. She knew with absolute certainty that it couldn't.

However, more than once in her life she'd been totally wrong. Romantically speaking, at this point in time, she was 0 for 3. What did she know, really, about any of this?

Sabra kept at it.

No, she wasn't ready to get up close and in person with these guys she was making contact with online. But at least by mid-May, she'd stepped up her game from mere messaging to Skype and FaceTime. It was so much easier to eliminate a guy once she'd seen him in action, heard his voice while his mouth was moving—and there she went again, thinking in terms of eliminating a man rather than trying really hard to meet someone new.

Finally, in June, she did it, took a giant step forward.

She agreed to meet a nice guy named Dave at the Astoria Farmer's Market. Dave seemed every bit as nice in person as he had during their messaging phase and on FaceTime. Too bad there was zero spark. None. A complete and utter lack of chemistry.

Worse, she felt like she was cheating on Matthias.

As they reached the last booth, Dave asked her out to dinner that night.

She turned him down. Dave got the message. She never heard from him again. Which was all for the best.

She did coffee dates after that. Several of them. During each one, she nursed a latte and wished she was anywhere but there.

She went out with a podiatrist who talked really fast and all about himself through a very expensive dinner. Then later, on the sidewalk outside the restaurant, he grabbed her and tried to choke her with his tongue down her throat. Somehow, she resisted the urge to smack his self-absorbed face and simply told him never to try anything like that again with her.

He called her a tease and a few other uglier names. And then, of all things, he grabbed her hand, kissed it and apologized profusely.

She said, "Apology accepted. Just please, never contact me again."

After the podiatrist, she took a break from dating. She figured she needed it. Deserved it, even.

Then, in late September, on CompatibleMate.com, she met a lawyer named Ted.

They went out to a concert and she had a good time. When he kissed her at her door, it was…pleasant.

And pleasant was pretty awful. A man's kiss should be much more than *pleasant*, or what was the point?

Still, that's what Ted's kiss was. Pleasant.

She experienced none of the goodness the right

kiss always brings—no shivers racing up and down her spine, no galloping heart, no fireworks whatsoever. In fact, what she felt was a deep sadness, a longing for Matthias.

But Ted really did seem like a great guy. She liked him.

He asked her out again two weeks later and she said yes to dinner and a show. That time, when he kissed her as they were saying goodnight, she knew beyond any doubt that she never wanted to kiss him again.

And when he called her a few nights later to ask her out for Friday night, she knew she should turn him down, tell him how much she liked him, explain somehow that merely liking him wasn't enough, that she was wasting his time and that wasn't right.

But there was nothing *wrong* with him—other than the simple fact that he wasn't Matthias. In no way was that Ted's fault.

She opened her mouth to express her regrets—and a yes fell out.

They went to dinner again. Ted seemed happy. Buoyant, even. He talked about his firm and how well he was doing there. He asked about the farm and he actually seemed interested when she proudly described the orchard of sapling fruit trees they'd put in that spring.

Over dessert, Ted leaned across the table, his dark eyes gleaming, a happy grin on his handsome face. "I have to tell you. I never thought this would work for me. But Sabra, now I've found you, I'm changing my mind about meeting someone online. I know we haven't really taken it to the next level, so to speak. But still. This is special, what's happening between us. Don't you feel it? Here we are on date three and I'm honestly thinking we're going somewhere."

Going somewhere?

No way.

Sabra kind of hated herself at that moment. She knew she had to stop this, that she had no right to go one second longer without getting real with the guy. "I'm sorry, Ted."

He sat back. "Sorry?"

"The truth is, you and I are never reaching the next level. We're going nowhere. I'm in love with someone else and I can't do this anymore."

Ted's eyes were no longer gleaming. "Tell me something, Sabra," he said, cool and flat. "If you're in love with someone else, why the hell aren't you with him—and you know what?" He shoved back his chair and plunked his napkin on the table. "Don't answer that because I don't even care."

Muttering invectives against online dating in general and, more specifically, crazy women who mess with a guy's mind, he headed for the door.

With a sigh, Sabra signaled for the check.

Late October...

"I'm done, you guys," Sabra said. "Finished. Not going there—online or otherwise. Because you know what? Ted was right. It's wrong to use one guy to try to forget another. And I'm never doing that again."

Her friends regarded her solemnly from the other side of her harvest table. "We do get it," admitted Peyton.

Iris, as always, asked the hardest question. "What will you do if he doesn't show in December?"

Her heart broke all over again at the very thought. But she drew herself up straight. "Die a little. Suffer a lot—and please don't look so worried. I love Matthias. I want him. No one else but him. I have to go all the way with that first. If he's not there on December twenty-third, *that's* when I'll have to figure out what comes next." She looked from one dear face to the other. "I know. I get it. I mean, who does what he and I have done? What two sane people make an agreement to have each other just for the holidays—and then keep that agreement for years? I know that sounds batcrap crazy, I do. But it worked for us. It was what we both needed. Our agreement created the space we both re-quired, the time and patience to learn to love again. I truly believe that if my dad hadn't died, Matthias and I would be married by now. But he did die and that threw everything into chaos for me. Matthias asked me for more and I answered no, unequivocally. I told him never. I said if he wanted more, he needed to go and find someone else. Which brought us here."

"Matthias should have waited," grumbled Iris, swiping a tear from her cheek. "He should have given you more space."

"Space? I had *years* of space. And he did wait. I knew it. I felt it, the year before I lost my dad. I knew he wanted more that year and *I* wanted more, too. But neither of us stepped up and said so. Still, when we parted that year, I knew that the next year, we would be taking it further. That didn't happen because the next year, I was a mess. But he *had* waited. He'd waited out that whole year."

Peyton said sheepishly, "Honey, we just want you to be prepared, you know? Just in case he, well, I mean…" Her voice trailed off.

Sabra put it right out there. "You honestly don't think he's going to be there, do you?" Both of her friends remained silent. But the truth was in their eyes. Peyton glanced away. And Iris gave a sad little shrug. Sabra said firmly, "There is no preparing for that. If he doesn't show, for me it's going to be as bad as it was last Christmas."

"But…" Peyton swallowed hard. "I mean, you *will* get through it, right? You'll be okay?"

Sabra did understand the deeper implications of the question. And she loved her friends all the more for venturing into this difficult territory. "I adored my dad. I miss him every day and I wish I'd done more to help him live without my mom. In many ways, I'm like him. A total romantic, devoted until death. But I'm like my mom, too. And my mom was stronger than my dad was, strong *and* practical." Sabra reached across the rough wood surface of the old table.

Her friends were there to meet her. Peyton's hand settled on hers and then Iris's hand covered Peyton's.

"You'll make it through, one way or another," said Iris. "That's what you're telling us, right?"

"One way or another, yes. If he doesn't show, I may curl up in a fetal position and cry my eyes out just like I did last year. I may spend a lot of time being depressed and self-indulgent. I may be miserable for months. It's possible that, after being with him, know-ing him, *loving* him, there's just no one else for me, that he's it for me, the one. Whatever happens, though, however it ends up with him this year, I promise you both that I will make it through."

December 23, this year...

An emotional wreck.

That described Sabra's condition exactly as she drove toward the cabin. An emotional wreck who almost ended up an *actual* wreck. Twice.

She kept spacing off, praying he would be there, then *certain* he would be there. And then *knowing* absolutely that she was deluding herself completely. He wasn't going to be there and how would she bear it?

It was during one of those spaced-out moments that a deer bolted out into the road and then stopped stock-still and stared at her through her windshield, as if to say, *Whoa. A car. Where'd that come from?*

She slammed on the brakes and skidded to a stop just in time. The deer—a nice buck, a six pointer—stared at her for a good ten seconds more before leaping off into the brush again.

She took her foot off the brake and carefully steered to the shoulder of the road, where she dropped her forehead to the steering wheel and waited for her heart to stop trying to punch its way out of her chest.

When her mouth no longer tasted like old pennies and her hands had stopped shaking, she set out again.

The second almost-wreck happened after she'd turned off the highway into the woods, onto the series of unimproved roads that would finally take her to the cabin and her own personal moment of truth. Really, she didn't know what happened that second time. She was looking at the road, both hands on the wheel.

But her mind? Her heart? Her whole being?

Elsewhere, far away, lost in memories of Christmases past. Of nights on the porch in a world buried in snow, of his hands—so big and yet deft and quick, whittling a small piece of wood into a porcupine, just for her, touching her naked body, showing her all the ways he could make her moan.

The giant tree seemed to rise up in front of her out of nowhere. With a shriek, she slammed the brakes again, sliding on the dirt road, her heartbeat so loud in her ears it sounded like drums, her whole body gone strangely tingly and numb with the sheer unreality of what was happening.

By some miracle, she eased the wheel to the right with the slide of gravel beneath her tires. The Subaru cleared the tree by mere inches. She came to a stop with the tree looming in her side window.

After that near-death experience, she turned off the engine, slumped back in her seat, shut her eyes and reminded herself that she'd promised Iris and Peyton she would get through this, one way or another. It would be so wrong for her to end up a statistic—especially if she finished herself off before even getting to the cabin and finding out that, just maybe, the man she hoped to meet there had shown up ready to try again, exactly as she dreamed he might.

He could be there right this minute, waiting to take her in his arms and swear that from this day forward, she was his only one.

Oh, if only that could really happen.

She was on fire to be the one for him, to claim him as hers. She yearned for this to be it, *their* year, the year they finally built something more than a beautiful Christmas together.

But none of that was even possible if she didn't keep her eyes on the road and get her ass to the cabin.

She started up the car again and put it in gear.

Five minutes later, her spirits hit a new low. The suspense was unbearable. And she really should face reality.

Her friends were right. Matthias had found someone else and she needed to accept that. She needed to stop this idiocy and find a way to move on as she'd once told him to do.

She should give up this foolishness, she kept thinking, give it up and go home. There was no point. She was only driving toward more heartbreak.

But she didn't turn around.

When she reached the last stretch of dirt road leading up to the cabin, her heart was hammering so hard and so fast, she worried it might just explode from her body. They would find her days from now, the front end of the Outback crunched against a tree, her lifeless form slumped in the seat, a gaping, empty hole in the middle of her chest.

She rounded the last curve and the cabin came into view.

Her nearly-exploded heart stopped dead—and then began beating again faster than ever as she pulled to a stop behind the muddy Jeep.

The gray world had come alive again. With anticipation. With promise. With her love that filled her up and overflowed, bringing the woods and the clearing, the rustic cabin, even the car in which she sat, into sharper focus, everything so vivid, in living color.

She heard a gleeful laugh. It was her own. "Yes!" she cried aloud. "Yes, yes, yes!"

Oh, it was perfect. The best moment ever. Her seemingly hopeless dream, finally, at last, coming true.

Golden light shone from the windows and smoke curled lazily from the stone chimney, drifting upward toward the gray sky. She managed to turn off the engine.

And then she just sat there, barely breathing, unable to move, still marginally terrified that she was reading this all wrong, that the man inside the cabin wasn't really waiting there for her.

Until the front door swung open.

And at last, after so long—*too* long, forever and a day—she saw him.

So tall and broad, in camo pants, boots and a mud-colored shirt, his dirty-blond hair a little longer than last year, every inch of him powerful, strong, muscular. Cut.

Joy burst like a blinding light inside her as her gaze met his. She saw it all then. In the blue fire of his eyes, in his slow, welcoming smile.

Mine, she thought. *All mine. As I am his. At last.*

Chapter Twelve

He came for her, moving fast down the porch steps, boots eating up the distance between them, eyes promising everything.

Love. Heat. Wonder. The kind of bond that weathers the worst storms. Joy and laughter and the two of them, together, forever and ever, building a family, making a rich and meaningful life.

She threw open her door just as he reached her. Popping the seat belt latch, she flung herself toward him.

He caught her, those strong arms going around her. She landed on her feet against his broad, hard chest.

"Oh, thank God…" They breathed the prayerful words in unison. And then his beautiful mouth crashed down on hers.

The clean, man-and-cedar scent of him was all

around her, encompassing her, exciting her even more. The kiss grew deeper, and his hold on her got tighter.

One minute, she had her two feet on the ground and the next, he swept her up against his chest, still kissing her, still holding her the way she'd dreamed he might again someday.

Like she was his and he was hers and he would never, ever let her go. He turned for the house, kissing her as he went.

Up the steps he took her, through the open door.

The scent of evergreen intensified as he kicked the door shut. He'd already brought the tree in and propped it up in the stand. Zoya lay by the fire, panting a little. She rolled over inviting a belly scratch and let out a whine of greeting. Sabra saw the tree and the dog in fleeting glimpses, keeping her mouth locked to his, worshipping him with that kiss.

Matthias kept walking, carrying her across the rough boards of the floor, to the stairs and up them.

The kiss never broke.

Until he threw her on the bed. She bounced twice, laughing.

"Take everything off." His eyes made a million very sexy promises. "Do it fast."

Not a problem. Not in the least. They stripped in unison, clothes flying everywhere. She'd worn one of those sexy bra-and-panty sets she'd bought the year before, but she gave him no time to appreciate them. She tore them off and tossed them aside.

And he?

Oh, he was everything she remembered, all she longed for—honed and deep-chested, with those sculpted arms that took her breath away. Such a big man.

Everywhere.

She held up her arms to him and he came down to her, grabbing her close again, slamming his mouth on hers.

It was frantic and hungry, not smooth in the least. Needful and desperate, necessary as air. They rolled, their hands everywhere, relearning each other, every muscle, every secret curve. There were more kisses, deep ones that turned her heart inside out. His fingers found the core of her, so wet, so ready.

They needed more.

They needed everything, to be joined, each to the other.

He produced a condom seemingly from thin air.

"Planned ahead, did you?" she asked, trying to tease him, ending up sounding breathless and needy.

His eyes burned into hers. "I want this, Sabra. Us. I want it forever."

"Yes," she said, before he'd even finished asking. "Forever. You and me."

"Don't leave me. Don't do that again. Don't drive me away." He stroked her cheek.

"I won't. I swear it. I'm ready now, Matthias. Ready for the rest of our lives, you and me. I love you. You're the only one, and you always will be."

"Sabra…" He kissed her again, wildly, his fingers tunneling in her hair, his mouth demanding everything, all of her. "My love," he whispered against her parted lips. "I love you, always. I was such a fool."

"It's not as if you were the only fool." She broke away enough to plead, "Let me…" And she took the condom from him, removed the wrapper and carefully slid it on.

Once she had it in place, he lifted her as though she weighed nothing. Stretching out on his back, he set her down on top of him.

She was so ready. Beyond ready. Rising to her knees, she lined him up with her heat and took him inside—all the way, to the hilt.

He groaned and she bent to him, claiming his mouth with hers, rocking her hips on him in long, needful strokes. He clasped her bottom with those strong hands, one palm on each cheek, and moved with her, surging up into her, sending her reeling.

She came with a gleeful cry.

And then he was rolling them, taking the top position. Rising up over her, he pushed in deep and true.

That time, when her second finish shattered through her, he joined her. They cried out in unison, going over as one, holding each other, Matthias and Sabra.

Together.

At last.

An hour or two later, they went downstairs naked. She greeted Zoya and admired the tree.

He didn't let her linger in the main room long, though. Pulling her into the bathroom, he filled the tub, added bath salts, climbed in and crooked a finger at her to join him.

She did, eagerly, settling in between his legs, leaning back on him. He really did make the firmest, most supportive sort of pillow. For a while, they floated in the hot water that smelled of lemons and mint.

He told her that he had a missing sister.

"What? You're kidding me."

He nuzzled her hair. "Nope. This past year, we found out that the oldest of my sisters, Aislinn, was switched at birth."

"So then, Aislinn isn't your sister by blood?"

"No. If she hadn't been switched, her name would be Madison Delaney."

"Wait." Sabra sat up, sending water sloshing. "Not *the* Madison Delaney, America's darling, the movie star?"

"Yes." Gently, Matthias pulled her back to rest against his chest. "We have a long-lost sister, and she is a movie star."

"Wow."

"Exactly. We've been trying to reach out to her. So far, our attempts have been rebuffed—either by her or by the people who protect her, we're not sure which."

"But you're not giving up." It wasn't a question.

He replied as she knew he would. "One way or another, we'll find a way to get through to her. As we will find Finn. Someday. Somehow…"

"I know you will," she whispered, and they were silent for a time.

But then, he bent his head to her and pressed his rough cheek to her smooth one. "Forever," he said gruffly. "I mean it. You still on for that?"

"Always." She lifted her arm from the water and reached back to slide her wet hand around the nape of his neck, tipping her head up to him for a quick kiss.

But one kiss from him? Never enough.

Already she could feel him, growing hard and ready, wanting her as she wanted him—again.

* * *

Sometime later, she told him that she'd moved back to the farm.

"When was that?" he asked.

"It's been a long time now. I moved in July, a year and a half ago."

He nuzzled her hair, which she'd piled on her head to keep it from getting too wet. "So then, you were already living there last Christmas, when I showed up just long enough to tell you it was over."

"Yeah."

He muttered something bleak. She couldn't make out the exact words, and she decided not to ask. Instead, she took his hand from the side of the tub and pulled it down into the water, across her stomach, so his arm was wrapped around her.

"Are you happy there, at your family's farm?" He bit the shell of her ear, so lightly, causing a thrilled little shiver to slide through her.

"Very." She slithered around, splashing water everywhere, until she was face-to-face with him. "I'm hoping to stay there."

"Hoping?"

"Well, I want to be with you. And maybe you want to stay in Valentine Bay." He kissed the end of her nose and she backpedaled, "If I'm moving too fast for you—?"

"No way. There is no 'too fast' when it comes to you and me, not anymore. We've wasted too much time already." He took her slippery shoulders and pulled her up so he could claim her mouth in a lazy, thorough kiss. When he finally allowed her to sink back into the cooling water, he said, "Yes. I'll move to your farm with you."

She reached up, pressed her hand to his bristly cheek. "You haven't even seen the place yet."

"I don't need to see it. You've moved home and that makes you happy. I love you and for me, home is where you are. You've mentioned that your farm is in Astoria, which means my field office is nearby. Getting to work won't be an issue—and do you realize you've never told me the name of this farm of yours?"

"Berry Bog Farm."

"Perfect."

"What's perfect?"

"Everything." He traced her eyebrows, one and then the other. "I'm going to need your phone number as soon as we get out of this tub."

"You got it."

"I'm serious, Sabra. I won't let you leave this cabin, not even to sit on the porch, until your number is safe in my phone."

"I'll get right on that."

"You'd better," he warned, but when she started to climb from the tub, he held her there. "Not yet. In a little while."

With a sigh, she kissed his square chin. "This is kind of nice, you and me, naked in the tub together…"

"*Kind of nice* doesn't even come close." He pressed his wet hand to her cheek, then made a cradle of his index finger and lifted her chin so their eyes met. "The thing with Mary…?"

Her heart felt caged, suddenly, hurting in her too-small chest. "That's her name? Mary?"

He nodded. And then he pressed his forehead to

hers and whispered, "I never should have started it with her. I was so hurt and mad at you."

She whispered her own confession. "I was so screwed up over my dad, screwed up and afraid, of you and me, of how powerful and good it was between us, of trusting what we have together—and then of someday losing you, like my dad lost my mom. So I told you to go out and look for what you needed. No way can I blame you for taking me at my word. I just hope… Oh, I don't know. I feel bad for her. For you. For all of it."

"It's been over with her for a year," he said. "A year, as of today."

She stared at him, confused. "You broke up with her on the twenty-third of *last* December?"

"That's right."

"The same day you drove up here to tell me you were with her?"

"That's the one."

"But I don't, I mean, how…?"

He pulled on a damp curl of her hair and then guided it tenderly behind her ear. "I knew it wouldn't work with her the minute I saw your face last year. I was just too damn stubborn to admit it right then. But as soon as I left you standing there alone, I knew what I had to do. I drove back to Valentine Bay feeling like a first-class jerk, wondering how I was going to break it to Mary that I couldn't be with her, that it was all wrong."

"Oh, Matt. And at the holidays, no less. What a mess I made. I'm so sorry."

But he gave her that wonderful, wry smile she loved so much. "It could have been worse. As it turned out, I didn't have to play the jerk, after all. Mary broke up with *me*."

She gasped. "No."

"Oh, yeah. We had a date to see a Christmas play that night. I went to pick her up and she asked me to come in for a minute. I stepped over the threshold— and then we just stood there by the door and she said how she'd been thinking, that it just wasn't working for her with me, that it wasn't love and she didn't feel it ever could be, that she and I needed to face the truth and move on. She really meant it," he said, his wry smile in evidence again. "We ended it right then, simple as that."

Sabra cradled his beard-scruffy cheek. "I do want to apologize sincerely, for hurting you, for sending you off to find someone else. I really messed that up. I could have lost you forever."

Matthias frowned. "I pushed too hard at the wrong time. You were all turned around over losing your dad. I wasn't patient and I should have been. As for losing me, you never could, not really. Somehow, I would always find my way back to you."

"And I. To you." They did that thing lovers do, having sex with their eyes. Then, with a happy sigh, she floated to her back once more and rested against him. "I have to ask…"

His warm breath stirred her hair as he pressed a kiss to the crown of her head. "Anything."

"All that time, from last Christmas to now. Did you know you would come to meet me today?"

"I did. No question, as sure as I knew I would draw my next breath. I also spent too many sleepless nights positive that you would give up on me, find someone else, change your mind. I could think of a million ways it was not going to work out, picture myself waiting here for hour after hour, alone."

"There's no one else, I promise," she said fervently.

He bent and pressed a kiss into that tender spot where her neck met her shoulder. "Baby, something in your voice says there's a story you're not telling me."

She blew out a hard breath and admitted, "My friends said I really had to try seeing other guys…"

He was suddenly too quiet behind her. Was he even breathing? "And did you?" he asked.

"I did, yes."

"And…?"

She winced. "You really want to hear this?"

"Damn straight I do."

She told him everything, all about her adventures in online dating, starting with the online chats and the coffee dates, moving on to the Farmer's Market day with Dave, the awful evening with the grabby podiatrist and the three dates with Ted.

When she first started putting it all out there, Matthias remained still as a statue behind her. But he slowly relaxed. He said he would like to go a few rounds with that foot doctor. And he made a sound of approval when she got to how she told Ted that she was in love with someone else and added, "Meaning you," just in case he had a single doubt by now who owned her heart.

Once she'd told him everything, she asked, "How come you didn't just come looking for me sooner? You could have saved me from all those bad dates, saved yourself from worrying that I wouldn't show up here for Christmas. I don't think I would have been that hard to find."

His hand stroked slowly along her arm, fingers brushing up and down. "That wasn't our agreement."

She slithered around again, getting front to front. "I can't believe you know that, that you understand that."

He looked vaguely puzzled. "*Should* I have tracked you down?"

"I have no idea." Sending water splashing, she rose up to kiss him and then settled back down against his broad chest. "What I do know," she said, "is that I've always felt that trying to find you between Christmases would be wrong. I felt it was important that we both respected the agreement we'd made together, that if the terms were going to change, they had to change at Christmastime."

He caught her face between his wet hands and pulled her up so her parted lips were only an inch from his. "Everything is changed, as of now. We're agreed on that, right?"

She bobbed her head up and down in his hold. "Yes, we are. I'm in. You're in. Both of us. A hundred percent."

"We're together now. We're taking this thing we have public and we're doing that before New Year's."

"Yes. You and me, in front of the whole world— have you got vacation time this year?"

His lips brushed hers again. "I'm off until January second."

"Good. We'll visit your family in Valentine Bay. I'm taking you to the farm—and we have to go to Portland. I need you to meet my best friends, Peyton and Iris."

He smiled against her mouth. "So then, we have a plan."

"Oh, yes we do."

"Make no mistake." He kissed her, hard and quick. "Marriage. We're doing it, the whole thing. The ring. The white dress. The vows—and what about kids? You do want kids?"

"Oh, Matthias. Yes. Definitely. All of the above. I can't wait to marry you."

"I think we've both waited more than long enough." But then he frowned. "Have I blown this? I should be on my knees now, shouldn't I?"

That time, *she* kissed *him*. "Naked in the bathtub is working just fine."

"All right, then." He pulled her closer and sprinkled kisses in a line along her cheek. When he reached her ear, he whispered, "We're not just each other's Christmas present anymore. What we have is for the whole year round."

"For the rest of our lives," she vowed.

And they sealed their promise of forever with a long, sweet kiss.

Epilogue

They stayed at the cabin for Christmas, enjoying all the traditions they'd created together in the years before.

On Christmas morning, he handed her a small package wrapped in shiny red paper and tied with a white satin bow. She opened it carefully, feeling strangely expectant, full of nerves and happiness.

Inside was a ring-sized box with a porcupine carved in the top. "You made this."

"Guilty," he said in that gruff, low voice that she loved more than anything—well, except for everything else about him. She loved all that, too.

She glanced up at him. He was kind of blurry. But that happens when a girl's eyes are filled with sudden tears. "Matthias. I love you."

He reached out a hand and eased his warm, rough

fingers under her hair. Clasping her nape, he pulled her in close. "Don't cry." He kissed her forehead. "It's a present. Presents shouldn't make you cry."

"Of course they should." She sniffled. "But only if they're really good ones." A couple of tears got away from her and trickled down her cheeks.

He kissed those tears, first on one cheek and then the other. Then he went for her lips. That kiss lasted a while. They were always doing that, kissing and forgetting about everything else.

Finally, Zoya gave a hopeful whine. They both glanced down to see the dog sitting at their feet, her vivid blue eyes tracking—Matthias to Sabra and back to Matthias again.

"Aww. Zoya needs love, too." With a chuckle, Sabra dropped to a crouch to give the dog a quick hug.

When she got up again, she held up the box and admired his workmanship. "It's beautiful." It even had two tiny brass hinges to keep the lid attached.

He gazed at her so steadily, a bemused expression on that face she knew she would never tire of looking at. From the speaker on the kitchen table, Mariah Carey sang "All I Want for Christmas Is You." Happiness crowded out every other emotion. She glanced away and swiped at more joyful tears.

"Sabra."

She met his eyes again. "Hmm?"

"Are you ever going to open it?"

A lovely, warm shiver went through her as she lifted the carved lid.

Inside, on a bed of dark blue velvet, a single pear-shaped diamond glittered at her from a platinum band.

"Oh, you gorgeous thing," she said, the words more breath than sound.

"It's okay?" he asked, adorably anxious.

"It is exactly right. Just beyond beautiful, Matthias. Thank you." She went up on tiptoe for another quick kiss. And then she passed the open box to him. "Put it on for me?"

He did as she asked, bending to set the box on the coffee table and then sinking lower, all the way to one knee. "Sabra Bond." He reached for her left hand.

She gave it, loving the feel of his fingers closing around hers, protective. Arousing. Companionable, too.

"I never expected you." His eyes gleamed up at her, teasing her, loving her. "You broke into my cabin and ran off with my heart." She gave a little squeak of delight at his words and brought her right hand to her own heart. "It hasn't been easy for us," he said. "We've both been messed up and messed over. And it's taken way too long for each of us to be ready at the same time. But now, here we are, four years from that first year. Finally making it work. And it all feels just right, somehow." He slipped the ring onto her finger. It did feel right, a perfect fit. "There is no one but you, Sabra. You are in my dreams at night and the one I want to find beside me when I wake up in the morning. I love you," he said. "Will you marry me?"

Those pesky, joyful tears were blurring her vision again. She blinked them away. "Oh, yes, I will marry you, Matthias Bravo—and didn't I say that two days ago, in the tub?"

He looked at her like he might eat her right up. "No man ever gets tired of hearing the word *yes*."

* * *

The next morning, as they were packing for their round-trip tour of farm, friends and family, Matt heard a vehicle drive into the yard.

He looked out the front window. "Terrific," he muttered, meaning it wasn't.

Sabra, descending the stairs with her suitcase in hand, laughed. "Oh, come on. It can't be that bad."

"It's Jerry," he grumbled. "He's here to check on us." Outside, his lifelong friend got out of his patrol pickup and hitched up his belt.

Sabra set the suitcase down at the base of the stairs. "Invite him in. We'll have coffee."

Jerry, mounting the porch steps, spotted Matt in the window and grinned. Matt scowled back at him.

Did a dirty look slow Jerry down? Not a chance. He kept coming, straight to the door.

Matt pulled it open. "What a surprise," he said flatly, because it wasn't. Jerry showing up with no warning was just par for the course. "Got a problem with your phone again?"

Jerry took off his hat. "You could have dropped me a text, man." He looked hurt. "Let me know that everything was working out. I kinda got worried. I just wanted to check in, make sure that you're all right."

Now Matt felt like the thoughtless one. Probably because Jerry had a valid point. "Okay. I apologize for not keeping you in the loop."

Jerry brightened instantly. "Thanks. And Merry Christmas."

Sabra, busy at the coffee maker, called, "Hi, Jerry. Coffee?"

That big, toothy smile took over Jerry's handsome face. "Sabra. Good to see you again. Coffee would be great."

Matt stepped aside and his friend came in.

Sabra served the coffee and offered some cranberry-orange bread to go with it. They sat at the table.

Jerry saw the ring and got up, grabbed Matt in a bear hug and clapped him on the back. "You lucky sonofagun. Finally, huh?" He turned to Sabra as he hitched a thumb in Matt's direction. "This guy. He's been waiting years for you."

Sabra just smiled her sweetest smile. "We've both waited. It's felt like forever. But now, at last, it's all worked out."

Jerry dropped back into his chair, ate a hunk of cranberry bread, and glanced around the cabin at the boxes on the counter and the suitcase by the stairs. "Where're you guys going?"

"All the places we didn't go in other years," Matt replied, knowing he was being needlessly mysterious—but doing it anyway because sometimes he enjoyed giving his friend a little grief.

Sabra sent him a reproachful glance and laid out their itinerary. "I have a farm in Astoria. We're going there for a couple of days, then down to Portland so I can introduce my hunky fiancé to my closest friends. And then on to Valentine Bay where I get to meet the Bravos."

"We would have been in touch when we got to town," said Matt. "I'm figuring we'll be having some kind of get-together, probably at Daniel and Keely's."

Back at the end of July, Daniel had married Lillie's cousin, Keely Ostergard, who had made the perennially grouchy Daniel the happiest guy alive—scratch that. *Second* happiest.

Now that he and Sabra were finally together and staying that way, Matt knew *he* was the happiest.

Jerry asked hopefully, "So are you saying I'm included for the party at Daniel's?"

"It's a promise," said Matt.

"What a great house," Matthias said when Sabra led him and Zoya up the front steps of the farmhouse.

"My great-great-grandfather built it," she informed him with pride.

She took him inside and showed him the rooms. He admired her new kitchen and agreed to start moving in right away, as soon as they were done with their holiday travels.

They left Zoya downstairs and Sabra took him up to see the second floor. She pulled him from one room to the next, saving the master suite for last.

She'd repainted it a soft blue-gray and changed out all the furniture. The new bed was king-size.

Of course, they had to try it out.

Matthias said it was a great bed. "But it could be a fold-up cot, as long as it has you in it."

An hour or so later, they put their clothes back on and went downstairs. Matthias got Zoya's leash and the three of them went out for a tour of Berry Bog Farm.

That night, Marjorie had them over for dinner. The Wilsons were so sweet, both of them beaming from ear to ear to learn that Sabra was engaged to her "young man," as they called Matthias. They were so pleased to learn that Matthias would be moving in with her at the farm.

In Portland, Sabra's friend Peyton welcomed Matt warmly. But he didn't miss the narrow-eyed looks Iris kept sending him.

They stayed in Iris's extra bedroom, which had become vacant when Peyton moved in with her long-time boyfriend a few months before. The plan was for two nights in Portland and then on to Valentine Bay.

The first night went well, Matt thought. They all got together at Peyton's. Matt liked her boyfriend, Nick. Peyton was a really good cook, so the food was terrific. They stayed late, till almost two.

In the morning, when he woke up in Iris's spare room, Sabra was still sleeping. He lay there beside her, watching her breathe, thinking that he'd never been this happy, loving the way her hair was all matted on one side of her head and admiring the thick, inky shine to her eyelashes, fanned out so prettily against the velvety curve of her cheek.

About then, as he was getting really hopelessly sappy and sentimental over this amazing woman who had actually said yes to forever with him, Zoya, over on the thick rug by the window, sat up with a whine.

She needed to go out.

He managed to get dressed, get his coat and the leash, and usher the dog out of the room without disturbing the sleeping woman in the bed.

At the door to the outer hall, he grabbed the key

that Iris kept in a bowl on the entry table. Outside, it was snowing, a light, wet snow, the kind that doesn't stick. He walked the dog to the little park down the street, where they had a big playset for kids and a tube mounted on a pole containing plastic bags for dog owners who hadn't thought to bring their own.

Zoya took care of business. He cleaned up after her and then walked her through the gently falling snow. They circled the block, pausing at every tree and rock and hydrant that happened to catch the husky's eye.

Back at the apartment, he let himself in, took Zoya off her leash and followed her to the kitchen where his nose told him there was coffee.

Iris was already up, sitting at the table sipping from a mug with Me? Sarcastic? Never. printed on the side. She didn't waste any time. "We need to talk. Before Sabra gets up. It won't take long."

Iris allowed him to get out of his coat, wash his hands and pour himself some coffee. When he slid into the chair across from her, she said, "This better be for real for you, that's all I'm saying."

The thing was, he understood her concern. Not because he was ever backing out on what he finally had with Sabra, but because of how long it had taken them to get here—and also the thing with Mary. That never should have happened. He would always feel like crap about that.

"I don't know how to say it, Iris. I love her. She's the happiness I never thought I'd find. I screwed up last year. I know that. But that was because of..." Anything he said was just going to sound like an excuse—worse. It would *be* an excuse. For his failure of belief when everything seemed hopeless, his failure to hold steady against all the odds.

Iris scoffed, "You got nothin'. Am I right?"

What could he say? "You *are* right. I should have done better. I took her at her word when she told me there was no future for us."

Iris glanced away. When she faced him again, she took a big gulp of coffee and set the cup down, wrapping her lean, dark hands around it, holding on tight.

He tried again, "The thing is, it *worked* for us, you know? The way it's all turned out, it was…right. It was what we both needed. Every step was important to find our way to this life we're going to make together from now on."

"You know that you sound just like her, right?"

"If I do, it's because she and I understand each other. You think *I* was happy when she told me that you and Peyton insisted she go out with other guys— and that she *did*?"

"She told you about that?"

"Yeah. She told me and, no, I don't like any other guy even having a prayer with her. But I get it. I get why you pushed her to do it. And I accept that it turned out to be something she *needed* to do."

Iris rose, refilled her mug and topped his off.

When she sat back down, neither of them said anything for several minutes. They sipped coffee as Zoya crunched kibble from the bowl Iris had put at the end of the counter for her.

Finally, Iris looked directly at him. "Okay, here's the deal, Matthias. I really didn't want to like you. But I kind of think I do."

* * *

In Valentine Bay, they stayed at Matthias's small house, which was perched on a hill overlooking his hometown. Now that he was moving to the farm, he would be subletting the place until the lease ran out.

Sabra liked his little house. It had two bedrooms and a small yard. In his room, he led her to his closet and shoved back a rod full of clothes to point out the calendar hanging there, every day marked with a big red X through the twenty-second of December.

"Note the large red circle around the twenty-third to the thirty-first," he said.

She grabbed him and kissed him, a long kiss full of love and wonder, just because he was hers.

When she finally let go of him, he explained, "I kept one every year from our first year—except last year," he admitted. "Last year, I bought the calendar, but then, well…"

"Come here." She pulled him close again. "I get it and there is no need to explain."

That called for another kiss, which called for another after that…

The house Matthias had been raised in wasn't far from his place. His brother Daniel and his family lived there now and also his youngest sister, Grace.

On December thirtieth, Sabra and Grace were together in the kitchen making sandwiches for lunch.

Grace mentioned Mary. Matthias's sister said that he'd brought Mary to the family Thanksgiving the year before.

"Mary's a nice woman," Grace said. "But we all knew she wasn't the one." She spread mustard on a slice of rye. "You, on the other hand..." She pointed the table knife at Sabra and fake threatened, "Don't you ever leave him."

Sabra had a one-word reply for that. "Never."

"Good answer." Grace dipped the knife in the mustard jar again and grabbed a second slice of bread. "So, have you set a date yet?"

"Not yet, but the sooner the better as far as I'm concerned."

"You want a big wedding?"

"No. Small. And simple. Just close friends and family."

"How about New Year's Day?" Grace slid her a sideways glance.

"*This* New Year's? The day after tomorrow?"

"Hey. It was just a thought..." Grace stuck the knife back in the mustard jar.

Sabra unwrapped a block of Tillamook cheddar. "I do like the way you think."

"Why, thank you." Grace held up a hand across the kitchen island and Sabra high-fived it.

"I would need to check with Matthias..."

Grace gave a goofy snort accompanied by an eye roll. "As if we don't already know what his answer's gonna be."

"...and then I would have to get on it immediately, see if my friends in Portland and at the farm might be able to swing it. And then, if they can, head for the courthouse in Astoria to get the license right away—and what about a waiting period? Isn't there one of those?"

"As a rule it's three days, but you can get the waiting period waived for a fee. I know because Aislinn got married this past year. She and her husband Jaxon went straight from the marriage license bureau to the church."

"Perfect—and what about a dress? Omigod. I need the dress!"

"Well, then, what are you waiting for? Get with Matt and then get on the phone."

They stared at each other over the half-made sandwiches. Sabra broke the silence. "I believe I will do that."

Grace let out a shout of pure glee and grabbed her in a hug.

On New Year's Day, Matt married the only woman for him. The ceremony took place in the family room right there at the house where he'd grown up.

Iris and Peyton served as maids of honor. Nils Wilson gave Sabra away. Jerry stood up as Matt's best man. Daniel's two-year-old daughter, Frannie, was the flower girl and Jake, Frannie's twin, the ring bearer. Both Zoya and Daniel's basset hound Maisey Fae had festive collars decorated with red velvet poinsettias. Matt wore his best suit. Sabra looked more beautiful than ever in a day-length, cream-colored silk dress with a short veil.

They said their vows before the big window that looked out on the wide front porch, a cozy fire in the giant fireplace. The family Christmas tree, resplendent with a thousand twinkling lights, loomed majestic across the room as snow drifted down outside.

"Always," he promised.

"Forever," she vowed.

Matt pulled her into his arms and kissed her—that special kiss, the kiss like no other, the one that marked the beginning of their new life together as husband and wife.

* * * * *